MAN
WITH A PAST

Who could beautiful executive assistant Kelsey Murdock trust? *Not* her foolish boss who'd sent her to the remote Caribbean island to hand deliver his sensitive documents. And *not* the suspicious men following her. That left tough but sexy Cole Stockton, who wanted to be her lover. Unfortunately, Cole also seemed to be hiding something from Kelsey....

TRUE COLORS

Charter-boat captain Cade Santerre had never met a woman like Jamie Garland. Soft, sweet, alive in bed, he wanted her for always. A visit from the authorities changed everything, and Cade abruptly left town. Weeks later, a question still burned within the devastated Jamie—one that could only be answered by seeking out Cade.

MAN
WITH A PAST

TRUE COLORS

Harlequin Books

TORONTO • NEW YORK • LONDON
AMSTERDAM • PARIS • SYDNEY • HAMBURG
STOCKHOLM • ATHENS • TOKYO • MILAN

HARLEQUIN BOOKS

First Harlequin Books edition published August 1991

JAYNE ANN KRENTZ REISSUE
© 1991 HARLEQUIN ENTERPRISES LIMITED

MAN WITH A PAST © 1985 Jayne Ann Krentz
First published as a Harlequin Temptation

TRUE COLORS © 1986 Jayne Ann Krentz
First published as a Harlequin Temptation

ISBN 0-373-83239-7

CONTENTS

About the Author

Talented Jayne Ann Krentz has been a leading author for the Harlequin Temptation line since it launched in 1984. In her novels, she likes to write about courage, loyalty, love and honor. "Good storytelling," Jayne says, "draws its strength from these enduring human values." Her many fans agree!

This versatile, prolific author also likes to experiment. She's delved into psychic elements, intrigue, fantasy and even futuristic romances. Two of her historicals, under the pen name Amanda Quick, have appeared on the *New York Times* bestseller list. Jayne has received numerous awards and honors in her field. Truly she is a publishing phenomenon and a reader's delight!

Dear Reader,

I began writing romance because I love the myths and legends that are unique to the genre. There is no other kind of fiction that taps into the forces of love and optimism and hope as powerfully as romance does. After ten years of writing my favorite type of story, I am more convinced than ever that romance is not only a vital part of women's fiction, it is the foundation on which all of the other genres are based.

I am delighted that Harlequin is rereleasing two of my early Temptation novels. I loved writing *Man with a Past* and *True Colors,* and I hope you will enjoy them. Both stories reflect a theme that continues to fascinate me as a writer: the importance of honor and trust between a man and a woman. And they contain another element I like to play with in my books, an underlying thread of danger.

Romance is fiction that is devoted to heroines and the heroic men they tame with love. It is fiction that celebrates life. Enjoy!

With best wishes,

Jayne

MAN WITH A PAST

Jayne Ann Krentz

The night was alive with promise

"I'm going to miss having you in my stateroom bunk," Cole murmured as he pulled Kelsey close. "Your apartment's a far cry from the cruise ship."

"But just think, no more squeezing into a *very* narrow bed," she countered lightly, her senses already reeling from his touch.

"Hmm . . . what sort of bed do you have here?" With a questing tongue, he tasted the curve of her neck.

Kelsey's breath caught in her throat as his palms teased her nipples. "That's a leading question," she gasped, nestling closer.

"So lead me on . . . ."

1

THIS WAS THE NIGHT she would have to tell him she was not going to see him again.

Kelsey Murdock stood in front of the floor-to-ceiling windows of her mother's beachfront home and gazed thoughtfully out into the darkness. It was raining again tonight. Not an unusual state of affairs during winter here on California's Monterey Peninsula. The weather fitted her mood she decided: quiet, meditative, vaguely regretful for what might have been.

But she was convinced of the rightness of the decision she had made. She'd played with fire long enough. If she didn't stop now she would very likely get burned.

Cole Stockton, the man she mentally labeled "fire," came up behind her, moving with the soundless stride she sometimes found intriguing and at other times unnerving. It didn't seem normal for a man to move with such hushed control.

"When your mother and stepfather return from their trip to New Zealand we'll have to find other excuses for your weekend visits," Cole remarked in the quiet, dark voice that matched the way he moved. "You won't be able to say you're just coming down to Carmel to water the plants and check the mail for your parents while they're away."

"No," she agreed, accepting the glass of Armagnac he had poured for her. Kelsey sipped the fine brandy and told herself she would wait a little longer before she explained that she wouldn't be needing any more excuses to make the drive from San Jose to Carmel. After tonight her only reason for the trip would be that of the occasional visit to her mother and stepfather. And as much as she loved her mother, Amanda, and liked the man her mother had married, she certainly had no intention of spending every weekend here in Carmel visiting them!

"You're very quiet," Cole observed as she turned to face him. He didn't smile at her as he raised the balloon-shaped glass to his mouth. Cole Stockton rarely smiled. But there was an expression of warm anticipation in his smoky-gray eyes.

"It's been a busy week at work." Kelsey excused her mood lightly, but inwardly she experienced a small frisson of uneasiness. With a sudden flash of feminine intuition she knew exactly what he was thinking. Tonight he intended to end the cautious, intricate dance of sensual attraction in which they had been engaged for the past month. Tonight Cole intended to take her to bed.

It was ironic, she thought, that Cole had decided to make his move the same evening she had made up her mind to end the dangerous relationship. He would not be pleased, but surely at his age he had learned the deal with rejection. After all he must be close to forty.

But it was almost as difficult to pinpoint Cole Stockton's age as it was to nail down anything else about the man. It was her inability to learn anything other than the most superficial facts about him that had led Kelsey to her decision to end the relationship before it became any more involved.

A man who, even under the most delicate probing, would reveal nothing of his past, who showed no interest in the long-term future, who calmly provided no explanation for his apparent financial security, who would discuss only the present as though he had materialized out of nowhere less than a year ago, such a man obviously did not believe in the kind of honest, open relationship in which Kelsey believed. The only wise course of action was to end the association before it could develop into a full-blown affair.

Mentally Kelsey cataloged the few obvious facts she did know about Cole. He was a friend of her stepfather's, she realized, but Roger Evans didn't seem to know anything more about him than did anyone else. It was obvious he genuinely liked the younger man. So did her mother, Amanda, for that matter. They had introduced Kelsey and Cole a month ago, shortly before leaving on their trip to New Zealand.

In addition to the knowledge that her parents liked their neighbor, Kelsey also knew that Cole had money. At least enough to afford one of the expensive beach-front houses here near Carmel. She had seen the outside of his home since he'd had the stone walls built, but for some reason she hadn't wanted to go inside. On the two occasions this past month when he'd suggested having dinner at his place she had graciously refused.

He hadn't objected when she'd neatly reversed the offers, inviting him to dine with her at her parents' house, instead, and Kelsey hadn't been forced to deal with the fact that she felt uncomfortable with the idea of entering the massive wrought-iron gate that opened onto his walled fortress of a home. It was as though a primitive part of her feared being trapped inside.

Probably the most arresting thing about Cole Stockton was his attitude of quiet watchfulness. He always seemed alert and aware, even when he was relaxing with a drink in his hand, as he was tonight.

There was a harsh strength stamped on his unhandsome face that Kelsey found far more riveting than conventional good looks. It also proclaimed a past, even though Cole flatly refused to acknowledge one. The smoke-gray eyes were normally as unreadable as everything else about the man. The only emotion Kelsey could be certain of in those fog-colored depths was blatant masculine desire, and even that was well-controlled, as always, this evening. The cordovan brown pelt of his hair was sleekly cut with a conservative razor.

Tonight Cole wore a black pullover of fine wool and a pair of black slacks. Both garments fitted his lean, smoothly muscled body well. Kelsey's mouth lifted in wry amusement as a thought struck her.

"Something's amusing you?" Cole inquired politely.

"I just realized you nearly always wear dark colors at night. Stand you outside on a rainy evening like this and you'd disappear into the background."

"I wasn't planning on standing outside in the rain."

"Do you even own a white shirt? Or a red one? I've never seen you in anything but khaki, browns and greens during the day and black at night."

"A limited wardrobe, I'm afraid. Perhaps I should take out a subscription to *Gentlemen's Quarterly?*"

He mocked her gently, but Kelsey realized he was faintly puzzled by the hint of annoyance in her tone. Criticizing the remarkably neutral colors of his clothing was ridiculous, and she knew it. But it was just one more tiny, unexplained aspect of his life she knew she would never be allowed to question. In a way it was the last straw. After a month of weekend dates she had had it with trying to dig beneath the surface of Cole Stockton. If he wanted to wear colors that allowed him to blend in with his surroundings, night and day, let him!

"I'm sorry," she murmured coolly. "That was rather rude of me."

"You're feeling quite tense tonight, aren't you? Was the week really that bad?"

"There was a lot to be done before I leave on my vacation week after next," she hedged, turning back to the window. Cole's quietly intimidating presence was disturbing her more than she wanted to admit. Perhaps because she had made up her mind she would not be seeing him again. A perverse part of her would always wonder what it would have been like to lose herself, however briefly, in an affair with Cole Stockton.

At least she would have the consolation of knowing it could never have amounted to more than an affair. A man like this one would never allow a woman anywhere near as intimate a relationship as marriage, she thought bitterly. She was giving up only the prospect of a short-term passion, not a long-lived, caring relationship.

"I've been thinking about that Caribbean cruise you've booked," Cole said slowly, glancing down into the rich Armagnac as he swirled it gently in the glass.

"What about it?" Kelsey only half listened, her mind on when and how she would tell him that this was their last evening together.

"There's no reason I couldn't come along," Cole mused.

Kelsey's breath caught in her throat as she considered that prospect. "The cruise was nearly sold out months ago. I was lucky to get reservations myself."

"I could always share your stateroom," he remarked, gray eyes gleaming with unsubtle male promise.

Kelsey forced a distant smile, determinedly squelching the small burst of panic that had flared to life in the pit of her stomach. "I don't think so."

"You might change your mind by the time you're scheduled to leave."

He didn't move, but she had the impression he had stalked a little closer. Kelsey resisted the impulse to back away. "Has anyone ever mentioned you have a tendency to be rather arrogant at times?"

Cole didn't respond to that. But, then, he seemed to find it easy to ignore questions he didn't wish to answer. Instead he watched her quietly for a moment, absently tasting his brandy. "You think that by the time you leave you won't be ready to share a bedroom with me?" he finally inquired, far too silkily.

Now was the moment to tell him she would never be ready to share a bedroom with him. But for some reason Kelsey hesitated, foolishly wanting to keep the evening alive just a little while longer. There wouldn't be any more of these charming, intriguing, frustrating weekends after tonight, and she was reluctant to bring them to an end. "Perhaps we should try discussing another subject," she suggested with an ease she was far from feeling.

"All right. How about your hectic week?"

Kelsey lifted one shoulder gracefully beneath the fire-red material of her dress. The close-fitting knit, with its long sleeves and tiny gold buttons down the front, gently outlined the small curves of her breasts, a slender waist and the flare of womanly thighs. She was five feet four inches and even with the high heels she had on tonight she was unable to meet Cole on an equal level. He was a notch under six feet, and in addition to the height, she knew she could never hope to match the lean, coordinated strength of him. It occurred to her to question whether she need fear that strength. Surely he would not lose control just because she told him she wouldn't be seeing him again. She seriously doubted there was much in the world that could make Cole lose control.

Then again, she knew so damn little about the man!

"My week really wasn't all that bad," she began determinedly, "just a lot to accomplish. My boss is set on finishing some important documents before I leave so that I can hand carry them to that flaky genius I told you about."

"The one who lives like a recluse on some Caribbean island?"

"Right. I'm going to go ashore at one of the scheduled cruise stops, hop a charter flight to the kook's private island and deliver the papers personally. The charter pilot will fly me right back to the port where the ship is docked. Shouldn't be any problem, and I'll get an interesting side trip out of it. Walt said my vacation was a case of perfect timing. If I hadn't been going on the cruise he would have had to pay another courier's fee. Whenever he sends business material to this guy he has to make certain it's hand carried."

"This way Gladwin has to pick up the tab for only a short charter hop between islands," Cole growled. "It would seem that, in addition to his other sterling qualities, Walt Gladwin is a bit cheap."

In spite of the growing tension, Kelsey allowed herself a quick grin, her near-green eyes sparkling with momentary mischief. "You've never liked Walt, and yet you haven't even met the man!"

"Maybe I just don't care for the way his name seems to come up so frequently in our conversations."

The humor faded from Kelsey's eyes. "I won't mention him again."

"Don't make rash promises," Cole advised dryly. "He's your boss, and since we discuss your work a great deal, I'm sure his name will continue to crop up."

"If I talk too much about my job at Flex-Glad perhaps it's because you never seem to want to discuss your work," she retorted crisply.

Cole lifted an eyebrow in vague surprise. "I'm willing to talk about what I do for a living, it's just that my various investment strategies always seem a little dull compared to your high-tech work. At Flex-Glad you're really on the cutting edge of the new computer technology."

"I'm a glorified secretary," Kelsey said wryly. "It's true my title sounds a little more prestigious, but I assure you that administrative assistants spend a lot of time running errands, putting out fires and convincing temperamental computer whizzes to cooperate with management in creating a marketable product. I don't do any of the real technical work. I just try to coordinate those who can do it and those who are trying to market it."

"You know something about the technical side of things. Look at the way you helped your stepfather set up his new home computer."

Kelsey shrugged. "You can't help but pick up a few things here and there when you work around the technical stuff all day long, I suppose. Frankly, I'd much rather hear about your investments. Is that really what you do all week long? Follow the *Wall Street Journal?*"

"That and several other economic news sources. I have a lot to learn, though. In fact, I've been thinking of having you help me set up a home computer like Roger's."

Kelsey refused to be sidetracked. "How long have you been managing your investments on a full-time basis?"

she pressed, trying for any small hint of his past that she could get.

"Almost a year."

"And before that? What did you do before moving to the Monterey Peninsula?"

His eyes narrowed consideringly, and she knew he was weighing every word, selecting the point at which he would cut off the flow of information about himself. It was always this way.

"I acquired the money I now have to invest," he offered calmly.

"How?"

"Here and there."

Blank wall again. Kelsey had known it would be there, of course. She was accustomed to running headlong into it. Every time she pushed for information that went further into his past than the year he had spent in the Carmel area she hit that barricade. Well, she assured herself bracingly, after tonight she wouldn't have to worry about it.

"Did you inherit your money, Cole?" she couldn't resist asking.

"No." He stepped closer and touched the tawny-brown sweep of her hair where it fell in a smooth, styled curve on her shoulders. "Let's talk about something else, Kelsey. The past doesn't interest me. Only the present. I've told you that."

"Several times," she agreed, stifling a small sigh. There was no point probing further. He would turn aside every question. Since this would be their last evening together she might as well endeavor to make it a pleasant one. With a bright smile she toasted him. "To the future."

His gaze roved over her. "To the present," he amended, raising his glass in an echoing salute. "Especially tonight. I've learned that the here and now is all you can really count on in life." Cole put the rim of his glass to Kelsey's lips and tipped it gently so that she was forced to take a small sip. Then, his eyes never leaving hers, he took a swallow of the brandy, setting his mouth to the same place on the glass that hers had touched.

Kelsey felt the heat of his implied intent. Her fingers tightened around her glass as she realized she was trembling slightly. "Speaking of tonight," she began quietly.

"A much more interesting topic than last year or next year."

"Yes, well, it's getting rather late, isn't it," Kelsey tried to say briskly.

"You didn't get here until rather late."

"The traffic out of San Jose was terrible," she explained quickly. "You know how it is on Friday afternoons. The freeways are jammed."

"Fortunately that's one of the aspects of modern life with which I don't have to contend. Living here on the peninsula has some definite advantages," Cole murmured. There was a pause before he went on deliberately, "But I suffer from the effects of your traffic problems in some ways."

"How?"

"I have to spend Friday afternoons waiting for you, never knowing just how late you'll be. And I worry about your driving."

"But I'm an excellent driver," Kelsey said in surprise. It hadn't occurred to her he might have been worried. The man didn't seem capable of such a useless emotion as worry.

"I've got news for you. Knowing you think you're a good driver does not keep me from being concerned," he told her dryly.

She wasn't certain how to take that. After all, this was the last weekend it would be a problem for him. "Any suggestions? Roller skates, perhaps?"

"I do have a few ideas on the subject I'd like to discuss with you," Cole said evenly.

"I'm listening." Her gaze focusing on the darkness beyond the windows, Kelsey was conscious of Cole collecting his words before he spoke. It was as if he wanted to approach this next bit very carefully.

"How important is your job to you?"

Startled by the question, Kelsey slanted him a curious glance over her shoulder. "It puts food on the table and gas in the car. It pays the rent and the taxes. I guess you could say it was very important."

"I could pay for all those things," Cole told her softly.

Kelsey froze. "You could what?"

"You heard me. Kelsey, I want you to think about moving in with me." There was a steady determination in his words that told Kelsey he meant them.

"Is this some kind of joke?" she whispered shakily. "We've known each other exactly one month. And during that time we've only seen each other on the weekends!"

"I'm not going to rush you," Cole soothed. "I just want you to start thinking about it. A long-distance arrangement would eventually be a strain on both of us."

"Yes," she agreed bitterly. "It would."

"Kelsey, have I upset you?"

"If I'm upset I have no one but myself to blame."

Cole slid his hand under the curve of her hair, fitting his palm to the nape of her neck as he gently forced her to turn and face him. "You're as tense as a strung bow tonight, honey," he said, stroking the sensitive area.

"Sorry, maybe it has something to do with the lack of romance in your little offer." Angrily she stepped out from under his hand. "Asking a woman to give up her job and move in as a full-time mistress is considered tacky in this day and age, Cole. I think it was always considered tacky. Did you honestly expect me to jump at the idea?"

"Calm down," he said softly, a thread of command in his voice.

And it was a real command, Kelsey decided fleetingly. Not just a warning. "I'm not becoming hysterical. Merely annoyed."

"I've told you I won't rush you."

"You're right. You won't rush me. In fact you will wait indefinitely. Cole, the last thing I'm ever going to do is give up my job."

"You're overreacting," he accused grimly. "I'm not asking you to give up your financial independence."

"No? That's what it sounded like to me!"

"Even if you stopped working tomorrow you'd still have your inheritance, wouldn't you? Or have you spent it all?"

She stared at him. "My 'inheritance'! What in the world are you talking about?"

He frowned. "Your mother happened to mention once that when she inherited her brother's estate there was a certain amount earmarked for you."

Kelsey was torn between fury and outright laughter. "Did she tell you just how much money I received from Uncle Curtis? I got exactly ten thousand dollars. Cole, that's not even a year's salary for me. How long do you think I could be financially independent on that? If you were thinking of getting your hands on my 'fortune,' better revise your plans. I'm not an heiress."

His fingers knotted around the snifter and the gray gaze became a swirl of ice crystals. "You know damn well I never had any such intentions."

"I hardly know you at all," she retorted bleakly. "How could I guess what your intentions might or might not be?"

"For God's sake, Kelsey, at least tell me you don't really think I was angling to get control of your money," he gritted.

In spite of her tension and resentment, Kelsey had the grace to back down on that issue. If there was one thing of which she was instinctively certain, it was that Cole had far too much pride to live off a woman. "Of course I don't think that," she said, relenting. "You're right. I am a little tense tonight."

"I honestly believed you had received enough from your uncle to enable you to feel financially independent. Your mother has implied you only work because you'd be bored otherwise."

Humor flashed in Kelsey's eyes. "My mother has been indulging herself in something of a fantasy world ever since she inherited this house and the income from my uncle's estate. She had to work long and hard to support me after my father died. Occasionally Uncle Curtis would condescend to send us a small check at Christmas, but that was all the help he ever gave her. He had never approved of my father, you see, and more or less felt my mother had got what she deserved for marrying an artist."

"Your father was an artist?"

"An unsuccessful one, I'm afraid." Kelsey smiled. "A dreamer. He was a lot of fun at times, but he wasn't a very good husband or father. He lived waiting to be discovered, and it never happened. He died when I was twelve. My mother really had a struggle on her hands holding things together financially. Five years ago when Uncle Curtis died she suddenly had money for the first time in her life. She's been enjoying it enormously. Trips to Europe, this lovely home and a wonderfully debonair, courtly new husband. She's having a great time and I'm very happy for her. But the truth is, she has very little control over the money. It's all invested, and by the terms of the will she can only live off the income. The estate is managed by my uncle's bank. My mother has the use of the income for her lifetime, and then the money goes to my uncle's favorite charities. Uncle Curtis didn't want to destroy my ambition by leaving me too much money too young," she concluded on a note of laughter.

Cole appeared to turn the situation over several times in his mind, and then he nodded. "Okay, so suggesting you give up your job is asking a lot. I understand that. But I'm prepared to make up for the financial loss. I'll take good care of you, Kelsey. Believe me, I can easily afford it. I could even pay you the equivalent of your present salary if that would give you a feeling of financial security."

Kelsey closed her eyes in silent disgust. "You're serious, aren't you?"

"Completely. I've thought about this a great deal."

She shook her head wonderingly. "Where have you been for the past ten years, Cole? The world doesn't work that way anymore."

"The hell it doesn't," he countered softly. "I want you and I think you want me. Your job is in the way because it separates us geographically. I have more than enough money for both of us. All that adds up to a very neat conclusion."

"Which is that I quit my job and move in with you?"

"Why not?" he asked earnestly. "If you really want to work in order to keep from being bored you can get involved with my investments. Or you can find something to do in Carmel."

"Open another cutesy boutique like the dozens of others that are already there?"

"Kelsey," he began warningly.

Rage simmered in Kelsey's veins. She controlled it with a supreme effort of will. "There's another alternative."

"What's that?" he demanded warily.

"You could move to San Jose."

It was his turn to eye her searchingly and ask, "Are you serious?"

"Why not?" she shot back flippantly. "Your work would appear to be more portable than mine."

"You'd rather live in San Jose when you could live here on the beach?" he taunted. "You would prefer the traffic and the smog and the crime and all the rest? Come on, Kelsey, you know as well as I do that you love this area."

"Everyone loves Carmel and the Monterey Peninsula," she tossed back icily. "But not everyone can afford to live here. You can afford it, and so can my mother and Roger. But I'm not in the same financial boat as the rest of you. It would probably take months for me to find another job around here. The odds are it wouldn't pay nearly as much or be nearly as interesting as the one I have now."

"I've just told you I can take care of you."

"And I've been trying to explain to you that I don't intend to become a professional mistress!"

Cole surveyed her flushed features and appeared to come to a quick conclusion. "I'm pushing too hard, too soon," he said soothingly. "I'm sorry, Kelsey. There's no need for us to have this argument tonight. And I certainly don't want to ruin the rest of the weekend. Let me have your glass. I'll get you some more of your stepfather's Armagnac. I'll say one thing for Roger, he knows his brandy. I shall have to buy him another bottle to replace the one you and I have been working on for the past month."

Before Kelsey could think of a logical protest, Cole had deftly removed the snifter from her hand. She watched nervously as he walked silently across the hardwood floor and the elegant Oriental carpet to pick up the bottle of French brandy that resided on a teak table. This wasn't going to get any easier, she thought morosely.

He had shaken her with his outrageous suggestion that she give up everything and become his concubine. It was alarming to discover that Cole had plunged ahead in his plans for their uncertain relationship. In her mind they were very much at the beginning of an association that, given time and appropriate circumstances, might have blossomed into something meaningful. She realized now that in Cole's mind the affair was an assumed fact. He was already planning the practical details.

"You look confused and very annoyed with me," Cole remarked as he glanced back over his shoulder at her. "There's no need for either emotion. Not tonight. I'm not going to rush you, Kelsey. I know you've grown accustomed to your independence. After all, you're what? Twenty-eight?"

She nodded, wondering where all this was heading.

"And you've been on your own a long time."

"Ever since high school," she agreed cautiously. "I worked my way through college."

"And you've never been married," he went on, carrying her brandy back across the room. "So you've never had to adjust your life-style to anyone else's, have you?"

"I've never been any man's kept woman, if that's what you mean," she flared.

"It's not what I mean," he growled. "And you know it. Haven't you ever made a commitment to a man, Kelsey? Surely you've cared about someone sometime during the past twenty-eight years!"

"Of course," she tried to say carelessly.

"Well?" he challenged. "Go on. Didn't you learn anything from the experience?"

"Only that you may be right about long-distance relationships," she said coolly, turning her back to him as she sipped the brandy.

"What's that supposed to mean?"

Why should she tell him, she wondered angrily. He had no right to pry into her past. Not when he refused to answer even the most superficial questions about his own background. She didn't have to let him dredge up that fiasco with Aaron Blake. She had put it firmly behind her, telling herself that all she needed to remember about it was the lesson it had taught her.

"A couple of years ago I was madly in love with a man who did a lot of traveling," she heard herself say stonily. "He was an executive with a firm back in the Midwest and he did business with the company where I worked. We could only see each other when his business brought him to town, but he made certain that was as frequently as possible. He was quite happy to let me adjust my schedule to his. Quite happy to let me make the commitment. And I was only too happy to do it." Kelsey inclined her head in self-mocking humor.

"Things didn't work out, I take it?" Cole asked roughly.

"No."

"Because the distance factor made a meaningful relationship impossible? Kelsey, that's just what I'm trying to tell you—"

"No!" she interrupted fiercely. "It wasn't just that there was a lot of geography between us, although I'm sure that eventually would have been a problem. It was that there were a lot of lies between us. The fact that we lived so far apart merely made it easier for him to hide those lies."

Behind her she could feel Cole going very still. "What kind of lies?"

"He was married," she explained bluntly. "It was months before I found out. Someone at work had to be the one to enlighten me. God, I felt like such a fool!"

"What did you do then?"

Kelsey yanked her mind away from the bitter, humiliating memories and tried to concentrate on the point of the story. "I quit my job because I couldn't stand having to see him on a business basis after that. I also got the pleasure of telling him what I thought of him. Other than a severe lesson on the importance of trust and honesty in a relationship, that was about all I did get out of the mess. Don't tell me I don't know what it's like adjusting my life-style to someone else's. Aaron Blake forced me to do some really major adjusting, including finding a new job!"

"Kelsey, everything you've just told me points to what I've been trying to explain this evening. Conducting an affair over long distance will be very hard on both of us. Aside from the fact that I already miss you during the week, there's the problem I'm developing worrying about that drive from San Jose on Friday evenings. I also don't like wondering where the hell you are when I call during the week and you don't answer the phone," he added with a sudden emphasis that told its own story.

Kelsey tilted her head. "I didn't know you called this past week."

His mouth twisted wryly. "Tuesday, Wednesday and Thursday evenings, to be exact. You were out all three times."

She reflected briefly, inordinately pleased that he had tried to call. Instantly she squelched the reaction. After all, she was about to end the relationship, not take it to a more intimate level. "Tuesday night I had dinner with a co-worker, Wednesday I went to a shower for a friend who's having a baby and Thursday...." She wrinkled her nose for a few seconds, trying to recall. "Thursday I worked late."

"Uh-huh. With good-old Walt Gladwin?"

"I explained that he's working very hard to finish up those documents before I leave on my trip," she reminded him quietly.

"All I knew was that you weren't home to answer your phone."

Kelsey swung around and found him studying her far too intently. It occurred to her in that moment that, if she had allowed the affair to commence, she would have found Cole Stockton to be a very possessive man. He must have seen the knowledge in her hazel-green eyes, because he continued to assess her expression for another long moment before nodding once.

"You're right," he told her. "I didn't like it. And I'm going to dislike it more and more. I want to know where you are and what you're doing. And I don't want to have to wonder three nights in a row if you're with another man."

Kelsey found herself reacting to the implied threat almost without thinking. "Don't worry. You won't have to concern yourself with that problem ever again."

A speculative gleam lit Cole's gray eyes. "Is that a promise?"

"I'm afraid so," Kelsey said wearily. She avoided his pinning gaze and walked across the room, feeling an urgent need to put some distance between herself and this man. She came to a halt in front of the fire that blazed in the black granite fireplace. Cole had kindled the flames just before they had sat down to the dinner of cracked crab and salad they'd prepared together.

"Kelsey, what are you trying to say, honey?" he asked softly.

"You missed the whole point of that little story I told you a few minutes ago, Cole," she said, gazing down into the flames. "The lesson I learned from that disaster two years ago was not that long-distance relations are difficult, but rather that any good relationship must be built on trust and honesty. I need to know that the man who's asking a commitment of me is being totally up-front and aboveboard. I don't want any hidden barriers, any secrets or any nasty surprises."

"Hell, I'm not hiding a wife and six kids somewhere," he told her with a flash of rare humor. "Word of honor." He held up one hand, palm out.

Kelsey looked up, refusing to respond to his attempt at lightness. "But I can't be certain of that, can I? I can't be certain of anything at all about you or your life before you moved to Carmel. You're a closed book to me, Cole. A locked chest. You refuse to discuss your past, you won't tell me anything except the most elementary facts about yourself. You don't seem to care about the future. You deal only in the present. There's no way I can really get to know you."

"Kelsey," he began harshly, "that's enough. I realize you're a little tense tonight and that you've had a hard week, but—"

"Cole, listen to me. I am not tense because of my hard workweek. I'm tense because I'm trying to find a polite way of telling you I'm not going to see you again. One solid month of trying to establish some kind of toehold in that wall you've built around yourself is enough for me. Our relationship, long distance or otherwise, is going nowhere fast, and I intend to end it before it becomes destructive."

Raw power and cold masculine fury crackled to life in the beautiful room with the force of an exploding incendiary grenade. Kelsey barely had time to assimilate the knowledge that she'd handled everything all wrong when the sound of splintering glass filled the air.

She watched, stunned, as the brandy snifter Cole had been holding seemed to disintegrate between his fingers. For an electric instant both she and Cole stared at the shards of glass as they dropped to the floor. Her mother's fine crystal had dissolved under the crushing force of his hand.

Cole snapped out of the frozen, charged silence that had gripped the room. "Don't even think of trying to run. You wouldn't make it through the door."

2

"COLE, STOP IT! You don't understand."

"I understand." Cole felt the anger and the hot desire flooding through him, a potent combination unlike anything he had ever experienced. "I understand everything. Did you think you could play games with me for a month and then walk out?"

"I wasn't playing games."

He watched her back away from him, one hand held out in front of her as if she could placate him or ward him off. He moved toward her with a cool stride, willing her to realize how inevitable the outcome of this confrontation was going to be for both of them.

"For a month we've been doing this your way," he said roughly. "I told myself I wouldn't rush you, that I'd give you all the time you needed. I wanted you to feel comfortable with me."

"'Comfortable'! How can I feel comfortable with a man who refuses to tell me anything important about himself?" she flung back. Still trying to maintain a distance between them, Kelsey was working her way steadily toward the sliding-glass doors at the other end of the room.

"I've answered your damn questions," Cole gritted. "We've had all kinds of long conversations. You seemed to like them so much that I've spent just about every weekend talking to you until two in the morning!"

"But you never tell me anything," she wailed.

"The hell I don't! I've told you everything you needed to know. Everything that affects our lives. You know where I live, what I do for a living, how I feel about the state of the economy, politics, Thai food and saving whales."

"But whenever I ask about your past you refuse to answer."

"That's because my past is not important to either of us," he informed her with cold arrogance. "It has no bearing on our relationship. Who do you think you are to demand explanations and answers just to satisfy your feminine curiosity? I have never lied to you and I never will lie to you. That's all you need to know. If there are matters I prefer not to discuss, you can take it they aren't important."

He saw the fury that sizzled in her near-green eyes and watched it do battle with the very female fear he had inspired. He wanted to see the wariness and uncertainty in her tonight because it meant that at last she was finally taking him seriously. But a part of him respected the anger and defiance, too. He had known from the beginning that he wanted Kelsey Murdock, and her pride was part of the package. Cole had promised himself he would handle that streak of pride and independence carefully. Until tonight he'd done a fairly good job, he thought.

"How can you claim your past isn't important?" she challenged, backing another step. "You could be a . . . a gangster or an international jewel thief. For all I know you could have been living here in Carmel under an assumed name for the past year. Maybe you're a syndicate hit man who only has to do a couple of big jobs a year and has the rest of the time to live in luxury. If you call living behind iron gates and high stone walls a luxurious manner of living, that is!"

"You've really let your imagination run wild, haven't you? I had no idea you were spinning such fantasies."

"What kind of fantasies did you expect me to dream up about your past when you won't tell me anything about it?"

"I expect you to ignore my past, not sit around making up fairy tales."

"You seem interested enough in what I've been doing for the past twenty-eight years," she retorted vengefully.

"Only because you've been willing to talk about it. If you hadn't wanted to discuss it, I would have respected that."

"I'm willing to talk about it because I have nothing to hide!"

"Implying I do? Forget it, Kelsey, you're not going to goad me into making any interesting confessions. If there were anything I thought you should know, I'd tell you."

She came to the sliding-glass doors and found herself forced to halt. Defiantly she lifted her head, and the recessed ceiling light fell on her taut features.

Kelsey was not a beautiful woman, but the lively intelligence in her eyes and the promise of tenderness and passion in her warm smile had tugged at Cole since the moment he'd met her. Technically, she probably only qualified as reasonably attractive. Emotionally, she drew him to her with a heady combination of factors. Kelsey could be charming and witty or soft and reflective. She could be gentle and perceptive or aggressive and teasing. The fundamental sensuality in her seemed to have been designed specifically to attract him. Even the scent of her was unique and intoxicating. In short, she had a power over Cole he couldn't fully explain but that he acknowledged completely.

What she didn't realize, apparently, he told himself ruthlessly, was that he had power over her, too. Or he intended to institute it. It was time she understood that.

"I'm not going to continue in a relationship that's conducted one hundred percent by your rules, Cole. I'll make my own decisions about what I think is important and what I should know."

"Arrogant little witch," he breathed, not without a hint of admiration. "Do you think you can just call off our affair because I refuse to satisfy every aspect of your curiosity?"

"Yes," she declared vehemently. "I do. I can call it off for whatever reason pleases me. Actually, to be perfectly factual about this association of ours, I don't think you can call it a relationship, let alone an affair."

"Because I've only kissed you good-night a few times? Because I've let you send me home to a lonely bed every night we've been together? Lady, if you think that means we haven't started an affair, you're deluding yourself. I wanted to give you time, damn it!"

"Why? So that I could get to know you better?" she asked scathingly. "That's a joke, considering your attitude toward questions!"

"I've been wasting my time, haven't I?" Cole drawled, halting a few feet away to study her. She was poised to make a frantic dash out through the sliding-glass door, he realized. Her fingers were hovering on the handle.

"I think I'm the one who's been wasting time," Kelsey told him evenly. "But perhaps you're right. Perhaps we're both making the same mistake. We're obviously not right for each other, Cole. I think that when you've had a chance to think about it you'll realize that. You need some mindless little powder puff who won't want a relationship that goes any farther than the bedroom."

"And what do you need, Kelsey?" he asked deliberately, watching her hand without appearing to do so. Her fingers were tightening around the door handle now. In another moment she would yank open the door and make a dash for it. He wondered almost idly where she thought she could run to that he wouldn't find her. Perhaps he'd let her flee for a short distance out into the misty night. It might teach her a lesson. A rain-soaked woman trying to run across a sandy beach while wearing a pair of ridiculously high heels would soon sense her own vulnerability.

"I need a man who can share all of himself—past, present and future. A man who believes in honest relationships. I also need someone who's in tune enough with me and the modern world to know that the last thing he should offer is to make me his paid mistress!"

With that she made her bid for escape. Cole watched with almost lazy indulgence as she flung open the sliding door and darted out onto the wide veranda that overlooked the beach. She turned anxiously to glance back at him before starting down the steps that led to the beach.

"Where are you going to go, Kelsey?" he asked softly as she stood tensed for flight. "My home is about the nearest source of refuge. It's a long walk into Carmel. And it's very wet and cold out there tonight, isn't it?"

He watched the effect of his words as she stood under the veranda light. The fury and the fear were still engaged in a fierce tug-of-war in her eyes.

"Why are you trying to terrify me, Cole? Just to get even for the fact that I've decided not to let you seduce me?"

"I'm not trying to terrify you. I'm going to make love to you. It's what I've been planning to do all evening and I'm not about to change my mind now."

Deliberately he stepped through the sliding-glass door, and her nerve broke. Kelsey turned and ran down the steps, out into the misty rain. Sighing at the prospect of having to get wet, Cole went after her. He was in no rush. She couldn't possibly run far in those shoes. Soon she would realize the hopelessness of trying to flee, and the psychological impact of that realization would be useful.

Besides, he reminded himself bleakly, this wasn't the first time he'd set an ambush in the rain.

It wasn't hard keeping her in sight. The fiery-red knit dress was a light, shifting patch of muted color against the darkness, and the pale skin of her legs provided an equally visible target.

Cole knew, without bothering to think about it, that in his black pullover and slacks he was probably already invisible to her. He watched her turn to the left as she hit the beach and saw her stumble a little on the damp, packed sand. She glanced back again to see if he was following. Standing near the twisted trunk of a Monterey cypress, Cole smiled grimly to himself. She couldn't see him at all now. That much was obvious. He saw her hesitate, trying to search the darkness. But fading into nearby cover was a skill that came so naturally to Cole he knew she couldn't possibly detect his presence.

Out on the beach, Kelsey tried desperately to assess the situation. It had been idiotic to allow him to frighten her into running outside. Running wasn't even possible in the high heels she was wearing, she had discovered. There was no sign of him as she glanced back toward the house, but the chilly, drizzling rain had already begun to soak the red knit dress and dampen her hair. She felt ridiculous.

To top it off, she'd let him chase her out of her own home, she thought furiously. Well, her parents' home. Same difference. He belonged in that walled fortress up the beach, not in her mother's beautiful, airy house. Kelsey wondered dismally how long he'd wait for her to come back.

Kelsey stood, miserable and wet, her heels sunk into the sand, and stared longingly back at the warmly lit house. Inside was a fire on the hearth, a hot shower and a glass of brandy waiting.

There was also Cole.

He had shocked her with his violent reaction to her decision to end the relationship. It had been stunningly clear that he'd planned to take her to bed tonight, and he hadn't liked her throwing his intentions off stride. She'd guessed he wouldn't like the rejection, but she hadn't been prepared for the fury it had elicited.

There was no movement on the veranda and none in the shadows that filtered through the misty rain. Behind her the surf tossed noisily, making it impossible to hear any other minor sounds. Not that Cole would make so much as a whisper when he moved, Kelsey thought nervously. A tangled cypress tree loomed in front of her as she stepped uncertainly back toward the shelter of her mother's home.

She couldn't continue to stand out here in the rain like a soggy terrier. Besides, she was very cold now. There was nothing to fear from Cole, not really, she told herself optimistically. After all, he was her parents' neighbor and friend. Surely he wouldn't risk incurring their wrath by assaulting her, she assured herself. It had been silly to allow him to intimidate her into running.

It was just that she knew so little about Cole Stockton. She couldn't really be sure of anything, including the notion that he might not resort to genuine violence.

She took another step closer to the house, drawn toward it now as a means of escape from the steady discomfort of the rain. Her own anger and the feeling of having been made to act idiotically fed her increasingly positive view of the situation. So what if Cole was still waiting for her inside, she asked herself. She could handle him. She'd call his bluff and tell him exactly where he could go.

Kelsey was bracing herself with that last thought when Cole's hand settled tightly around her wrist. She opened her mouth instinctively to scream and promptly felt his palm across her lips as he materialized from the shadow of the cypress.

"It's not that I'm afraid anyone will actually hear you and come to your rescue," he rasped softly. "It's just that I'd like to protect my own ears."

She panicked as she sensed the inescapable quality of his hold. All thoughts of being able to handle him faded. Frantically she tried to struggle, beating at Cole with her free hand until he somehow managed to lock it between their bodies. The strength of him was overwhelming. He wielded it with a casual ease that told her precisely how little her efforts mattered.

When she managed to get in one good kick that caught his leg a solid blow, Cole abruptly turned impatient. Binding her to him so that she was crushed against his chest, he captured her face and brought his mouth close to hers.

"Did you think you could run from me tonight?" he asked against her lips as the rain fell gently. "I've been waiting for you for a whole month. I know you want me as much as I want you, so sheathe your claws, Kelsey. Tonight you're going to find out what's really important between us."

Kelsey grabbed for her courage. "Let me go, you bastard. I've had enough of your way of conducting a 'relationship.' I'll bet you actually do have something to hide, don't you? An honest man, a man with any sensitivity wouldn't dream of behaving like this!"

She got no further, because he was driving the abusive words back into her throat with the force of his kiss. Kelsey tasted the rain on his mouth, and then he was inside her own. There was a savage possession in his kiss that she sensed could only be satisfied with her complete surrender. She could feel the demand in every part of her body.

For a month she had been tantalizing herself with fantasies of what it would be like to make love with Cole. Until now she knew the few kisses she had received had been carefully restrained, designed to warm the fires of attraction that flared between them but not intending to set them ablaze. Cole had been biding his time, she realized dimly. He had hidden the full extent of his passion from her with a self-restraint that was incredible.

Kelsey had sensed she would find excitement and fire in his arms, but she had not guessed at the depths of the desire that would flame within her when Cole released himself from the barriers he had established. The chilled rain was forgotten under the intensity of his kiss. His arms were locked around Kelsey with such force that she knew she could not escape. His tongue swept into the farthest recesses of her mouth, taunting, daring, conquering, until she went limp against him.

"What made you think you could end everything we've started just because you weren't getting some answers to your foolish question?" he grated as he dragged his mouth damply away from hers.

Kelsey could only stare up at his face, stricken with the knowledge of just how helpless she was. A part of her longed fiercely to surrender to the passion he ignited, but another part of her rebelled at the way it was all happening. She had made her decision before leaving San Jose, she tried to remind herself. It had been the right one—she was sure of it. At least she had been sure of it in the cold light of day. But tonight . . .

"You have no right to force me into bed with you," she bit out desperately.

"'No right'? When I can make you tremble like this just by kissing you? You're the one who's so gung ho for truth and honesty, Kelsey. Why don't you admit you want me? I've seen it in your eyes. I've felt it in your touch. You're only resisting now because you're so independent and stubborn. I told you earlier this evening that you are going to have to learn to make some compromises in this affair, and I'm going to start teaching you the meaning of the word tonight."

"Cole, no! Put me down," she objected as he swung her into his arms and started back toward the house.

"I'll make love to you in the rain on some other occasion, Kelsey. It's too damn cold out here tonight. We need a hot shower and a warm bed."

"That isn't what I want." Her nails sank into the wet fabric of his pullover.

"It's what you want, all right. It just isn't happening quite the way you wanted it to happen. I would have done things your way, Kelsey, if you hadn't thrown down the gauntlet tonight." He was on the steps leading up to the veranda now. "I would have given you all the time you wanted, within reason. But you had to push a little too hard, didn't you? You have a lot to learn."

"I refuse to begin an affair with a man I can't trust," she flared.

"Tell me you still refuse and that you don't trust me after we've spent the night together," he challenged tightly. "By morning the world is going to look very different to you, Kelsey. I'll see to that."

"One night in bed with you isn't going to change anything," she protested wildly as he carried her inside the house.

"Tell me that in the morning," he taunted. Cole balanced her easily as he slammed the sliding-glass door shut. Then he started down the hall to the bedroom that Kelsey used when she stayed in her mother's home.

Torn between panic and desire, Kelsey caught her breath and began to struggle again as Cole walked into the cream-and-yellow bedroom. "You can't do this to me and you know it. I don't care what kind of attitude you've got toward the rights of others, you can't treat me like this!"

His cool gray gaze swept over her as he stood her on her feet. "I'm an old friend of the family's, remember. All I'm going to do is take care of you, see that you get properly warmed after that stupid dash out into the rain."

"Cole, listen to me," she pleaded, her voice wavering under the impact of his relentlessness. "We need to talk. Communicate. That's what's been wrong with this...this relationship of ours since the beginning. You keep drawing lines and putting up walls. You haven't let me get to know you."

His fingers went to the first of the gold buttons on her red dress. "You'll know everything you need to know by morning."

"Damn you, I won't let you do this to me!" Tears of frustration and rage burned in her eyes as Kelsey tried to slap aside his hands. She was cold and wet and miserable. She was also more than a little frightened. She knew she was dealing with a man and a situation that had, in a matter of minutes, flared out of her control. And the most shattering aspect of the matter was that she was no longer in full control of herself, either.

"Stop fighting me, Kelsey," Cole urged huskily as he caught her wrists and pinned them quite gently behind her back. "I'm doing this for your sake, as well as mine."

"At least spare me the self-righteous act."

"Look at me, Kelsey," he ordered softly, using his free hand to lift her chin. "Look at me and tell me you don't want me."

"I don't want—" she began heatedly, only to have the words cut off as he stopped them with a warning kiss. Kelsey's mind and body absorbed the threat along with the heavy passion behind it. Every inch of her was tingling with awareness and longing. She could no more stop her response to this man than she could stop the rain in the night.

"The truth, Kelsey. Give me that much at least."

"Why should I?" she breathed painfully. "You won't give me the same in return."

"You've always had the truth from me. You always will," he vowed. "I may not tell you everything you want to know, but what I do choose to tell you is for real."

"That's not good enough!" she cried.

"It's going to have to be good enough." Once more he kissed her, crushing her against the length of his body until she could feel the hard planes and angles of him through his damp clothing. When he lifted his head this time there was raw, insistent demand in his bluntly hewn features. "Admit you've wanted me this past month. Tell me you've known from the beginning that sooner or later we would find ourselves in bed together."

"There was nothing inevitable about it," she said shakily, and knew now that she lied. It was shockingly, brilliantly clear to her senses that this moment had been preordained from the first time she had met Cole Stockton. Why was she trying to deny herself this night, she wondered.

"Kelsey, Kelsey," he murmured huskily. "I can feel you trembling in my arms. Don't lie to me, honey." He drew his hand down the line of her vulnerable throat and once more found the gold buttons of the red knit dress. This time he undid them methodically, each action a caress. By the time he had finished, Kelsey was leaning helplessly into his strength, tiny tremors of desire racing through her, sapping her will. When Cole finally slipped his hand deliberately inside the parted material of the dress and found her breast she had to swallow her instinctive cry of longing.

"Oh, Cole..."

"I can feel what you're trying to tell me, sweetheart. Just relax and let it all happen as it was meant to happen." He allowed her to bury her face against the fabric of his sweater as if he knew she would find it easier that way.

"Cole, this won't change anything," Kelsey managed, but her voice was thick with emotion. "In the morning..."

"I'm not interested in anything but the present. We'll worry about tonight now. The morning will take care of itself." He stroked the dusky rose tip of her small breast with the pad of his thumb. "Your nipples are like hard little berries, Kelsey. Earlier this evening I could see their outline through your dress and I knew you hadn't worn a bra. You wanted me to know, didn't you? It was an invitation. A small act of intimacy. And it made my head spin just thinking of what it meant."

"Cole," she said, sighing. "You don't understand." But in a way she knew he did. He certainly understood the depths of the physical attraction between them. And he seemed to comprehend completely just how thoroughly he could dominate her senses.

"Hush, Kelsey," he soothed, lowering his head to kiss the sensitive skin just under her ear. His fingers toyed with the damp strands of her hair. "I'm not going to wait any longer for you." He paused, letting the tip of his thumb graze her flowering nipple again. "Want me, Kelsey?"

She shuddered, giving up the pointless battle. "I want you, Cole. But it won't change anything in the morning."

"For our purposes tonight the future is as nonexistent as the past." Then he covered her mouth with his own, holding it captive, while he stripped the red knit dress from her body.

In one mind-shattering moment, Kelsey found herself naked in front of him, shivering from the cold of the rain and the heat of desire. He freed her hands and she moaned gently, wrapping her arms around his neck.

"Kelsey, I've wanted to see you like this for so long." Cole's palms slicked down her sides, following the contours of waist and thigh with a hungry touch. She heard the deep groan in his chest. "Come on, honey. We need a hot shower. We're both too cold and wet."

He led her into the bathroom, tossing aside his sweater and stepping out of his shoes and slacks with impatient efficiency. Kelsey was unable to take her eyes from the strong, lean body, revealed as he undressed. When he reached out to shove aside the yellow shower curtain and turn on the water, the muscles of his broad shoulders moved with smooth coordination.

Cole turned to confront her as the shower came on, and Kelsey felt a rush of nervous anticipation as she saw the full extent of his arousal. He smiled one of his very rare smiles as he took in the expression in her eyes.

"Come here, Kelsey. You know as well as I do that there's no turning back now." He held out his hand.

After the briefest of hesitations, Kelsey put her fingers in his and allowed him to tug her under the hot spray. The water chased away the shivers that had been caused by the cold rain but not the tremors of rising passion. They only seemed to increase.

"You're so sleek and soft, Kelsey," Cole whispered into her wet hair as he pulled her against him. "Feel what you do to me."

"I've already seen what I do to you," she blurted out unthinkingly, and then flushed at the passionate amusement in his eyes. "I mean—"

"I couldn't possibly hide my reaction to you. Why should I?" He accepted his body's fierce arousal with arrogant complacency. "But I want you to feel it, not just see it."

He captured her wrists and drew her hands down his chest. Kelsey stared in fascination as her wine-tinted nails trailed through the crisp hair that tapered down to his flat stomach. She found herself flexing her fingers just to feel the taut hardness beneath his skin.

"Little cat," he muttered, and then he forced her hands even lower.

"Do you really want me so badly?" she heard herself ask tremulously, a strange sensation of feminine power springing to life in her.

"I think I'd lose my mind tonight if I didn't take you." He released her wrists and cupped her breasts, bending down to nip at the exquisitely sensitized tips with teasing hunger.

Kelsey shuddered delicately as he reached around her waist to grasp her hips. She felt him drawing her tightly into the hardness of his lower body.

"My God, lady. What made you think I'd let you walk away from me tonight?" He began to probe gently between the softness of her thighs, his fingers searching and finding the part of her that was dampening of its own accord, not because of the shower. "And what," he added meaningfully as he felt the slick evidence of her longing, "made you think you could deny either of us?"

She didn't answer. There was no point trying to deal with the complex emotions storming through her, at least not on an intellectual basis. Right at this moment Kelsey could only feel and respond. Everything tonight was beyond anything she had ever experienced. For a month she had been tormenting herself with fantasies and dreams, all of which she had decided must not be fulfilled. But if she had been able to estimate even a fraction of what the real thing with Cole would be like she would have known the decision was out of her hands.

Slowly, with an intensity that left her shaking, Cole explored her body. In harsh, heavy whispers he urged her to return the intimate favor. At the mercy of the unfamiliar passion and need, Kelsey obeyed. She touched him with every emotion from delight and shyness to tenderness and aggression.

Cole welcomed all her myriad responses, clearly glorying in her uncontrollable reactions. Under his hands she drifted further and further into the whirling vortex of his desire and was barely aware of the moment when he turned off the shower. She was vividly conscious of her rising impatience as he insisted on towel-drying her hair and her body, however. When he had finished the task she was flushed and tingling with need.

"Please, Cole," she pleaded, clinging to him as he quickly dried himself.

"I told you," he reminded her thickly, "I told you that in the end you'd be begging me."

Later she would remember both the words and the satisfaction in his voice, but right now they were unimportant. "I want you," she admitted almost violently.

"And I want you. Believe me, I want you more than anything else on the face of the earth." He picked her up again, striding back into the darkened bedroom. There he settled her in the middle of the turned-back bed, coming down beside her with a dark growl of desire.

Cole gathered Kelsey to him, heating her body with his own, inflaming her with ancient words and even more primitive caresses. Kelsey was a shivering, demanding, uninhibited female creature by the time he rose above her.

"Now, sweetheart. It has to be now. I can't wait another moment for you. Open yourself, Kelsey. I'm going to make you mine."

Something in his words got through to her; perhaps the grim promise in them when instinctively Kelsey knew she should be hearing a passionate plea. Whatever it was, combined with the bold, aggressive manner in which he parted her legs and lowered himself to her, it caused her to surface briefly. A sensation of real danger and a vague realization of the incredible emotional risk she was taking made Kelsey stiffen in belated resistance.

"No, Kelsey. It was all over for you weeks ago," Cole rasped as he felt the sudden tensing of her body. Deliberately he moved his hand to her thighs, stroking the throbbingly sensitive bud of passion hidden there.

Kelsey cried out, her nails digging into the skin of his shoulders. Her head arched back in invitation as she lifted her lower body against his hand.

"See, honey?" he groaned. "It's much too late." He fitted himself to her soft, warm opening and before she could summon any further protest he thrust deeply. "Ah, Kelsey, Kelsey...."

Her body accepted the invasion and Kelsey gave herself up to the shimmering excitement, thrilling to the crushing weight of the man who held her so tightly. He set the pace of the lovemaking, dominating the rhythm as if intent on imprinting her body with his own. Every small moan in the back of her throat, every pleading arch of her hips, every urgent demand of her hands he took with passion and satisfaction.

Kelsey felt filled, her body stretched deliciously tight until each nerve ending threatened to explode. On and on the heavy, thrusting rhythm went, driving her higher and higher up a spiral staircase of need. She had never climbed to such heights, never seen the highest steps with any man. Tonight the rapidity with which she gained the top was dazzling.

"Cole, oh, my God, Cole...!"

"Hang on to me, Kelsey. Just hang on to me. I'll take care of you...."

And then they were both crying out each other's names, over and over again as the pulsing completion spun them away from the last vestiges of reality.

Cole felt himself recovering slowly, a sensation of infinity coalescing around him. It took him a moment or two to realize that the soft, exciting gasps of the woman under him had become long, relaxed breaths. Kelsey's lashes fluttered restlessly and then lifted. He found himself gazing down into the bottomless depths of her eyes. In the shadowy light of the bedroom he could not begin to read the mixture of emotions swirling there.

"Kelsey?" he whispered as he reluctantly unsealed their bodies. "Are you all right?" He settled down beside her, cradling her in the crook of his arm.

"Yes."

He smiled. "You scared me there for a moment. You looked somewhat shell-shocked."

"Yes."

His faint smile disappeared as he watched her close her eyes again. Damn it, what was she thinking, he wondered, experiencing the first touch of uncertainty he'd had all evening. He'd felt the total response of her body, heard the words of desire on her lips. And he knew beyond a shadow of a doubt that he'd given her complete satisfaction. So why was she closing her eyes and trying to shut him out?

Because he had the distinct impression that was exactly what she was doing. Uneasily he stirred beside her, tangling his legs with hers. She didn't resist the small intimacy, but neither did she open her eyes.

"Kelsey, where the hell do you think you're going?" he demanded as he realized she was drifting away from him, trying to isolate herself.

"Is it all right if I go to sleep, Cole?" she asked with a suspicious meekness.

"Kelsey, I want to talk to you."

"You said we'd talk in the morning."

Cole stifled an impatient sigh and reached out to smooth the tendrils of her tawny hair off her cheek. He knew he was growing angry and knew, too, that it was a ridiculous reaction on his part.

He'd achieved his goal, he reminded himself. After tonight Kelsey would never be able to deny the passion they generated in each other. And, he told himself forcefully, she wouldn't be able to pretend she was free any longer. He knew by the way she had responded tonight he could repeat the experience anytime he wished. She was his on a very fundamental level. No matter what she tried to tell herself intellectually, he only had to reach out and take her in order to remind her of the bonds he had put in place.

But somehow all the conviction in the world wasn't countering the growing uneasiness in his gut. He'd pushed her hard tonight, Cole admitted as he stared up at the ceiling. He'd lost his control when she'd startled him by saying she was going to end the relationship. Of all the words he had expected from her tonight, those were the last he'd thought he would hear.

He'd been furious that she could even think of withdrawing. And, if the truth be told, he acknowledged, he'd felt the cutting edge of something close to panic.

Panic was an alien reaction for Cole Stockton. The necessity of surviving under deadly conditions had taught him self-control a long time ago. It had taken Kelsey Murdock to introduce him to the recklessness and panic only true desperation could produce.

He'd had no choice tonight, Cole decided grimly. It was a case of either acting forcefully or running the risk of having Kelsey walk out.

But he'd really pushed her, another part of his mind reminded him. She was going to have some adjustments to make in the morning. He should allow her some time now to come to terms with herself and with him.

Cole turned his head on the pillow and saw that Kelsey had gone to sleep. Initially he'd planned on spending the night in her bed, but now he asked himself if he shouldn't provide her with some breathing space.

He'd like to be here in the morning. It would be very pleasant to make long, slow love to her at dawn. Then they could fix breakfast together and spend the rest of the day talking about their relationship....

But perhaps that schedule, satisfying though it would be for him, wouldn't give her the private time she might need to deal with what had happened. He realized now that he wasn't quite certain what to do next.

Uncertainty was almost as alien to him as panic, Cole thought with a grimace. Kelsey was teaching him a great deal tonight, and he didn't particularly appreciate the lessons. On the other hand, he assured himself, rising carefully from the bed, he'd taught her a crucial lesson, too.

He stood for a long moment, looking down at her curved body, and then he reached to draw the quilt up over her shoulders. He was tempted to crawl back under that quilt with her. In the end he resisted.

He'd been stalking his quarry for a month now, and tonight he'd been forced to close the trap far more aggressively than he'd ever anticipated. The hunter in him sensed that he should back off a bit and allow Kelsey time to accept what had happened.

At least Cole thought it was his hunting instincts that issued the advice. A cold prickle of wariness warned him it might be the strange new element of uncertainty guiding his actions. Or the panic. He could no longer be sure.

Retrieving his still-damp clothing, Cole dressed and prepared to leave the bedroom. He hesitated a moment in the doorway, feeling the invisible pull of the sleeping woman. She had been everything he had dreamed or imagined she would be in his arms—passionate, exciting, soft and captivating. He had to work at summoning the self-discipline he needed to leave the room. But Cole had a lot of experience calling on self-discipline.

He walked down the hall and stepped out into the night, disappearing into the shadows and the misty rain as if he were a natural part of the darkness around him.

3

KELSEY AWOKE EARLY the next morning, struggling upright in bed with a gnawing sense of doom. Memories of the night flooded back. Nothing had gone right. Nothing had gone as she had planned. The small twinges she felt in her thighs as she pushed back the covers and got to her feet reinforced the knowledge that she had fouled up very badly. She must have been a fool to assume she could handle Cole Stockton in a straightforward, honest, civilized manner.

She had sensed he could be dangerous, Kelsey reminded herself as she padded wearily into the bathroom. But she hadn't realized just how completely he lived by his own rules. And if she was honest with herself she had to acknowledge she hadn't dreamed just how primitive her own responses could be under such circumstances.

Last night. She couldn't quite believe what had happened last night.

She must have gone crazy, Kelsey thought as she sought refuge in the shower. She should have fought Cole, threatened to call the police, screamed rape. Instead she had allowed herself to be whirled away on a tide of passion unlike anything she had ever known. It had all seemed so inevitable, so irresistible last night. He had pursued her, captured her and claimed her, and she had accepted his right to do so. On some fundamental level she had accepted him.

Kelsey closed her eyes in anguished memory. Never had she been so much at the mercy of her own desire, let alone the mercy of a man. It was almost impossible to comprehend her actions.

Where had it all gone wrong, she questioned time and again as she went through the ritual of showering and dressing. She had known that every weekend in Carmel was becoming increasingly risky. She had realized the attraction between her and Cole was a smoldering fire that could easily singe her fingers if she wasn't careful. Well, last night she had not been careful enough, and more than her fingers had been burned. Kelsey felt as if her whole body had gone up in flames.

He had been so furious when she'd tried to tell him she wouldn't see him again. Accustomed to his controlled, quiet responses to almost any situation, Kelsey simply hadn't been prepared for the sudden blazing power that had erupted in him. In her mind she would see that shattered brandy glass for a long time to come.

Kelsey winced as she pulled on gray pleated trousers and a long-sleeved persimmon sweater. Her body was going to be a long time forgetting last night, too. Cole had been a demanding, overwhelming lover. He had gone about eliciting her responses with a bold aggressive passion that had been captivating.

Angrily Kelsey tugged on low suede boots and stalked out into the living room. Passion, physical attraction, *sex*. That's all it could have amounted to, given the fact there was no basis for any genuine relationship between Cole Stockton and her.

He had steadfastly refused to allow her close in any meaningful way. He had refused to confide in her, or let her get to know anything about the forces that had shaped his life. He wouldn't answer questions about his past, and he arrogantly assured her she had no need to know the answers.

And in addition to all his other sins, she decided furiously, the man hadn't even stayed through the night. He'd walked out right after seducing her.

Not that there was any reason he should have remained, Kelsey told herself bitterly as she poured dry cereal into a bowl and located a carton of milk. He got what he wanted, didn't he? He had his revenge. He'd made a mockery of her cool decision to end the relationship. Then he'd calmly walked out.

Kelsey sat tensely on the stool in front of the marble counter, her booted feet hooked over the bottom rung. She munched cereal while she waited for the coffee to make itself in the drip machine, and she thought about her own foolishness at great length.

It wasn't until she was on her second cup of strong coffee that her basic spirit began to revive. Every woman made a few mistakes in her life when it came to dealing with the male of the species.

"So why can't I calmly sit here and write off last night as a bad error in judgment?" she said aloud.

It just wasn't going to be that easy. Picking up the mug of coffee, Kelsey wandered into the living room, noting gloomily that the rain had stopped. She must have been crazy to make that dash outside last night. No, she hadn't been nuts. She'd been scared. Panicked by a man at her age. Well, with good reason, as it turned out, she thought with a sigh.

Unfortunately that sense of panic had not completely vanished. A part of her insisted on feeling that something elemental had changed in her life and she wasn't going to escape the consequences.

One thing was certain. She couldn't stay here this weekend. Not when Cole Stockton lived virtually next door. The thought of running into him in Carmel or during a walk on the beach sent real shivers down her spine. Her instincts this morning were to go into hiding, she realized wryly.

Absently she began to water her mother's plants. The little task was, after all, supposed to be her chief excuse for coming down to Carmel each weekend during the past month. She would carry it out as usual this morning, and then she would run.

Promising herself the escape did not lighten Kelsey's feeling of tension. It was as if deep down she knew that running away this morning wasn't going to do any more good than running away last night had done. But she forced herself to concentrate on getting away from Cole Stockton as she walked through the house with the brass watering pot.

In her stepfather's study she paused to look at the sleek home computer she had helped him select a few months ago. Roger Evans had been as delighted with his new toy as any child. He had a passion for order and precision when it came to maintaining his personal financial records and the computer was a perfect mechanism for providing this. With the expertise she had naturally picked up working at Flex-Glad, Kelsey had been able to give her stepfather a lot of advice and assistance. She had even presented him with a copy of the new, very sophisticated accounting program Flex-Glad had recently perfected.

Working together on the project had established a firm friendship between Roger and her. Kelsey had been quite pleased at her mother's decision to remarry, and she had found Roger to be charming from the first. But it wasn't until she had helped him choose his computer and had taught him how to use the accounting program that she had really had a chance to get to know Roger Evans.

Impulsively she sat down in front of the terminal. She was curious to find out how far her stepfather had gone with the accounting potential of the new Flex-Glad program. With the computer warmed up, she shoved the correct diskette into the drive and called up the list of files she and Roger had established.

IRS
JOURNAL
GEN LEDG
A.E. INV

That last file was the one in which Roger tracked her mother's investments. There wasn't much either of them could do about the decisions regarding the administration of the money, as it was all in the hands of the bank, but Roger loved to keep up with the bank's choices all the same. He simply thrived on the intricacies of orderly accounting procedures. It was much more than a hobby.

"You should have been an accountant," Kelsey had told him once.

"Probably should have been," Roger had replied with a chuckle. "But I came from a family of lawyers, and there was never much choice about my career, I'm afraid. It was either law or utter disgrace."

"Ah, the perils of being born into East Coast preppydom," Kelsey had teased affectionately.

Roger had agreed with a surprising degree of seriousness. "One's background can place a great many limitations on one. There are times when it would be very pleasant to simply close the door behind yourself in life and open a new one. But it takes courage. A lot of it."

Kelsey thought about that conversation now, wondering if that was exactly what Cole Stockton had done. Perhaps he had closed a door behind himself and started over.

Bringing with him the money he'd made in his other life, she reminded herself firmly. Mustn't forget that little fact. What kind of life could it have been that it had provided him with so much money he could now afford to sit back and simply manage his investments? Or perhaps, as she had speculated last night, his other life still called to him occasionally. For all she knew, he really could be a very high-priced hit man.

"No more questions about Cole Stockton," she advised herself aloud as she idly glanced down Roger's list of files. "Didn't you learn your lesson last night?" Why was it that after the trauma of last night she found herself more curious than ever about Cole, she wondered unhappily. Roger, she was pleased to see, had become very creative. In addition to the initial financial record files she had helped him establish there were a few new ones.

EC. IND.
5 YR
STOCK

That first one was probably short for something like "Economic Indicators." The second probably stood for "Five-Year Trends." Roger had mentioned starting such a file for tracking the vagaries of the stock market. And that last file must be another stock-market record. Out of curiosity she called up the actual file in order to see what was inside.

A few seconds later she found herself staring at, first in perplexity and then in shock, the careful notations Roger Evans had entered under the file titled Stock.

The first thing she realized was that "Stock" was not short for a longer file name having to do with tracking the stock market. It was short for Cole Stockton.

The sense of impending doom that had been hovering over her when she awakened intensified by several quantum jumps. She ought to get out of the file right now and shut down the computer. She had no business viewing these records, she told herself. Although up until now Roger had encouraged her to examine what he had been doing with the computer so that she could offer advice, she knew immediately that he would never have intended for her to see this particular file.

There could be no doubt about the type of transaction she was witnessing. Roger was clearly making regular payments to Cole in the amount of a thousand dollars a month.

"My God," Kelsey breathed, staring at the evidence before her eyes. It didn't make sense. *A thousand dollars a month!* Horrifying possibilities danced through her head. Blackmail. A loan. Hush money. She couldn't even guess what else might be included on such a list.

Kelsey's imagination ran wild as she tried to come up with a logical explanation for why Roger should be paying off Cole Stockton. Quickly she backed out of the file and turned off the computer. Then she simply sat staring at the darkened display screen for a very long while.

More questions about Cole Stockton. Always there seemed to be more questions. Never any answers. She remembered the sensation of danger she'd had more than once around the man. Her instincts had been right.

Sudden fury assaulted her, driving her to her feet and out of the study. The brass watering pot sat forgotten beside a small ivy plant as Kelsey stormed out of the room.

It was bad enough that he had invaded her life, demanding that she accept him as a lover without any explanations of his past. It was humiliating that he had offered to set her up as his mistress. It was excruciatingly painful that she would have to live with the fact that he had been able to seduce her so easily.

Damned if she would allow him to intimidate her stepfather on top of everything else!

Snatching up her red calfskin checkbook, Kelsey slammed out of the house. The anger and the hurt of last night fed her recklessness, until she was almost running as she covered the hundred yards separating her mother's home from Cole's fortress.

For the first time since she had met him, Kelsey found herself outside Cole's heavy wrought-iron gate. Viciously she stabbed at the buzzer embedded in the rock wall near the coded lock mechanism.

There was no verbal response through the speaker implanted above the buzzer, but a moment after she had leaned on the button, the front door of the austere white-stucco house opened.

Cole stood in the doorway, watching her intently from across the distance of the neat lawn that ringed his home inside the garden walls. She could not hope to read any nuance of emotion in his face. Cole was a master at concealing his reactions. Except, of course, when he'd lost control last night, Kelsey reminded herself abruptly.

The thought of how he'd become very dangerous very quickly gave her a split second of panic over what she was about to do, but she damped it down under the more fiery anger.

Wrapping her right hand around one of the wrought-iron bars of the gate, she met his eyes. "I've come about the Stockton file," she told him starkly.

Whatever he had been expecting from her, clearly that remark was not it. The cool gray gaze narrowed, and then Cole stepped through the door, starting toward the gate.

He was wearing the familiar neutral khaki slacks and shirt today, and his cordovan brown hair gleamed faintly in the cold sunlight. Kelsey caught her breath as all the remembered intimacy of the night washed over her.

By the time he came to a halt on the opposite side of the huge gate she was having to grab for every ounce of nerve she possessed.

"What in the world are you talking about, Kelsey?" he asked quietly. His hand curled over her fingers as she clenched the iron. When she tried to free herself he tightened the grip, until her fingers were biting into the metal.

"The Stockton file," she repeated evenly. "It's one of Roger's new computer files. And it says he's paying you a thousand dollars a month."

Cole studied her for a long moment before saying very softly, "You've been busy this morning, haven't you? What the hell do you know about that thousand a month?"

"Nothing yet," she snapped. "But I want to know everything. Why is my stepfather paying you that kind of money, Cole?"

He released her to unlatch the heavy gate lock, muttering a short, highly explicit oath as he did so. But his next words were unexpectedly polite. "Have you had breakfast?"

She brushed the question aside impatiently. "Cole, I'm not here to have a pleasant chat over a cup of coffee. I want to know what's going on between you and Roger."

"Come on inside, Kelsey," he instructed. "You may not be in the mood for coffee, but I am." Without waiting to see if she intended to follow, he turned to lead the way toward the house.

Reluctantly, not seeing any other alternative, Kelsey strode after him. Warily she glanced around the walled garden. "Are you expecting a revolution?" she asked caustically. The place reminded her of a military compound.

"It wouldn't be the first," he retorted as he pushed open the heavily paneled front door.

Kelsey stared at his back, astonished. "What's that supposed to mean?"

"Never mind. The breakfast room is this way."

He led her down a tiled hall and through a living room that had been furnished in wicker, wood and bamboo. The serene, almost tropical look surprised Kelsey, and then she reminded herself she hadn't really known what to expect. She hadn't even known enough about Cole to hazard a guess as to the type of environment he would choose for a home. The realization increased her wariness.

The fabulous view of beach and ocean had not been completely sacrificed for the sake of another high stone wall, but it had been impeded somewhat by the tall, wrought-iron grillwork that stood between the house and the beach.

"You have to use a key just to get back and forth to the ocean," she muttered.

"The former owners had the wall built," he told her dismissively.

"I saw the outside of this house a couple of years ago, when the Hendersons lived here. The wall was half its present height in front and there was no wrought-iron fence between the house and the beach."

Cole shrugged as he indicated a wicker chair in the airy breakfast room. "So I made a few modifications."

"You take the phrase 'a man's home is his castle' seriously, don't you?" she scoffed. Kelsey sat down at the glass-topped table, watching as he stepped over to the counter and switched on the coffee machine.

"Kelsey, you didn't come here to make nasty remarks about my home. You've made it clear you don't like the place. Let's move on to another subject."

"The monthly payoffs Roger is making to you?" she suggested boldly. She hadn't cared for the thread of command in his words.

"How about discussing last night, instead?" He leaned back against the counter and pinned her with a brooding expression.

In spite of her determination to remain calm and in control, Kelsey felt the flush that stained her cheeks. "Last night is not on my list of topics open to discussion," she bit back tightly.

"It's about the only one I'm interested in discussing."

His quite resoluteness nearly unnerved her. "You can't expect me to believe that. You're the one who makes it a policy never to rehash the past, remember?"

"That policy applies to my distant past, not the immediate one, and you know it."

"Do you have any idea how incredibly arrogant you are?"

His expression hardened. "I've made a few rules for myself and I live by them. You can call that arrogant if you like—"

"I do."

"I prefer to call it reasonable and prudent. I also call it my prerogative."

Kelsey yanked her eyes from his. Concentrating on the view of the ocean as seen through a row of iron bars, she said, "Forget last night. Any man who truly wanted to discuss last night would have stayed at least until morning." God, she shouldn't have brought that up, she told herself furiously.

There was silence behind her, and then Cole was beside the table where she sat. His movement across the kitchen had been virtually soundless. Kelsey felt his fingers on her chin, lifting her face.

"Is that what this is all about?" he demanded softly. "Are you on the warpath this morning because I didn't stay the whole night?"

"No, damn it, that has nothing to do with the reason I'm here," she protested violently.

He sank down onto the chair next to hers, still cradling her tense face. "Believe me, Kelsey, if I handled that scene all wrong it wasn't intentional. I told myself that you'd need a little time to yourself this morning. I didn't want to push you—"

"You're joking! You didn't want to push me? After you'd already pushed me straight into bed?"

The brackets around his mouth tightened and emotion flickered briefly in the icicle-gray eyes. "You wanted to be there as much as I did."

She flinched, but she was too proud to let her eyes falter. "I will admit I learned something last night, Cole; I found out I'm no more immune to the power of sexual attraction than anyone else."

"Are you going to tell me that's all it was for you?" His thumb moved on her jaw with faint menace. "A bit of sexual adventure?"

"What else could it have been?" she got out flippantly. "Assault?"

"Kelsey, don't push me too hard, okay? When I'm around you I find my self-control isn't quite what it should be," he warned gently.

"I found that out for myself last night."

He shook his head and released her. Silently he got to his feet and went to pour two cups of coffee. "That's about the same time I discovered it, too," he announced dryly. "Along with a few other interesting things."

Kelsey took a grip on her determination. "As I said, I'm not here to discuss last night."

"Ah, yes. You want to know about the thousand a month." Cole carried the mugs of coffee over to the table and sat down again. His attention seemed to be focused entirely on not spilling the coffee, as if a man who moved as smoothly as he did needed to be concerned about such a minor act of coordination. "How did you find out about it, Kelsey?"

She reached for one of the mugs, more out of a desire to find something to do with her suddenly restless hands than because she wanted more coffee. "The records are all neatly stored in Roger's computer," she muttered.

Cole's mouth twisted. "I should have guessed. Roger and his passion for accuracy. Of course he would have entered the information into his new computer." Cole took an experimental sip of his coffee. He gazed thoughtfully out the window now, not looking at Kelsey. "So you went snooping this morning, hmm?"

She stiffened, aware of a lingering sense of guilt. "I wasn't prying. I helped Roger set up those records and I've been into the files a dozen times with him."

"But not that file."

"This file didn't exist the last time I looked at the list in the computer," she gritted.

"And once you saw my name on it, you couldn't resist going into it, right?" Cole appeared half amused and half resigned. "Poor Kelsey. You and your endless questions. You've got the curiosity of a cat, along with a few other feline characteristics, don't you?"

"Cole, I want some answers."

"I know you do. But as usual, you're not going to get them."

She swallowed uncertainly, not liking the blunt finality in his voice. "I mean it, Cole. I want to know what's going on. Why is Roger paying you that money?"

"That's between Roger and me."

"What about my mother?" she demanded.

"Amanda knows nothing about it, either. It doesn't concern her. Furthermore, if you mention the subject to her I'm going to be definitely annoyed," he said mildly.

"Do you honestly expect me to let it drop there? Pretend nothing's going on?"

He gave her a level look. "Nothing *is* going on. At least nothing that concerns you. I've explained that this is entirely between Roger and me."

"Did you loan him money?" Kelsey pressed.

Cole said nothing.

"Are you blackmailing my stepfather?" she asked wildly.

Cole took another sip of his coffee, obviously deliberating his response. "That's a pretty heavy accusation, Kelsey."

"I'm not accusing you. I'm asking you. But you have this policy of not answering questions, don't you?" she reminded him angrily. "A policy of non-communication except when it suits you. How dare you sit there calmly drinking coffee and telling me none of this is my business? If the situation were reversed would you let me tell you to mind your own business? If you thought I was blackmailing a relative of yours would you simply back off and leave the whole matter alone? Hell, I don't even know if you have any relatives!" she concluded in frustrated fury.

"Do you really believe I'm blackmailing Roger?"

"I don't know what to believe. I know virtually nothing about you, thanks to your total failure to communicate!" Lord, she was nearly shouting at him now. Kelsey's fingers trembled around the hand of her coffee mug. It was nerve-racking to lose your temper with a man who was still very much in control of his own.

"We communicated last night, Kelsey."

"That's your idea of communication?" she yelped, leaping to her feet as her emotions threatened to overwhelm her. "You're out of your mind. What in heaven's name made me think we could ever develop a long-term relationship? Forget last night, Cole. It's past history, and we don't talk about past history, remember? I only want to know what you're doing to Roger."

"I'm not doing anything to him."

"Are you blackmailing him?" she demanded.

The gray gaze was as cold as the ocean on a winter's day. "What do you think?"

"That's not an answer!"

He got to his feet with lazy grace, taking a step toward her, which drove Kelsey back against the kitchen wall. "Do you believe I'm blackmailing your stepfather?" Cole lifted his hands, flattening his palms against the wall on either side of her head. There was cool intimidation in every inch of his hard body.

"Cole...."

"Answer me," he ordered.

"I've told you, I don't know what to believe."

"*Answer me.*"

"I don't want to believe it," she gasped.

"But do you?"

She sensed the threat in him and realized he was cold-bloodedly furious. "No." Kelsey dropped her eyes, staring at the first button of his khaki shirt. "No, I don't think you're the blackmailing type."

He straightened, letting his hands fall away from the wall. Grim-faced, he went back to his chair. "Well, thanks for that much at least."

She glared at his back. "Don't act as if it's such a small matter. Considering your high-handed, strong, silent style, it's a wonder I'm even willing to give you the benefit of a doubt!"

He shot her a mocking glance. "I'll look on it as a small step toward trust."

"A very small step," she flung back, seething.

"Sit down, Kelsey. We've got some talking to do this morning."

"Are you going to tell me what's going on between you and Roger?"

"No." He smiled faintly. "Other than to tell you that it's a personal matter between Roger and me, I'm not going to discuss the subject with you, and you should realize that by now."

She held herself very still for a long moment, reading the implacable set of his face. "Then there's nothing else to talk about, is there?"

"There's last night."

"Really?" She moved determinedly back to the table, reaching for her red checkbook.

"Kelsey, what are you doing?"

"I'm writing out a check for three thousand dollars. That should cover my family's obligation to you for the next three months. During that time I will find out just what in hell is going on, and then I'll decide what to do next."

"Don't be an idiot."

"I've been an idiot for the past month. I'm trying to recover some lost ground." She industriously bent over the check, filling in the blanks and scrawling her name with a flourish.

"Forget the check, damn it, and look at me, Kelsey." He put out a hand to cover her fingers just as she finished signing her name. When she raised her eyes, resentment and wariness clear in them, he went on steadily, "I'm sorry if you were hurt by the fact that I left you alone last night. I honestly didn't know quite how to handle things. I intended to walk over this morning, maybe take you for a long hike on the beach while we discussed the situation. I thought you'd want some time to yourself when you awoke, though. After all, last night you didn't want to talk at all, remember?"

Last night she hadn't wanted to deal with the traumatic emotional events that had just taken place. She had been struggling between a longing to let herself drift in the physically pleasant afterglow of satisfaction and the knowledge that she was involved in a dangerous dilemma. She had chosen to give herself over to the physical languor.

Meeting Cole's steady gaze now, however, Kelsey realized there was no point trying to explain all that to him.

There wasn't much use trying to explain anything to a man who didn't believe in open, honest communication.

"I remember," she whispered.

His expression softened and so did his voice. "Last night was good, wasn't it, Kelsey?"

"Depends what you use to judge it," she told him with surprising calm.

He refused to react to the deliberate provocation, shaking his head with a whimsical smile. "I'm judging it by the way you wrapped yourself around me. By the fierce little demands you made. By the way you called my name and by the way you went up in flames in my hands. Going to deny it?"

"No," she said honestly. "By those standards, it was good. Want to know the truth? It was unlike anything else I've ever known. It was fantastic." She got to her feet abruptly, the check in her hand, aware that she had at last managed to take him by surprise. "I'll be sure to call you, Cole, the next time I'm in the mood for a terrifically interesting one-night stand. Here's the three thousand. You can cash the check on Monday. It won't bounce."

"Where do you think you're going?" he snarled as she picked up her checkbook and headed for the door.

"Home."

"What makes you think you can walk out like this?" He was right behind her.

"Common sense." She was almost at the door.

"You know full well you can't end everything between us just by walking out that door!"

"What are you going to do? Tie me up and lock me away here in your fortress?" She reached for the doorknob, aware that her hand was shaking. She wasn't at all

certain but that Cole might just do something that crazy.
She had to escape from his prison of a home.

"Kelsey, listen to me," he began.

"Anytime you feel like talking, *really* talking, I might
just decide to listen. In the meantime I've got better—"

She got no further as his hand clamped down on her
shoulder and he spun her around.

"You want a relationship based on total communication? Well, I want one based on total trust."

"You can't have one without the other," she cried.

He seemed to be making an effort to control his temper. "Kelsey, we're both talking in terms of extremes, and
that's not the way it has to be. We need to calm down and
start over."

"An excellent idea," she agreed very politely.

He searched her face with suspicion. "We need to start
over," he repeated cautiously, "but that doesn't mean we
can forget what happened last night."

"Don't worry," she told him with great depth of feeling. "I will never forget what happened last night."

"Don't twist my words, Kelsey," he warned. "Last
night I made you mine, and there's no going back to a
time when you didn't belong to me. That part of the situation remains carved in stone, understand?"

"I hear every arrogant word you're saying."

Something very much like anguish seemed to appear
in the normally unreadable gray eyes, startling Kelsey.
Whatever the emotion was it disappeared almost at once,
and she succeeded in convincing herself it hadn't been
there at all. Cole's fingers bit deeply into the persimmon
sweater.

"Kelsey, believe me, there are reasons for the rules I've
made for myself. It will be better for both of us if you'll
just trust me."

"When was the last time you trusted anyone, Cole?" she asked sadly. Before he could respond, she slipped out from under his hand and walked through the door.

Cole stood on the threshold, hands clenched at his sides as he watched her open the heavy iron gate. Her tawny hair danced around her shoulders as she swept out of the garden. He remembered the feminine strength and the softness in her that had been his last night, and he swore under his breath.

She was upset this morning because she'd accidentally come across those financial records of Roger's. Why the devil had the man put them on his computer, Cole wondered in disgust. Perhaps if Kelsey hadn't found that file she would have been in a much different mood this morning.

Or perhaps not, he conceded, slamming the front door of his home and heading back to his unfinished coffee. Kelsey was a cautious little thing, inquisitive and careful.

But last night he had proven to both of them that she was capable of abandoning herself in his arms. It was a start. In bed, at least, he could overcome her wary, prudent approach to their love affair. Given time he could teach her to trust him.

Cole's eyes fell on the check for three thousand dollars, lying on the table. Irritated, he picked it up and tore it into several very small pieces.

Monday he'd call a local travel agency and get himself booked on Kelsey's cruise. A week's vacation at sea might be the perfect way to reestablish the foundation of the affair he intended to have with Kelsey Murdock.

At least on a ship she wouldn't be able to run far.

4

"I WANT YOU TO KNOW how much I appreciate your dropping these analysis runs off at Valentine's island," Walt Gladwin told Kelsey for what must have been the hundredth time. "You're saving the company a couple of grand in courier's fees. And in addition I'll have the peace of mind of knowing the documents are in good hands."

"It's no problem, Walt. To tell you the truth, I'm somewhat curious about Mr. Valentine and his island. It should be an interesting side trip."

"The guy's a first-class eccentric, but he's also a genuine genius." Walt smiled, stuffing the computer printout sheets into a heavy black-leather attaché case that stood open on his desk. "This set of printouts is evidence of that. It's an analysis of his latest theories. He sent us the theoretical data on artificial intelligence that he wanted put through our computer and we're sending him back the results. They hold tremendous potential. He's making incredible strides in computer technology. He's got his own hardware on the island, but it's only a small, personal computer. He can explore some of his theories on it and work out the logic needed to analyze them, but he needs our mainframe to actually do the analysis of this kind of stuff. You won't have to worry about keeping track of the keys to these locks, by the way. Valentine has his own set. One less thing to think about."

Privately Kelsey thought the case with its shiny chrome locks looked like something out of a sophisticated fashion magazine for spies. She was going to feel a bit self-conscious carrying the thing aboard ship the next day.

It was typical of Walt Gladwin to supply such an exotic-looking case, however. When it came to personal items, Gladwin always treated himself to the best. One of the outstandingly successful young executives in the volatile world of computer technology, Gladwin had made a great deal of money very quickly, and, as he was fond of telling anyone who was interested, he fully intended to enjoy it while he was in his prime.

Gladwin's clothes were from the trendiest Italian and French designers. His hand-sewn shoes were made of the softest kid leather and his three cars were from three different European nations. Tonight he was driving Kelsey home in her favorite, the Ferrari. The Mercedes was lovely, too, of course, and she couldn't say she didn't like the Lotus. But there was something about the fire-engine-red Ferrari that appealed to her sense of humor.

She needed a bit of humor this evening, Kelsey decided with an inwardly stifled sigh as Walt closed up the office and escorted her out to the parking lot. It had been a long and not particularly fun-filled day in the office with Walt, readying the last of the documents she was to take to the man called Valentine.

In addition to the fact that she had put in some long, hard hours at work, Kelsey was forced to acknowledge that there had been no call from Cole.

She knew she had been expecting a phone call.

Over and over again she had told herself that the last thing she wanted was to hear from the man. But another small voice had assured her he wasn't the type simply to let her walk out the door. He would contact her. Kelsey had rehearsed several pithy phrases to use if and when she did hear from him, but to date there had been no occasion to use any of them.

It was just as well, she reminded herself as Walt opened the Ferrari door and ushered her inside. Whatever relationship she had hoped to build with Cole Stockton had been doomed from the beginning.

"Are you all packed?" Walt inquired easily as he piloted the high-strung car out of the parking lot.

"I think so. Just a few last-minute things to go in the suitcase." She cast a rueful eye on the attaché case. "Am I supposed to chain that to my wrist?"

Walt grinned, his good-looking features adjusting readily to the expression. Walt Gladwin was an attractive, open-faced man in his mid-thirties who smiled a lot. But, then, he had a lot to smile about, Kelsey reflected. Wealthy, successful and handsome, he seemed to have life in the palm of his hand. He also had a number of women there, too. Kelsey, for reasons she had never really stopped to analyze, had politely refused the one or two suggestions Walt had made that she join those women. Her lack of interest hadn't concerned Gladwin. He'd cheerfully gone on to the next flower, and Kelsey's relationship with him had remained strictly professional.

"Wouldn't be a bad idea," he mused pleasantly as he turned the Ferrari in the direction of Kelsey's apartment complex.

"You're kidding!" she said, laughing. "Are those reports that valuable?"

"Oh, they're valuable. To the right people, that is. Most folks probably wouldn't have any notion of the real worth, even if they did happen to see them. This artificial intelligence stuff is right out there on the edge of current technology. There are only a handful of people in the world who have any idea of what it's all about."

"They say that when we can teach computers to think like a human and actually make judgments that are based on human-type logic we'll have a whole new generation of machines," Kelsey noted.

"It'll be called the fifth generation. That's what Valentine is working toward." Walt nodded. "But it's a long way off. The small slice of the future we're working on at Flex-Glad is highly theoretical at this point."

"And Valentine is capable of understanding these reports?"

"Valentine created the basic theory on which these analysis sheets and reports are based. He doesn't have access to the kind of computer equipment he needs to test his ideas and theories, so Flex-Glad and Valentine have made a mutually beneficial bargain. We pay him to think and he allows us to test what he dreams up. If and when we hit the jackpot he'll get a share of the profits."

"If he needs access to sophisticated computers in order to verify his work, why does he live on that island?"

"He's a nut," Walt said with a shrug. "A certified eccentric. Who knows how he thinks? If he did his thinking in a normal way he wouldn't be very useful to us."

"I suppose you've got a point. He is expecting me, isn't he?"

"Yes, don't worry. He's made arrangements to meet you at the small landing strip that serves the island."

"Does anyone else live on that island?"

"A few people. Mostly fishermen and their families. From what I understand, Valentine ignores them and they return the favor. It's one of the least developed islands in the Caribbean, and that's saying something. The whole area isn't exactly rich."

"Do I just hand these papers over to him? I mean, should I get him to sign a receipt, or something? How will I know I'm dealing with the right man?" Kelsey asked curiously.

Gladwin chuckled. "There's only one Valentine. I met him a year ago. He's a huge bear of a man with long hair and a beard that falls halfway down his chest. He wears a pair of wire-rimmed glasses and he has an attitude about him that makes you think you're taking up his valuable time. You won't be encouraged to stay. All Valentine wants is to be left alone with his brain and the small computer he's rigged up on that island. Lucky for us he can't install the kind of hardware he needs to test his programs and theories. Otherwise he wouldn't need Flex-Glad. But there's no way he could put the highly sophisticated monsters into his shack. Nor could he afford them."

"He hasn't made a lot of money yet with his theories?"

"Just between you and me, the man's not much of a businessman," Walt confided. "Is this where I turn?"

"Yes, the next street. You can pull into the parking lot and I'll hop out."

Walt looked comically astonished. "What? No bon-voyage drink?"

Kelsey blinked. "Oh. Well, if you'd like to share one with me..."

"Sure. After all, I'm sending you off with a portion of Flex-Glad's future. I think that deserves a drink."

Gladwin parked the Ferrari and jumped out to open Kelsey's door. Together they walked up the stone path to her garden apartment.

"Nice place," Walt said as he glanced around at the small patio while Kelsey dug out her key.

"Thanks. I like it."

"Not as nice as your mother's place in Carmel, though, I'll bet. I'm thinking of picking up some beachfront property down there myself."

He probably would do just that, Kelsey decided as she turned the key in the lock. Walt was indulging himself these days. He might save money wherever he could in business, but he certainly didn't worry about stinting in his personal life.

Carmel was not a place she wanted to think about at the moment, however. The memories of her last night there still haunted her dreams and the pain of that final scene with Cole bit deep.

"Your phone's ringing," Walt observed helpfully as he pushed open the door. "You go ahead and answer it, and I'll see what you've got in your kitchen in the way of farewell toast material."

Kelsey watched him blithely walk into her sunny papaya-and-tan kitchen while she automatically reached for the phone. Walt certainly made himself at home easily. He'd never even been in her apartment before and already he was opening cupboard doors. Cole had a far more restrained attitude about such things, she reflected.

But, then, Cole had been far more restrained and cautious around her in every regard. Until that last night, of course.

Kelsey shivered and spoke quickly into the phone, anxious to erase the small chill that had coursed down her spine.

"Hello?"

There was a pause on the other end and even before she heard the soft, dark voice, Kelsey's instincts sensed the identity of the caller.

"It's about time you got home. It's almost ten o'clock."

"Cole."

Feeling unaccountably shaken, Kelsey sank down onto the leather-and-chrome chair beside the phone. After a week of silence he had decided to call. She wasn't at all certain she wanted to learn why. The palm of her hand grasping the white phone felt damp.

"What do you want, Cole?" Kelsey kept her voice low, aware of the tension in it. She prayed Walt would busy himself in the kitchen for a few more minutes. Frantically she tried to think how best to handle the situation. All the sharp little phrases she had been practicing seemed to have fled her mind.

"For starters, you could tell me where you've been all evening," he suggested a bit too blandly.

"Working." There, that was definitely short and pithy.

"I see."

"Look, Cole, I can't imagine why you're bothering to call tonight, unless—" She broke off as an overoptimistic thought struck her. "Unless you've finally decided to explain about that file in Roger's computer." She could feel the knot of uncertainty coiling in her stomach.

"You've got a one-track mind, haven't you, honey?" Cole said, sighing. "Well, as it turns out, so do I. Are you alone?"

"No, I'm not," she told him with a fierce hint of defiance. "My boss is having a bon-voyage drink with me. I can't really talk very long, Cole. Please say what you have to say and leave me alone."

"You mean, leave you with Gladwin," Cole growled. "Get rid of him, Kelsey."

Quite deliberately she maintained her silence in the face of the clear-cut command. Damned if she would allow this man to order her around.

"Kelsey? I mean it. You know better than to play this kind of game with me."

"I don't play games, Cole. You're the one who likes games," she accused tightly.

"Nothing," he vowed gently, "that I have ever done to you has been in the nature of a game. And I'm not playing one now. Kelsey, you've been seeing me for a month. Don't you know me well enough yet to realize I won't share you with another man, now that you belong to me?"

Kelsey swallowed, aware of the claim he insisted he had on her. The unpleasant truth was that she did know him well enough to believe he meant every word now. And she had no right to involve Walt in the firefight.

"Did you only call to harass me?" she managed coolly as Walt walked into the living room, holding a bottle of cognac and two glasses. He grinned cheerfully and sat down across from her on the white sofa.

"To be honest," Cole said calmly, "the answer is no. I called to see if you had made arrangements to have your parents' plants taken care of while you're gone. You're leaving tomorrow, aren't you?"

She drew a deep breath. "That's right." With a small smile she accepted the cognac Walt handed to her. "And you don't have to worry about the plants. I notified mom's housekeeper to start looking after them. Thank you for thinking of them, though," she went on in a deliberately chatty tone. "I believe everything's under control. I'll let you know how the trip was when I return. Thanks for calling to wish me goodbye."

Before Cole could respond she gently hung up the phone. "Just a neighbor calling to say so long," she explained lightly to Walt.

"Well, here's to a fun trip for you and a potentially profitable one for Flex-Glad," Walt said pleasantly, lifting his glass in a toast. "Be sure to send us all a postcard."

"Of Valentine?" she teased.

He laughed. "Never mind Valentine. Pick a shot of a nude beach. Much more interesting."

She was going to have to get rid of him quickly, Kelsey thought. Poor Walt. He had no idea of how he'd just been caught in the cross fire. But he was a nice man and she couldn't bring herself to involve him further.

True, Cole had been calling from Carmel and there wasn't much he could do about Walt tonight, but she instinctively knew that wasn't much protection for her boss in the future. She'd already had a sample of Cole's potential for violence and she knew just how implacable he could be. He had told her to get rid of Walt and—uneasily—Kelsey decided to do exactly that. It would be much safer for everyone, including herself.

God, she was letting Cole's threats get to her. A week of wondering if he would pursue the relationship as he had promised must have eaten away a portion of her brain.

But she had unfinished business with Cole Stockton, and until it was cleared up she had an obligation to keep others out of harm's way.

Fifteen minutes later Kelsey had politely maneuvered her boss to the door.

"Don't let that attaché case out of your sight, Kelsey," Walt warned on an unexpectedly serious note just as she was about to close the door.

"Don't worry, I'll take good care of it," she promised.

"I don't doubt that for a minute," he said with a grin, lifting a hand in farewell. "You're just about the best administrative assistant I've ever had. Take care and have a good trip."

The phone rang again just as Kelsey firmly shut and locked the door. With a sense of deep foreboding she picked up the receiver.

"Is he gone?" Cole asked blandly.

"What do you think?"

"I think he is."

He sounded so disgustingly sure of himself that Kelsey wanted to scream. It took a strong effort of will to hang on to her temper. "Then why bother calling back?" she asked politely.

"Just for the reassurance, I suppose."

"I didn't think you were the kind of man who needed any reassurances," she snapped. "You always seem so very damn sure of yourself."

There was a slight hesitation before Cole asked quietly, "Would you believe me if I told you there are times when you make me feel a little uncertain?"

"No," she retorted flatly. "Any man who has learned to put up the kind of walls you've built for yourself and your house hasn't got room for any emotion as soft and wishy-washy as uncertainty. Good night, again, Cole."

Very firmly Kelsey replaced the receiver, and then she unplugged the phone. Her mouth curving ruefully at the small, probably meaningless act of defiance, she headed for the bedroom to finish her packing.

THE FOLLOWING EVENING Cole flicked another glance at the face of the stainless-steel watch on his wrist. It was nearly nine o'clock and Kelsey still had not made an appearance. She had not shown up for the second seating at dinner, which was just ending, and there had been no

sign of her earlier in any of the three cocktail lounges.
Cole had checked them all.

He had wound up sharing dinner with the other couple who had been assigned to his table. June and George Camden were pleasant enough, even though one could get tired of hearing of George's exploits on the golf course. But the cheerful middle-aged couple certainly hadn't made up for the empty place across from Cole.

He had tipped well to have Kelsey reassigned to his table, but she, apparently, had had something better to do this evening than join the rest of the passengers in the main dining salon.

If he had been a less controlled man, Cole's fingers would have been drumming restlessly on the white tablecloth. Or perhaps he would have begun to snap his responses to George Camden's running monologue on golf courses he had known and loved.

But Cole allowed none of his growing unease and impatience to show. He knew she was on the ship. He had watched her come aboard late that afternoon in Puerto Rico. She had arrived in San Juan to catch the liner about an hour after he had. He hadn't seen her since she had disappeared with a cabin steward in the direction of her stateroom. Quite deliberately Cole had kept out of sight, wanting to time his appearance.

"Will you be going on to one of the lounges after dinner, Cole?" June Camden asked politely. "The entertainment should be starting soon."

"There's always a nice variety of young women looking for a little fun and games on these ships," George advised with a wink. "If I were you I'd take advantage of the opportunities available. The trick is to get moving before the ship's officers have picked out the best of the bunch."

"George!" his wife exclaimed in vast annoyance. "What a horrid way to talk! As if you knew!"

"Remember, I'm a golfer, my dear," George pointed out complacently. "I'm quite capable of observing the way the ball lies."

June got determinedly to her feet. Her comfortably rounded figure was sheathed in a vividly patterned silk dress of green and turquoise that set off the equally vivid blue of her lively eyes. "I think you will have to excuse us, Cole. It's time I took George into the nearest bar and bought him a drink. A few Scotch and sodas and he'll decide I still look good enough to dance with."

Cole gave her a serious, intent smile. "Believe me, June, you look good enough for that right now and I haven't even had any Scotch and sodas."

June laughed, delighted, and George arched bushy gray brows in mock warning as he rose beside his wife. "Hands off, my boy. You'll have to find a woman of your own tonight. This one's already spoken for!"

"Oh, George," and June chuckled, clearly pleased.

"Have a good evening," Cole said politely as they took their leave. "Perhaps I'll see you around later. After I've found my own lady for the evening."

"Good luck," George said, grinning.

Luck, Cole reflected as he watched them leave, should have nothing to do with it. Everything had been carefully engineered from his end. If there was one factor he did not like to have to depend on, it was luck. But something had gone wrong tonight. Kelsey should have been sitting opposite him all during dinner. What the hell had gone wrong?

Perhaps George was right. Maybe one of the ship's officers or a fellow passenger had already made his move. Cole rose, his face set in a cold, hard expression that made the hovering steward fear for his tip at the end of the cruise.

If she hadn't been hungry she might have spent the past couple of hours browsing around the huge luxury vessel, Cole told himself. He'd start with the sun deck and work down, systematically checking all the public rooms and lounges. She had to be somewhere on board.

With a methodical approach he moved from one deck to the next, pushing through a crowd of disco dancers in one lounge and then forging a path through the small gambling casino that had just opened up for the evening. From there he wandered outside to search the floodlit pool area.

It took quite a while to convince himself he'd covered every possible public place on board, but in the end Cole had to admit Kelsey wasn't anywhere to be found.

Surely she wouldn't have spent the first evening in her small stateroom, he told himself, realizing there was nowhere else to look. A woman like Kelsey didn't book herself onto an expensive Caribbean cruise and then sit alone in her room the first night out!

Still, he had pursued every other possible option. He might as well check her stateroom. Cole took the ship's elevator to the fourth deck and paced along the carpeted hall. He'd calmly bribed a cabin steward to get her room number earlier. It hadn't been a problem. Cole knew how to get information when he needed it.

Cabin number 4063 was one in a long row of outside staterooms. Cole paused in front of the orange door and found himself hesitating a fraction of a second before he knocked.

The faint twinge of uncertainty that stayed his hand was irritating but not unexpected. He was learning just what thoughts of Kelsey Murdock could do to him. The biggest question now was how she would react when she realized he was on board. He knocked on the cabin door.

There was a faint shuffling movement inside, and then a very low voice begged softly, "Please go away. I told you I didn't want any dinner."

Frowning at the weak sound of Kelsey's mumbled words, Cole knocked again. "Kelsey? Are you all right?"

There was another sound of movement and then the door was opened a distance of about three inches. One very weary, hazel-green eye stared at him balefully.

"Oh, my God," Kelsey breathed in shock. "Now I'm hallucinating." She slammed the door.

Prepared for that eventuality, Cole had thrust his foot over the threshold. "Kelsey, what's wrong? I was wondering what had happened to you."

Inside the small room, Kelsey leaned back against the door, fully aware she was too weak to counter the steady pressure he was applying. This was all she needed, she thought morosely. On top of everything else, Cole Stockton was on board ship with her.

"Kelsey, let me in."

The force of his one-handed push sent the door swinging inward. Kelsey was propelled forward. She managed to maintain herself in an upright position by grasping frantically for the edge of the bathroom door. It stood conveniently open because she had already made several trips through it.

Turning to glare at him, Kelsey found herself oddly distracted by the dark, powerful image he made dressed in a formal black evening jacket and a gray dress shirt. His deep-brown hair was combed into the familiar severe style.

By contrast she felt distinctly rumpled and frumpy. Her hair was hanging in tangled tendrils and her peach-colored bathrobe was knotted untidily. She knew she looked drawn and pale. Valiantly she struggled for her self-possession.

"This is a tropical cruise," she noted dryly. "Couldn't you have found something else besides a black dinner jacket? Something a little lighter in color? White socks might have added a nice touch."

"You know me and my limited wardrobe," he remarked, eyeing her closely. "But right now I'll have to say that I'm better dressed for life on a cruise ship than you are. What's the matter, Kelsey?"

She was too drained to make even a token protest of his presence. "I've never been at sea before." She closed her eyes briefly. "Apparently I'm not much of a sailor. Excuse me, Cole. I have a date with the bathroom." She lurched through the open door as another wave of nausea assailed her.

Cole was beside her instantly. "Take it easy, honey. It'll be all right," he soothed gently, holding her as the spasms shook her body.

"Go away," she pleaded. "Let me die in peace."

"You're not going to die."

"You don't know that for sure. Oh, Lord, I feel awful."

"As soon as I get you back to bed I'll dig up the ship's doctor. He'll be able to give you something for the seasickness. Here, let me wash your face."

She stood like a sick child, meekly allowing him to rinse her face and hands. Then he prepared her toothbrush with a dab of minty toothpaste and wrapped her fingers around the handle. "You'll feel better if you brush your teeth," he advised.

"How do you know?" she muttered belligerently. But she obeyed the soft command in his voice and leaned over the wash basin. "If only this ship would stop moving. Why didn't someone tell me it would be like this?"

"Because most people don't have any problems on a perfectly calm sea," Cole murmured, handing her a glass of water. "After you rinse your mouth out I want you to drink a little of this."

"I couldn't possibly," she groaned, staring at the glass as though it were a snake.

"Just a few sips. How long have you been sick?"

"Since an hour after I came on board."

"Then you're bound to be somewhat dehydrated. Take a couple of sips of water, Kelsey."

"It'll just come right back up," she warned miserably.

"Give it a chance," he urged, holding the glass to her pale lips.

She saw the concern in his smoky eyes as she obediently took two small swallows of water, and the knowledge that he was actually worried about her health fascinated her for a moment. "What are you doing here, Cole? You're supposed to be safe behind your high stone walls back in Carmel."

"Around you I find myself willing to take a few risks," he growled. "That's enough water. Now back to bed while I go dig the doctor out of the cocktail lounge."

"How do you know that's where he'll be?" She allowed herself to be guided across the small room to the single bed. She wasn't particularly surprised that Cole's arms felt strong and supportive, but she was vaguely astounded they also felt rather reassuring.

"Where would you hang out on the first night of a cruise if you were the ship's doctor? The infirmary?"

"Well, no, I guess not. Oh, Cole, I have never felt so terrible in my whole life. I just want to get off this ship and go home. Maybe I'll throw myself overboard."

"You'll feel entirely different in the morning. Trust me."

"I can't. I hardly know you, remember?" Kelsey wasn't quite sure where she found the energy for the small spurt of resentment. Given the way she felt, she was startled she could summon up even such a minor act of rebellion.

"The lady has a one-track mind," Cole said with a sigh as he tucked her into bed. "Stay put until I find the doctor, okay?"

"Believe me, I'm not going anywhere in my present condition."

A small smile crooked Cole's mouth as he stood looking down at her. "If you were always this cooperative, I wouldn't have any problems."

"I am not amused," Kelsey tried to say regally.

"I'll be right back." Cole turned to leave, and the toe of his shoe struck the black-leather attaché case sitting beside the bed. "Ah, let me guess. I'll bet that's Gladwin's little courier pack, isn't it? The one you're supposed to take to the kooky genius?"

"I've been instructed not to let it out of my sight. Lord, Cole, if I don't feel better by the day after tomorrow I may not be alive to deliver the papers!"

"I keep telling you to trust me," he muttered as he walked out the door.

Kelsey lay with her eyes closed, dreading each gentle movement of the ship, and wondered bleakly at what point during his mysterious past Cole had learned to be such a good nurse.

He certainly wasn't the squeamish type. But she couldn't help wondering if any man could maintain much interest in a woman who looked like death warmed over. A man in love might be able to handle his lover in the throes of seasickness, she decided grimly, but what about a man who was only interested in hiring a mistress? Her stomach turned violently at that moment, successfully changing the focus of her thoughts.

Cole arrived with the doctor who was young, good-looking and possessed of a brilliant bedside manner.

"Believe me, you're going to feel like a new woman in the morning," he promised cheerfully as he filled a hypodermic needle. "This stuff will fix you right up. Wouldn't want you to spend the cruise here in your bunk. Over you go now."

"Over where? Over the side?" Kelsey gritted her teeth as another wave of sickness threatened to consume her.

"Over on your stomach," the doctor said, chuckling, standing with the needle at the ready.

"Uh, couldn't you give me the shot in my arm?" she asked uncertainly, conscious of Cole's standing a foot away.

"Come on, honey, let's get it over with." Cole glided forward, sitting down beside her and pulling her lightly into his lap. Gently he smoothed aside the robe.

Kelsey swore softly and turned her face into his black jacket as the doctor delivered the medication. She felt abused and annoyed and embarrassed. In her disgruntled state of mind it was easy to suddenly blame Cole for the entire situation. If there had been even a hint of sensuality in his touch on her bare thigh, Kelsey would have bitten him. There was nothing but firm gentleness, however.

"That should take care of everything, Ms. Murdock. I'm sure I'm leaving you in capable hands. Check in with me in the morning if you have any further problems. I can give you some tablets if you need them. I have a hunch you'll be fine, however. Good night."

"It's okay for him to be so damn cheerful. He's headed back to the bar, I'll bet," Kelsey groaned. Hastily she re-adjusted her robe and wriggled off Cole's lap. "And I'm sure that's where you'd like to go, too. Thank you for the help, Cole. Please don't worry about me. I'll be all right. You've done more than enough."

But Cole was already getting to his feet and shrugging out of his jacket. "I'll stay until you're safely asleep. The doctor said the stuff he gave you would put you out like a light."

"Really, Cole, there's no need—"

"Honey, you're in no shape to kick me out, so you might as well accept the inevitable gracefully." He hung the jacket in her closet and came back to the bed.

Kelsey lay staring up at him through slitted lashes, absorbing the impact of his solid, dark presence here in her tiny shipboard bedroom. Through the welter of sensations, both physical and mental, that she had been experiencing during the past few hours, she suddenly realized that everything about her association with Cole Stockton took on overtones of inevitability.

Looking back, it seemed inevitable that they should meet. Having met, it seemed equally inevitable that he should have seduced her. And after the seduction it seemed inevitable that he should claim her as his own. Therefore, her blurry mind decided, it was probably inevitable that he should be standing here in her room.

"I think that shot the doctor gave me is affecting my brain," she told Cole drowsily.

"Were you really surprised to see me, honey?" Cole asked softly, as though he'd read her mind. "You shouldn't have been. You should have known I'd come after you."

"You didn't show much interest during the past week," she tried to say flippantly. "You called only once."

"And found you having a farewell drink with Gladwin."

She heard the hardening in his voice and took refuge in her illness. "Oh, Cole, my stomach..."

Immediately he hunkered down beside the bunk. "Want me to carry you into the bathroom?"

"No, I, uh, think I'll be all right this time. I'm feeling very sleepy, though." She closed her eyes, relieved to have found a way around the faint menace that had crept into his words. It was far more pleasant to have Cole in this helpful, concerned mood. "You're rather good at this nursing business. You must have done it sometime during your past, hmm?" Even on the verge of sleep, her body feeling devastated by the seasickness, Kelsey still found herself struggling for information about this man. She was drawn to him like a moth to a flame.

"No, Kelsey, I was never a nurse."

She thought there was a tinge of amusement in his tone, but she could no longer be sure. She could no longer be certain of anything, in fact. The blurriness in her mind seemed to be overwhelming her thought processes. Sleep beckoned as an escape after hours of fighting the seasickness, and she gave into it with a vast sense of relief.

She awoke only once during the night, turning sleepily onto her side in the dimly lit room. Cole had switched off all the lights except the small one over the dresser. He was still here, she thought, aware of a deep sense of comfort at the knowledge.

He stood in front of the dresser, reading intently. Perhaps he'd found a magazine. She started to close her eyes again and was almost asleep, when something registered on her drowsy brain.

The black leather attaché case stood open on the floor beside him. The papers he was examining must have come from the case.

The attaché case had been locked, she thought, unable to fight the pull of the drug-induced sleep. She knew it had been locked. Big, shiny chrome locks that Walt Gladwin had closed. He hadn't given her the keys, saying that Valentine had a set of his own.

Cole had no right to be prying into that case, Kelsey tried to tell herself, but it was useless to struggle against the pleasant oblivion that was claiming her. She sank heavily back into the depths of slumber.

5

KELSEY WAS IMMEDIATELY aware of two things the moment she awoke: the first was that Cole wasn't in the room and the second was that her stomach felt calm. It was some time before she realized the black attaché case was gone. She was on her way to the shower, glorying in her victory over the seasickness, when she remembered the midnight vision of Cole poring over the contents of the attaché case.

Half-convinced the memory was a dream, she automatically glanced around for the case. It wasn't in the room.

Brow furrowing in concentration, she checked the small closet, glanced under the bunk and then yanked open the dresser drawers. Nothing. Surely Cole wouldn't have taken it. He could have no possible interest in a bunch of computer printouts and analysis sheets. And she must have imagined that late-night scene of Cole studying the papers.

This morning what she really wanted to remember was the way he had taken care of her last night. She had awakened with a sense of loss at the realization that he wasn't with her. During the night he had offered comfort and practical assistance. His touch had been gentle and soothing.

She certainly hadn't looked like anyone's idea of a glamorous mistress last night, Kelsey reminded herself as she gave up the search for the case and went on into the bathroom. There was no denying that Cole's concern had been deeply comforting. Somehow it had soothed much of the inner anger and resentment she had been experiencing all week.

She ought to have known better. After all, Kelsey thought savagely, nothing had changed in their relationship. She knew no more about him than she ever had.

Except now she knew he could deal very competently with a sick female.

And what had he done with her attaché case, she wondered nervously. For that matter, where was Cole? One thing was certain, she thought with dark humor: he couldn't have got off the ship. They had been underway all night and weren't due to dock in a port until tomorrow morning.

Again she thought of his actions during the previous evening. She had been too ill to be terribly astonished at the sight of him. Instead she had decided that his presence was inevitable. At least that was the way it had seemed to her weary brain last night.

Now she had to ask herself just why Cole had followed her and why he had taken care of her. And most of all why he had broken into the attaché case.

The conclusions she was forced to arrive at in the shower were nerve-racking. Walt had said the information in that case was extremely valuable but that only a handful of people could understand it. He certainly hadn't implied that anyone might resort to stealing it.

Cole had never seemed particularly interested in computers in general, but they had spent a lot of time talking about her job, Kelsey reminded herself anxiously.

But she had met him so casually! There had been nothing suspiciously coincidental about it. Or so she assumed. He had simply been a reclusive man who had eventually made friends with his next-door neighbors and, ultimately, with their daughter.

He hadn't even known she worked for Flex-Glad until after he had met her. Unless her stepfather had mentioned it, she added in silent anguish.

God, she was going crazy this morning, trying to figure out the whole mess. She had to get control of herself and the situation. The first order of business was to get back that attaché case. Walt had entrusted her with it. She couldn't bear to confess she had been stupid enough to get seduced by an industrial spy who had now stolen the data she was supposed to deliver to Valentine.

Nor could she bear to believe that Cole would do such a thing to her. Kelsey shuddered as she slipped into a white collarless linen shirt and matching wide-legged linen pants. Sliding her feet into a pair of bright-red sandals, she paused to run a brush through her hair and clip the tawny stuff back behind her ears.

She had to keep things in perspective. With those words of caution echoing in her head, Kelsey left her stateroom and headed for the dining room. For the first time since she had arrived on board she found herself thinking about food.

Perhaps after a cup of coffee she would be able to sort out the truth of the situation. Then she would confront Cole and demand some explanations. This time he wasn't going to get away with simply refusing to discuss certain subjects, she promised herself.

The sea air was fresh and invigorating. This morning the endless blue waters were a delight to the eye. Sunlight danced on the waves and the gentle motion of the ship no longer bothered her. The day was already turning warm. Kelsey took a brisk walk on deck before seeking out the dining room. It was still early, and only a handful of people were at breakfast. She saw Cole almost immediately.

Kelsey hesitated at the realization that she was going to have to deal with him before she'd had the promised coffee and more time to think. Then her natural spirit surged to the surface. Lifting her chin, she walked straight toward the table where he sat alone. Cole watched her come toward him, a politely unreadable expression on his hard face.

"Good morning, Kelsey. We have the table to ourselves. The Camdens appear to be late risers. How are you feeling?" He got to his feet to hold her chair.

"Much better, thank you," she declared with a breeziness she was far from feeling as she accepted the chair. "Where's the attaché case?"

He blinked lazily under her steady, demanding gaze. But he made no move to sidetrack her. "It's safe enough for the moment."

Kelsey took a deep breath. "I want it back, Cole. And I also want back all the papers that were inside."

He handed her the breakfast menu and said casually, "You act as though you think I might have stolen something, Kelsey. Be careful what you say next."

"Have you stolen anything, Cole?" she asked stonily. "I saw you looking at the printouts that were in that case."

His gray eyes chilled. "Do you believe I'd take them from you?"

"I'm asking because, as usual with you, I don't know what to believe!"

Cole reached for the silver coffeepot that had been set on the table. "Are you ever going to trust me, Kelsey?"

"I told you once you couldn't have trust without genuine communication," she bit out tightly. Kelsey leaned forward. "I want that case back. I have a responsibility to deliver it. I do not want to have to admit to myself or to Walt Gladwin that I allowed a man who had seduced me to make off with those printouts. If you have any respect or . . . affection for me at all, Cole, you will stop playing games and give me back that case."

He stared at her intently for a long moment, studying her tense features. "And if you trusted me at all you wouldn't accuse me of industrial espionage."

Kelsey paled, but her voice stayed even. "I guess we know where we stand with each other, then, don't we? All the evidence would seem to indicate you've taken advantage of me."

"Do you truly believe that? Last week you accused me of blackmailing your stepfather. Now I'm supposedly a thief. Last night you didn't think so badly of me. But if you are prepared to make accusations this morning why don't you call a ship's officer and do it right?"

Kelsey bit her lip and shifted restlessly in the chair. "I don't think there's any need to go that far. Just give me back the case and we'll forget about the whole thing."

"No, we will not forget about the whole thing. If you honestly believe I've stolen those printouts, then do something about it. Call an officer and report it. A search will be made of my room and the case will be found. You will identify it and that will be that. You'll probably be able to press charges when we get home." Cole smiled one of his rare smiles, but his eyes were colder than ever. "Go ahead, Kelsey. Act on your beliefs. Make a formal accusation."

"Stop it," she told him, infuriated at the way he was pushing her. She couldn't report him, and he must have known that. "I don't want any dramatic scenes. I just want that case. If it's in your room we can go and get it after breakfast. I won't ask you why you took it—"

"How forebearing of you," he mocked.

"Damn it, how would you feel this morning if the situation were reversed? If you'd seen me going through the contents of that case in the middle of the night and then awakened to find it gone?"

"This reminds me of the conversation we had last week," he mused as a chilled grapefruit was set in front of him. "At that time you were asking me how I'd react if I discovered someone was blackmailing one of my relatives."

"I'm trying to make you understand how ridiculous it is of you to keep demanding that I take everything you say or won't say on trust!"

"Are you going to order breakfast?" he interrupted gently as the steward hovered.

"The last thing I'm thinking about at the moment is breakfast!" she raged stiffly.

Cole glanced up at the waiter. "You can bring her some poached eggs and toast. She was a little seasick last night, so I think we'll keep it simple."

"Yes, sir," the man responded respectfully.

"Cole," Kelsey began as the steward disappeared. "Please stop harassing me. I don't understand you. What do you want from me?"

"You know what I want from you." He calmly started eating the pink grapefruit.

"The printouts?" she challenged.

With great care he put down his spoon. "No, Kelsey, I do not want the printouts. I want you."

"Really?" she retorted sardonically. "Then why take the printouts instead?"

He looked at her with steel in his eyes. "I've told you that if you think I've stolen those printouts, you'd better do something about it. Are you going to call a ship's officer and report me, or not?"

"Don't you dare push me, Cole," she blazed.

"I am pushing you, lady. Either make a formal accusation or stop threatening me. You're ruining my breakfast."

"What do you think you're doing to mine?" she wailed furiously.

"I'm the guy who made it possible for you to eat again this morning, remember? If it hadn't been for me you'd still be lying in your bunk in between running to the bathroom!"

"Cole, you're being utterly ridiculous, expecting me to accept your actions without any explanation."

"There's an explanation. There's always an explanation. Blame yourself for not being able to see it."

"I'm blaming you!" she snapped, outraged.

"So it would seem. So do something or shut up. Call a ship's officer or else let me eat my breakfast in peace."

"You're so damned unreasonable."

"Is it unreasonable to want a little trust from the woman I've asked to come and live with me?"

"This is hardly a 'little' trust, and you're out of your mind if you think your offer is anything terrific in the first place."

"You're getting a bit loud, Kelsey," he pointed out.

"So why don't you do something about it? Call a ship's officer and complain," she suggested, throwing his challenge back in his face.

"You know, I think you were more pleasant when you were sick to your stomach." Cole set down his grapefruit spoon with deliberation. He folded his arms on the white tablecloth and assumed his familiar, aloofly alert expression. "Well? What are you going to do?"

Kelsey had never experienced such a combination of fury and exasperation in her entire life. She ought to take him up on his dare, go ahead and report him to someone in authority. After all, she'd seen him examining the contents of that case and he'd admitted he'd taken it. Why she was hesitating was beyond her.

But she knew, even as she sat there infuriated, that she wasn't going to report him as a thief. What really unnerved her was that Cole probably knew it, too.

"Kelsey?" he prodded softly.

"Eat your breakfast in peace, Cole. You know damn well I'm not going to turn you in for stealing that case." The emotion drained out of her, Kelsey threw down her napkin and made to rise. Cole's hand swept out in a smooth movement, closing around one of her wrists with a pressure that kept her anchored in her seat. His strength could be quite appalling, she thought distantly, staring at his fingers.

"Why aren't you going to call for help, Kelsey?" he asked huskily

"Probably because I'm a fool." She refused to meet his eyes, continuing to stare down at her trapped wrist.

"You're not a fool and we both know it. So why aren't you yelling for the captain?"

That brought her head up proudly. "Why don't you tell me?"

"All right, I will," he said, surprising her by agreeing. "I think you're going to back off from doing anything rash this time for the same reason you didn't scream blackmail to the authorities last week. The same reason you got rid of Gladwin so quickly the other evening after I called. You belong to me now, Kelsey, and on some level I think you recognize that. Our battles are too private, too intimate to allow you to drag others into them. Furthermore, I think you trust me more than you even realize."

"I don't know what could possibly give you that impression," she gasped, ignoring the rest of his words.

"Last night gave me that impression." His expression softened slightly. "You let me take care of you last night, honey. I saw the way you looked at me just before you went to sleep. You weren't frightened of me, were you?"

"I was too sick to waste any energy being frightened," she argued. But it was true. She had found his presence vastly comforting. Even when she'd awakened in the middle of the night and discovered him going through the attaché case she hadn't had the sense to be worried. It wasn't until morning had arrived and she'd realized both he and the case were gone that she'd started questioning his actions.

"Kelsey, deep down do you really believe I've stolen your precious attaché case?"

"Cole, this is not a good time to push me," she gritted, not wanting to be forced into answering.

"I can't seem to find a good time so it will have to be now. Tell me the truth, honey."

She sucked in her breath, knowing she was thoroughly trapped. "I expect you've got some justification for what you did," she temporized coldly.

His mouth crooked wryly. "Your generosity overwhelms me."

"Will you at least give me this much, Cole?" she asked tightly. "Just tell me why you took the case."

Impatience flickered in his eyes, and his voice hardened. "Because I don't like the idea of Gladwin forcing you to chaperon a locked case, that's why. For God's sake, Kelsey, anything that has to be kept under double locks must be valuable. This whole situation bothers me. It has since you first mentioned it. I decided to take the case to my room so that you would no longer have to be responsible for it. Couldn't you have figured that much out for yourself?"

"I saw you looking at the papers inside that case," she whispered.

"Simple curiosity. I wanted to know whether you were carrying anything that could get you into trouble. That's the only reason I opened the case. If it's any consolation, I'm no wiser than I was before I opened it. Those printouts look like so much gibberish."

She considered that broodingly, knowing that, for some totally irrational reason, she actually believed him. The man was so calmly arrogant about the whole situation, though. It made her want to keep pushing and prying and demanding, even when common sense told her she'd probably gone far enough. You'd have thought that by now she would have learned to observe the strict limits Cole set, Kelsey reminded herself.

"Simple curiosity got you through two very sophisticated locks without using keys?" Kelsey remarked with mocking politeness.

"Curiosity is a powerful motivator," he murmured equally politely.

"You are an unreasonable, incomprehensible, totally frustrating man," she said with a sigh, knowing she was beaten.

"Who wants you very much," he added.

Kelsey flushed under the coolly sensual remark. "But not badly enough to risk a little honest, open communication."

Cole shook his head wryly as her plate of poached eggs and toast was set down along with his mushroom omelet. "Kelsey, honey, you are the victim of all that junk pop psychology that's always being pushed in the media. I can't imagine where everyone got the notion that total communication was always a great thing."

"You're saying you don't believe in honesty?" she gritted, relieved the eggs were actually tasting good and that her stomach was accepting them without a whimper.

"I'm saying I believe more strongly in the right to privacy," he returned easily.

"You certainly weren't respecting my boss's right to privacy when you went through those printouts last night!"

"That's different."

"How?" she demanded forcefully.

"It involves you. Your rights are far more important to me than those of Walt Gladwin. I don't want you being used."

"I am not being used. I am carrying out a small task for my employer. And you had no right to get into that case without permission! Furthermore," she declared recklessly, "if anyone's guilty of using me in the recent past, it's you, not Walt!"

A warning flashed in Cole's eyes, but his voice was silky smooth. "You'd rather be used by an employer than by a lover?"

"At least I get paid by my employer!" Kelsey shot back without pausing to think. She regretted the rash words the moment they were out, but it was far too late.

"I told you last week, I'm willing to pay," he reminded her with a devastating coldness.

Kelsey felt the blood drain from her face. Her stomach, which had been accepting the toast and eggs without complaint, tightened into a savage knot. "Yes, you did, didn't you," she murmured, carefully folding her napkin and setting it beside her plate. "How could I possibly forget your generous offer of bed and board? Excuse me, Cole, I seem to have lost my appetite."

Cole said nothing as she got to her feet and walked out of the dining room. But silently he called himself every name he could think of that meant blundering idiot.

On the other hand, he asked himself savagely, what choice did he have? He wasn't going to unlock all the doors he had closed, not even for Kelsey Murdock. She wouldn't like what she found behind them, anyway. Damn it to hell, why couldn't the woman leave well enough alone? Why did she have to keep pushing and provoking until he found himself deliberately retaliating the way he had a moment ago?

Reminding her of his offer to compensate her for the salary she would lose when she came to live with him was not exactly his brightest move lately. He had already learned she didn't think much of his proposal.

Cole's eyes narrowed as he gazed unseeingly out the nearby dining-salon window. The situation was complicated, but he had the rest of the week to reestablish the basis of the affair.

It was far from hopeless, he told himself. He'd had some proof lately that when it came down to the bottom line, Kelsey knew whose woman she really was. The way she had responded to him the night he had made love to her, the way she had obeyed him the other evening when he'd phoned and discovered Gladwin was with her and the way she had trusted him to take care of her last night. All the reasons he had listed for her earlier were valid.

But she was hung up on this communication business. Cole went back to his omelet while he considered that roadblock. He'd either have to find a way around it or he'd demolish it.

Because one thing was certain: no one was allowed past the gates that guarded his past. He was a different man now, a man Kelsey could respect and to whom she could give herself without reservation once she accepted the situation. The past had been put behind him by an act of will. He intended to keep it there.

He could allow her some time, but he could not allow her any real choice in the end. Cole didn't kid himself. He wanted her, but more than that he needed her. She was the element that would complete his new life, an element he'd sensed vaguely had been missing but that he hadn't been able to define until he'd met her.

He'd be a fool to let her escape, Cole knew. A lot of people had called him a great many names in the past, but no one had ever labeled him a fool. Foolishness and survival did not go together. Cole was a survivor.

KELSEY FOUND A LOUNGER on the sun deck and flung herself into it. She had brought a magazine to peruse, but it was proving impossible to concentrate. From beneath the canvas awning that provided shade for this portion of the deck she idly watched the bright bikinis and swimsuits gather at poolside. White-jacketed stewards circulated platters of iced tea and rum punches to the cheerful crowd as bodies coated with tanning oil glistened in the sun.

Still feeling a little weak from her ordeal the day before, Kelsey had opted not to go swimming this morning. Today the gentle swells of the sea were beautiful to behold, instead of nausea inducing, she thought with wry amusement. Tomorrow they would be docking in St. Thomas, one of the U.S. Virgin Islands. From there she would take her short charter hop to Valentine's little island.

Always assuming she could get that damned attaché case back from Cole, she added disgustedly. She ought to have put up more of a battle to repossess that case. Instead she had allowed him to send her fleeing from the dining room.

Well, perhaps she hadn't exactly fled, she consoled herself. She had simply walked away from the insult he had delivered. The problem was, Cole didn't seem to understand that what he was offering was an insult.

Perhaps he'd never asked a woman to give up everything and come and live with him. She had no way of knowing what his previous history was with women because she had no way of knowing anything about his previous history, period.

As usual, total frustration set in on that thought, and Kelsey deliberately opened her magazine. She tried very hard to read the fashion article in front of her, but all she could think of was the conflict she was experiencing internally.

Kelsey knew she had been hoping that the cruise would provide the time she needed to make the break psychologically with Cole. She had been counting on the change of atmosphere and the change of pace to enable her to put her life back in perspective.

Now he was here, making all that impossible. She might as well face the fact that this week was going to be one of the most difficult of her life. She had to deal with it because there was no longer any way to run from it. He had seen to that.

"I brought you some iced tea." Cole materialized behind her and took the empty lounger on her left. He set the glass of tea down within her reach. "Not going swimming?"

"How do you manage to sneak up on people so quietly, Cole?" she demanded, asking the first question that popped into her head as she met his eyes. As usual, she hadn't even heard his approach.

He studied her with a flicker of wariness, obviously surprised by her words. "Soft-soled shoes?" he offered hopefully.

His flippancy infuriated her. "Can't you even answer a simple question like that one?"

"Hey," he pleaded, holding up a hand in a placating gesture, "I'm sorry. I didn't mean to be evasive."

"You're always evasive."

"That's not true," he pointed out reproachfully. "I never evade your questions. Sometimes I simply refuse to answer them. There's a difference. In any event, this time around I asked you a question first."

"To which the answer is self-evident," she muttered. "No, I am not going swimming this morning. And it looks like you're not, either," she added, glancing at the rolled-up sleeves of his khaki shirt. "Wearing your normal daytime attire, I see. Delightfully neutral khaki. Don't you have a pair of khaki swim trunks?" she asked innocently.

"If you hadn't been so ill last night, I'd be tempted to put you across my knee. Drink some of your iced tea, honey, and stop trying to bait me. It could be hazardous to your health."

"The tea or baiting you?"

"Guess," he suggested dryly.

"Threats, Cole?" she dared, driven by some indefinable desire to provoke him. It was always like this around him. She felt she had to keep pushing until she found out what made him tick. Incredibly stupid, of course. No woman in her right mind went around probing time bombs to find out what made them tick.

"If they are, I think you know me well enough to be sure they aren't idle ones."

Kelsey glared at him and made a show of returning to her magazine article as if he didn't exist.

"You see, Kelsey?" Cole went on almost cheerfully, "You know more about me than you think. You know when to quit."

It was the amusement in his voice that got to her. "On top of everything else, Cole, please don't laugh at me."

She felt him tighten beside her on the lounger. Aware of the sudden tension in him, Kelsey felt a pang of remorse. Cole's attempts at humor were rare enough as it was. For some crazy reason she wished she hadn't squelched this last poor attempt.

"I am not laughing at you, Kelsey," he told her quietly.

"Then what were you doing?" She set down the magazine and met his eyes very squarely.

"Trying to lighten the situation, I suppose." He leaned back in the lounger with a rather wry curve to his mouth.

"Why bother?"

"I wanted this cruise to be a fresh start for us, honey." He was watching the swimmers, not her face.

Kelsey experienced another wave of inner regret. For one solid month she had wanted nothing more than to have her relationship with Cole succeed. After the traumatic events of last weekend she had told herself nothing could salvage the situation between them. Yet here she was, longing to believe there might be hope. The knowledge that Cole still wanted her seemed to cut through all the rational reasons why she could not possibly risk a love affair with him.

"Do you really think that's possible, Cole? With all that stands between us?" she whispered.

His head snapped toward her, the gray gaze ruthlessly intent. "Nothing stands between us but your stubborn female curiosity and arrogance."

Kelsey drew back as if he'd slapped her. "Thank you, Mr. Stockton, for your succinct analysis of the situation!"

Cole said something explicit and savage. Then he appeared to take a tight rein on his temper. "Please, Kelsey. Just give us another chance, will you? Give us this week together. That's all I'm asking of you."

To have Cole Stockton asking—no, *pleading*—for such a favor was a distinctly unsettling shock, Kelsey discovered. It took away her breath for a timeless instant. She was a fool to allow him so close, an idiot even to listen to him. But she could not deny her emotional response. A week ago she would not have believed that Cole would resort to pleading for anything, let alone a woman's patience. Kelsey touched the tip of her tongue to her lower lip, her pulse picking up speed as she acknowledged the yearning inside her.

"Cole, if you would at least tell me about those payments Roger is making to you..." she began uncertainly, seeking some kind of compromise, any kind of compromise.

He closed his dark lashes, every line of his face unyielding. "It doesn't concern you, Kelsey. It's between Roger and me. Your stepfather wants it that way, and he trusts me to keep my word on the matter. I can't discuss it with you."

"I'll just have to trust you, is that it?" She sighed.

He lifted his lashes. "Is that too much to ask?"

"In all honesty, I think it is," she told him quietly. "But that's not going to stop you, is it? You're going to ask it, anyway."

He sat up on the lounger, reaching out to capture her hand in a compelling grip. Kelsey shivered under the stark intensity in him. She felt mesmerized beneath the force of the power he was wielding over her.

"Yes, I'm going to ask for your trust. I've told you that I think it exists. I just want you to acknowledge it so we can build on it."

Wariness blazed in the depths of her eyes as she sat very still under his grasp. "And what are you prepared to give me in return, Cole?"

"Anything I can," he answered simply.

"Except the truth about you and your past," she concluded. *Or your love,* she added in painful silence. If Cole did not understand why she needed to know everything there was to know about him; if he didn't realize why she had pushed and prodded and tried to force open, honest communication between them, then he didn't understand anything at all about love. If he didn't comprehend it, he could not give it. There was no future for her with Cole Stockton.

"I have given you my word that I will never lie to you," he countered roughly.

"Oh, Cole," she breathed helplessly.

"Just give us a chance, honey. That's all I'm asking. I give you my word, I won't push you into bed this week. I only want to spend the time with you."

"It won't change anything," she tried to protest, hearing the uncertainty in her own words and cursing it. "Too much has already gone wrong between us...."

"That's in the past, Kelsey," he told her. "And I've learned how to put the past behind me."

"Just close a door and walk away?" she asked sadly.

"Whatever it takes," he said, shrugging.

"And you call *me* arrogant," she murmured, shaking her head in wonder.

"Kelsey?"

She sought for some rational, face-saving way out of the dilemma. "The ship isn't that big," she tried crisply. "I can't very well spend the next week running from one end to the other just to avoid you, can I?"

His mouth crooked and the relief was plain in his eyes. "Is that a roundabout way of telling me you're not going to try to pretend I don't exist for the next few days?"

She looked at him gravely. "Cole, I might try to run from you, I might try to ignore you or I might try to strangle you, but I don't think I could ever pretend you don't exist!"

Kelsey heard the capitulation in her own words, and the flash of satisfaction in Cole's icicle eyes told her he had heard it, too.

"I'll show you how it's done, honey."

"How what's done?"

"How to close a door and start over."

"You're an expert?"

He brushed the question aside, lifting a hand in a negligent gesture that brought a steward hurrying over to the lounger.

"Another glass of iced tea, please," Cole ordered politely. "The ice in this one seems to have melted."

"Yes, sir." The steward started toward the poolside bar to put in the order.

"And speaking of melting ice," Cole began firmly, turning back to Kelsey.

"Were we speaking of it?"

"Oh, yes," he assured her gently. "We most certainly were."

Kelsey didn't miss his meaning. She fully understood he was referring to her. But privately she thought he was wrong. True, she might have softened a little this morning under the heat of his insistence, but it seemed to her the real melting action had just taken place in Cole's ice-colored eyes.

Her wary, very cautious agreement to spend the week with him had raised the temperature in those eyes by several degrees. She couldn't help speculating on what her outright surrender would accomplish.

It was too bad that the risks remained so high. Because the urge to allow herself to love Cole Stockton was a singing compulsion in her veins.

6

"THAT'S CIBOLA COMING UP straight ahead." His voice raised so the passengers could hear him over the whine of the Cessna's engine, the pilot indicated a patch of gray-green looming above the ocean surface. "And that little cluster of shacks near the harbor is what passes for a village. The rest of the island is just about empty."

"Thank goodness we're almost there." Sitting in one of the rear seats of the four passenger plane, Kelsey's fervent comment went unheard by either the rather taciturn pilot or Cole, who was sitting in the right front seat.

They had left the airport on St. Thomas half an hour earlier, and as soon as the little plane had leaped skyward Kelsey had begun to question the decision to hire a small plane for the hop to Cibola. Actually, she had questioned the plan even before that. The moment she had seen the heavyset pilot with his mirrored sunglasses and his sweat-stained shirt she had wondered aloud about the wisdom of flying to Cibola.

"Would you prefer to swim?" Cole had inquired laconically.

"I don't like people who wear mirrored sunglasses," Kelsey had grumbled.

"You don't have to love the guy. All we need to worry about is whether he's qualified to fly a plane to that island where your genius lives."

Ray, the pilot, didn't appear to bother with the formality of a last name. He had been ready and waiting for them at the airport when Kelsey and Cole had arrived.

"Only supposed to be one of you," Ray had pointed out skeptically, eyeing Cole, who was carrying the attaché case.

"Plans have changed slightly," Cole had told him calmly. "Ready to leave?"

"Yeah, I reckon so."

Kelsey had told herself she could hardly criticize Ray for his sweat-dampened clothing. Her own yellow cotton safari-style shirt was clinging uncomfortably to her skin as she followed the pilot across the hot pavement. The heavy humidity combined with the heat of the day made it impossible to stay serenely cool. She wished she had worn a short skirt instead of the white jeans. It might have been more comfortable.

Cole didn't appear particularly affected by the muggy heat. Dressed in his customary khaki clothes and a pair of low leather boots, he had looked quite at ease in the tropical surroundings.

In fact, Kelsey told herself now, as she watched Cibola coming closer on the horizon, one could even say Cole looked almost at home.

She'd had plenty of time to speculate on Cole's behavior during the past twenty-four hours. The noise of the Cessna engines had made conversation a strain. So she had sat quietly in the rear seat and reflected on the wary relationship she had allowed herself to enter.

Not that she'd had much choice in the basic decision, she decided wryly. It was either compromise with Cole or try to escape the ship. It hadn't taken any great degree of intelligence to reason that much out. Cole was on board with only one purpose in mind, and that was to force her back into a relationship on his terms. Kelsey was learning the hard way that when he set himself a goal he allowed nothing to get in his path.

She had surrendered at least partially, Kelsey knew, but she had been prepared for the whole fragile situation to collapse under the weight of the first major confrontation. And she had assumed that confrontation would take place at her stateroom door last night.

Cole had made no secret of his desire during the evening they had spent together. But he'd behaved as the polite, quietly restrained escort he had been on the weekends this past month. By the time she had eaten dinner with him, attended the cabaret show and then danced with him out on deck under the stars, she had finally begun to relax.

No, Kelsey told herself with rigorous honesty, she had more than relaxed. She had begun to slip back under the spell of the man. It had done no good to remind herself what had happened the last time she had attempted to break free of that emotional sorcery. She had still found herself going willingly into his arms as they danced, her tawny head on his shoulder and her body luxuriating in the feel of his hands on her waist.

When the moment had come, as she had known it would, and they found themselves standing in the hall outside her stateroom door, only her hard-won caution had prevented her from surrendering completely to the magic and the man.

"Kelsey?" There had been a hungry question in the way Cole had said her name as he feathered a kiss along the line of her throat. And demand had been buried just beneath the question.

"No," she had managed starkly, focusing on the first button of his dark, formal shirt. Her crimson-tipped nails had flexed unconsciously into the black fabric of his jacket sleeve. She had been violently aware of the tension in him, and for a precarious instant she wondered if he would explode the way he had that fateful night in her mother's home.

"Kelsey, honey, I'll make it good for you. I'll make you forget the fear and the caution and all the questions."

Kelsey had shivered under the rough honey of his words and the sensual glide of his fingers as he stroked the nape of her neck. He had felt that telltale tremor. She had known he felt it, because she had immediately sensed the leaping satisfaction in him. Perhaps it had been that knowledge that had given her the fortitude to stand by her decision.

"No," she had said again, very softly but very firmly.

He had hesitated then, and she had felt the strength in his hands as he tightened them ever so slightly on the curve of her shoulder. But Cole had nodded, as if to himself, and stepped back, gray eyes as unreadable as fog.

"Good night, Kelsey. I'll pick you up for breakfast."

She had stood in the corridor and watched him walk away. He hadn't looked back.

Now Kelsey sat watching the approach of Valentine's island, and told herself for what must have been the thousandth time that she had made the right decision last night. She had known from the beginning that Cole Stockton was fire and that she was in danger of being consumed by the blaze. She must stay just out of reach for her own safety. There was no doubt that the intricate dance at the edge of the flames was a dangerous one.

Ray made a competent landing on the small dirt strip that had been hacked into the leeward side of the tiny island. He taxied to the far end and shut down the engines. The strip paralleled the rocky shoreline. As far as Kelsey could see the only respectable patch of sandy beach was that lying in a crescent framing a small bay not far away. It was protected by a rock-strewn, craggy cliff.

"I don't see anyone waiting for us," Kelsey said, peering through the window at the heavy foliage that began at the edge of the dirt strip and climbed back to the hills forming a backbone down the long, narrow island.

"That's not my problem," Ray noted. "How long you want me to wait?"

"We'll give the guy half an hour to show," Cole said decisively, unlatching his door to let some breeze into the cabin of the plane.

Kelsey frowned. "I can't leave until I've delivered that case."

"Time on the ground is the same price as time in the air," Ray reminded them curtly.

"Half an hour," Cole repeated. He stepped easily out of the Cessna and then turned to help Kelsey.

"Cole, I have a job to do. I can't leave until that case has been turned over to Valentine."

"'Valentine'?" Ray interrupted. "The weirdo who messes around with computers?"

"That's right," Kelsey replied quickly, glancing back into the plane where Ray still sat. "Do you know him?"

"I've brought other deliveries to him." Ray nodded. "He's got a shack up in those hills. Not too far. He usually walks down to meet the plane."

"Maybe he forgot this was the day I'm supposed to arrive," Kelsey said thoughtfully.

"Honey," Cole said, "on an island this small he's bound to have heard the Cessna coming in for a landing. Even if he did forget the date, he probably remembered as soon as he heard the plane. He'll be down soon. If he's coming at all."

Kelsey was beginning to realize just how completely Cole was taking over. On an hour-by-hour basis the number of little decisions he made for her was growing. Last night most of the decisions had been disguised as suggestions, she acknowledged. Still, she had wound up with the Cabernet wine he had brought to her attention and the scallops in basil sauce he had mentioned at dinner. Later he had begun ordering her drinks without consulting her. This morning he had organized the trip from the ship into Charlotte Amalie, the port town. It was Cole who had commandeered a taxi to the airport and located the one-man charter service run by Ray.

It was true that all his actions had been very helpful, Kelsey thought, but Cole's helpfulness was beginning to turn into something more direct. Now he was starting to decide how she should handle her business on Cibola. It was time to remind him she was still in charge of herself and her task.

"We'll give him fifteen minutes," she declared calmly. "And then we'll go check his house."

Cole slanted her a strange look, as if deciding how to deal with Kelsey's deliberate assertiveness. She had the impression he was on the verge of issuing a clear-cut command, and then he appeared to think better of the idea.

"Kelsey, believe me, if he's anywhere in the vicinity, he'll have heard the plane arrive. If he doesn't come down it must be because he's not particularly interested in the printouts. I don't think we ought to track him down. You've told me, yourself, the guy's a little strange."

"Fifteen minutes and then we'll go check his place," Kelsey repeated firmly. She pretended to ignore the flash of irritation that came and went in Cole's expression. Whatever he had done in his past, she decided, he had been accustomed to being in command.

One more tiny little clue to his background. As if there were any point in collecting such tidbits, she reminded herself sadly. Cole was not likely ever to fit the pieces of the puzzle together for her.

"We'll see," he temporized.

But fifteen minutes later Kelsey decided to act. The thick heat was making her think longingly of the air conditioning on board the ship. She stood up from where she had been sitting on the attaché case under the shadow of the Cessna wing and announced the next step.

"Come on, Cole. Let's go see if we can find him."

Cole, who had been hunkered down on his heels beside her, got slowly to his feet, frowning. "Kelsey, I really don't think he's around."

"I have to make certain. Walt is going to be very upset if I don't deliver this case."

"And Walt's getting upset matters?" Cole inquired wryly.

"Of course it does. He's my boss!"

"The road up to Valentine's shack starts over there," Ray offered. He was sitting in the Cessna, clearly bored by the entire matter. "How long do you want me to give you?"

"How long will it take to walk there?" Kelsey asked.

"No more than ten minutes."

Cole took over, speaking coldly. "You'll wait until we get back," he told the pilot. "Regardless of how long it takes. Don't worry, you'll be paid. All right, Kelsey. If you're dead set on this, let's get going." He picked up the attaché case and started in the direction Ray had indicated.

Kelsey followed quickly, stepping out from the shelter of the wing and into the full heat of the day. "This climate is awfully humid. I don't think I'd like to live in the tropics."

"You get used to it," Cole said absently.

"It doesn't seem to bother you," Kelsey noted, unable to resist the delicate probe.

"Stop fishing for information, honey," Cole retorted dryly. "Save your breath for the walk up to Valentine's place. You're going to need it."

You'd think I'd learn, Kelsey thought grimly. Then she decided to take Cole's advice. The walk through the thickening foliage required an effort. For one thing, the path they were following hardly constituted a "road," Kelsey decided. Ray had been generous labeling the narrow dirt track as such. It was overgrown with a variety of unidentifiable greenery and it had obviously never been used by a vehicle larger than a motorbike. It climbed quite steeply up into the hills and with every step the surrounding plant life seemed to grow heavier."

"This is turning into a real jungle," Kelsey observed.

"I don't like this," Cole said quietly, coming to a complete halt in the middle of the track. "I don't see any signs of Valentine's shack and I just don't like the feel of the place."

"Well, I'm not exactly enjoying this little afternoon stroll, either," she tossed back irritably. "If you want to go wait with Ray, feel free."

"Don't be an idiot," Cole growled. "Do you really think I'd go back to the plane and leave you to continue this crazy hike by yourself?"

Kelsey looked up at him through lowered lashes. "Uh, no."

Cole abandon her at this juncture? Impossible. He would no more leave her alone in this overgrown garden than he would fly. Kelsey knew that with such certainty that it seemed ludicrous even to question it. Cole was right, she thought uneasily. In some ways she did know him and trust him. It made no sense, but she couldn't deny the facts.

"I don't like anything about this job you've got," Cole went on darkly as he turned to continue along the path. "But what I like least is that Gladwin would send you on a stupid task like this one just to save himself a few bucks in professional-courier fees."

"I offered to do it! He didn't force me." Kelsey defended her boss automatically.

"But it was his idea."

"So what? It was a perfectly reasonable idea."

"'Reasonable'? To send a woman alone into a jungle like this?" Cole demanded almost fiercely.

"Walt's never actually been to Cibola himself. He had no way of knowing it was quite this primitive. Sitting in an office in San Jose, Cibola sounds very appealing. A picturesque tropical paradise," Kelsey informed him frostily.

Again Cole halted, swinging around with an abrupt decisiveness that took Kelsey by surprise. His face was set in implacable lines. "This is far enough, Kelsey. We're on a fool's errand. Turn around and start back toward the airstrip."

Kelsey almost found herself obeying without question. Cole wasn't making a suggestion; he was issuing an order, and in a manner that elicited instinctive compliance. If she hadn't been trying to fight him on one level or another for the past week, she probably would have followed orders. As it was, it took an astonishing amount of willpower to dig in her heels.

"Cole, I came here to do a job. I'm not going back until I've given it my best—"

The sudden revving of an aircraft engine shattered the silence.

"Damn it to hell." Cole uttered the oath with weary resignation rather than any real heat.

"What's going on?" Kelsey turned to gaze back toward the landing strip, but she could see nothing through the foliage. "Is that the Cessna?"

"I'm afraid so." Cole was looking up toward the sky now, and Kelsey followed his gaze. The Cessna was already several hundred feet in the air, heading back in the direction from which it had come.

"He's leaving! Ray's leaving us here!" she gasped. "He can't do that. How will we get back to the ship?"

"An excellent question," Cole said dryly.

"But why would he leave us behind?" Kelsey looked up at him in total bewilderment.

"I think our old friend Ray conducts business on a very straightforward version of the free-enterprise principle," Cole murmured thoughtfully. "In other words, he'll work for whoever pays him the most. Just on a hunch I'd guess someone paid him more to leave us here than he was paid to take us back to the ship."

"But why would anyone want to . . . oh, my God." Kelsey's eyes opened very wide as she glanced at the black attaché case Cole was holding. "You don't really think someone would go to these lengths to get hold of those, do you?" she asked weakly.

"Kelsey, the more I get to know about your job and your boss, the less I like either."

"I don't see why you have to drag Walt into this," she snapped, thoroughly annoyed. "It's hardly his fault."

"Well, if it makes you feel any better, I can't find anything particularly wonderful to say about myself right now, either. I must have been out of my mind to let you go through with your plans to deliver these papers. I should have listened to my head instead of my, uh, hormones. Come on, let's get moving." He started back up the path with a swift, ground-eating stride.

"But, Cole...!" Kelsey found herself hurrying to keep up with him. The stylish yellow safari shirt was clinging to her damp skin in earnest now as Cole's pace forced her to exert herself in the heat. "Why go any farther in this direction? Shouldn't we go back to the airstrip? Maybe someone else will come along. Or there's that little fishing village on the other side of the island. The one Ray mentioned. Maybe we should head for it."

"Those are probably the two directions we'll be expected to head. So I think we'll skip both," Cole tossed back over his shoulder.

Kelsey stared at his back as he continued to forge easily ahead on the trail. "What do you mean by that? Cole, do you actually think someone might be waiting for us down at that landing strip?" It was taking a while for the reality of the situation to sink in, Kelsey realized, slightly dazed. She couldn't yet quite believe all the frightening implications of the fact that Ray had abandoned them.

Cole, on the other hand, seemed to have accepted the worst possibilities with hardly a flicker of an eyelash. As if he had been half expecting this bizarre turn of events.

"I think it's very likely someone will be watching for us to dash back to the strip. It's what most people would instinctively do if their transportation had just disappeared. And once out in the open we'd be a couple of sitting ducks."

"You're certainly adjusting to the situation with remarkable ease," Kelsey gritted caustically. "None of this seems to have fazed you in the least."

"Save your breath, Kelsey," he advised laconically. "You're going to need it. This trail is getting steeper."

Kelsey bit back a sharp retort, aware that he was right. The patch was climbing rapidly now, and the pace Cole was setting, combined with the oppressive heat, was taking a lot out of her.

So Kelsey stopped flinging questions and comments at Cole's impervious back and started thinking, instead. And the first thing that occurred to her was that the bottom line so far contained a very simple entry.

Simple and alarming. Cole had the attaché case and she was alone with Cole.

Kelsey caught her breath as she finally put the facts together. Cole had known all about this side trip. He'd known she'd be taking the case full of printouts to the mysterious Valentine. He had examined the contents of the attaché case and then he'd calmly removed the case from her room. And it had been Cole who had located Ray back in St. Thomas. Now it was Cole who was leading her deeper into the island jungle.

Kelsey came to a halt in the middle of the trail.

Ahead of her, Cole sensed at once that she had stopped. He turned back, annoyed at having to deal with more questions when he was trying to think his way through the mess.

"Kelsey?" he growled. Perhaps she was exhausted already. This heat could get to someone who wasn't acclimated. It was even beginning to affect him, although he'd had all those years in one steaming hellhole after another to get used to it. One year of civilized living in Carmel had been sufficient to undo a fair amount of conditioning, he decided wryly. "Kelsey, I know it's hot and you're getting tired, but we have to keep going."

"Do we?" she asked with a distant politeness that finally told him what the problem was. "Who says we have to keep going, Cole?"

He felt a shaft of cold anguish as he realized what was going through her head. Then he flicked an assessing gaze over her, noting the way the yellow shirt was outlining the curve of her breasts as she inhaled deeply to catch her breath. Her tawny hair was no longer a neat, sophisticated frame for her face, now perspiration-dampened. Instead it was beginning to get tangled from too many brushes against the persistent greenery along the path. The snug-fitting white jeans were rapidly becoming dirty, and when she wiped her forehead with the back of her hand she left a small smudge. She glared at him with wary, defiant eyes, her slender body poised and tense.

"You know," Cole said with perfect honesty. "For some reason that utterly defeats me, you look as sexy as hell."

The off-the-wall remark startled her, as he had intended it should. While it was nothing less than the truth, because she always looked sexy to him, he had said the words aloud as a way of breaking through the fear he saw in her eyes.

"This is not a joke, damn it. Tell me what's going on!"

Better to have her angry than fearful, Cole decided. "How should I know what's going on? You're the one who insisted on coming to this island."

"You're the one who insisted on coming with me." Her eyes darted downward toward the black case. "And you're the one who has his hands on those printouts."

Cole felt himself tighten under the uncertainty and accusation he saw in her eyes. "You haven't got much choice, Kelsey," he told her brutally. "You're going to have to trust me."

"You've been saying that in one way or another since the day we met. And like an idiot, I keep letting you talk me into giving you one more chance. Now I find myself stranded on a lonely island in the middle of the Caribbean with you and that attaché case."

"The problem is that I can't be sure just how lonely we really are," he explained coldly. "For you this is going to be a clear-cut case of 'better the devil you know than the one you don't.' Your Mr. Valentine is still floating around out here someplace and Lord knows who else. It's a safe bet we're not completely alone on this island. Someone must want the printouts, and whoever it is won't be satisfied until he has the case."

"How do I know you aren't that someone?" she flared.

"Trust me," he grated, and started back up the path.

"Damn you, Cole Stockton! You've told me to trust you one too many times! You may be good at giving orders, but I am not so good at taking them blindly. In any case, trust is the one thing you can't force someone to give. I want answers, Cole. And I want them now."

Cole considered his options. There weren't very many. He was going to have to handle this as ruthlessly and efficiently as possible. For all he knew her life depended on his getting her completely under his control. When it came to protecting her he'd do whatever had to be done.

The decision made, he followed through on it the way he always did on his decisions. It was one of the old habits that he'd probably never completely shake. Survival had never favored those who vacillated over their decisions.

He saw the shock that replaced the anger and uncertainty in Kelsey's hazel eyes as he moved toward her with flowing speed. She never even had a chance to run. Cole closed his fingers over her shoulder, letting her feel the weight of his strength. Then he hauled her very close, trapping her startled gaze.

"I don't have any answers for you, Kelsey." Deliberately he threw all the hard intimidation he had at his command into the words. He had to break her stubborn will to resist, and do it quickly. "No answers, but I do have a few observations. I'll give it to you short and sweet. We are in a very unpleasant situation. Potentially dangerous. You are not equipped to get either of us out of this mess. Therefore you will have to rely on me, whether you fully trust me or not. *You have no choice, Kelsey.* Do you understand? Absolutely no choice. You will do as I tell you, no questions asked, and you will do it when I tell you. You will do it as quickly and as obediently as you can, because if you don't you will find I won't hesitate to do whatever it takes to enforce my orders. And I will give you fair warning, Kelsey. I am not at my most thoughtful and charming when I'm in a situation like this. In fact, I am a complete bastard. If you can't trust me in any other way, you'd better believe in that much. Now move on up that trail or I will drag you up it."

He stepped away from her, letting her see the absolute confidence he had in his own authority. Only he realized that the intimidation tactic wasn't going to work unless she genuinely feared or trusted him on some deep level.

When she slanted him a seething glance and then turned to stride ahead of him up the trail, Cole was left to ponder the inevitable question he had posed for himself. He could not be certain if it was fear or trust motivating her to obey. He could hope that it was trust, pray that it was trust. But he could not be certain.

It didn't matter, Cole told himself as he moved to follow Kelsey. As long as she obeyed him when the crunch came, it really didn't matter why she did it. But he knew he was lying to himself.

Ahead of him on the path, Kelsey was furiously trying to assess her own behavior and that of the man behind her. She could not fully explain why she had backed down so readily under the force of Cole's intimidation. She was, she acknowledged uneasily, a little afraid of him. When he claimed he could be a bastard in certain circumstances—dangerous circumstances—she believed him.

There was an underlying ruthlessness in Cole Stockton, Kelsey realized. She'd known that since the traumatic night he had taken her to bed. There was also an innate self-confidence and authority that he wore like a cloak. He was accustomed to being in command, both of himself and others.

Oh, yes. She believe him when he told her he could be a bastard. But that was about all she could realistically believe in, she cautioned herself. As usual around Cole, there were a lot more questions than answers. For the moment she would obey him. But she couldn't say why.

Perhaps it was simply that she had no choice.

Because she was in the lead, it was Kelsey who first saw the odd octagonal house in the jungle clearing. She slid to a halt, and Cole, who was only a step behind her, reached out to grasp her arm.

"That's far enough," he muttered, sweeping the cleared area with eyes that missed nothing.

"Valentine's place do you think?" Kelsey peered at the roughly hewn wooden house. She rather liked the strange octagonal design. The rooms would probably be pie shaped, she thought fleetingly. There were windows on all eight sides, and a heavy-duty generator was housed at the rear. There was no sign of a huge man with a long beard and wire-rimmed glasses.

"Must be," Cole said quietly. "You wait here. I'm going to have a look."

"I'll come with you," she began automatically, not particularly wanting to stay behind in the dense jungle when something as civilized as a house was beckoning.

"You'll stay here. And hang on to this." Cole thrust the attaché case into her hands. "Give me ten minutes."

"But, Cole—" Kelsey broke off at once as he switched a hard-eyed gaze at her. "All right," she muttered. "I'll stay here."

"You're learning," Cole grunted. He started to slip away into the nearby foliage but stopped when he felt Kelsey's fingers touch his sleeve.

"Cole, be careful," she heard herself whisper.

He looked startled, and then he briefly touched her fingers as they clung to his khaki shirt. "Yes," he agreed. She thought he was going to say something else, and then she decided he must have changed his mind.

He slipped away, and a few seconds later he had disappeared into the jungle. Kelsey stayed very still, holding the attaché case and thinking how easy it was for Cole to fade into the jungle.

When Cole reappeared a few moments later he was emerging from the dense growth on the opposite side of the clearing. She watched anxiously as he stepped out of the protective cover around him and calmly entered the house through a door that stood open. Kelsey held her breath until he materialized again in the doorway. Then he moved quickly back across the open ground and into the underbrush. A short time later she whirled, startled to see him suddenly appear beside her.

"You move like a ghost," she accused softly.

"And you look like you've just seen one. It's okay, honey. The place is empty."

"No sign of Valentine?"

Cole shook his head. "No, but someone has recently been through that place with a fine-tooth comb. It's been torn apart. Somebody was looking for something." He glanced down at the attaché case. "My guess is he didn't find it."

"What about Valentine? He wouldn't have torn his own house apart."

"Your guess is as good as mine. We're not going to stick around and see if he shows up, however. It's going to start getting dark in another hour or so. We're going to have to find someplace to spend the night."

"Couldn't we stay in Valentine's house?" Kelsey asked wistfully. But even as she asked the question she knew the answer. Cole had already decided they wouldn't be using the obvious source of shelter, and although she was putting up a brief argument about it, Kelsey also knew she would abide by his decision.

"Anyone who knows we're stranded on this side of the island will also know that this place is standing here like an open invitation."

"And you don't accept open invitations?" she hazarded.

"Only from you," he returned without any hesitation. "But I don't get many of those from you, do I?"

Kelsey would not have believed that in her bedraggled, perspiration-soaked, anxious state she could be capable of turning a rather vivid shade of red. "You don't usually bother to wait for them!"

Cole picked up the attaché case. "We're wasting time. Let's go."

Swallowing her protests, Kelsey obediently fell into step behind Cole. He led her off the trail and straight into the heavy undergrowth. The going was rough, and she had to fight to keep up the pace he set. But Kelsey didn't bother with complaints. There was no point, she decided realistically. Cole was not deliberately punishing her, he was simply doing what had to be done in order to find shelter before nightfall.

It occurred to Kelsey to question her growing confidence in Cole, but she was much too tired now to pursue that line of thought. She was lost as soon as they left the trail, vaguely aware only that they were heading downhill. Blindly she followed Cole, concentrating on the task of keeping up with him.

When they at last broke out into the open again it was at a point some distance from the airstrip. Across the wide, rocky beach the foaming water beckoned invitingly.

"What I wouldn't give for a swim right now," Kelsey murmured, eyeing the gentle waves wistfully. Eagerly she started forward, thinking she could at least get her feet wet.

"Later," Cole ordered softly. He reached out and unceremoniously yanked her back.

"Must you be so heavy-handed about everything?" she snapped, massaging her shoulder as she glared up at him. He wasn't looking at her, though. He seemed to be listening.

"At times like this, yes," he answered almost absently. "I tend to get heavy-handed when complications arise. And we've got another one."

"Another complication?" She stared up at him, perplexed.

"That's right."

"Now what?"

"Someone followed us down the hill, Kelsey."

"'Followed us'? Oh, my God!" She twirled, trying to peer into the jungle behind her, but it was impossible to see more than a few feet. "Where is he?"

"Several yards back. He stopped when we did. Probably waiting to see what we'll do next."

"What *are* we going to do next?" she asked evenly.

"Make our visitor welcome, of course." He caught her wrist and led her along the edge of the beach.

At no point did they actually step out into the open. Cole hugged the cover of the undergrowth with a skill that Kelsey knew had come with years of practice. Pulling her along in his wake, he somehow managed to assure her of cover, too.

The rocky beach grew into a cliff that rose a short distance above the surf. Huge chunks of stone littered the landscape from the edge of the jungle to the sea's edge. Cole wove a path between the boulders until he seemed to find what he was looking for.

"This will have to do. Down you go, Kelsey, and stay there until I tell you to get up. Clear?" He urged her behind a pile of tumbled boulders, using his weight to push her down to a crouching position. When she glanced up at him she shivered at the sight of the lethal expression that carved his features.

"Cole?"

"Just stay put, Kelsey." He handed over the attaché case again, and then he seemed to melt into the landscape, losing himself amid the heavy stone shapes that surrounded him.

Kelsey watched him go and realized she was suddenly very afraid. And her fear was not of Cole. Rather, she admitted silently, it was for him. The thought of anything happening to him in that jungle filled her with a dread that had nothing to do with her own situation.

It was then that Kelsey began to realize how inevitably committed she was becoming to Cole Stockton. In spite of the fact that she knew almost nothing about him and in spite of her suspicions that whatever had shaped his past had not been particularly civilized, her own fate was now inextricably bound up with his. She waited alone behind the shelter of the stone, and knew how her female ancestors had felt when they waited in caves for the return of their men from the hunt.

7

HE WAS A GIANT OF A MAN, but it wasn't his size that made him dangerous, Cole knew. It was the way he moved like a cat through the jungle.

A rather out-of-practice cat, Cole conceded as he tracked his quarry. The big man wasn't quite as silent or as careful as he should have been, but Cole was willing to bet that at one time Valentine had been very skilled, indeed.

It had to be Valentine. From the brief glimpses he got as he circled around behind the man, Cole decided no one else could fit the description Kelsey had been given. Huge, a long beard and gold wire-rimmed glasses.

No one had apparently bothered to tell Kelsey that the man called "Valentine" had once done something far more lethal than program computers. Perhaps no one had realized it.

But as soon as he'd become aware of being followed, Cole had understood one or two crucial facts about their pursuer. The first was that he was a trained hunter and the second was that the game Valentine had once been taught to hunt was probably the two-legged variety.

It takes one to know one, Cole thought grimly as he closed in behind the massive Valentine. He could only hope that the big man's skills might have grown a shade rustier than his own.

Silently he glided to a point a few feet behind the bearded man. Balanced lightly, feet spread slightly apart,

Cole collected himself physically and then called out softly.

"Valentine's Day is going to be a little late this year."

The huge man spun around, and Cole found himself being rapidly scrutinized and assessed by a pair of very perceptive blue eyes. For a moment the two men stood poised, confronting each other across the short distance.

"I don't know whether or not Valentine's Day is going to be late this year, but I surely do know that today hasn't been it. Just one damned thing after another. And now you." Valentine's voice was a low, bearlike growl. Perfectly suited to the man.

"And now me," Cole agreed laconically. "If it makes you feel any better, today hasn't exactly been one of my red-letter days, either."

"You're with the woman." It was a statement, not a question.

"Yeah, I'm with the woman."

"Do you mind telling me in what capacity?" Valentine flexed his big hands a little, as if they were stiff.

Cole noted the small movement, and his mouth twisted into a faint smile. He instinctively checked his own balance and decided it was as good as it was going to get. It had been a long time, and nothing stayed well honed if a man didn't practice frequently.

"You could say I'm looking after her," he explained very politely to Valentine.

"Protection, hmm. Paid or unpaid?"

"I look after her because she belongs to me," Cole said with deadly simplicity.

At once Valentine seemed to relax. "That," he rumbled gently, "explains a few things. Not everything, but a few things. I think, sir, that we may be on the same side."

"And what side would that be?" Cole felt the tension lessening, but he didn't change his balanced stance.

"Opposite from the one those two jokers who tore up my place are on." Valentine absently fingered his beard, but his piercing blue eyes continued to peer perceptively through the wire-rimmed glasses. "Like I said, it hasn't exactly been Valentine's Day around here."

"Two of them?"

Valentine nodded. "And armed."

"Unlike us," Cole said wearily.

"Unlike us," Valentine agreed.

"It's going to be a long day. I suppose I'd better introduce you to the lady who came all this way to see you."

"Your lady," Valentine clarified.

"Mine. Although I'm not sure she knows it yet." He motioned slightly with one hand. "After you."

Valentine arched a shaggy brow, mild amusement flickering behind the lenses of his glasses. "Cautious sort, aren't you?" He swung around and started to make his way toward the rocky beach.

"These days I prefer to think of myself as just well mannered, not cautious." Cole fell into step behind Valentine.

"Do you succeed in fooling yourself?"

"Sometimes," Cole said. "How about you?"

"Sometimes I get lucky and fool myself, too," Valentine said very softly.

"I guess we're a pair of real con artists. Out to deceive the toughest audience in the world—ourselves."

"I think," Valentine said slowly, glancing back over his broad shoulder, "that being con artists is probably better than what we were before."

The two men exchanged a look of masculine understanding that spoke volumes. And then Cole shrugged. "That's what I keep telling myself."

"Where did you hide your lady?" Valentine asked curiously as he emerged from the undergrowth and stood scanning the boulder-strewn landscape.

"Valentine!" Kelsey, who had been watching the edge of the jungle for any sign of Cole's return, leaped to her feet and came racing toward the two men. "You must be Valentine." She grinned, liking the big man on sight. "I'm so glad it was you following us. I've been worried sick, wondering what Cole was doing charging around in that overgrown weed garden. Are you okay? Cole said your house was ransacked. What's going on here, anyway?"

Valentine's white teeth flashed through his beard, and Kelsey decided that any resemblance the man might have had to Santa Claus ended with that smile. The thick beard could not hide the hint of a hunting wolf gleaming within the grin. In that moment she realized the expression reminded her rather forcibly of Cole's rare smiles.

Two of a kind. The thought went through her head in a burst of intuition that she immediately discounted. What a ridiculous notion. Valentine and Cole were as different as night and day. One was a big, bearded, eccentric computer genius. The other was a reclusive, frustratingly uncommunicative, arrogant businessman. But her female intuition was telling her something else.

"I'm fine. You must be Miss Murdock. Sorry about the change of plans around here. I assure you, it wasn't my idea. Just as well you brought your friend here along."

Kelsey wrinkled her nose at Cole. "I didn't have much choice. Cole insisted on coming with me."

"'Cole'?" Valentine asked blandly.

"Haven't the two of you introduced yourselves? Valentine, this is Cole Stockton." Kelsey glared from one to the other.

"Oh, we introduced ourselves," Cole drawled. "We just didn't get around to exchanging names." He nodded formally to Valentine.

"My pleasure," Valentine murmured.

Kelsey was aware of the cryptic overtones in the air, but she couldn't understand them. It was as if Valentine and Cole knew far more about each other than either let on, and yet she knew neither had met until a few minutes ago.

"So much for life's little pleasantries," Cole said smoothly. "I suggest we get on with a few of its necessities. In case no one else has noticed, it's starting to get dark. This is your territory, Valentine. Any suggestions of where we might stash Kelsey for the night?"

"'Stash' me!" she echoed, astonished. "What's that supposed to mean?"

"It means hide you," Cole explained, as if to a child.

"What about you two?" she demanded, not liking the direction of the conversation.

"Your man and I have a little business to take care of, Miss Murdock," Valentine said gently. "There are a couple of other folks on this side of the island. Not your average tourists, I'm afraid."

"The people who ransacked your house? Who are they, Valentine? Are they after these printouts?" Kelsey tapped the attaché case with the toe of her sandal.

"That's the theory I'm going on at the moment. Come on, Kelsey, I'll show you and your man a nice, safe spot."

Kelsey flushed, darting a quick glance at Cole, who was already moving to take her arm and guide her in

Valentine's wake. "He's not 'my man,'" she felt obliged to mumble. "His name is Cole."

Valentine and Cole both ignored the remark. Cole's face was set in hard lines as he steered Kelsey after the other man. She felt a little awkward around these two, Kelsey decided resentfully. Both of them moved with that silent, graceful stride she had always found unnerving in Cole.

"You two didn't happen to be ballet dancers sometime in your past, did you?" she muttered at one point as Cole kept her from tripping over a tree root. As the sun set on the other side of the hills that divided the island, night descended quickly. It was getting difficult to see.

Valentine chuckled softly up ahead in the gathering shadows.

"Don't pay any attention to her," Cole advised. "She's addicted to the game of twenty questions."

"And you don't like to play it with her, right?" Valentine asked with what sounded like complete understanding.

"Not when the questions always center around ancient history," Cole murmured.

"You want some current questions?" Kelsey gritted, infuriated at the way the two men were discussing her. "I'll give you a couple. Number one, what are you two planning to do tonight? And where are those two people who went through your house, Valentine? What exactly happened here today?"

"Actually," Cole interrupted mildly, "I'm a little curious on that subject myself, Valentine."

"I'll tell you everything I know, which I'm afraid isn't much, as soon as we get to the cave."

"A 'cave'?" Kelsey considered that. "I hate caves. They give me the willies."

"If this cave solves the problem of keeping you safely hidden tonight, then you will learn to tolerate the 'willies,'" Cole informed her bluntly.

"One of these days," Kelsey retorted seethingly, "we're going to have a long talk about your infuriating arrogance!"

"But not tonight," he said.

Kelsey remained silent for the rest of the hurried hike to the cave Valentine had selected. As soon as she saw it buried in the shadows of a cliff face, Kelsey knew she was going to hate every moment spent inside its dark mouth. But there was no doubt about the degree of security it offered. Heavy foliage concealed the entrance until one was virtually in front of it. It faced toward the ocean, but no one standing out on the rocky beach would have noticed it unless he knew exactly where to look. She couldn't deny it would serve as an excellent hiding place. With a giant effort of will she managed to conceal her shudder as Valentine led her and Cole inside.

"What about bats?" she asked suddenly.

"There aren't any," Valentine assured her.

"Rats?"

"The only kind of rats we have to worry about tonight are the two-legged variety," Cole told her as the three of them stood in the mouth of the cave and surveyed it in the fading light.

"Snakes?"

"A few lizards," Valentine said reassuringly. "That's all. There's even a nice, freshwater spring near the entrance. Have a seat, both of you. Welcome to my vacation cottage." He indicated a couple of large rocks off to one side.

"Lizards, huh?" Kelsey glanced around skeptically. "And I'm supposed to wait here while you guys go off to see what's happening?"

Cole and Valentine exchanged glances. "Something like that," Cole agreed dryly. "Let's hear your story, Valentine. What did go on today?"

Valentine sank down onto a rock, shaking his shaggy head. "Beats me. I've been trying to put two and two together, and the only thing I can come up with is that someone wants those printouts. There are a heck of a lot of unknowns. All I do know for certain is that I left the house at dawn for my usual run on the beach. I was about halfway through my normal course, when I spotted a launch moving very quietly into that small bay near the landing strip. Two unsavory types came ashore and the third took off in the launch. Presumably he'll be returning at a prearranged time."

"What did you do?" Kelsey asked.

Valentine lifted one massive shoulder. "Being of a basically inquisitive nature, I followed the two gentlemen who came ashore. It didn't take long before I realized they were heading for my place. I got there just as they were about to go inside. I thought about doing something dramatic at that point, and then I decided to give the situation a little time. For one thing, I knew you were due later on today, Kelsey, and I didn't think Flex-Glad would appreciate my letting one of their lady administrative types walk into an awkward situation like this. Especially not when she was carrying some important printouts." Valentine broke off to smile meaningfully. "Of course, I didn't know you'd be bringing along your own protection."

"The printouts are the only things our two visitors could possibly want?" Cole asked quietly. "No chance this isn't something, uh, personal?"

"Cole, what a crazy question!" Kelsey gasped. "How could it be personal? Who would want to hurt Valentine? He lives all alone and bothers absolutely no one."

Valentine grinned. "Just your average, lovable island eccentric who asks nothing more out of life than to be left alone with his computer."

"And who happens to be a con artist," Cole tossed back smoothly.

"Takes one to know one," Valentine quoted.

"What on earth are you two talking about?" Kelsey burst in, thoroughly annoyed. She swung accusing glances from one to the other.

Valentine's derisive grin faded. "Nothing, Kelsey. Just a private joke."

"The two of you have hardly known each other long enough to have developed a repertoire of private jokes!"

"You're absolutely right," Cole said firmly. "So let's get back to business. You're sure the printouts are the problem here?"

Valentine nodded, sobering completely. "I'm sure, Stockton. The analysis of the theoretical data I've been working on could give someone a real jump ahead in the fast lane of artificial intelligence. I've been approaching some fundamental problems from an entirely new direction. Hate to sound so immodest, but the truth is, that stuff in the attaché case is worth someone's while to go after. Besides, none of this bears the marks of any unsettled personal business. I don't know those two jokers. Furthermore, after they finished demolishing the inside of my home and went their merry way, I had a look to see if I could tell what they'd been searching for.

Everything near the computer, including all my hard-copy files had been torn apart. I decided to remove a certain personal possession I value highly and vacate the premises temporarily. Thought it might be interesting to wait and see what happened. The two from the boat blundered around for a while trying to find me. By now I think they've assumed I must be over in the village. I watched them go down the hill to wait for the plane."

"How would they know what to look for if they are after this artificial-intelligence data?" Kelsey asked.

"Not a bad question," Cole said, sounding mildly surprised. "I had a look at that stuff in the attaché case, Valentine. If I hadn't known it was important enough for someone to keep under lock and key, I would never have been able to guess. It would take an expert to identify those printouts as valuable."

"Not if they'd been instructed to look for the alpha numeric code on each page. Gladwin and I worked it out back at the beginning to keep the data from getting mixed up with other kinds of material."

"Would they have known I was bringing the data to-day?" Kelsey wondered.

"I'd say it's obvious they did," Cole offered. "Some-one had to bribe good old Ray to take off without us."

"I heard the plane leaving," Valentine said. "I'm afraid good old Ray will do anything for a buck."

"Why did you follow us, Valentine? Why not just show yourself when we arrived at your place?" Kelsey fixed him with a curious glance.

"Because he wasn't sure where I fitted into the pic-ture," Cole explained for the other man.

"But now I know," Valentine murmured.

"You two certainly seem to have arrived at a fair de-gree of mutual understanding during that short introduction in the woods," Kelsey complained. What was it with these two men, she wondered.

"We ex-ballet dancers recognize each other on sight," Cole told her sardonically.

Kelsey snapped her head around, outraged. "Damn it, I do not intend to sit here while you two crack little inside jokes. Tell me why those two men didn't attack us!"

"Probably because they couldn't figure out what Cole was doing with you. He's the wild card in all this," Valentine explained.

"Now tell me what happens next. You both seem to have devised all sorts of clever schemes in the space of a few short minutes. In fact, everyone around here except me seems to have some idea of what's going on. I can think of a couple of reasons why that state of affairs exists!"

"What reasons, Kelsey?" Valentine asked, sounding genuinely curious.

"The first possibility, of course, is the fact that you're both just a hell of a lot smarter than I am," she remarked scathingly.

"And the second?" Cole inquired too softly.

"The second is that everyone already knows what's going to happen next because the whole thing's been planned from the start. I'm just playing the role of pawn."

Utter silence greeted that comment. Kelsey shivered, and it wasn't from the creepiness of the cave. The tremor went through her because she had just now realized the truth of her words. She was sitting meekly between two men who seemed to be taking a dangerous situation with a frightening degree of calm. That calm could easily stem from the fact that they both knew exactly what was going on.

It was Cole who broke the tense silence. He looked across at Valentine and his mouth curved wryly. "I believe I mentioned earlier that Kelsey doesn't quite understand she's not an independent anymore."

"Not an independent what?" she demanded fiercely.

"He only means that you belong to him, Kelsey." Valentine spoke soothingly. "It's all right. You've had a rough day and this is all very confusing. You just sit tight here in this cave while Stockton and I go have a look around. We won't be gone long."

"But how will you know where to look? Cibola may not be very large as islands go, but there's still a great deal of terrain out there where someone could be hiding. Especially at night."

"Well, I've been keeping tabs on the situation since dawn." Valentine smiled gently. "I have a pretty good idea of where to look for our two visitors. They were watching the landing strip when Ray dropped you off. They started to follow you back to my place to see what you'd do. Stockton lost them when he dragged you back down the hill taking the scenic route. Our two friends are sticking to the few footpaths we have around here. They don't seem very comfortable in the wilds. In fact, I get the feeling they've spent most of their lives on city streets."

"So where will they be now?" Kelsey asked.

"Where would you spend the night around here if you had a choice?" Valentine asked blandly.

"If I had a choice? Your nice, comfortable house, complete with food and power!" Kelsey answered unhesitatingly.

"And that's probably exactly what our friends will do." Cole got to his feet and walked to the cave entrance. "It will be completely dark in another half hour.

They won't want to be caught out in the open. They also know we aren't likely to try hiking over those hills to the village. Not at night."

"They've probably got someone keeping an eye on things in the village, anyway, just on the off chance that we did make a try for it. Possibly the guy who piloted the launch away from the bay this morning," Valentine added consideringly. "The town is very tiny. It would be easy to watch the harbor entrance to make certain no one left aboard a boat."

"So we assume they'll spend the night on guard at your place, planning to resume the search for us at dawn. That gives us most of the night. The launch will probably return in the morning."

"No sooner than that," Valentine agreed, rising to his full height. "This whole side of the island is protected by some rough reefs. That little bay you saw is one of the few points a boat can be brought close to shore, and even it would be too tricky to try at night. You have to be able to see what you're doing out there."

"I wonder why those two thugs didn't arrange to have the launch return and take them off the island before nightfall," Kelsey mused aloud.

"I imagine they've been paid very well to get those printouts, Kelsey," Valentine said. "If they leave the island they run the risk of losing track of us completely."

"What I don't quite understand," Kelsey went on very carefully, "is just what you two are planning to do. What can you hope to accomplish running around out there in the dark? If you think you know where those creeps are spending the night, why go observe? Let's just all stay hidden here until dawn and then hike on over to the village to call for help."

Both Cole and Valentine turned to stare at her as if she'd just said something outrageous instead of highly practical.

"Honey, you don't understand," Cole finally said. "Tonight is simply too good an opportunity to miss. Those two are all alone up there in Valentine's house. If we move tonight, we can take them out."

"Take them out where?" Kelsey asked blankly, and then realization dawned. "Take them! You're going to go up there and try to capture them?" Horrified, she jumped to her feet. "I forbid it! As the highest ranking representative of the Flex-Glad Corporation present, I absolutely refuse to sanction such an action."

"Kelsey," Cole began carefully while Valentine turned politely away to study the landscape. "You may be the highest ranking Flex-Glad employee present since you're the *only* employee here, but—"

"Don't forget Valentine," she snapped.

"He isn't exactly an employee, is he?"

"More like an independent contractor," Valentine put in soothingly. "I don't take orders from anyone. Not any more."

Kelsey was incensed. "I do not intend to split hairs. On behalf of Flex-Glad, I am refusing to let you carry out such a ridiculously dangerous project." She stood with her hands planted on the hips of her stained jeans, her hazel eyes almost green as they flashed her anger and frustration.

Cole stepped forward, capturing her face between rough palms. His gaze burned down into hers. "Kelsey, honey, this is the way it has to be."

"According to you!"

He nodded once. "According to me. I know what I'm doing. You're going to have to trust me."

"You keep saying that," she wailed helplessly, knowing already that she didn't stand a chance of stopping him.

"I suppose I keep saying it because I keep hoping that you will."

She brushed that aside. "This isn't a matter of trust. It's a question of logical behavior under difficult circumstances. You and Valentine are not behaving in a practical, logical fashion!"

A strange little smile played briefly around Cole's mouth. "Don't expect logic from an ex-ballet dancer. I go for style."

"Damn it, Cole, this is not a joke!" She could feel the tears burning at the back of her eyes and only an effort of will kept them from falling. "My God, why am I even trying to reason with you? I have absolutely no influence at all over you, do I?"

"How can I help but be influenced by you, Kelsey?" he asked her grittily. "You're the reason we're here!"

She stared at him. "Then listen to me. Don't go chasing off into the jungle tonight. Stay here and in the morning we'll find a way over to the village to get help."

Valentine interrupted in a husky growl. "Kelsey, there isn't any help to be had in the village. There are only a few fishing families there, none of whom will want to get involved in this fracas. By the time I can summon help from one of the larger islands, those two at the house will be gone."

"Let them disappear!"

Cole dropped his hands from her face, his expression remote and hard. "No, Kelsey. We can't do that."

He seemed to lose interest in making her understand and Kelsey was stricken numb by a tangle of emotions that contained everything from fury to despair. Wordlessly she sank back down on the rock she had been using for a stool, her arms wrapped tightly around her as she stared sightlessly out into the darkness.

Time passed. She was aware of Cole and Valentine deciding to wait for the rise of the moon so they could use its light to make their way up to the octagonal house. She heard Valentine speaking quietly of something he had taken out of the house that morning and left stashed near it. She knew that Cole tried more than once to discern her expression, but the shadows concealed her features well. Time passed, during which she said nothing, continuing to sit perfectly still in the darkness. Kelsey paid no attention to the low discussion going on between Cole and Valentine. For some strange reason everything seemed remote and unreal now.

Finally Cole reached out to put a hand on her shoulder. "It's time for us to go, Kelsey."

She didn't move. "Have fun," she said bitterly.

Valentine's huge bulk shifted in the darkness. "Kelsey, if something happens . . ."

She stiffened under Cole's touch but refused to acknowledge the implications of Valentine's words. Cole finished the sentence.

"Kelsey, if we don't come back in a few hours, you're to stay here in the cave until you hear or see that launch arrive and take our visitors off the island, understand? You'll be able to see the bay without being seen if you crawl outside and use the natural cover. When they've gone, start walking and don't stop until you reach the other side of the island. It will take you several hours to get there. Go down to the village and hire one of the fishermen to take you back to St. Thomas."

She ignored that, making one last plea. "Cole, please don't go."

"I'll be back as soon as I can, Kelsey." His fingers tightened on her shoulder for an instant, and then he and Valentine were gone. They both seemed to vanish into the darkness the moment they left the cave.

Kelsey put her head down onto her folded arms and let the tears flow.

A lot of thoughts went through her head during the endless time that followed. Logic insisted she recognize the fact that she really had no proof the mysterious thugs from the launch even existed. She had seen only Valentine and Cole on this island. The whole situation could be an involved plot to take the printouts without throwing any blame on either of the two men. But even as she reminded herself of that possibility, Kelsey couldn't bring herself to really believe it. Perhaps, she decided bluntly, she just didn't want to believe it. She could take just about anything from Cole except that. It was unbearable to think that he might have lied to her from the beginning.

No. Cole didn't lie to her. He just wouldn't give her all the answers.

One thing was certain: Valentine had certainly done something more in his past than play with computers. Just as Cole had done something other than play with his business investments.

Two of a kind. Men who walked like large hunting cats through the jungle. Men who seemed familiar with the prospect of violence. She had always known there was another, darker side to Cole, but Kelsey was aware she hadn't really believed her own wild guesses about him being a part-time hit man or a loan shark.

Now she shuddered in the darkness as she contemplated just what kind of background would give Cole grim confidence in his own ability to handle the dangerous situation on the island.

It was after she had considered all those possibilities that Kelsey finally remembered something else about Cole Stockton.

Until tonight he had waged a successful campaign to keep his past locked behind closed doors. It was because of her that he was opening those gates. If she had never brought him to this island, he would not have been forced to use the dangerous skills he had learned in his other life.

The sudden pain that coursed through her at the thought of having caused Cole to unlock a past he obviously wanted to escape told Kelsey all she needed to know.

She had fallen in love with him.

THE REMOTE-CONTROL computer keyboard was lying undisturbed exactly where Valentine had left it. He pushed aside a pile of palm fronds and picked it up.

Cole grinned savagely in the moonlight as he glanced at the keyboard and then at Valentine's satisfied expression. They were several yards from the house, which was ablaze with lights. There was no doubt the unwelcome tourists were inside.

"The computer controls just about everything in the house, including a few special touches I've installed over the past couple of years," Valentine murmured.

"And you control the computer with that keyboard." Cole nodded. "Kelsey has told me about the remote controls on some of the new home computers. The keyboards don't have to be connected physically to the machines. How does it work?"

"Infrared signals. I've beefed this sucker up quite a bit. It will function at a distance of up to a hundred feet."

Valentine patted the object in his hand with paternal pride.

"So we use it to douse the lights. That should give our friends a start," Cole remarked.

"And then I'll key the storm shutters to lock in place. That will seal up the windows. No one ever understood why I wanted locking metal shutters on all my windows," he said dryly.

"No one ever understood why I doubled the height of my garden walls when I bought my home in Carmel. I think Kelsey was scared to death to go inside for fear she'd never get out again. She calls it a fortress."

"It's hard to explain to a woman how one picks up such extreme security habits," Valentine wryly pointed out.

"Yeah. Something tells me she didn't buy the dance-school bit," Cole muttered sardonically.

"What have you been telling her up to this point?"

Cole sighed. "Nothing. Nothing at all."

"And you expect that to work?"

"It hasn't been what you'd call incredibly successful. She's as curious as a cat."

"And you've been stonewalling."

"I figured she'd hate the truth far more than she'd hate the silence," Cole said with a shrug.

"Hard to say. Women are funny creatures." Valentine was quiet for a moment, his thumb idly stroking the keyboard in his big hands. He studied Cole's face in the moonlight. "Start out in the military?" he asked finally.

Cole nodded. "You?"

"Southeast Asia. I was very young. It all seemed like an adventure back then. When the sense of adventure wore off it just seemed unreal."

"I know. And then one day you realize it's become a business. At least it did for me. You wonder what the hell you've turned into." Cole glanced toward the house.

"You went free-lance?"

"When I got out of the army I had no reason to go back to the States. I stayed in Southeast Asia. There were plenty of jobs for men who knew their way around that part of the world and who weren't too fussy about how they earned their pay. Some of the most lucrative were those Uncle Sam was offering," Cole added.

"High paying, short-term contracts. No questions asked, no help from the government if you screw up."

"But lots of cash quietly deposited in a numbered account in Switzerland. I took the jobs. There didn't seem any reason not to."

"I know that feeling of not having any reason not to take the contracts." Valentine was silent for a moment as they both let the truth lie unvarnished between them. "The trick in life seems to be making your own reasons for doing things. I went the mercenary route for a few years. Africa and South America mostly, fighting other people's wars. And then I discovered I have this... empathy with computers. Long story."

"With an ending here on Cibola, hmm?"

Valentine nodded seriously, shaking off the past. "This is home. And right now two uninvited guests are intruding."

"I know how I'd feel if I found someone had got past my garden walls without an invitation," Cole said evenly. "What else can that gadget do besides seal the windows and douse the lights?"

"It can trigger the valve on a canister of gas I keep tucked into the ceiling. Very unpleasant gas. As soon as it's released we're going to have two very miserable men lurching through the front door, gasping for air."

"Then we'd better have the welcome mat out." Cole reached for the palm fronds that had been shielding the computer keyboard and began to bind them together. He worked until he had a long, tough rope of vegetation. When he was finished he glanced up at Valentine. "Ready when you are, maestro."

They moved together toward the edge of the clearing. Every room in the octagonal house was lit, but whoever was inside was prudently steering clear of the windows.

"They probably know we're unarmed," Valentine mused. "Ray would have told them you weren't carrying anything lethal, and when they went through my place at dawn they were bound to see I had no ammunition stores. I'm sure they feel very safe in there. The bastards."

Cole understood the sentiments. "Hit the lights," he ordered softly.

Valentine depressed three keys on the board and instantly the house went dark. Cole didn't wait to see if there was any reaction from within. He moved out into the open, crossing the clearing as rapidly as possible. It would take a while for the two inside to decide what was going on, and he had to take advantage of those few seconds of disorientation. They'd assume something had gone wrong with the generator.

He went down on his belly in front of the door, slinging the crude rope around the post that held the awning. Letting it lie loose on the ground, he waited for Valentine to trigger the next sequence of events.

There were sounds coming from inside the house now. Hoarsely muttered commands and angry oaths. A second later there was a grating, metallic rush of noise as

Valentine ordered the computer to seal the windows. Now there was only one exit: the front door.

Someone inside panicked. A shot roared through the night, and the bullet pierced the door panel over Cole's head. He hugged the ground and waited for the next step.

Cole never heard the hiss the escaping gas made, but he was well aware of the reaction of the men inside the house. Screams of panic gave way to retching, gasping sounds. Two more shots slammed through the door, and then it was shoved open. Firing wildly, two men floundered over the threshold.

Cole used the palm-frond rope to trip the first yelling man. Already reeling, the guy hit the dirt with a thud, allowing time for Cole to deal with the second intruder.

Coming to his feet in a smooth arc of energy, Cole brought the side of his fist down on the second man's neck. He fell as if he'd been pole-axed.

A wave of the noxious gas caught Cole as it seeped through the doorway. He backed off hurriedly, frantically inhaling fresh air. The first man was struggling to his knees as Cole swung around. It was almost an unconscious reaction to put the guy out with a blow from the heel of his hand.

Cole left both men where they lay and raced out of reach of the dissipating gas. "Hell, Valentine, that stuff is god-awful!"

"I'm glad you approve," Valentine drawled as he came forward. "A little something I picked up while working for a very technologically oriented sheikh. I keep a gas mask in the drawer beside my bed. Always thought I'd probably be in the house myself, if I ever had to use it."

"Well, it's a cinch no one's going to be able to spend the night in there," Cole growled as he helped Valentine secure the two men on the ground.

"I suggest you leave these two with me. They don't look like they're going to give anyone any trouble. I've spent many a night out in the open. We'll ask them a few pertinent questions before you leave, and then you can go spend the night in that cave. I've got some food I can send with you. Your lady will be waiting."

Cole glanced up as he finished binding the feet of the second unconscious intruder. "Waiting to do what?" he wondered aloud. "Scream at me? Accuse me of plotting this whole mess? Demand that I never come near her again?"

Valentine tilted his head in the moonlight, his rather savage grin gleaming through his beard. "You won't know what kind of a welcome you'll get until you go down to the cave and find out, will you?"

8

HE HAD KNOWN nights such as this one before now. They always ended in a strange tangle of emotions that were better buried than examined.

Cole made his way down the path toward the sea, veering off in the direction of the cave as he came out onto the beach. He didn't need the flashlight Valentine had provided. The huge tropical moon bathed the landscape in a pale glow that could have been romantic to another man. Cole had never thought of moonlight in such a way. It was usually a factor to be cursed because it illuminated too well. Yet occasionally he had been very grateful for the light.

It had been a while since he had used the gleam of such a moon to find his way home after an evening of violence—no, "home" was the wrong word. He had never used the moonlight for that purpose because he had never had a home to which he could return afterward. He had simply used it to walk away from one job to a place that served as a resting point before going on to another.

Home had never been waiting at the end of the moon's path, and neither had a particular woman. Tonight there would be a cave and Kelsey. Tonight seemed very different from all the other nights.

The violence this evening had been minimal. He had known far worse. Strange that the aftermath was as fierce as it had ever been. The adrenaline was still throbbing in his bloodstream and the primitive but controlled sensation of savagery still simmered along with it. Both would fade. He knew that much from long experience. What usually followed was a restless depression. It was that which he had come to dread.

But tonight there was a new element mixed in with all the others. Tonight he was walking out of the jungle to find his woman, and he realized that what he was feeling on top of everything else was a heightened sense of anticipation and anxiety.

The two emotions flared through him, tangling and writhing until he felt as though they were pulling him apart.

Brutally he tried first to crush the anticipation. There was no reason to think Kelsey would throw herself into his arms. It was sheer fantasy to imagine such a scene. She had been sitting huddled into herself when he had left, completely withdrawn. Her despair and anger had been palpable in the confines of the cave. The most he could expect from her was a polite, remote concern. She would want to know what had happened. Probably ask after Valentine. Then she'd ask about the two in the cabin.

Questions. That's what he could expect tonight. A hundred cool questions. And she had a right to hear the answers this time. She had been a part of it. When he had given her all the explanations she would probably turn her back on him and try to get some rest. It was unreasonable to think she would forgive him for not trying to do things her way. Kelsey would not understand the need for the violence.

It was also unreasonable for him to expect complete trust tonight. She had every right to question his role in this mess. Every right to wonder if she wasn't a pawn in some elaborate scheme concocted by him.

In time that end of things could be straightened out, but it wasn't likely to happen tonight. He had no proof to offer that he had acted only to defend and protect her.

If he was totally honest with himself he had to admit that in her place he probably would be formulating conspiracy theories, too. No, not *probably*, definitely. After all, he was accustomed to thinking in terms of betrayal and violence. It would be natural for him to question the role of those around him. Kelsey was an intelligent woman. He could expect cautious, intelligent questions and a prudent degree of distrust when he gave her the answers.

After that lecture to himself, it wasn't too hard to suppress the sense of anticipation that had been welling up in him. The anxiety replaced it easily.

Cole's night vision was good. With the aid of the moon it was no major task to work his way through the tumbled rocks that littered the bluff above the beach. With an unerring sense of direction that he long ago had learned to take for granted, he headed for the tangled undergrowth that shielded the cave entrance.

The adrenaline had dissipated, but the tension remained. He was strangely weary, but he knew already he wouldn't be able to sleep for a long while yet. Cole could read his immediate future as if it were written in stone. He could expect to lie awake for hours tonight, aware of Kelsey beside him, holding herself physically and emotionally apart. The image caused a grim despair to course through him.

Kelsey never heard his approach, but she was aware of his presence the moment he appeared in the wide mouth of the cave.

She leaped to her feet, staring hungrily at the dark shape of him. Desperately she tried to read his face in the dim glow of the moon. All she could see was the familiar, hard planes of his jaw and the stern line of his mouth. The gray eyes were far too shadowed. There was no way she could discern the emotions in them.

"Cole! Oh, my God, Cole! I've been so worried." She waited in absolute stillness, and then the paralysis broke. Kelsey hurled herself forward, straight into his arms and buried her face against his shoulder.

He was safe. Nothing else mattered just then. The knowledge sang through her, pushing aside all the doubts and agonizing fears of the past few hours.

"Kelsey?"

There was an odd note of disbelief in his voice. Perhaps it was confusion. She ignored it, wrapping her arms fiercely around his lean waist and clinging as though her life depended on it.

"You're all right? You aren't hurt?" she demanded huskily.

His hands moved slowly, almost tentatively on her back and then circled her with sudden power. Cole lowered his head, seeking the shell of her ear. "I'm okay. I'm fine. Kelsey, I . . ."

"And Valentine? Is he okay?"

"Yes. Everything went like clockwork. Valentine's staying at the cabin tonight to keep an eye on the two we caught. We're going to have to sleep here, I'm afraid. Valentine's house isn't habitable at the moment." He broke off as if searching for other words. "Kelsey, I'm sorry about tonight. I didn't have any choice. Please believe me, if there had been any other way—"

"Hush," she whispered, aware of the strange tension in him and wanting nothing more than to soothe. Her fingers trailed tenderly along the muscles of his neck, massaging the skin beneath the collar of his khaki shirt. "Hush, darling. You need to rest. There's no reason to talk just now. Is there anything else you have to do tonight? Is it all over?"

"It's over for tonight," he said, sighing. "In the morning we'll have to pick up the third man. The two we caught at the cabin said he was due right after dawn. But for tonight it's over. Kelsey, I know this has been hard for you."

"All I had to do was sit in the dark with a bunch of lizards. You were the one who had to go out and exert yourself." She smiled tremulously, slipping free of his arms to take his hand. "I disobeyed orders a couple of times, though." She started leading him to the far side of the cave.

"What are you talking about?" Sudden disapproval flashed into his voice and he halted at once. "Kelsey, what have you done?"

"A relatively small act of insubordination. I just ducked outside earlier and gathered some ferns to spread on the ground. There was a lot of greenery growing very thickly near the cave entrance. Since we're going to have to spend the night here, it's lucky I found something to cushion these rocks, isn't it?"

He continued to stand, unmoving. "You shouldn't have left the cave without permission. Kelsey, I told you to stay put."

She came back into his arms. He sounded so weary, yet so determined to stay in command of the situation. What he needed was rest and time to recover from whatever had happened up at the cabin. With feminine intuition guiding her, Kelsey nestled against him. "I'm sorry, Cole. It won't happen again."

"Oh, hell, what am I doing," he muttered, letting her push him down onto the bed of ferns she had contrived earlier. "There was no harm done, and the last thing I want to do tonight is yell at you."

"You rarely yell," she assured him gently. "Are you certain you're all right?" She came down on her knees beside him. "What have you got there?" she asked, glancing at a packet he was carrying.

"You rarely yell," she assured him gently. "Are you certain you're all right?" She came down on her knees beside him. "What have you got there?" she asked, glancing at a packet he was carrying.

"Valentine sent some cheese and bread."

"Thank goodness. I'm starving."

They munched the food in silence. When it was finished, Kelsey leaned toward Cole.

"What are you doing, Kelsey?" He stared down at her hands as they moved in the moonlight. She was unbuttoning his shirt.

"You're as tense as a coiled spring. I'm going to rub your back for you. Otherwise you aren't going to sleep a wink tonight."

His head lifted abruptly. "You want to rub my back?" He sounded disoriented.

"That's right. Turn over and use your arms for a pillow. My God. Every muscle is like a sheet of steel," she muttered as he slowly did as she directed.

"I must smell like a herd of buffalo," he growled.

"Not quite. But then I'm not exactly a rose garden myself at the moment. It's been a long day."

"You always smell good," he said with great certainty. "I used to think about your special scent at odd times during the week when you were in San Jose."

"Did you?" she asked shyly. Her hands worked on his broad back and she took satisfaction in the slow relaxation of his body.

"Yes." He paused as if gathering his thoughts. "Kelsey, I know you must have a lot of questions," he finally began hesitantly.

"You can tell me all the details in the morning. Right now you need to stop thinking and just relax. You need sleep."

"I need you," he said with sudden harshness. "I've never needed you more than I do tonight."

Kelsey heard the raw hunger in him and her hands stilled. "I'm here, Cole."

He turned over slowly on his back, seeking her face in the moonlight. "Just like that?"

She sucked in her breath, her love for him sweeping aside everything else. "Just like that," she agreed gently. She leaned over and feathered his lips with her own, longing to give him whatever he wanted from her.

"Oh, Kelsey!" Cole put his arms around her with a strength that told its own story. He pulled her down on top of his bare chest, his legs snarling with hers.

The strong male scent of his body filled Kelsey's nostrils and the power in his grasp conveyed an urgency she had no wish to deny. She did not fully understand this man; knew that she would never be privy to his secrets; recognized that he wasn't the tender, communicative lover she had always wanted for herself. But this was the man with whom she had fallen in love.

Tonight he had gone to battle on her behalf, dealing with a dangerous situation in the only way he knew. Now he was back, needing her.

She felt his fingers move roughly down the row of buttons of her stained yellow shirt, impatiently yanking the fabric free until the once-stylish garment hung open. Cole slipped his hands inside the shirt, exhaling deeply as he grazed his palms across the tips of her breast.

"Kelsey, honey, I didn't dare let myself believe it would be like this tonight. You don't know how badly I want you. There have been women, but there's never been a particular woman waiting. Oh, hell, I can't explain it."

"Don't try." She drew her fingertips lightly over his shoulders, kissing him softly at the curve of his throat. He shuddered beneath her and gave up trying to talk.

Kelsey felt the snap of her jeans being undone, and then he was sliding his hands inside the white denim and pushing the fabric down over her hips. Her panties went the way of the jeans, and when she lay naked along his half-clothed length Cole touched her demandingly, as if he couldn't get enough of her.

She trembled under the intensity of his caresses. When he probed between her thighs she gasped. His fingers moved gently, stroking until the dampening warmth he elicited told him of her arousal.

"I promised myself after last time that I would take all the time in the world when I finally got you back in my arms. But I didn't know it would happen like this," he said huskily. "I didn't think it would be on a hard floor of a cave, and I couldn't know it would be after I'd spent the evening trying to straighten out the mess you'd got yourself into. Kelsey, honey, why is it I never seem to be in complete control on the rare occasions I make love to you?" he concluded hoarsely.

"You've always told me I'm the one who asked too many questions." She moved a little so that she could reach the buckle of his belt.

"Are you telling me to shut up?"

She heard the rueful humor in him and put her mouth to his. "Yes," she muttered against his lips.

He took her command literally. Without a word he set her aside, sitting up so that he could yank off his boots and khaki slacks. Then he lay down beside her, cushioning himself on the ferns and moss she had gathered. Wrapping his strong hands around her waist, Cole pulled Kelsey astride his lean hips. Kelsey was abruptly, vividly aware of his heavy arousal.

"Cole?"

"No more words. Not now," he reminded her thickly. He fitted himself to her softness and held her steady while he surged upward. In one powerful thrust he invaded her clinging warmth, and her soft cry was lost beneath his groan of need.

Although Kelsey was on top, it was Cole who set the rhythm of their passion. Anchoring her at the waist, he moved within her, filling her totally and then withdrawing over and over again until Kelsey was a shivering creature of pulsating desire.

"Yes, Cole, oh, yes, *please*," she begged. Her nails scored the skin of his shoulders, and she nipped a little savagely at his hard flesh.

"Sweet she-devil," he rasped as he felt the touch of her small teeth. "There are times when you are not as civilized as you'd like to pretend!"

She couldn't answer him. His driving passion was swamping her senses, leaving her unable to think. She could only feel now; knew only the sense of being filled with his manhood; was aware only of the power in him as he held her in place for his thrusting body.

The shimmering convulsions swept up out of nowhere and shook her. She gasped brokenly, her whole body tightening.

"Kelsey!"

Cole was sucked over the edge into the vortex of the climax, his body following hers as men have always followed women. He grated her name again and again as the release pounded through him. The rough cries filled the cave and then slowly, slowly disintegrated until there was nothing left but profound and complete silence.

It was a long time before Kelsey stirred along the length of Cole's sprawled form. When she finally did he opened his eyes lazily. "Going somewhere?"

"Your backside must be a bit raw by now," she murmured, sliding down to lie alongside him. "These ferns I picked don't exactly constitute a mattress."

He allowed her to readjust her position but kept her snug against his body. Reaching for their discarded clothing, Cole spread it out beneath them, padding the mossy floor of the cave as well as he could. Then he lay back, his fingers sliding along her arm with absent pleasure.

"Thank you, Kelsey. I haven't felt this good since the last time I had you in my bed."

"This isn't your bed," she reminded him lightly. It was satisfying to feel his relaxed state and know she had been the cause of it.

"Details," he assured her dismissingly. "Wherever you are, when you're lying with me, I'm in my bed. It was just like coming home tonight when I walked into the cave and you ran into my arms. I tried to tell you there's never been a woman waiting for me," he said simply.

"Go to sleep, Cole. You must be exhausted."

"You must have a million questions," he said hesitantly, the sleepiness clear in his voice. He stifled a yawn with the back of his hand.

Kelsey took a breath. Her decision had been made during that long wait alone in the cave. "No, Cole. No questions. At least not about the past."

She felt him grow unnaturally still beside her. "What are you trying to say, Kelsey?"

"Only that I've decided to do things your way. Keep your secrets, Cole. You have a right to them. I had no business trying to pry them out of you. I trust you."

His hand tightened around her shoulders. "You do?"

"I wouldn't have stayed here waiting for you in this horrid cave if I didn't trust you," she said gently. "I won't push you ever again."

"Kelsey, honey, don't make rash promises." He sounded distinctly skeptical.

"It's not a rash promise. I had plenty of time to think about it while you were gone tonight. You're entitled to draw the lines in your life and I have no right to cross them." She touched the edge of his mouth with the tip of her finger. "I won't ask any more questions about your past. For you and I there will be only the present. I promise."

He caught her fingers and crushed them tightly in one large hand. "Kelsey, you won't regret it, I swear. I'll give you anything I can."

"I don't need anything, Cole. Only you."

"All I needed was to know you trusted me. Believe me, the past doesn't matter. The present is the only thing that counts between us."

"Yes," she whispered. "Only the present."

No past, Kelsey thought silently as she cradled her head on Cole's shoulder. *And no future. Only the present.* She would take life on a day-to-day basis. No more trying to build a future based on understanding and acceptance and communication. Cole could not offer that. She would take what she could get for as long as it lasted.

No past and no future. Only the present.

The promise had been made to herself during the interminable wait in the cave. It didn't mean the questions would go away. They still hovered in the wings. She would always wonder what kind of past Cole had that had taught him to take violence in stride. She would be curious about the likeness between Valentine and him. She was certain they had never met before yesterday, but Kelsey was equally sure they had recognized some quality in each other on sight. Even she had noted the disturbing similarities in the way they chose to deal with the dangerous situation they had encountered.

Every time she thought of her stepfather she would find herself thinking of the Stockton file locked in the computer. The question of those thousand-dollar-a-month payments to Cole was another issue that would not simply fade away, now that she had made her decision.

And every time she spent the night with Cole in his walled home she would ask herself why any man would build such a fortress in which to live.

No, the questions would never cease. Her curiosity about the man she loved would last as long as the relationship. Longer, she forced herself to acknowledge. She could not allow herself the luxury of thinking of a future. Cole lived only for the present, and if she would spend that present with him then she must learn to think in those terms, too.

The questions would continue in her mind, but Kelsey vowed they would not be asked aloud. She would rely on the basic, underlying trust she had finally acknowledged during the long wait in the cave.

With that promise floating in her mind, Kelsey closed her eyes and crowded deeper into Cole's protective embrace. He was sleeping, his lean hard body relaxed at last. But she felt his arm tighten instinctively around her. A few moments later, in spite of the uncomfortable bed provided by the cave, Kelsey fell asleep.

She awoke hours later to the very faintest rays of an island dawn seeping through the vegetation that guarded the cave. Then came the realization that Cole was gone. Her next awareness was of the stiffness in her muscles.

"Oh Lord. I may never recover from this cave," she groaned, sitting up slowly and glancing around. "Cole?" she called tentatively, thinking he must have stepped outside.

An intelligent-looking lizard, brilliantly illustrated in shades of green and blue, blinked at her from a nearby rock.

"Voyeur," Kelsey accused, reaching for her crushed and stained clothing. The lizard watched her dress, clearly fascinated, and then it skittered off on more important business.

Cole had not returned by the time Kelsey had finished pulling on the garments. She stretched, trying to limber up the muscles that had been cramped and bruised by the hard bed, and then she went to the cave entrance.

"Cole?" she called again, frowning into the pearling morning light.

Still no answer. She pushed her way through the vegetation that protected the entrance and stood looking down at the sandy beach far below. Maybe Cole had decided to take a swim as a substitute for a bath. She could use one herself.

Her gaze swept across the jagged, rock-strewn slope that formed the bluff above the beach. Still no sign of Cole.

A trickle of nervousness assailed her. Damn the man. Trust was all very well and good, but this habit of disappearing in the mornings was getting to be more than a shade annoying. He had disappeared that first morning after he had made love to her, the morning after her had nursed her through the sea-sickness and now this morning. Kelsey decided her resolution not to question his past did not apply to details of his present actions.

If she was going to be forced to learn the ultimate meaning of compromise, Cole could darn well learn something about that fine art himself. Irritably Kelsey started away from the cave, moving along the rocky bluff in the general direction of the cliff that ringed the bay. She would find the path that led to Valentine's house and see if the big man knew what Cole was up to this morning.

It wasn't until she came in sight of the bay and saw the small launch anchored in it that Kelsey suddenly remembered the unfinished business Cole had alluded to last night.

A wave of panic sent her flat on her stomach. The boat carrying the third man Valentine had mentioned was down there, and a figure stood in the bow. She inched her way to the edge of the cliff and looked out. The man in the boat was armed. He was holding a high-powered rifle on Cole, who stood on the sandy beach.

Kelsey thought her breathing had stopped. A terrifying sense of helplessness seized her. She was too far away to do anything. Cole had seemed so much in command of the situation yesterday, and she knew he and Valentine had been expecting the third man's arrival. How on earth had he managed to get himself trapped down there on the beach?

Then she realized the attaché case was sitting on the sand in front of him. Cole stood easily, his booted feet planted slightly apart, his stance seemingly relaxed.

There was an air of balance in the way he stood watching the man with the rifle. Kelsey moved uncertainly, straining to see exactly what was happening. All the natural fighting balance in the world wasn't going to do much good against a man with a rifle.

Kelsey glanced around, frantically trying to find any sign of Valentine. Surely he would have accompanied Cole to this dawn rendezvous. The two men had worked together last night. She couldn't believe they hadn't planned this morning's events as a team.

The fact that Valentine was nowhere in evidence could be cause for further panic on her part, Kelsey thought morosely. Or it could mean the huge man was hidden somewhere behind a boulder on top of the cliff. Perhaps he was providing cover for Cole's actions from behind one of the tumbled piles of rocks at the bottom of the cliff.

There was no way of knowing what was really happening, she realized as panic and fury mingled in her. Neither of the two men had thought fit to inform her about what was planned for this morning. She was left to stare in horror as the man she loved stood unarmed in front of a thug with a rifle.

"Make up your mind," Cole called roughly to the man in the gently rocking boat. "It's a fair price considering what I'm offering in exchange."

"How do I know you've got the genuine article for sale?" the rifleman called back.

"You don't. Not until you come ashore and have a look at the samples I've got in the case," Cole told him laconically.

"Seems like it would be easier to kill you and then come ashore," the other man drawled consideringly.

"Easier, except you wouldn't have a snowball's chance in hell of figuring out where to start looking for those documents. They could be hidden anywhere on this island. No, I think killing me would be very risky under the circumstances. I suggest we do business together, instead."

"What about Keller and Matson?"

"Your friends are out of the picture, I'm afraid. Simple all the way around, though, isn't it? This way you get to keep whatever you make from handing over the printouts to whoever hired you. No splits."

"Except what I have to pay you," the man in the boat reminded him coldly.

"All I'm asking is fifty thousand. That seems reasonable, given the value of those papers."

"I don't have any fifty G's with me."

"So I'm prepared to wait while you go arrange things. I'll still be here when you get back."

"What about the crazy hacker who was supposed to be somewhere on the island?"

"Like your pals, he's no longer involved," Cole said succinctly.

"And the woman."

"I'll handle the woman."

Kelsey grimaced at the cold-blooded way Cole said those last words. He could sound incredibly ruthless, she thought uneasily. Perhaps because he *was* incredibly ruthless. Or had been in his past, she corrected herself. Once again she tried to scan the rock cliff top, searching for Valentine. She couldn't believe he wasn't up here somewhere, supplying cover. Cole and Valentine were two of a kind, and neither was stupid.

"I'd have to see those printouts for myself before I could agree to any deals," the man with the rifle declared.

"I'm willing to show you a couple of pages. Not the whole lot. The remainder is my insurance policy, as I'm sure you can understand." Cole indicated the attaché case with a careless glance. "If you want to come ashore and take a look, it's fine with me."

"How do I know I can trust you?"

Cole shrugged. "You don't. I brought along a sample of the product for sale. Do you want to see it or not?"

"Yeah, I'll come take a look," the other man finally decided. "Open the case and leave it on the sand. You stand over there." He waved the rifle to a point about twenty feet from the case.

Cole obediently moved away as the rifleman stepped over the side of his boat into knee-deep water and started wading to shore.

Kelsey's fingers clenched fearfully into a small fist. Where was Valentine, she asked herself once again. She flicked a hopeless glance around the cliff, and just then light from the rising sun glinted off something metallic.

A gun barrel, Kelsey told herself, drawing a deep breath. It must be Valentine. He wasn't more than twenty feet away from her, using the huge rocks as cover.

She glanced down at the drama on the beach. The rifleman was halfway to shore now, his weapon trained unwaveringly on Cole.

Kelsey was holding her breath, wondering how and when Valentine would act when the brightening sunlight caught and held something more than the wicked sheen of metal. It illuminated the gloved hand holding the rifle. And the hand inside the thin leather glove was not one of Valentine's huge fists. Even as Kelsey watched in stunned comprehension, the gleaming metal moved forward. A second later she saw the head of the man who held the weapon. He was crawling through the rocks toward the edge of the cliff.

It wasn't Valentine. This man was small and wiry and very ratlike.

The significance of what she was seeing registered immediately. Valentine might very well be covering Cole from some other point, but neither he nor Cole could be aware of this new intruder.

She could see the stranger quite clearly now as he moved from the cover of one boulder to another. He was concentrating totally on his goal and had not spotted her.

Twenty feet away, she thought shakily. *He's only twenty feet away.*

Hidden behind her own rocky protection, Kelsey tried frantically to think. The light sound of the surf was bouncing up the face of the cliff, providing some assurance that the newcomer would not hear her if she was to move. And since the gunman was focusing intently on the scene below, he might not see her if she was exceedingly careful.

There was no way of knowing exactly what Valentine and Cole had planned. She was operating completely in the dark. But surely they could not have anticipated this new element. Valentine had been telling Cole from the beginning that there were only three men involved.

The man off to her right was clearly a backup for the one in the boat. If Valentine and Cole made a move to capture the guy down on the beach, this one would probably shoot to kill.

The image of Cole lying dead in the sand forced Kelsey to act. If she was going to do something, it had to be now. Cautiously she tried to move, and for a split second Kelsey was afraid that the combination of terror and stiff muscles might make even a small movement impossible. Then the short-lived paralysis died beneath the necessity of saving Cole.

Ever so slowly, hugging the uneven surface of the top of the bluff, Kelsey slid toward the shelter of another rock. If the gunman didn't glance back she should be safe. He was at the edge of the cliff, looking down. His rifle was aimed with steady hands. She knew his whole attention was on the scene below. Kelsey made it to the cover of a second boulder.

Ten feet away, she crouched behind a rocky projection and risked a peek around the edge. The second gunman was flat on his stomach, holding the rifle.

What now, she asked herself. Hastily she examined the limited selection of weapons at hand. Rocks and pebbles of all different sizes littered the terrain. Her insides turned sickeningly at the thought of trying to use one of the jagged stones against the intruder's head.

What if she missed, she wondered frantically. On the other hand, what if she didn't miss? The image of a crushed skull was almost her undoing.

But the overpowering mental picture of Cole's blood seeping into the sand was far more persuasive. There was no time to debate the issue. The joker from the boat would be walking up the beach now toward the attaché case. At any second Valentine would probably act, popping out from some hiding point at the base of the cliff to surprise the intended victim.

And when all that action took place, it was a sure bet that the second rifleman would act. Someone was almost bound to be killed in the ensuing melee. Someone like Cole.

Kelsey's hands closed around a rock the size of her two fists. Rising to her knees, she looked over the edge of her protective boulder and caught her breath. The second gunman still lay flat, pointing the rifle downward. With all her strength, Kelsey leaped to her feet and hurled the rock straight for his balding head.

She heard the sickening thud, for which she had tried to prepare herself as the rock struck the man, but the sound was drowned out almost immediately by the ferocious roar of the rifle. Her victim had squeezed reflexively on the trigger as the blow had landed.

Before Kelsey could race forward to see if the gunman was truly out of commission, a second shot rang out. She threw herself flat and scrambled frantically to the cliff edge. Beside her the second gunman lay awesomely still. His weapon had fallen from his hands. She was afraid to look at his head.

Down below on the beach there was a hoarse cry. By the time she looked over the edge, Cole was sweeping up the rifle the first gunman had dropped. The man from the boat was down on his knees, clutching at his shoulder. Even as she watched, Cole swung the rifle upward, aiming for the spot where she lay. Valentine was surging up from behind a clump of rocks he had been using for cover near the base of the cliff. The gun he had just used on the man from the boat was also swinging in her direction.

"Hey, guys, it's me!" Kelsey yelped, getting hastily to her feet. "Don't shoot. I'm on your side, remember?"

A mild form of hysterical relief seemed to be assailing her. It died almost instantly as she realized that both Cole and Valentine were still aiming their weapons in her direction. She suddenly understood just how dumb it had been to leap up and yell at them.

Both men were balanced on a knife-edge of violent readiness. They were reacting to the rifle shot that had come from the top of the cliff. She suddenly realized she was lucky to be alive. It would have been second nature for either of these men to shoot first and ask questions later. Kelsey froze. The fact that she was still standing on the edge of the cliff and not lying dead at the bottom was a fact that could be credited only to the lightning swift reaction times of both Cole and Valentine.

Kelsey swallowed uncomfortably as both men slowly lowered their weapons. In that moment she recognized how dangerous both Cole and Valentine really were.

"Kelsey! What the hell do you think you're doing? Get down!"

Kelsey leaned over and picked up the rifle beside her. "It's okay, Cole," she called out unsteadily. "The guy up here is out of commission."

A low oath sliced through the air, and then Cole was racing for the uneven cliff path, covering the distance to the top in only a few seconds. Behind him, Valentine examined their captive.

Kelsey turned to face Cole as he came toward her. She read the chilling expression on his face and shivered. He halted in front of her, his glance going briefly to the unconscious man at her feet and then to the rifle in her hand.

"What in blazes are you doing out here, lady? You're supposed to be back in that cave. Who gave you permission to leave it?" He snapped the weapon from her fingers and did something quickly to the mechanism. Then he tossed it down and reached for Kelsey, giving her a fierce shake. "Answer me, woman! How dare you disobey orders like this! You could have been killed."

"So could you," she managed, although her heart was pounding as the fear-induced adrenaline shot through her. "You didn't know about this one up here, did you?"

"No, by God, I didn't. But that is absolutely no excuse for you to be running around out here in the open. Hell, Kelsey, I ought to use my belt on your sweet tail. I ought to make sure you couldn't sit down for a week! Do you have any idea just how close you came to getting yourself killed?"

From out of nowhere, Kelsey's natural assertiveness finally revived. "It's all your fault, Cole Stockton," she shot back, infuriated by his actions. "You and your little secrets. You didn't bother to tell me what was going on. You didn't see any need to explain the plans you and Valentine had developed. You didn't think it was necessary to keep me informed or to involve me in any way, did you? Your secretiveness almost got both of us killed. But don't let that small fact interfere with the way you've chosen to run your life. Go ahead and wall yourself up behind your damn secrets! There may not be much of a future in that but, then, you don't care about the future, anyway, do you?"

She whirled, intent on getting away from him before she disgraced herself with tears. She almost stumbled over the man she had struck with the rock.

First things first, Kelsey thought with a sigh as she knelt down beside the too-quiet gunman. Right now she had to face the consequences of her own act of violence. With shaking fingers she tentatively touched the back of the man's head. He was bleeding.

"He'll live," Cole said brusquely, dropping down beside her and investigating the wound with an expert touch. "You didn't kill him, Kelsey."

She looked across at him with mute thankfulness and had the impression he understood how hard it would have been for her to accept that she might have killed someone, even a ratlike thug such as this.

9

THEY CAUGHT the cruise ship at its next port of call. Kelsey had several reservations about continuing with the trip, and she didn't hesitate to make them known. By the time Cole managed to get her back to her stateroom he was feeling a vast sense of relief. He needed the next few days alone with Kelsey. Instinct told him that while he had won a great deal during that day and night on Cibola, the groundwork of his affair with Kelsey was still vague and shaky in many areas.

Before he could risk taking her home and finding himself competing once again with the other forces in her life he needed to establish the basis of the relationship.

He had never worried very much about relationships, he'd reflected more than once during the trip on the strongly scented fishing boat. Worrying about relationships came into the same category as panic and uncertainty. A very alien thing.

"Matters such as this have to be reported to the authorities," she had exclaimed when Valentine casually announced he could arrange to have a fishing boat from the village take them to the island where the luxury liner was due next. "Cole and I can't just take off and leave you to explain everything."

"I don't see why not," Valentine had said politely.

"But the authorities will have a lot of questions when they come to pick up these four men," Kelsey had pointed out.

"Maybe. If the authorities who were going to show up were proper FBI types and if they were arriving at your doorstep in San Jose to take these four jokers into custody. But the folks who will be coming to Cibola aren't going to be representing the U.S. government. This isn't U.S. territory, remember? Cibola is part of a very loosely knit group of islands under independent rule. Frankly, our version of the 'authorities' could care less about such exotic things as industrial espionage."

"What will they do with these four?" Kelsey had glanced worriedly at the well-secured men who had been brought around the island on the launch to the small village.

"Officially, they'll probably be accused of breaking and entering," Valentine had offered slowly.

"And unofficially?" Kelsey had pressed.

"Unofficially, their biggest crime is being four off-islanders who bothered a local resident. Being an off-islander around here is bad enough. Bothering a local is just about the worst crime in the book."

"What makes you a local? Aren't you an off-islander, too?" Kelsey had demanded.

"Not anymore," Valentine had said, chuckling. "I did a favor for the governor on the main island a few years ago. Since then I've had official 'local' status."

"What sort of favor?" Kelsey had gone on to ask.

Cole had decided he'd better step in at that point. There was no telling what sort of dirty work Valentine might once have done for the governor, and whatever it was it would probably put even more questions into Kelsey's head.

"That's enough, Kelsey. Just take Valentine's word that he can handle matters, okay? There's no need to go into detail. You've caused enough trouble for one day."

"*I've* caused enough trouble!" she'd flared. "I may have saved your lives by being up on that cliff when I was!"

"She's right, you know," Valentine had put in mildly, obviously amused by Cole's heavy-handed approach to dealing with Kelsey.

Cole had shot him a sardonic glance. "I know, but I don't think she realizes how close she came to getting herself killed."

"Believe me, I'm well aware of it!" Kelsey had muttered.

Cole knew she was remembering the precarious seconds she had stood on the top of the cliff, facing the weapons he and Valentine had instinctively aimed in her direction. He suppressed a grim shudder. It was going to be a while before he forgot that little scene himself.

The distraction had worked. Kelsey had been successfully led away from any more questions about the favor Valentine had done for the governor. After that there had been plenty to do, what with finding an obliging fisherman, securing the four thugs in the storeroom of a local bar and saying goodbye to Valentine.

"I'll send a cable to Gladwin and let him know he's got a leak somewhere," Valentine had promised Kelsey when she expressed a few more concerns about leaving the scene of the crime. "He'll know how to handle it. These four were obviously just hired hands."

"How will Walt know where to start looking for the real source of trouble?"

"I'm sure our pals in the storeroom will be glad to give us some leads," Valentine had said easily. "I'll have a chat with them before they get taken off Cibola."

Kelsey looked dubious. "'A chat'?"

Once again Cole had deemed it prudent to step in. "Come on, Kelsey. The guy with the boat is waiting."

"But, Cole, I still think we should do something more, well, official about all this," she had protested worriedly.

"This isn't the States, Kelsey. Things work differently in other parts of the world. Valentine knows what he's doing. Let him do it," Cole had ordered firmly as he'd pulled her determinedly toward the waiting boat.

She'd turned to Valentine, who was pacing alongside her. "You're sure you'll be all right?"

"I'll be just fine, Kelsey."

"You'll come and see us if you ever get back to the States?"

"Send me an invitation to the wedding and see if I don't show up," Valentine had replied with a grin.

Cole had experienced an odd rush of annoyance when Kelsey had looked startled, and then had hastened to explain there was no wedding planned.

"Cole and I don't think too much about the future," she'd told Valentine very seriously.

Valentine had given Cole an empathic glance, and then he'd shrugged his massive shoulders. "Sometimes the future has a way of forcing itself on you. Take care, you two. I have a feeling we'll be seeing each other again sometime."

Cole had watched Kelsey brush Valentine's cheek with her soft mouth, and then he'd shaken the huge man's paw.

"If you, uh, ever need anything," Cole had begun gruffly, "yell."

"I will. And the same goes for you." Valentine had stepped back to let Kelsey climb on board the bobbing boat, and then he grinned at Cole. "Don't worry. I'll be giving Gladwin that version of the story we agreed on this morning. And about that favor I did for the governor a while back," he'd murmured for Cole's ears alone. "All I did was computerize the island's government records. The governor loves the prestige of having the most sophisticated filing system in the Caribbean. Gives him all sorts of clout when he mingles with the leaders of the other islands."

"I'll tell Kelsey," Cole had remarked wryly.

"You do that. The woman already has to deal with enough secrets. See you."

HOURS LATER Cole dressed for dinner in his own stateroom. The shower had felt terrific, and although he wasn't wild about wearing dinner jackets and ties, the dark color of his fresh clothing was comfortable and familiar nighttime attire.

He knotted the tie with impatient efficiency and met his own brooding gaze in the mirror. He had been trying to decide on how to deal with Kelsey tonight and he still wasn't certain of the right approach.

That damned uncertainty again. Something about that woman left him feeling suspended in midair. He turned away from the mirror and reached for his jacket. One thing *was* certain. She was going to be spending the night with him. No more excuses, rationalizations, protests or other crazy, illogical feminine reasons for keeping him at arm's length.

She'd committed herself last night. Cole had no intention of allowing her to wriggle free of the implied and implicit surrender she had made there on the floor of the cave.

That knowledge brought some sense of relief, but it didn't dispel the uncertainty he was feeling. He glanced at the neatly made bunk and mentally pictured Kelsey lying in it. His body hardened at the image.

Inhaling deeply, Cole stalked toward the cabin door, wondering how it was possible to simultaneously want to take a woman to bed and yell at her. He still hadn't recovered from the close call that morning.

He strode down the corridor toward the elevator, lost in glowering thought. Kelsey had given him a great deal last night. He knew that at last she had given him her trust.

It should have been enough, he told himself as he waited for the elevator. It had certainly constituted the biggest hurdle. She had promised there would be no more questions about the past, and then she had given herself to him unreservedly.

It should have been enough. All that was left now was to work out the details of the affair. He could afford to compromise for a while, he decided as he stepped into the elevator and punched the number of Kelsey's deck. He could afford to accommodate himself to her life-style for a time.

Aware of a pleasantly magnanimous feeling, he stepped out of the elevator and headed for Kelsey's room. Now that he had the essential element of trust from her he would be generous and allow her to reshape her life at her own pace. He was not an unreasonable man, he assured himself. He could make compromises.

Just so long as he knew that one way or another he could be certain of having Kelsey in his bed.

KELSEY MOVED TO ANSWER the knock on her stateroom door with a sense of determination. She had dressed for the evening knowing that in some ways she was going into the kind of negotiations that always followed a battle. Cole had won the war. Now she faced the task of working out the terms of her own surrender.

The bold, fluid shape of the chili-colored wrap dress swirled lightly around her knees. The neckline was an exciting plunge that was halted by the firm clasp of a wide, silver-studded belt. High-heeled sandals in the same shade as the dress added the height she felt she needed tonight. After spending nearly an hour in the shower washing the dirt of Cibola out of her hair, Kelsey had brushed the tawny mass until it moved around her shoulders in a smooth, well-behaved style. She was as ready as she would ever be. Kelsey opened the door.

"I think," Cole murmured thoughtfully as he stood examining the deep neckline of her dress, "that we may have to buy you a few new items for your lingerie wardrobe."

"Like what?" Kelsey hadn't been prepared for the remark.

"Like some new bras. Don't you ever wear one?"

"To work," she assured him promptly, stepping through the door to join him in the corridor. "I had no idea you were so conventional, Cole." Her mouth curved faintly.

He appeared to be waiting for a follow-up remark as he took her arm in a possessive grasp and started her toward the elevator.

"Don't hold your breath, Cole," she said gently. "I'm not going to say it."

"Say what?"

"Something about how your conventional feelings about lingerie just goes to show what little I know about you," she said readily. "You needn't worry, I'm really quite reformed. I meant it last night when I said we would ignore the past."

Beside her Cole nodded once, his expression intense. "You won't regret it, Kelsey. I've said from the beginning that the past doesn't count."

"Only the present," she agreed softly.

They dined on stuffed roulade of veal, Caesar salad and rum mousse. June and George Camden greeted Kelsey and Cole with pleasure and a great many questions about where they had spent the preceding day. Kelsey smiled serenely and let Cole handle the good-natured inquiries. He was the one who was the expert at turning aside unwanted questions, and she told him so with her bland gaze as he sat across the table from her.

"Thanks," he growled wryly as they walked out on deck after dinner. "I had no idea you could be such a reserved little creature."

"You were doing such a great job of handling all their questions I didn't want to interfere. You have a wonderful knack of being able to tell the truth without telling anyone anything," Kelsey said, laughing. "The bit about visiting an acquaintance who lives on a nearby island was masterful. At least you didn't try to give the Camdens the line about Valentine and you being ex-ballet dancers."

"You were the one who invented that one."

"So I was. Lucky for your story tonight I didn't try to give the Camdens that added tidbit." The laughter in her eyes faded as they came to a halt beside the rail.

It was a beautiful night, balmy and warm. The foaming wake of the ship was a splash of brilliant white against the darkness of the sea. Behind her the music from the cabaret sounded faintly. "Being on board ship is like being in a world apart, isn't it?" she observed after a moment. "It's as though the rest of the world with all its demands didn't exist. As though none of the problems of real life can bother you."

Cole watched her profile in the moonlight. "That's why I didn't want you to insist on going straight back to San Jose," he admitted calmly. "We need this time alone together, Kelsey. Time without any outside distractions."

She didn't pretend not to understand. "A sort of honeymoon without the wedding, hmm?"

His eyes narrowed. "You could say that. There are things we need to settle between us, honey."

"Such as?" Kelsey tried to keep her voice light and flippant. Cole's sense of humor had never been his most impressive characteristic, she reminded herself. And when he was serious, he tended to be *deadly* serious. Even Valentine, who seemed to have a lot in common with Cole, had more laughter in him than Cole would ever have.

"First of all," Cole began carefully, "I should tell you that even though I was furious with you for getting involved in that scene this morning, I was also proud of the way you handled that fourth gunman." Cole's hands flexed around the railing. "You kept your head and you pulled off a very dangerous stunt. Valentine and I may owe our lives to you. Valentine had the guy in the boat covered every second, so he was under control. But we didn't guess that a fourth man had swum ashore at another point before the boat pilot brought the launch into the bay. Since Valentine had only seen three men in the beginning, we were assuming there weren't any more. Valentine had questioned the two men we'd caught last night and they apparently didn't know about the fourth man, either, or he would have had the information out of them."

"I see. Well, it's very generous of you to thank me, Cole," Kelsey murmured dryly. "I know you've been simmering all day over that episode this morning."

"You scared the hell out of me," he told her frankly.

"I was rather scared myself." She didn't look at him, pretending to study the darkened horizon.

"Don't ever disobey me in a situation like that again, Kelsey," he ordered flatly.

"Will there be a great many more such situations, do you think?" she asked flippantly.

"I hope not. And don't make it sound as though it were all my fault," he warned. "It was your job that got you into that mess."

"And you haven't liked my job from the beginning, have you?"

"No," he said grittily. "But I am prepared to live with it for a while.

Kelsey turned her head in astonishment at the unexpected concession. "Would you mind repeating that?"

He drew a deep breath and then announced brusquely, "You heard me. I'm willing to work out a compromise regarding your job at Flex-Glad. For a while."

"What sort of compromise?" Kelsey asked cautiously.

"I'll stay with you in San Jose from Monday through Friday. I can manage an office in your apartment, I think. The weekends, holidays and vacations you will come back to my home in Carmel. Fair enough?"

"You're certainly making matters much simpler than I had expected. I was prepared for a major bit of negotiating this evening," she told him honestly. "I thought I'd have to do a great deal of talking in order to get you to agree to an arrangement like that." Inwardly she experienced a vast sense of relief. The biggest hurdle had been jumped.

Cole's gray gaze swept over her. "You'll be happy with that arrangement?"

"I think it will work." She pulled free of his assessing eyes and gazed down at the foaming wake several decks below. "Thank you, Cole."

"For what? Not forcing you to give up your work? I want you to be satisfied with the relationship, Kelsey. I realize you have a fear of giving up your job and your independence to come and live with me. I'm hoping that after a while you'll feel relaxed enough about the situation to risk it, but in the meantime I'm willing to make compromises."

Something in the way he said that caused her lips to lift in amusement. "You're being very generous," she assured him smoothly.

"I am," he agreed roughly. "And if you had any sense, witch, you wouldn't laugh at me because of it."

Suddenly contrite, she moved closer, reaching up to touch the side of his jaw. "I'm not laughing at you, Cole. I think I'm just greatly relieved that my job isn't going to be a problem." Her near-green eyes were wide with reassuring warmth.

Cole caught her fingers and kissed the tender heart of her palm. His eyes burned into hers. "I told you once I'd give you anything I could."

"I think you mean you'll give me anything you feel is good for me. There's a slight difference," she teased.

He let that pass, his intensity still engraved on his hard features. "There are other things that need to be considered, Kelsey."

"What things?" She was feeling too thankful for the unexpected concession to worry about what might be coming next.

"There's the possibility you could be pregnant."

The warmth in Kelsey's eyes turned to shock, and she dropped her fingers from the side of his face while she absorbed the implications of his statement.

Cole gave her a moment to respond, and when she didn't and merely continued to stand very still by the side of the rail staring out to sea, he went on determinedly.

"It's something we have to think about, Kelsey. On the two occasions I've made love to you I haven't taken any precautions. Unless you're on the pill . . . ?" He left the question hanging.

Before stopping to think that it might be better to lie, Kelsey found herself shaking her head. "No. No, I'm not using anything. There hasn't been any need, I mean there hasn't been anyone—" She broke off, angry at the way she was beginning to flounder.

Cole's hands closed over her shoulders and he pulled her back against the hard planes of his body. "I'm not complaining, honey," he murmured into her hair. "I like the fact that when you're in my arms you forget everything else. But it's something we should think about."

"I agree," she said fervently. "From now on we must be careful. Until we get back to the States there isn't much I can do, so I'll have to rely on your handling the details, won't I?" The tension in her must have communicated itself to Cole, because he began to knead her upper arms soothingly.

"I'll take care of everything," he said quietly. "But that's not the main problem. What we have to think about is the possibility that you already are pregnant."

"No."

"No, you're not?" he queried politely.

She shook her head quickly. "No, we won't think about the possibility that I'm pregnant. You have a policy of not concerning yourself with the future, remember? If there's anything on this earth that has 'future' written all over it, it's a baby. Therefore we will not deal in such iffy matters. Stockton's Second Law of Survival. The first, of course, being that we don't talk about the past. However, since I shall be left to deal with the future on my own, I expect you to take those precautions you spoke of a moment ago."

"Kelsey," he began huskily.

She straightened away from his hold and spun lightly around to confront him. Deliberately she summoned a brilliant smile. Knowing her eyes were probably not reflecting that brilliance, Kelsey tried to compensate with a tauntingly light tone of voice.

"Only the present, Cole. Remember? And right now I think I would like to dance."

She felt the hesitation in him, and he failed to respond to her beckoning smile.

"Kelsey, you can't just ignore this."

"Of course I can. You've taught me how to ignore a great deal. Come and dance with me, Cole."

"But, Kelsey..."

"This is our imitation honeymoon. Are you going to ruin it by being so deadly serious the whole time?"

"Damn it, woman, I want to talk about this!" he exploded tightly, refusing to budge as she tugged lightly on his wrist.

"But I don't want to talk about the future, Cole. It's all so uncertain, isn't it? Are you going to stand out here all night?"

"No," he gritted. "As a matter of fact, I think I'd like to go inside and have a stiff drink."

Kelsey wasn't quite certain how to take that, but she relaxed when he allowed her to lead him inside to one of the crowded lounges. And when she slipped into his arms on the dance floor, she told herself she could do what she had promised herself she would do. She would live life with Cole the way he chose to live it. She'd live by his rules.

Hours later, when he crushed her heavily down into the crisp sheets of his stateroom bunk, Cole told himself that he had got everything he wanted. Why the damned feelings of uncertainty wouldn't leave him alone, he couldn't understand. And, as always, just under the uncertainty lay the threat of panic.

Perhaps it was that buried threat that compelled him to wring the shuddering cries of satisfaction from Kelsey's lips over and over again that night. She gave herself without reservation, eagerly and with a delicious abandon that made him glory in his manhood. He derived an incredibly intense pleasure from the feel of her silky legs wrapped around his thighs. The peaks of her breasts were hard little berries that he nibbled with exquisite gentleness. And the warm moistness that flowed from the center of her desire welcomed his thrusting passion in a way that made him throb with an excitement that was more satisfying than anything he had ever known.

But when he awoke at dawn the next morning, Cole knew he hadn't managed to throttle that strange sense of unsureness.

It continued to needle him at odd moments throughout the day. After lunch he threw himself down on a lounger to watch Kelsey swim, and he found himself staring at her slender waist.

What if she was pregnant? He had begun taking precautions last night and he would honor his commitment to take care of her in that way. But that didn't answer the question of what was to be done if she already had conceived.

And she simply wouldn't discuss the issue.

Irritably Cole studied the sleek lines of the tangerine swimsuit Kelsey was wearing. He would feel very uncomfortable, far too visible and exposed, in anything that bright, but he liked the brilliant plumage on Kelsey. Of course, the suit was cut too low in the back and it didn't seem to have a built-in bra, but it was exciting to watch her in it.

Everything about Kelsey was satisfying and exciting, he was thinking when a white-jacketed steward walked through the crowd calling Kelsey's name.

"Miss Kelsey Murdock. Message for Kelsey Murdock."

Cole snapped his head around and frowned. Kelsey had just gone underwater. She wouldn't hear her name being called.

"I'll take it for her," Cole said calmly, extending his hand with a commanding air, which hopefully would cause the messenger to respond without thinking. "She's in the pool. It's all right. I'll give it to her."

"Okay," the steward said agreeably. "I was going to leave it under her door, but the guy who left the message said he'd already been unable to reach her on the phone. And he said it was urgent."

"Miss Murdock is spending the remainder of the cruise in my room," Cole informed him coolly. "Have any further messages transferred there."

The attitude of command worked, as it usually did, and the steward cheerfully pocketed the tip Cole gave him. Glancing toward the turquoise water to assure himself that Kelsey was still doing laps under the surface, he quickly ripped open the white envelope. The message inside had been taken by the ship's communications officer. It was from Walt Gladwin.

Kelsey, call ASAP. What's going on? Had message from Valentine. Request more details at once.

Gladwin

Cole reread the short message and then calmly shredded the piece of paper in his hands. Gladwin wasn't going to be allowed to interfere with this crucial week. Besides, the man deserved to stew in his office in San Jose. Cole was never going to absolve the other man of blame for having been the one to blithely send Kelsey into the dangerous situation on Cibola.

Getting to his feet, Cole deposited the shredded message in a nearby trash bin and then turned to glance back at the pool. Kelsey was just climbing up the ladder, her wet hair streaming behind her.

As he watched, Cole could see the outline of her sexy nipples as they pushed against the fabric of the tangerine suit. He wasn't the only male near the pool who noticed the enticing shape of her breasts, he realized at once.

Seizing an oversized towel from her lounger, he stalked forward to meet her at the edge of the pool. She blinked the water out of her eyes and smiled up at him as he approached.

"Something wrong, Cole?" she asked politely.

He knew he was glowering at her. "Cover yourself, woman. That suit is attracting too much attention."

She grinned recklessly, her eyes alight with mischief. "And you think yours isn't? I'll admit you look good in basic black," she told him, glancing down at the sleek black trunks he was wearing, "but I don't think it's the color that's attracting that redhead's eye."

Cole was astounded at the warmth he knew must be staining his cheekbones. He swore softly at the very idea that his body was capable of embarrassing him at his age. But he could feel the tightness in his loins and the pressure of the black swim trunks against his manhood.

"This," he informed Kelsey, "is all your fault." He grabbed the towel back from her and wrapped it around his lean hips, trying his best to look nonchalant. "If you hadn't come out of that pool wearing little more than a wet handkerchief this wouldn't have happened. You can damn well come on down to my stateroom and take care of the problem."

Kelsey giggled. "I can handle it right here."

Before he realized her intention, Cole felt her flatten her hands against his naked chest and push. An instant later he was sinking with a splash into the turquoise pool.

The thing about Kelsey, Cole told himself grimly as he resurfaced, was that even if he were able to overcome the odd feeling of uncertainty he experienced around her, he would never find her totally predictable. He saw her watching him from the edge of the pool and knew from the look in her eyes that she wasn't quite sure how he was going to take the playfulness."

"Nervous?" he drawled meaningfully. "Don't be. You solved the problem."

She relaxed back into teasing laughter. And quite suddenly Cole was vastly pleased with himself for being able to make her laugh.

The scene at the pool set the tone of their remaining time on board the ship. There was laughter during the days as they explored the ports of call and passion each night in Cole's stateroom.

There were also two more messages from Gladwin, both of which Cole managed to intercept before they reached Kelsey. He would probably have some explaining to do when they returned to California, Cole reminded himself occasionally, but that was in the future. No sense letting it spoil the present.

For the present was very good, indeed, and if he couldn't succeed in completely banishing the flickering moments of unease he had whenever Kelsey refused to discuss anything other than the present, Cole at least managed to keep the underlying panic at bay.

10

THE IDYLLIC WEEK came to an end the moment Kelsey turned the key in the lock of her San Jose apartment. The phone was ringing violently.

"Oh, for heaven's sake!" she grumbled, tossing down her lightweight carryall and hurrying forward to pick up the receiver. Cole appeared in the doorway behind her, loaded down with his suitcase and her own. He stood for a few seconds curiously absorbing the interior as Kelsey answered the ringing summons..

"Walt!" she exclaimed after the initial hello. "Hey, wait a minute before you begin shouting at me. I just walked in the door. What? Yes, it was very exciting. Did Valentine tell you everything? He's absolutely charming, Walt. I liked him enormously." She paused as her boss fairly exploded in her ear. At last it began to dawn on Kelsey that this was not just a welcome-home call.

"I have one hell of a lot of questions for you, Kelsey Murdock. Stay right where you are. I'm coming over." Walt slammed down the phone on his end, leaving Kelsey staring at her own instrument.

"He's very worked up over that business on Cibola," she explained slowly to Cole as he prowled her apartment. "He's on his way over here. He sounds furious and I can't figure out why." She chewed her lower lip. "I knew I should have done something more official about that whole mess. After all, I was representing Flex-Glad's interests."

"So was Valentine," Cole replied, shrugging. "And he knew a lot more about the local government than you did. As an off-islander you wouldn't have been able to accomplish much. I like your apartment, Kelsey."

She blinked at the abrupt change of topic. "Oh? Well, thanks. Maybe Valentine ran into some trouble trying to handle things on Cibola."

"Valentine can handle trouble. The only problem with this apartment is that it's wide open." Cole examined the window-locking mechanism. "You need better locks on everything. The ones you have are almost worthless. I suppose the first thing I'd better do is upgrade the security system. I should have done it a month ago."

"You've never seen my apartment before," Kelsey reminded him irritably. "How could you have known a month ago that my locks weren't the best?"

"Knowing you, it was a safe bet. You're not really much into security measures." Cole absently fingered the inexpensive lock on her front door.

"Well, I'll admit I wouldn't want to put up ten-foot-high walls around the place," Kelsey murmured, watching him curiously.

"You mean like the ones I have in Carmel. You've never liked my home, have you, Kelsey?" He glanced back at her over his shoulder. "You always made excuses not to have dinner with me there. The only time you came inside was that morning you discovered my name in your stepfather's computer."

Kelsey's expression softened as it occurred to her for the first time that her wariness of his home might have hurt him on some level. She got to her feet and walked across the room to put her arms around his neck. "I think I was afraid of getting trapped inside and never being allowed to leave," she confessed lightly.

Cole didn't respond to the lightness. His palms slid down the sides of her oversized white shirt and came to rest possessively on the snug-fitting denim that encased her hips. "That may have been a legitimate fear," he remarked wryly, bringing his mouth down on hers.

He had barely begun the kiss, when the angry roar of an expensive automobile engine filled the air. Kelsey pulled away reluctantly. "That will be Walt. With the Ferrari, it sounds like."

"Oh, by the way, Kelsey. About the story we give Gladwin . . ." Cole tossed out almost negligently.

"What do you mean, 'story'?" she demanded, startled.

"I just wanted to mention that Valentine intended to keep us out of his report as far as possible. The official line from him is that he caught some armed men going through his possessions on Cibola. Upon questioning them, he decided they were after the attaché case. He was going to let Gladwin take it from there. According to Valentine, you arrived on the island after the fracas was all over. And you came alone. I wasn't with you."

"But why?" Kelsey was dumbfounded.

"I'll explain it all later, okay? Trust me."

Kelsey clenched her teeth, telling herself that if she heard that request one more time she would probably come apart at the seams.

Her brow furrowed in angry tension, she went to open the door and found an irate Walt Gladwin on her doorstep.

"It's about time you got home. I've been trying to get in touch with you for days. Why didn't you respond to any of my messages, Kelsey? Did you think that when you're on vacation you aren't working for me, or something? For Pete's sake, I've been going nuts here trying to figure out what was going on."

"Come on in, Walt." Kelsey stepped back to allow the annoyed man inside. "And tell me what messages you're talking about. I never had any messages from you. Oh, and this is Cole Stockton," she added quickly as the two men surveyed each other with critical eyes.

"Stockton." Walt nodded curtly at the taller man and then turned back to Kelsey. "I sent three messages to the ship, not to mention trying to call you twice. It was obvious right away that I was never going to get you on the phone. Apparently you didn't spend much time in your own room," he added, sliding an annoyed glance at Cole.

"No, she didn't spend much time in her room. She spent most of her nights in mine," Cole said blandly.

"Cole, please," Kelsey gritted. "I'll handle this." Cole's possessiveness was going to be a problem on occasion, she knew, if not an actual source of embarrassment.

Cole ignored her with monumental indifference. He stood easily, watching Gladwin with chilled eyes. "I decided it was safer for her in my room. After all, working for a boss who sends her off into messy situations such as she apparently encountered on Cibola isn't good for a woman's health."

"What the devil is that supposed to mean?" Gladwin demanded furiously. "And just how much do you know about all this?"

"Cole, will you please stay out of this?" Kelsey begged, horrified at the way matters were rapidly escalating beyond her control. "Why don't you go fix us some coffee, or something?"

"She keeps the coffee next to the brandy," Gladwin tossed out with the air of a man who obviously knew his way around a woman's home. "You can't miss it."

"Both of you, stop it this minute!" Kelsey yelped, genuinely frightened now by the glacier cold in Cole's gray eyes.

"She told me that the man called 'Valentine' had his house searched by some armed thugs before she arrived. If she'd got to Cibola a little earlier, she might have been in the middle of things. I don't take kindly to a man who casually sends a woman off on little ventures like that," Cole went on conversationally.

"I don't particularly care how you take to me, Stockton. Kelsey works for me. I can send her where I want, when I want. Just who do you think you are, anyway?"

"The man who intercepted all your messages on board ship," Cole said politely.

"What messages?" Kelsey pleaded frantically. "Will someone please tell me what's going on? I didn't get any messages, Walt."

"That's because loverboy here apparently saw to it that you didn't," Walt shot back seethingly. He jammed his hands into his jacket pocket and glared at her. "I tried to reach you because, believe it or not, I would have liked to have had a report on exactly what happened. Do you realize I've had to call in the FBI? Ever since Valentine phoned and explained that things had got 'adventurous'—I believe that was the word he used—I've been running around like crazy."

"What's happened here, Walt?" Kelsey asked hurriedly. She'd get back to the matter of the intercepted messages later, she told herself. Right now a distraction was definitely called for, or she might find herself witness to more violence. There wasn't much doubt about which of the two men she'd be nursing afterward, either. Kelsey had seen enough of Cole's dangerous abilities to know Walt would be lucky to be able to crawl away from any battle between the two of them.

"I'll tell you what's going on here," Walt rasped, switching his glare back to her. "After Valentine gave me some names and information he said should be turned over to the FBI, I took his advice and called them in. They came down on Flex-Glad like a ton of bricks. Then two days ago Tom Bailey disappeared."

"Bailey? From the software planning department? Where did he go? Does the FBI suspect he might be the leak?"

"That's the current guess. From what we can piece together so far with Valentine's information it looks like Bailey was trying to sell those printouts to a representative of a not-so-friendly foreign power. He'd promised delivery several weeks ago, but he hadn't counted on the tight security Flex-Glad imposed here in corporate headquarters. But he did find out approximately when the printouts were due to arrive on Cibola."

"So he arranged to have the attaché case snatched on Cibola?" Kelsey asked uncertainly.

"The Bureau thinks he probably didn't know how to go about arranging that kind of thing himself. They suspect he simply told that representative of another country when the printouts were going to be delivered. The professionals took over from there." Gladwin ran a hand through his light-colored hair. "Valentine told me most of what went on, but he's a little hard to talk to at times. I was trying to get in touch with you in order to get the full story."

Cole interrupted coolly, "Just what did Valentine tell you?"

Gladwin shot him a fulminating glance. "Only that some armed thugs had come ashore and torn his place apart. He seemed more upset about that aspect of the situation than anything else."

"It was his home," Cole pointed out dryly.

"Yes, well, those printouts were worth a great deal more than his island home!"

"Maybe not to Valentine."

"Look, Stockton, will you just stay out of this? You're not involved as anything other than a nuisance, so I would appreciate it if you'd butt out."

"'Nuisance'?" Cole flicked an amused glance at Kelsey's tense face. "Just what did Valentine tell you?"

"Well, after he explained that his place had been searched but that the timing had been wrong—"

"'Wrong'?" Kelsey inserted curiously.

Gladwin nodded brusquely. "He explained that you hadn't yet delivered the attaché case. He caught the men responsible with the help of a friend and turned them over to the local authorities. I realize that by the time you arrived on Cibola everything was under control and we can't get our hands on those men who came looking for the printouts, much less prove that's what they were after, but that doesn't mean I didn't expect a full report from you. Kelsey, you were the only Flex-Glad employee on the scene. Valentine is hardly an employee, you know. You should have got back to me immediately."

Kelsey sent a questioning frown at Cole, who shrugged. He gave her a hard glance warning her that this was no time to dispute Valentine's story. She turned back to Walt.

"I'm sorry I didn't get in touch with you, Walt. Valentine told me he'd handle everything."

"Well, he did, I guess," Walt admitted peevishly. "But I still wanted to speak to you."

"I gather the FBI didn't feel compelled to talk to me, or did I miss some messages from them, too?" Kelsey narrowed her eyes as she looked over at Cole.

It was Walt who answered. "Valentine talked to them. Told them you couldn't add any further information, since the whole thing was over by the time you hit the island. The local agent said they'd get a statement from you when you returned to San Jose."

"I see." Kelsey wasn't sure what to say next.

Cole was not nearly so reticent. "If you've finished chewing her out for what wasn't her fault, why don't you run along. Kelsey and I would like to unpack and get settled. There's really not much else Kelsey can tell you, anyway."

Gladwin looked disconcerted. "But I haven't even talked to her yet!"

"It's true you've been monopolizing the conversation," Cole agreed.

"Look, Kelsey, we have a lot to discuss. Get rid of this guy, and then we can sit down and go over your report."

"Kelsey's still on vacation, in case you haven't noticed. If she sits down anywhere, you can bet I'll be right beside her."

Kelsey decided to act. The entire scene had gone far enough. "Walt, I feel a little disoriented. Give me a few hours to readjust to real life, okay? How about overnight? I'll be in your office first thing in the morning."

Gladwin sent one more infuriated glance at Cole and then apparently decided discretion was more comfortable than insisting on his rights. It was becoming clear that Cole would be equally insistent and that he might be able to defend his rights as a lover more ruthlessly than Gladwin could defend his as Kelsey's employer.

"Eight o'clock tomorrow morning, Kelsey."

"I'll be there, Walt," she assured him quickly. She held the door for him as he stalked out. Shutting it with a groan of relief, she leaned back against it to confront Cole. The flicker of relief changed to simmering anger as she faced his implacable expression. "So you took it upon yourself to intercept messages meant for me?"

Cole didn't answer her immediately. He assessed her flashing eyes and then walked over to stare out the window. "I had to, Kelsey."

"Why?" The single word was clipped and loaded.

"I needed that time on board ship with you," he finally said simply. "I was afraid that if Gladwin got in touch, he'd insist you fly home at once. Even if I could convince you not to obey his summons, it was bound to distract you. I didn't want any distractions. That time was for us."

"But Cole, he's my employer!"

He spun around with the smoothness of a coiling snake. "And I'm your lover."

She ought to be protesting his arrogance, telling him exactly where his rights and privileges as a lover ended, letting him know she would not tolerate his interference in her life.

But as Kelsey stood staring at his hard, set face, she read something more than arrogance in those usually unreadable eyes. Something close to desperation.

She was imagining things, she told herself. Cole had all the self-confidence in the world. He knew exactly what he wanted and he'd do whatever he had to in order to get it. Arrogance. Domineering, heavy-handed arrogance. That's all she could possibly see in those icy eyes.

But she had spent a very intimate week with him. They had been through a great deal of danger and passion together. Perhaps she really was getting to the point where she understood him on some levels. Maybe she shouldn't discount what her intuition was telling her.

"And as my lover you felt you had the right to keep Walt's messages from me?"

"We needed that time alone together, Kelsey," he insisted stubbornly.

"Why?"

"To establish the basis of our relationship!" he threw back roughly. "I wanted us to have time to get to know each other. Time apart from the world. You said yourself that being on board ship was like being in another world. I knew we'd have to come back and deal with real life soon enough. But I wanted us to come back united. Oh, hell, I'm not explaining this very well."

She thought about that. For the first time she wondered why a man who did not believe in the past or the future would make an effort to establish the groundwork for an affair. Affairs were, by definition, fleeting things, easily dissolved. Why wouldn't such a man simply take what she was obviously willing to give and be content. Her stomach knotted with a strange tension as she considered the ramifications of Cole's words. He was talking as though he were trying to build the basis for a real future. She wondered if he even realized what he was doing. Her poor stomach became even tenser as she allowed herself to wonder if Cole could eventually learn to believe not only in the future but in love.

"Cole Stockton, you can be absolutely infuriating. But the damage is done now. I'll be lucky to have a job tomorrow morning," she said with a sigh, sinking down onto the couch.

"Kelsey, I only did what I had to do."

"Uh, huh." Wisely she let that drop. Nothing she could say would convince him he shouldn't have kept those messages from her. "You never did like my job," she said wryly.

To her surprise he lifted his shoulder in an offhanded gesture of disinterest. "I think Gladwin's the kind of hustler who will take advantage of your loyalty to the firm, but I guess he's no worse than most other employers."

Kelsey's eyes opened wide in astonishment. "Well, that's a new line. Since when did you decide Gladwin's no worse than any other boss?"

Cole's mouth twisted ruefully. "Since I realized the two of you aren't particularly interested in each other on a nonbusiness level. Oh, Gladwin would probably take anything you offered, but you're not offering, and he's not going to make a grab for it. You're safe enough around him—at least when it comes to a physical relationship."

"Good grief! You determined all that just now?"

He came toward Kelsey, sitting down beside her. Cole's expression was very serious. "I still think you need someone to keep him from taking advantage of your willingness to work. But you'll have me around to do that now, won't you? I'll make certain he doesn't send you off on any idiotic delivery trips or require that you work weekends and nights. I think I can live with your job, Kelsey."

She bit off the sarcastic, "Gee, thanks," that sprang to her lips as she realized just how much that admission meant, coming from Cole Stockton. "I'm, uh, glad," she managed, not knowing quite what else to say. She seized on the other point that was plaguing her. "Tell me why Valentine kept us out of the story he gave Gladwin."

"That was mostly for my sake."

"Well?" she prompted when he didn't continue. "Why?"

"He was protecting my privacy," Cole explained simply.

"Why?" she pressed.

"Because the last thing I want to do is get mixed up with an investigation of any kind." He uncoiled from the couch and paced toward the kitchen.

Kelsey sprang up to follow him. "But, why, Cole?"

He was already running a glass of water for himself in the kitchen sink. He didn't look at her. "Because even the most casual investigations have a way of resurrecting things that are better off left buried. Take my word for it, Kelsey. It's easier this way."

Take my word for it. Trust me. Was she going to spend her whole life running up against this brick wall he'd built to guard his past, Kelsey wondered.

She answered her own question at once. No, she wouldn't be spending her life beating her head against his walls. She would only have to spend the short time he wanted her for an affair.

"All right, Cole," she agreed gently. "I'll take your word for it. I trust you."

He set the glass down on the counter with a snap and swooped across the kitchen, catching her up in his arms. His eyes were blazing with sudden desire.

"I was right about that time on the ship, wasn't I? It made a difference for us."

"Yes, Cole. It made a difference." Spearing her fingers through his hair, she lifted her face for his kiss. His mouth was fierce on hers. A week ago she would have read some of that near violence as an example of his determination to dominate her physically.

But for the second time that day she wondered if there wasn't something more beneath the surface of his actions. It seemed now as though he were somehow trying to reassure himself of her commitment.

Nonsense, Kelsey thought fleetingly. She had already given him everything he'd asked for. He could not possibly need any reassurance.

When he eventually lifted his mouth from hers, Cole did so reluctantly. "I'm going to have to go back to Carmel for the remainder of this week, honey. I have business to attend to, and I've got a lot of work to do, getting ready to shift files and records here to your apartment."

"I know, Cole." They had discussed this briefly on the return flight. Cole could not move in immediately. He had to arrange for the transfer of his business. "Mom and Roger are due home next Friday. I'll pick them up at the airport and drive them on down to Carmel."

"And on Sunday evening we'll come back to San Jose together," he concluded firmly.

"Yes."

He nibbled persuasively at the corner of her lips as he pulled her white shirt free of the jeans. "I'm going to miss having you in my bed this week." Cole stroked his palms up under the shirt until he found her breasts.

"Just think, no more having to squeeze the two of us into a narrow stateroom bunk," she teased lightly.

"I rather liked the squeezing."

"That's because you're bigger than I am. You always wound up with the lion's share of the bed."

"Size has it privileges. What sort of bed do you have here?" He tasted the curve of her throat with a questing tongue.

"That's a leading question if I ever heard one," she complained, nestling closer as his palms tantalized her nipples.

"So lead me on," he invited in a husky growl.

FRIDAY AFTERNOON Kelsey met her mother and stepfather at the airport as scheduled and spent the drive to Carmel delicately trying to explain about her relationship with Cole.

"He'll be coming over for dinner tonight," Kelsey said at one point after going through a long explanation of how he had accompanied her on the cruise.

"And you'll be going back to his home afterward, is that what you're trying to tell us?" Amanda Evans asked cheerfully.

"I think you've got the picture, Mom."

"When's the wedding?" Roger demanded easily.

"It's a subject we don't discuss," Kelsey said calmly.

"Well," Roger mused, "even if Cole doesn't discuss such things, I don't think I'll have to get out the shotgun. Stockton's a man who will honor his obligations, one way or another."

Kelsey slanted a speculative glance at her charming gentleman of a stepfather and smiled, but she said nothing. Whatever that business was involving Cole and Roger, there didn't appear to be any anger or bitterness between the two men. Just secrets.

"The two of you look marvelous," she noted, opting to change the subject as she changed lanes on the freeway. The Friday traffic was worse than usual tonight. "I gather New Zealand agreed with you."

"Wonderful place," Amanda enthused excitedly. "Roger and I are thinking of going back next year, aren't we, dear?" She leaned forward over the front seat to smile at her husband. Her short, stylish gray hair emphasized the wide hazel-green eyes Kelsey had inherited. Amanda Evans was a trim, outgoing woman who was thoroughly enjoying the new lifestyle her money had bought her. It showed in the way she wore her expensive designer fashions with obvious delight and in the laughter in her smile.

"I'm holding out for that cruise to Tahiti we discussed," Roger said, giving his wife an affectionate grin. His patrician features relaxed easily when he smiled at Amanda. "Just look at what a cruise did for Kelsey. She looks terrific."

"I don't think the cruise is responsible for that," Amanda murmured. "I think that's love."

"Speaking of the cruise," Roger went on conversationally. "How did your little side trip to Cibola go? Did you find your eccentric genius?"

Kelsey drew a deep breath. "Thereby hangs a tale," she said. And then she told them exactly what had happened during the twenty-four hours on Cibola.

When Cole strolled through the front door of the Evans home that evening wearing the familiar black pullover and black slacks he'd worn the fateful night Kelsey had tried to end their relationship, Roger greeted him with a drink and a demand for details.

"I want to hear all about Cibola, too," Amanda had warned as she swept in from the kitchen carrying a tray of herbed caviar puffs. "Sit down, Cole, and tell us everything. We've already heard Kelsey's story."

Cole's eyes narrowed as he looked at Kelsey over the top of her mother's head. Having no difficulty at all in reading the disapproval of his gaze, Kelsey smiled brilliantly and came forward to brush his mouth in a light kiss of greeting. She moved away before he could pull her closer.

"I told them all about it, Cole. The real story. And I explained that Valentine has already given Gladwin a slightly different version." She picked up her glass of wine and sat down beside her mother on the cream-colored sofa. The slim lines of her narrowly cut turquoise dress made a bright splash of color against the light background. She lifted her chin with just the smallest hint of assertiveness as Cole continued to frown at her.

"It might have been better if we'd all stuck by Valentine's version. For the sake of consistency, if nothing else," Cole said pointedly.

"I can keep secrets from some people but not from the ones I love," Kelsey told him with a quiet calm she was far from feeling.

"Kelsey never could abide secrets," Amanda interjected nonchalantly. "She can keep them when she has to, but she hates having to do it any more than necessary. And her natural curiosity drives her crazy when she knows someone is keeping a secret from her."

"Not unlike her mother," Roger put in smoothly before Cole could respond. He turned back to the younger man. "So since we know all, Cole, you might as well fill us in on some of the gory details. I must say, I'm very glad Kelsey took you along on that little jaunt. Just how did you and Valentine smoke out the two thugs in his house? Kelsey was a bit vague on that point."

Cole surrendered to the inevitable, relaxing as he sipped the drink Roger had fixed for him. "Fortunately Valentine had a few tricks up his sleeve. The dicey part was the next morning when Kelsey decided to get involved. I'd given her strict instructions to wait in the cave."

"No, you didn't," Kelsey felt obliged to protest. "You were gone when I awoke. I merely went looking for you."

Cole gave her a wry glance. "You've already told the tale from your standpoint. How about letting me give it from my point of view?"

"Because I get the feeling it's going to be decidedly biased!"

"Listen to this, Amanda," Roger said, chuckling. "Their first argument and they're not even married yet."

Kelsey felt the warmth rush into her cheeks. To cover her sudden restlessness she got to her feet. "I've explained about marriage, or rather the lack thereof, Roger. Remember? Now if you'll excuse me, I'll let Cole give you his no-doubt-male-oriented view of the story while I go check on the lamb marinade." She paused a moment longer to throw Cole a cool look. "And for the record you can bet this isn't our first argument."

She swept out of the room with a flourish, and didn't realize her mother had followed until she came to a halt in the elegant white-and-chrome kitchen and found Amanda right behind her.

"I take it Cole would have preferred you not tell us the full story of what happened on Cibola, hmm?" Amanda poked at the apricot marinade on the lamb chops.

"Cole's big on keeping secrets," Kelsey said, opening the refrigerator door to pull out the salad.

"And you think that makes him unique?" Amanda asked, amused. "Roger's got a few of his own."

In spite of herself, Kelsey shot a quick, questioning glance at her mother. "Serious ones?"

"He thinks they are," Amanda said gently. "He's sharing a secret with Cole, but he'd be traumatized if he thought I knew about it."

Very slowly Kelsey set the crystal bowl full of salad greens down on the counter and turned to face her mother. "And you do know about it?"

Amanda cocked an eyebrow at her daughter's very sober expression. "I get the feeling you know about it, too. What happened? Did Roger put the little matter of his debt to Cole on the computer?"

"Mom, I didn't mean to pry," Kelsey explained hurriedly. "I was just browsing through the computer to see how Roger was doing, and I found the file. I . . . I was shocked. I couldn't imagine why Roger would be paying Cole a thousand dollars a month."

"I found the file when it was still being kept in Roger's accounting books, before he transferred it to the computer." Amanda took the salad bowl over to the other side of the counter and reached for the dressing she had prepared earlier.

"And you went through it?"

"Well, of course, darling. What wife wouldn't?"

Kelsey grimaced. "Maybe the men are right to keep secrets from us."

"Nonsense. They don't do it because we can't be trusted. At least men like Roger and Cole don't keep secrets for that reason. Deep down they know we wouldn't betray them. We may be deeply curious about them, but we are also intensely loyal to them."

"Then why . . . ?"

"Because they try to protect us, naturally." Amanda tossed the salad with a theatrical air.

"'Protect us'?"

"Certainly. Also themselves."

"Mom, I don't understand," Kelsey protested.

"Well, take Roger, for instance. He's hiding that debt to Cole because he couldn't bear to have me find out his financial status isn't as strong as he'd like it to be. He lost a great deal of money in the stock market last year and that loan was to cover his losses. It was either ask Cole for the loan or ask me. His handwritten notes were very explicit."

"He couldn't bring himself to ask you?"

"He's afraid I'll not only worry about the money but also think less of him for having taken the heavy losses."

"It's all wrapped up with his ego?"

"Kelsey, dear, almost everything a man does is somehow wrapped up with his ego. Male egos are very fragile things. But men seem to function to a large extent on them. Along with a few other basic instincts and drives such as possessiveness, protectiveness and pride."

"I'm learning," Kelsey sighed. "I know Cole can certainly be overly possessive, overly protective and overly arrogant. And he's always insisting that I trust him."

"Do you?"

Kelsey flung out her hand in a helpless gesture. "For some strange reason that utterly defeats me, I do."

"Well, in that case there's nothing to worry about, is there?" her mother said with a grin. "As long as you can trust a man the rest is merely a challenge."

Kelsey burst out laughing as she went across the tiled floor to hug her mother. "When did you pick up all this feminine wisdom, Mom?"

"Unfortunately it only comes with age. Believe me, I'd have given a great deal to have had it when I was younger. Now are those chops ready to go under the broiler?"

"They're ready."

The meal was a pleasant success, with the conversation moving on from the events on Cibola to Amanda's and Roger's experiences in New Zealand. Kelsey would have enjoyed the homecoming meal far more, however, if she hadn't been intensely aware of Cole's frequent, searching glances.

They came at odd moments during dinner. She'd pass the salad bowl to him and find him studying her. Or she'd ask for the butter dish and have it handed to her along with a speculative gleam in a pair of gray eyes. After dinner there were more such looks, and they made her uneasy. She began to lose some of her bright, charming mood.

Kelsey didn't think anyone noticed she was becoming increasingly quiet until her mother said sympathetically, "You look a little tired, dear. Hard week?"

"There was a lot to catch up on after that Caribbean cruise. I had to put in a lot of overtime." Kelsey heard herself use work as an excuse for her more silent mood and grew even more uneasy. That was the excuse she had used to explain her attitude that night she had decided to tell Cole goodbye. It was as phony then as it was tonight. In both cases it was Cole who was responsible for her tension.

"That probably explains why I wasn't able to reach you on the phone Thursday evening until after eight," Cole said deliberately.

Kelsey stirred with a tinge of restlessness. "Yes." He had called her at eight-thirty that evening, but he had never mentioned until now that he'd tried earlier. She found herself gnawing gently on her lower lip and stopped at once. She was not going to let him make her tense like this. It was ridiculous.

But the atmosphere between them continued to vibrate with an escalating sense of danger. By the time she kissed her mother good-night and allowed Cole to lead her outside into the chilly darkness, Kelsey was feeling very strained.

They walked in silence down the private road that led to Cole's walled fortress. At the heavy wrought-iron gate, Cole entered a code into the computerized lock and stood silently aside, waiting for her to step into the garden.

As she hesitated and then brushed past him, Kelsey felt the tightly balanced tension in his body and suddenly realized she was not the only one on edge tonight. Cole was as remote and wary as he had ever been around her.

The gate clanged shut with a solid sound behind her, and Kelsey turned to glance back at it. In the light of the well-lit garden she found Cole gazing down at her.

"You were right about one thing," he said coolly. "Once inside the walls, you can't get back out."

"Cole, please don't tease me."

"But it's true, Kelsey." He took her arm and led her toward the front door. "Oh, you'll be able to come and go in a physical sense. But in another sense I could never let you go free."

She tried a tremulous smile. "Your possessive instincts are showing."

"I never knew I had any before I met you," he countered with deadly seriousness. He unlocked the front door and guided her down the hall to the living room. Without a word he escorted her to one of a pair of rattan chairs that faced the ocean. Then he paced silently across the room to pour two glasses of cognac.

Kelsey accepted one of the snifters with an odd sense of déjà vu. This was the kind of glass from which she had been drinking brandy that crucial night in her mother's home. She sipped carefully, her gaze on the darkened ocean that surged beyond the wrought-iron fence.

"Kelsey?" Cole didn't sit down in the other chair. Instead he moved to stand near the window, his back to her.

"Yes, Cole?"

"I've been doing a lot of thinking this past week."

Kelsey felt the faint trembling of the glass in her hand and knew it was due to the distinct tremor in her fingers. Oh, God, she had been right to be aware of tension in the atmosphere. Something was badly wrong. What had happened to Cole during the past week, she wondered frantically. Fear for the fate of her newfound love coursed through her. With a fierce effort she kept her voice calm.

"Have you, Cole?"

"We need to think about the commitment we're making by deciding to live together."

Kelsey's stomach tightened, but from somewhere she found the courage to say very evenly, "There's no need to think of our relationship in terms of commitment, is there? We're only dealing with the present, after all. If you—" She broke off to moisten her lower lip. "If you change your mind about our arrangement...I mean, you're perfectly free, Cole."

She thought the controlled tension in him went up another notch.

"Am I perfectly free?"

"I doubt there's a person on the face of this earth who could make you do anything you don't wish to do, Cole."

"Not even you?"

"Least of all me," she tried to say lightly.

He braced one hand against the window frame and lifted his glass to his mouth with the other. He was still staring intently out into the night as if he could see something she could not. "That shows how little you understand our situation, Kelsey."

She swallowed the fear that was threatening to choke her and tried to replace it with anger. "I don't know why you're choosing to go melodramatic on me all of a sudden. I thought everything was very clear-cut between us. All the ground rules have been worked out, remember? We're doing this exactly the way you wanted it. No past and no future. We take things on a day-by-day basis."

"And if I decide I don't like that kind of arrangement?"

"Then you're free to leave, aren't you?" she tossed back. "This is the way you wanted it, Cole."

He took a long drag on the brandy. "For someone who was once very big on long-term commitment, you've certainly changed your tune."

"I suppose I've learned from you," she retorted with savage spirit.

"What would you say if I asked you to marry me, Kelsey?" The question was ground out in a stark, steel-edged tone.

She caught her breath, struggling for the answer. "I'd say no. I'd *have* to say no." *Because it wouldn't be what you wanted,* she added silently to herself.

"And if it turns out you're pregnant?" he demanded grittily.

"I'm not. I found out for certain this past week. It was sweet of you to be concerned, Cole, but you really don't have to worry about that aspect of the situation any longer."

For the second time since she had known Cole Stockton, Kelsey found herself totally unprepared for the sensation of controlled violence that ripped through the room. As if in a dream, she watched him twist around with feral grace and slam the glass he had been holding on an end table. It met the hard surface with such force that the delicate stem snapped. Fragrant brandy spilled out on the table. The crackle of broken glass stunned Kelsey, but Cole hardly seemed aware of it.

"'Sweet of me to be concerned.' *Sweet* of me! My God, woman, haven't you learned yet there is nothing remotely *sweet* about the way I feel toward you?"

Instinctively Kelsey got to her feet, poised to run, as he stalked toward her. "Cole, wait, you don't understand!"

"Don't give me that bit about not understanding. You're the one who's missed something along the way. I'm not going to let you treat our relationship as a short-term affair, Kelsey Murdock. You belong to me now, and you'll belong to me fifty years hence. You've made a commitment and you're going to honor it. We're talking long-range, lady. We're talking about the future. And I'm finished with listening to you try to avoid that particular topic. There's no way you can run from me, Kelsey. Or from our future. It exists. Tonight I'm going to make you admit it."

11

SHE WASN'T GOING TO RUN this time. Cole realized that almost immediately. Kelsey was physically poised for flight, but he was hunter enough to know from the look in her eyes that she wasn't going to flee.

"It wouldn't do you any good, anyway," he rasped as he moved a few steps closer.

"I know," she affirmed gently.

His eyes slitted warningly. "If you did try to run I'd have you before you got to the door."

"You don't have to tell me that, Cole. I've seen you move. I could never outrun you."

"I'm going to take you into my bed and keep you there until you realize that you belong there tonight, tomorrow night and every other night."

She said nothing, but she didn't move. Cole deliberately stalked to a point only a hand's reach away and halted. Kelsey faced him with wariness but no real fear. He searched her expression. "You're not afraid of me, are you?"

"Should I be?"

"I'm going to revise this entire relationship," he declared vehemently. "Doesn't that make you nervous?"

"We've been doing everything your way from the beginning, haven't we?" she countered.

He shook his head at the ludicrousness of her response. "You've fought me every inch of the way."

"You've won every battle." It was a simple statement, not an accusation. "Got everything you wanted."

Anguish shot through him. "Kelsey, I never wanted it to be war between us!"

"Why not? War is an art you know well, isn't it?"

Panic flared deep inside. Cole felt as though it would strangle him. He'd never experienced anything like it. It seized him by the throat and wrenched at his guts. And it took every ounce of willpower he had ever possessed to control it just to the point where only his hands shook.

"What do you know of that?" he heard himself whisper fiercely.

"Very little," she admitted calmly. "But no one could watch you or Valentine for any length of time and not know that at some time in your past you were warriors."

She knew. Or she had guessed. She had seen the past in him.

"That's why you won't talk about the future, isn't it?" he charged roughly. "That's the reason you no longer care about a long-term commitment. The reason you won't marry me. You'll let yourself indulge in an affair with me, but you're no longer interested in any future with a man who might have blood on his hands."

"Cole, listen to me."

"It's too late, Kelsey," he gritted, closing the small distance between them. Deliberately he reached out to place his hands on her shoulders. "You're going to have to learn to live with these hands on you." He used his thumbs to force up her chin. It seemed to Cole that her eyes had never been closer to true green than they were in that moment. He could feel the shimmering tension in her and see the faint tremor of her soft mouth. "God, Kelsey, there's no way on earth I could keep my hands off you.

I want everything. All of you. And that includes your future."

He was expecting anything but the tender smile that curved her lips. Kelsey lifted her hands, her cinnamon-tipped nails sliding around the collar of his khaki shirt. "You can only have that if you're willing to give it in return," she murmured.

He shuddered heavily and wrapped her against him, burying his face in the compelling scent of her hair. "I've told you over and over I'll give you everything I can."

"I wasn't sure you really knew what that meant," she admitted gently. "You always seemed to talk in terms of making me a well-kept mistress."

He closed his eyes. "I suppose I thought that was all I had to offer. I wanted you so badly and I didn't know how to hold you. Kelsey, please say you'll marry me."

"I'll marry you," she breathed against his shoulder.

His hands tightened on her. It wasn't enough, Cole realized. He wanted something else. "Why?" he finally asked boldly.

"Because I love you, of course. What other reason could there possibly be?"

That, Cole realized, was what had been missing. "You love me?" he repeated uncertainly. Even though he had the words from her, he didn't quite dare to believe them. "You *love* me, Kelsey?" He raised his head to look down at her, needing confirmation of this more than he had needed anything else in his life.

"I love you, Cole."

"Just like that?" he asked dazedly, remembering vaguely that he had asked that question in almost the same way on Cibola when she had given herself to him after the battle at Valentine's house.

"Just like that." She smiled, clearly remembering the prior occasion. "Just like that."

"In spite of what I might have been in the past?" He had to know, Cole told himself. He had to be certain.

She brushed his lips with the tips of her fingers. "The past is no longer important, Cole. Whatever it was, you've closed the door on it. I trust you to keep it closed."

"Oh, Kelsey," he groaned. "I love you."

"I believe you," she whispered against his mouth. "You've never lied to me."

"Kelsey...." He couldn't say anything more. Anything coherent, that is. Cole swept her up into his arms, violently aware of the warmth of her thigh as it reached him through the turquoise silk.

She cradled her head against his shoulder as he carried her down the hall to his bedroom. The door of the darkened room stood open and he walked through it, leaving the lights off. Then he put Kelsey down in the middle of the wide bed and stood for a moment looking at her in the pale moonlight.

Beyond the wall of windows the surf crashed in counterpoint to the throb of his own pulse. Cole saw the smile of feminine warmth and welcome on Kelsey's lips and realized he was shivering from a combination of physical desire and emotional need.

"You are the only one, Kelsey," he tried to explain as he shrugged out of his clothing. "The only one who can give me what I've been needing for so long." Naked at last, he came down beside her in a heated rush, gathering her close. "I didn't even know I needed love before you came into my life. I thought I had provided myself with everything a man like me could want."

Kelsey felt the surge of hunger that went far deeper than physical desire in him, and she stroked the hard planes of his back. "I love you, Cole."

"Just keep saying it. I'll never be able to hear it enough. Oh, Kelsey, I love you so much. When I realized you weren't even willing to discuss a future between us I nearly panicked. Lord, woman, I'm not accustomed to panic. I'm not even used to this god-awful uncertainty that's been plaguing me since I met you."

He growled the last words into her throat, his hands on the fastenings of the thin silk dress. Kelsey moaned softly as he stripped it from her with a long, sensuous movement that left her completely nude.

"So soft and warm and inviting," he whispered. His palms slid possessively along the curves of her body, finding all the secret places that responded so readily to his touch.

Kelsey arched against him, drawing a fierce groan from his lips. Enthralled with the response, she trailed her fingertips down his back, pausing to clench them urgently into the lean flesh of his buttocks before moving to cradle the throbbing evidence of his desire.

"I love the feel of you," he muttered thickly. "And the scent of you. I think I'm addicted." He tasted the skin of her breasts and then went on to sample the silk of her stomach. Lower he moved, nipping with exciting gentleness along the delicate inside of her thigh. His fingers stroked the flowering heart of her until she cried out for him.

"Cole!"

Kelsey clung to his shoulders, pulling him up along the length of her and imprisoning him within the circle of her legs.

He came to her swiftly, as though he, too, could wait no longer for the throbbing union of their bodies. Kelsey gasped as he surged into her, filling her completely. And then she once again surrendered willingly to the mind-spinning rhythm of the passion they generated together.

When the pulsing climax overtook them they called each other's names over and over again until they plummeted as one into the depths of the bedding. Damp and languorous and content with a heavy warmth flooding her, Kelsey lay curled against Cole, her palm resting lightly on his chest.

"Kelsey," he finally said quietly. "I want to tell you."

"No, Cole. There's no need." She knew at once what he was going to talk about.

"I think there is. I don't want any more secrets between us."

She raised her head and smiled down at him. "Keep your secrets, Cole. I don't need them."

"Are you still afraid of them?"

"No."

He nodded, his eyes holding hers. "Then I can tell you."

She realized he had to talk now. Gently she touched the side of his face. "And then we'll close the door again and leave it closed."

Cole took a deep breath and began to talk. There in the darkness he told her what it had been like in that special unit of the military in Southeast Asia. He explained the remote, controlled facade he had developed to keep himself together emotionally when he was sent out on the top-secret missions that so often culminated in violence. He explained succinctly how that remote, carefully controlled wall had become more than a facade. It had become a part of him. And when he left the military, he continued to take the dangerous jobs that now paid so very well. The inner walls protected him.

"And then one day they weren't enough," Cole said evenly. "I wanted out. I wanted to start over. So I just disappeared. As far as the people I worked for are concerned, I never came back from my last mission. It seemed simpler that way." He stirred a little, folding Kelsey closer. "No one seems to have cared. As far as I can tell no one bothered to go looking for me. They just wrote me off as a disposable commodity that had been all used up."

"So you came to Carmel and started over," Kelsey concluded, soothing him with her hands.

"And built a few more walls," he said, grimacing. "Walls that made you wary of me and of my home."

"I understand them now."

"Kelsey, there aren't any more barriers between us, are there? I love you."

She heard the raw truth in the husky words and smiled up at him as he leaned over her.

"No more barriers, Cole. And we don't need to concern ourselves with the past. We have a future now."

"Speaking of which, we must remember to invite Valentine to the wedding."

"Absolutely. Something tells me he'll be here with bells on."

"Valentine with bells on may be more than Gladwin can handle," Cole mused. Then his brief amusement faded. "Everything's really okay, sweetheart?"

"Everything's perfect," she said, gently laying the remnants of his uncertainty to rest. "And now that we've discussed the past and the future, I think it's time to consider the present."

"My pleasure," he growled. "Right now I'm very interested in the present." His mouth closed over hers in a kiss that sealed their love for all time.

TRUE COLORS

Jayne Ann Krentz

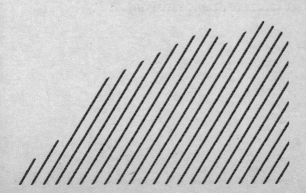

"Were you looking for me, Jamie?"

Cade stood in the hallway wearing only a pair of briefs, dark hair slightly tousled from sleep, sleek shoulders looming powerfully in the shadows. "What woke you?" he asked softly.

The words soothed and beckoned, promising warmth and passion in place of irrational fear. "I—I had a bad dream," she whispered, hugging her arms to her breasts.

"Did you? Come here, sweetheart, and I'll help you forget all about it." He held out a strong, square hand.

Jamie trembled, but not from fear. Heart racing, she slowly put out her own hand.

"You won't have any nightmares in my bed," he promised huskily, tugging her gently forward. "I'll make certain all your dreams are deeply satisfying...."

1

THE REPORTERS DESCENDED like a swarm of vampire bats, surrounding the tomato-red Audi before Jamie Garland could even get the door open. A flash of the simmering anger she had been trying to control for three days slammed through her. With all her strength she shoved at the Audi door. When that didn't work she leaned back and braced one foot against it.

"Come on, Miss Isabel, we'll have to make a run for it." The door gave slowly as the press of photographers, newsmen and related vultures jockeyed for position.

"My God," the older woman sitting beside Jamie breathed in genuine shock, "where did all these people come from?"

"These aren't exactly people, Miss Isabel," Jamie informed her caustically. "They're reporters." She got the door open a little farther, and a microphone was shoved in her face. Jamie ignored it, reaching behind her for Miss Isabel's hand. "Get out on my side of the car and stay close. Don't say anything, just concentrate on making a dash for the front door, understand?"

Isabel Fitzgerald's old-fashioned silver bun bobbed as she nodded. "I understand. But why are they here?" Her bewildered gray eyes swept the loud crowd.

"They want a story," Jamie said bluntly.

"About Hadley?"

"I'm afraid so."

"But how could they know so soon?" Isabel whispered sadly as she inched across the seat in Jamie's wake.

"The same way the authorities knew to walk in and seize Hadley's records and books yesterday," Jamie told her grimly. "Cade Santerre must have let them in on the results of his brilliant investigative work."

Isabel gasped. "Surely Mr. Santerre wouldn't have informed the press and sent them down on us like this? He always seemed like such a nice man, even if he did . . ." She couldn't finish the sentence.

Jamie drew a deep breath as she shoved once more against the car door with her sandaled foot. "Mr. Santerre is the kind of man who does anything he wants, regardless of who gets hurt. He's a ruthless—" she paused to slide out of the opening she had created, dragging Isabel behind her "—conniving, lying, deceitful son of a . . ."

"Would you repeat that into the mike, Miss Garland?" a reporter demanded. "And tell us whom you were describing, please."

Before Jamie could tell the man that she could easily have been describing one of the fraternity of newspeople who surrounded the car, a dark growl of a voice intervened.

"Leave her alone," Cade Santerre ordered, pushing three photographers aside as he waded through the crush toward Jamie and Miss Isabel. "She doesn't want to talk to the press."

"Our readers deserve answers. Some of them were among Hadley Fitzgerald's victims," a woman reporter snapped. She edged toward Isabel, reportage instincts telling her the older woman was the weaker prey. "Miss Fitzgerald, we understand you're a painter. How involved were you in your brother's tax-shelter schemes?"

"I had no idea," Miss Isabel whispered despairingly. "I mean, I never knew anything about it. I'm sure there's an explanation for it all. Hadley would never do such a thing."

"What about you, Miss Garland?" Another microphone blocked Jamie's path. "Is it true you were Fitzgerald's private secretary? His mistress? True that he confided everything in you and that you helped him in the fraud?"

"I said leave her alone," Santerre gritted, reaching Jamie's side at last. His fingers closed around her arm.

Jamie flinched as the strong, blunt hand chained her to Cade's side. Memories of the last time he had touched her flamed in her mind. That had been two nights ago. Then the strength in his hands had been a source of wonder and excitement. He had wielded his masculine power so easily, Jamie recalled with a vivid clarity that stained her cheeks even now. So very easily. And she had been such a fool, giving him everything she had to give; both promises and passion. Neither, it seemed, meant much to Cade Santerre.

With his free hand Cade grasped the quivering Isabel and started on a path toward the front door of the beautiful Fitzgerald home. In spite of themselves, reporters and photographers gave way before the implacable, savage intent reflected clearly in Santerre's unyielding features.

"Don't do us any favors, Cade," Jamie hissed as she was hauled through the jostling crowd. "It's a little late for that kind of thing."

"These guys are like vultures," Cade muttered, guiding the two women up the flagstone walk.

"I can deal with vultures," Jamie retorted, ignoring one particularly persistent cameraman who was running alongside. "After all, they don't show up until after the kill. It's the predator who brings down the victim in the first place who's really dangerous."

"I assume it was me you were describing a minute ago when you climbed out of the car?" Cade observed as they reached the front door. He waited with obvious impatience while Jamie sorted out the right key. Miss Isabel clung to his arm, peering around anxiously. When one or two newsmen tried to move in again Cade warded them off with a chilling glance. Santerre had the kind of eyes well suited to such glances, Jamie thought vaguely. They were a feral, tawny brown, laced with small flecks of gold. The eyes of a hunting cat.

"I'm . . . I'm quite sure Jamie didn't mean you, Mr. Santerre," Miss Isabel hastened to assure him as she ducked her head to avoid a camera. Even in a crisis her good manners and fundamental faith in people came to the fore.

"Of course I meant him," Jamie said coldly as she turned the key in the lock. "Who else do we know who fits the description so perfectly?"

"Jamie, I've got to talk to you." Cade reached over her shoulder to push open the door. He urged both women through into the hall and then slammed the door shut again, right in the face of the aggressive cameraman.

Jamie ignored Cade, her attention on her employer. She spoke gently to the older woman. "Go on upstairs, Miss Isabel. You need to rest. You didn't sleep last night and you've had a horrible day. I'll be up in a little while with some hot tea."

Miss Isabel looked uneasily at her personal assistant and then at the grim-faced man standing behind her. "Are you quite sure, dear? I don't mind staying down here if you'd rather not talk to Mr. Santerre alone."

"She's perfectly safe with me," Cade muttered.

Jamie nodded in agreement, her eyes narrowed behind the lenses of her stylish oversize glasses. "That's right, Miss Isabel. I'm quite safe with Cade now. He's already gotten everything he wanted from me. Go on up-stairs. You need some rest."

She sensed behind her Cade's sharply indrawn breath, but he said nothing as Miss Isabel walked slowly up the carpeted stairs and disappeared. Jamie watched her sadly. She'd never seen her employer in such a condi-tion. The older woman appeared astonishingly frail to-day. Her normal energy and enthusiasm had been drowned beneath the weight of shock and worry. And there was nothing Jamie could do except try to offer sup-port and friendship. Her own sense of guilt just made the situation all the more depressing.

Jamie waited as long as possible, but when she heard the door to her employer's room close she knew she could no longer delay facing Cade Santerre. Summoning up the full extent of what remained of her inner fortitude, she swung around and confronted the man who had made passionate love to her only two nights ago.

"Why are you still hanging around, Cade? Haven't you done enough damage?"

"I'm not leaving until I've made you understand ex-actly what happened," he vowed harshly. "It wasn't supposed to end like this. I've been trying to tell you that since yesterday but you wouldn't even take my calls. That's why I'm here. I'm going to talk to you, Jamie, and you, by God, are going to listen!" He shoved his blunt fingers through the gray-flecked brown pelt of his hair and stalked across the sleekly beautiful, elegantly mod-ern living room.

Hadley Fitzgerald's Santa Barbara home had ap-peared an ideal place to spend the summer, or so Jamie had thought two months ago when she had arrived with Miss Isabel. The Pacific Ocean was almost at their front door, and the warmth of a California beach summer had seemed to hold so much promise. In the summer Santa

Barbara was alive with artists, craftspeople and tourists. The charm of the town's Spanish architecture combined with the picturesque locale to create a California fantasy. Jamie realized she had taken Cade Santerre's hand and stepped all too willingly into that inviting fantasy. But now the chill of fall was in the air, hastened by the same man who had created the warmth. Jamie eyed him uneasily as Santerre came to a halt by the wall of windows that looked out on a serene Japanese-inspired garden.

Cade Santerre had transformed a pleasant working vacation at the beach into a passionate summer affair that had culminated in a night of shimmering love. That had been two evenings ago. The next day, yesterday, he had destroyed Jamie's newfound world of light and magic, leaving it in a pile of glittering shards at her feet. Only the need to protect her employer had kept Jamie functioning during the past forty-eight hours. She had focused everything on her job. Never had Isabel needed her more.

Jamie studied the man by the window, trying to see him with new, more realistic eyes. But there was little about him that she didn't already know far too intimately. It was just that she had either ignored the evidence that had been before her for the past two months or else she had chosen to interpret it falsely. Fantasies were tricky that way. And heaven knew she'd always tended to view reality from a gentle perspective.

Cade's tawny gold eyes still mirrored cool intelligence and unwavering intent. It was her own fault, Jamie told herself, that she hadn't labeled that gaze with the proper adjective. Ruthless was the word that truly described those eyes.

He was not a particularly good-looking man, but the stamp of inner strength and power was plain on his bluntly hewn features. That same strength and power was echoed in the compact, smoothly muscled body. Jamie closed her eyes briefly, remembering the feel of that body as Cade had crushed her passionately into the tangled sheets. Fleeting pictures of how the moon had gleamed through the yacht's cabin window behind his sleek shoulders came back along with the memory of the rhythmic motion of the sea. Her own husky promise returned to taunt her. *I'll come with you, Cade. If you really want me, I'll come with you.* But he hadn't really wanted her to sail away with him. Cade had been merely making the seduction total. He had wanted complete surrender and he had gotten it from her. Cade was a very thorough man, she had learned.

Frantically she pushed aside the disturbing images, trying to concentrate on the man he really was, not the fantasy lover he had been two nights previously. Today he was dressed in jeans and a dark olive long-sleeved pullover that emphasized the hard lines of stomach and thigh. He always seemed to be casually dressed, Jamie realized, but, then, that was true of just about everyone here in Santa Barbara during the summer. Cade's clothing hadn't gotten in the way of convincing Hadley Fitzgerald that he had money, a great deal of it. Of course, the crisp clean lines of the expensive yacht tethered in the nearby marina had lent credence to the image.

"You fooled us all, didn't you, Cade?" Jamie observed softly. "Hadley, me, even Miss Isabel. You probably missed your calling. You should have gone on the stage. But perhaps that line of work doesn't pay as well as the betrayal business."

He spun around, his movement quick and highly controlled. The tawny gold eyes glittered for an instant. "I didn't betray you, Jamie. I don't care what else you choose to believe about me, I didn't mean for you to get caught in this mess. I want you to know that. Know it and believe it."

She nodded thoughtfully, straining inwardly to keep the leash on her fury and despair. Whatever it cost her, she would not lose her self-control in front of this man. Not again. That night of abandon in his arms had been quite enough. Slowly she walked across the room and sank down onto the white leather banquette that fronted the fireplace.

"Whatever you say, Cade. Would you mind leaving now? I've got a job to do. I'm still working for Miss Isabel, remember?"

The tension in him radiated across the room but he didn't move. "Don't you dare sit there and pretend that it's all over. You know better than that, Jamie."

"Do I?" She met his eyes unflinchingly. "Let's see, this is the day I was going to sail away into the sunset with you, wasn't it? It's difficult to keep the schedule straight. So much has happened recently. But I believe the scenario went something like this: I was going to explain to Miss Isabel that I had to take some time off without any notice because you were being called away on business and you wanted me to come with you. You couldn't leave without me, I think that was how you expressed it. You were quite certain Miss Isabel wouldn't mind me taking a little impromptu vacation. After all, she approved of you. She thought our little romance was charming. You didn't know how long you were going to be gone and you couldn't take the risk of leaving me behind here in Santa Barbara. I assumed, naturally, that you were so passionately captivated by me that you couldn't bear to be without me, not even for a few weeks. You spin a lovely fantasy, Cade. I believed you in the end. I believed you completely. It's incredible now when I think about it, but I was actually prepared to give up everything for you. If you'd asked me to quit my job entirely I probably would have done it."

"Everything I promised was the truth," Cade bit out savagely. "I was going to take you with me. I had it all planned, Jamie. If the people I was working with hadn't screwed up the whole operation at the last minute, you would have been safely out of the picture when the authorities and the reporters moved in on Fitzgerald. I meant to keep you out of it completely. I wanted to protect you."

She widened her eyes behind her glasses, the bitter mockery plain in the gray-green depths of her gaze. "Why would you want to keep me out of it when I had been so much a part of everything up to this point? After all, I'm the one who so stupidly and unintentionally kept you informed of Hadley's comings and goings, wasn't I? I'm the one who was dumb enough to mention his second office here at the house. I'm the one whom you so casually pumped for so much useful information. Surely I deserve to be here at the end. I'm only surprised you didn't have me arrested when Hadley himself slipped through your fingers."

"Don't be a fool. You know damn well I never meant to implicate you."

"Don't tell me you're so naive that you thought you could drag Hadley Fitzgerald down into the mud and not get Miss Isabel and me splattered, too! Do you know what they're saying about me in the papers this morning? They're speculating on whether or not I was Hadley's mistress. That's a joke, isn't it? No one seems to have figured out that I was your mistress, not Hadley's. They're also speculating about Miss Isabel, wondering how much she knew about what was going on. The fact that she's a rather successful painter makes her fair game as far as the press is concerned. She's got a name they can work with, after all. I'm just a nobody who will probably be forgotten fairly quickly. But Miss Isabel's career could suffer because of this."

"Her career won't suffer. Artists can always use a little notoriety. And before I leave here today I'll make damn certain those reporters know you weren't Fitzgerald's mistress!"

"I'd appreciate it if you didn't accomplish that by telling them the truth! I have even less desire to be known as your mistress than as Hadley's. My God, but you're callous," Jamie whispered starkly. "How could I have ever believed you cared for me? I'll bet you've never cared for another living soul in your whole life!"

"Jamie, you're upset and I can understand that," Cade began carefully, clearly trying to hold on to his temper. "You've been through a lot in the past couple of days."

"No kidding? I must say one hasn't lived until one innocently opens the door bright and early in the morning and finds a man outside holding a search warrant. It does add a certain level of excitement to the scene when a team of government financial investigators walks in right behind him and proceeds to confiscate just about everything of a personal and private nature they can get their hands on!"

"They were only after Fitzgerald's records. After all, they're out to prove fraud, remember? Don't exaggerate, Jamie. They didn't take anything personal and private of yours, did they? Or of Miss Isabel's."

She threw him a derisive look. "Sorry if I seem to be embroidering the issue a bit. Wouldn't want to bore you. It's just that I get so little excitement in my life. When something like this comes along I want to get all the charge out of it that I can. It's not every day that a man seduces me for information he can use to set a trap for someone I happen to like."

"I didn't use you!" Cade exploded roughly.

"No? That's sure what it felt like."

"Those agents weren't supposed to show up on the Fitzgerald doorstep until tomorrow. The whole operation got fouled up when some fool higher up made an executive decision to carry it out two days early. That's what you've got to understand, Jamie. I had everything planned so that you'd be clear when the roof fell in on Fitzgerald."

"I don't believe you, but even if I did, do you honestly think that would make me feel one bit better about being used?" she demanded furiously. "And what about Miss Isabel? Did you have any plans to protect her?"

Cade stared at Jamie intently, utter ruthlessness underlining every hard feature in his face. "You were the only one I was worried about protecting. I'm a realist. There was no way to save Miss Isabel from being hurt. She's Fitzgerald's sister, his only living relative, so she was bound to get caught up in the scandal. The best thing she could do for herself now is take a long cruise somewhere. You should probably get her out of the country until the whole thing blows over."

"Your suggestion comes a bit late, but we'll certainly consider it," Jamie shot back, privately thinking that it really was a good idea. Perhaps she would mention it to Miss Isabel later.

Cade took a step toward her but halted when she went very still on the white banquette. "Jamie, I did what I had to do. I tried to set things up so that you wouldn't be here when the authorities moved in, but something went wrong. I'm sorry about that part of it. I swear it. I didn't plan for things to go that way."

She lifted her chin challengingly. "My only consolation is knowing that Hadley got away. You really blew it there at the last, didn't you? You were so busy seducing me the other night that you forgot to double check to see if Mr. Fitzgerald had made any last minute changes in his plans. I could have told you that he left unexpectedly for San Diego a few days early."

"I didn't seduce you in order to gain information." Cade ignored Jamie's sharp exclamation of disbelief. "The original plans would have worked out just fine if everyone had followed orders. Fitzgerald was supposed to be back tomorrow," Cade said heavily. "And the authorities weren't supposed to close in until after we were sure he was back. That idiot Gallagher has a lot to answer for. We had Fitzgerald in the bag. If Gallagher hadn't decided to play Lone Ranger, we'd have had Fitzgerald as well as the documents."

"Gallagher being the one who made the decision to act yesterday? Well, as far as I'm concerned, more power to Gallagher!"

Cade's expression was hawklike. "While you're cheering for Hadley Fitzgerald's side, you might spare a couple of thoughts for all the people he bilked. Miss Isabel's charming, gentlemanly brother cleared hundreds of thousands of dollars on his tax-shelter schemes. None of the victims is likely to get his money back, either, especially now that Fitzgerald himself has escaped. He's probably out of the country by now."

Jamie drew in a steadying breath. Her palms felt damp from nerves and tension. "I only have your word that Hadley was guilty of fraud and, quite frankly, Cade, your word isn't worth much around here these days. You've been lying to me and to the Fitzgeralds for almost two months. What's more, you put me in an untenable position. How do you think I feel knowing that I was unwittingly supplying you with information about Miss Isabel's brother? I work for the woman, Cade, and you made me betray the person she cares most about in the world. You used me and I swear I'll never forgive you for that. But I doubt that matters to you, does it? Why should you care what I think about you now? You've got everything you wanted, with the exception of Hadley, of course! But I'm sure you're enough of a *realist* to know that we seldom get absolutely everything we want in life."

Cade moved abruptly, striding across the white Italian tile floor to where Jamie sat on the banquette. She tried to shrink back out of reach but she didn't move quickly enough. Familiar strong fingers locked around her wrist, drawing her to her feet. Cade held her firmly in front of him, his hands gripping her shoulders. Jamie could feel the tightly controlled anger and frustrated tension in him.

"Let's get one thing clear, Jamie Garland. I'm going to say this once more and that's all. You were not responsible for betraying your employer's brother. Hadley Fitzgerald sealed his own fate the day he tried to pull his scam on my sister and her husband."

"Your sister!"

"She and her husband poured twenty thousand dollars into one of Fitzgerald's mining ventures. Unlike some of his clients, Meg and Bill couldn't afford to take that kind of loss. Especially not with a new baby to plan for. When they realized what they'd done they asked me to see if there was any way to get the money back. I started checking into Fitzgerald's operations and realized he wasn't just a fast-talking salesman; he was a crook."

"You were qualified to make that kind of judgment?" Jamie blazed passionately.

"Yes."

She blinked owlishly at the single word, not knowing how to argue the point further. She was only beginning to realize just how little she actually knew about Cade

Santerre. It was frightening to acknowledge that after two months of seeing him and after that night in his bed she really knew nothing about him. What a fool she had been. "It sounds to me as though you decided to institute some kind of personal vendetta against Hadley just because your relatives were unwise enough to invest money they couldn't afford in a high-risk venture."

"They weren't involved in a legitimate high-risk deal," Cade rasped impatiently. "They got conned. There's a difference. I decided to go after Hadley and at least put him out of business, even if I couldn't get Meg and Bill's money back for them."

"And I was a convenient tool, wasn't I? Don't try to deny it. You came to Santa Barbara posing as a wealthy vacationing executive investigating ways of shielding his taxable income and Hadley took you on as a client. But you didn't stop there. You started dating me. You admired Miss Isabel's paintings. You took Hadley for cruises in your boat. You made yourself a friend of the Fitzgeralds and a—" She broke off, unable to put the rest into words.

Cade had no such inhibitions. "And a lover to you," he concluded evenly. "Jamie, you must believe me. I didn't plan that part of the operation. It happened. But our relationship had nothing to do with closing the trap on Fitzgerald."

"I don't believe you. I can't believe you. Are you going to deny that you pumped me for information whenever we went out together?"

Cade's eyes narrowed. "I did what had to be done. I'm a practical man and I wanted to bring down Fitzgerald as quickly as possible. No, I'm not going to deny that I asked you a few casual questions and got some useful answers, but the end result would have been the same. I was out to close down Fitzgerald's operations and I would have done it regardless of whether or not you answered a few questions."

Jamie felt as if she would break into a thousand pieces. Pain and fury seemed to be fighting for control within her. "You're a practical man, a realist. You do what has to be done." Cade stood motionless as she flung his incriminating words back at him in a scathing tone. "You use whatever tools come to hand and I certainly came to hand, didn't I? I was right in your palm. But was it really necessary to take the seduction of Jamie Garland all the way? Couldn't you have called a halt before humiliating me completely?"

"What the hell do you mean, humiliating you?" he grated.

"You let me make a complete fool of myself the other night on your damn boat!"

"I made love to you. I didn't make a fool out of you!"

"Somehow it seems to have amounted to the same thing!" she shot back violently. "Why, Cade? Why did you do it? You knew what was going to happen. Except for the fact that your pal Gallagher seems to have fouled up his end, your plans were in place and ready to be carried out. You didn't have to make your victory so complete. But you did it anyway because you're a thorough man, aren't you? A ruthless, arrogant, deceitful but thorough man!"

"I made love to you the other night because I wanted you," he said between clenched teeth. "And because I needed to make certain you would come with me on the boat today for your own protection. I thought that once we'd been together in bed you would—" He snapped off the end of the sentence, aware that what he was about to say would only infuriate Jamie more.

But Jamie wasn't about to let the words remain unsaid. She knew exactly how to finish the sentence. "You thought that after you'd taken me to bed I'd be even more in your power, didn't you? You thought that by seducing me completely you could control me completely. What I don't understand is why you were worried about having that kind of control unless . . ." Shock went through her. "Unless," she continued very slowly, "you were afraid that something might go wrong at the last minute with your precious operation and you wanted to cover all the bases. That was it, wasn't it? If Hadley did manage to escape you wanted to make sure you still had a spy planted in the household. And that's why you're here now, isn't it? Hadley did slip away and you're looking for a way to find him if and when he tries to contact Miss Isabel."

Grim lines marked the edges of Cade's mouth as he stared down at her. "You're letting your emotions and your anger run away with you, Jamie. I didn't plan anything of the sort."

"Get out of here, Cade. You're not going to get any more from me or from the Fitzgeralds," Jamie said, her eyes unnaturally bright behind her glasses. "I won't play the fool for you again. You obviously have a very low opinion of my intelligence if you think I will. But, then, I guess I haven't given you much reason to think highly of my intellectual abilities, have I?"

"Jamie, you won't even let yourself try to understand. You're allowing your pride and your temper to control your thinking." Cade pulled her stiff, resisting body against his chest, aware that his own frayed temper was almost at the breaking point. For the past two days nothing had gone right. Gallagher had botched the job. Jamie felt used and betrayed. And he, Cade, was frustrated and coldly furious because of both. He knew deep down he had only himself to blame for having blown the whole business.

Everything had seemed to be going so smoothly two nights ago when he had led Jamie on board the yacht and down into the shadowy cabin. She had come with him, full of trust and a sweet, rather shy anticipation that had made him feel both infinitely protective and wildly victorious. The combination of emotions had been entirely new to him. They had formed a potent brew, singing through his bloodstream like a rare and exotic drug. The night had been magic. He had undressed Jamie so slowly and carefully, savoring the soft, rounded curves of her breasts and thighs.

There had been warm, gentle invitation in the depths of those wide gray-green eyes as he had slid the oversize glasses off her short, tip-tilted nose. The mass of dark auburn hair had tumbled tantalizingly around her shoulders when he'd pulled it free from the pins that held it in a casual swirl on top of her head. Cade remembered how he'd run his fingers through the rich stuff, delighting in the deep fire.

There was no overt classical beauty in her face, but the lively expressive features had caught and held him every time he'd looked at her during the past two months. She was twenty-nine years old and still suffering from what he considered a romanticized view of life and people. Cade had suspected she would probably never outgrow the charming touch of naïveté. He didn't mind. He found it somewhat amusing, even strangely pleasant to know that Jamie saw him through a rose-colored haze. It was a sure bet that few people had ever viewed him that way.

He'd known from the first day he'd walked into Fitzgerald's beautiful home that there would come a time when he would take Miss Isabel's intriguing employee to bed. But Cade had waited, willing to bide his time and do it right even though he was cognizant of her growing awareness of him. He'd liked her honesty in that regard.

She hadn't played games. The initial shyness had been real but so had the initial attraction she'd felt for him.

For some reason it had seemed unduly important that the seduction of Jamie Garland be carried out carefully and properly. He still couldn't explain the way he'd handled that end of things. There had been no reason not to push matters much farther, much faster. But a part of him had insisted on taking his time and making everything perfect for her. And so the two months had drifted past in a haze of gathering sensual attraction and intellectual pleasure until they culminated quite naturally in an evening of exquisite passion. The only shadow on the horizon was that Cade knew he had to get her free of the Fitzgerald home before the authorities made their move.

Cade had thought his timing had been faultless. When he'd pushed her deeply into the cabin bunk and felt Jamie blaze with passion at his touch, he'd known she would follow him on board the yacht two days later. She would have done anything he'd asked of her. Glorying in her response to him, he'd lost himself in her that night. There had been a sense of wonder and power and warmth in taking Jamie Garland so completely. The two months of courtship had culminated in a night Cade knew he would never forget; a night that had left him starving for more even as it had satisfied him completely.

If all had gone well, the two of them would have been safely away from Santa Barbara by now. She wouldn't have been caught up in the scandal. The knowledge that everything had gone wrong instead had been eating at him for the past forty-eight hours and there wasn't much left of his self-control. Jamie's infuriatingly obstinate response to his attempts to explain the situation came close to making his temper snap completely. And something else was chewing on him; a sense of panic.

"Please go, Cade."

"Jamie, this mess with Fitzgerald has nothing to do with you and me."

"I'm not in the mood to appreciate your odd sense of humor."

"I'm not joking, damn it! I'm laying it on the line. We have a *relationship*, you and I."

"Is that what it's called?" she asked flippantly.

Cade sensed the high-strung emotions that were searing her nerves and knew he should back off for a while. Cade Santerre knew people. He had a talent for analyzing them and predicting their behavior. It was a skill he used almost unconsciously and it had often served him well. But although he knew intellectually what his course of action ought to be now, emotionally he wanted to force Jamie to understand and accept what had happened. He was afraid, Cade realized, afraid that she was going to slip through his fingers the way Fitzgerald had. But while losing Hadley Fitzgerald was annoying, after all the work that had been put into trapping the man, losing Jamie didn't even bear thinking about. She belonged with him now, Cade told himself for the hundredth time that day. They belonged together.

"I'm not interested in having any kind of relationship with you whatsoever," Jamie said stonily. Before Cade could reply the phone shrilled loudly. Automatically she turned to look at the white instrument where it sat on a glass-topped end table. "I suppose that's the press again. Why won't they just go away? Can't they get it through their thick heads I'm not going to talk to them?"

Cade released her and strode over to the ringing phone. "I'll handle it." He lifted the receiver and delivered a cold, unencouraging greeting. A familiar gruff voice responded. "Oh, it's you, Gallagher."

Jamie absently rubbed one shoulder where Cade's fingers had been unconsciously sinking deep into her skin and watched belligerently as Cade listened in unemotional silence.

"I see," Cade said finally, his eyes on Jamie. "No, I'm here; I'll tell her. You're absolutely sure it was Fitzgerald's boat?" There was another pause while he listened, and then he said a brusque goodbye and replaced the receiver.

Instantly on the alert, Jamie stared at him. "What is it? What's happened?"

Cade hesitated and then said coolly, "They finally located Hadley Fitzgerald's cabin cruiser. It's been missing from the marina since very early yesterday morning."

A quick frown brought Jamie's dark brows together. "His boat? Where was it?"

Cade sighed. "It was found drifting a couple of miles offshore. All indications are that Fitzgerald has committed suicide at sea."

Jamie's mouth fell open in stunned amazement. "Suicide!"

"Gallagher says that it looks like he must have thrown himself overboard," Cade concluded quietly.

"Oh, my God." Jamie's knees suddenly felt as if they wouldn't tolerate her weight. She dropped down onto the nearest chair, hugging her arms tightly to her breast. "Suicide. I never dreamed he was the type. I never thought...I just assumed he would lie low until he could prove his innocence. What will I tell Miss Isabel?"

Cade came toward her, crouching down beside her and reaching out to put a hand on her jeaned thigh. "I'll tell her for you, Jamie. You don't have to be the one. Let me handle it for you."

Jamie turned her head slowly to look at him. With great dignity she said very clearly, "Neither Miss Isabel nor I need any more bad news from you. You've done enough. Get out of here, Cade. I will be the one who tells Miss Isabel what's happened to her brother."

Cade read his complete and utter dismissal in her eyes and knew there was nothing more he could do in that moment. The sense of panic flared again. This time he dampened it with a hefty dose of logic. Time was what Jamie needed. She needed time to remember how good it had been between them these past two months. Time to reconsider his side of the story. Time to get over the shock of the events of the past two days. Time would be his ally. It would allow Jamie to regain her perspective, allow her to remember.

Even as he told himself all that, it occurred to Cade that time might provide something else.

There's just a chance, Cade realized, *that she might discover she's pregnant.* He was startled at the odd jolt of pleasure and possessiveness the thought gave him. If she were pregnant she would need him. She would have to come to him. And he would take care of her.

Cade got slowly to his feet and walked over to the end table that held the phone. Reaching for the note pad and the silver-plated pen that stood beside the telephone, he wrote quickly. Then he straightened and tore off the page.

"You can find me at this address, Jamie. If you need me for anything at all, or if you discover when you've calmed down that you don't want to throw away what we have going between us, look me up. I'll be waiting."

"You'll wait until hell freezes over," Jamie managed starkly.

"Jamie, honey, sometimes things happen..."

"Isn't it the truth!"

Cade reined in his sense of frustration and quieted the uneasiness he was feeling. He kept his voice gentle. "I meant sometimes our actions have certain, uh, ramifications. Unforeseen consequences . . ."

"Goodbye, Cade."

"Jamie, listen to me. If anything happens, anything at all, I want you to know I'll be waiting. Do you understand, honey? I'll be at that address. Waiting."

"Goodbye, Cade," she said again.

There was nothing more to be said. Cade left.

2

SHE MUST be pregnant.

Cade felt an odd twist of excitement somewhere deep inside. Satisfaction rippled through him next, and finally, incredible relief. It had been a long shot. After all, he had only been to bed with her once. But the timing fit, he thought with a sense of exultation. It fit perfectly.

After six weeks of alternating bouts of desperation countered by logical reassurance that he was doing the right thing by waiting, Cade realized he felt almost lightheaded with relief. Determinedly he took control of his emotions. The last thing he wanted to do was to ruin everything now by mishandling the situation again.

He lounged in the stern of the oceangoing fishing boat he'd named *Loophole* in a rare moment of whimsy and watched as Jamie Garland walked hesitantly toward him. She held a scrap of paper in one hand and was glancing at the names of the boats tethered in the marina as she moved slowly along the bobbing, planked walk. In another couple of seconds she would spot the *Loophole*. When Cade had glanced up a few minutes ago and seen her poised in the sunlight at the gate of the marina, he had told himself very forcefully that he had been right to wait.

Six weeks. That was long enough for a woman to find out she was pregnant. At least he assumed it was. Cade's strong fingers closed fiercely around the can of beer from which he had been drinking. Six weeks. He had almost given up hope. The cold, clear-thinking side of his nature, the side that had always given him an instinctive ability to outmaneuver others, had insisted he wait as long as two months if necessary. It would all be so much easier if she came to him. And she would come to him eventually, he had assured himself over and over again. One way or another she would come to him.

At least that's what he had told himself during the long nights of the past six weeks when another side of him clamored for action on his part. The second aspect of his nature had surprised him at first with the extent of its power. Never had his emotions threatened to so completely overwhelm the logical, calculating elements of his personality. But during the past six weeks he had frequently found himself in the grip of a frustrated, raging male panic that almost convinced him he should ignore his intellect and go after Jamie.

Thank God he'd had the sense to maintain his self-control and wait for her. It would be much better this way. Jamie had obviously been forced to face the fact that she needed him, either because she had found herself pregnant or simply because she couldn't forget what they'd shared. Either reason, or a combination of both, suited Cade. He was, after all, a pragmatic man. He'd use whatever worked; whatever brought him the results he wanted. Pregnancy and passion were powerful forces in a woman. One or both of them was undoubtedly responsible for bringing Jamie to him at last. Given the proud, angry manner in which she had told him to get out of her life just a few weeks ago, he was inclined to lean toward the pregnancy theory. Nothing like finding out she was having a baby to make a woman reconsider her feminine pride, Cade decided with what he considered shrewd insight into the behavior of the female of the species.

He wasn't going to ruin everything now by letting her know he had dissected and analyzed her behavior. He'd play this cautiously. He wouldn't throw her pride back in her face. She'd admit the truth to him and to herself in her own good time. For now it was enough that she was here. Things were back on track. The sense of overwhelming relief turned into euphoria that had to be strictly controlled. Firmly he clamped down on his own reactions.

Cade took a long swallow from the can in his hand in an effort to steady himself. His fingers were trembling a little, he realized in wry disgust. The waiting was over, so why in hell was he succumbing to nerves? Ruthlessly he suppressed the sign of uncertainty. He watched Jamie's approach through eyes that were narrowed partially against the warm Southern California sunlight and partially in hungry assessment. It had been so long. . . .

She looked wonderful coming toward him. The rich auburn hair was twisted into the familiar sweeping knot on top of her head. She wore her dark prescription lenses instead of the clear ones, and the frames were even more oversize and stylish. The white pants she wore were pleated and full at the waist, cropped at the ankles. A rakish, white linen shirt, open at the throat completed the outfit. Her bare feet were only minimally enclosed in a pair of thin-strapped sandals, and she carried the bulging, oversize shoulder bag she had toted everywhere during those two months in Santa Barbara. He'd teased her more than once about the large purse, but she'd only laughed and told him he ought to be grateful. It had carried more than one picnic to the beach.

Cade concentrated on her waist for a few seconds, wondering when a pregnant woman first began to show that fact to the world at large. Not this early, apparently. Of course, he reminded himself, there was always the possibility that she wasn't pregnant, but on the whole he was rather inclined to think that that reason fit the timing of her appearance best. Vaguely he understood that he wanted her pregnant because it gave him such a useful tie to hold her with. It was a tie she couldn't break. She was far too honest to deny him his fatherhood.

Jamie glanced once again at the name scrawled at the bottom of the slip of paper she held in her hand. The paper, containing the address of the marina in the little town just up the coast from San Diego, had become wrinkled and smudged during the past six weeks. She was lucky she had it at all, Jamie decided with a touch of irritation. She'd very nearly tossed it in the trash after Cade had walked out of the Fitzgerald home. She probably should have thrown it out. In fact, Jamie still wasn't sure why she hadn't discarded it and instead stuffed it unceremoniously into a zippered compartment of her purse. It had probably been sheer force of habit. She was so accustomed to tossing loose odds and ends into the bag that she'd added the scrap of paper without thinking about it.

But even as she reassured herself, Jamie knew she was lying. She hadn't kept the paper by accident. She might as well admit it.

The *Loophole* struck her as an odd name for a boat. She was quite certain it hadn't been the name of the elegant yacht Cade Santerre had used for two months in Santa Barbara. She was hardly likely to forget that particular boat. It had been called *Dreamer II*, and in her idiotically enchanted state of mind this past summer Jamie remembered thinking it was a lovely name for a beautiful craft on which dreams had become reality. The yacht had been brilliantly white, trimmed in rich teak. The cabin had been intricately outfitted, providing every luxury. There had been expensive wine in a small rack, pâté and caviar in the tiny refrigerator, and a stereo system stocked with classical music. And the view through the windows of the moon silvering the sea was one she would never forget.

She really was going to have to get control of this unfortunate tendency she had to romanticize life, Jamie told herself brusquely.

She moved on to the next boat slip and almost walked right past the *Loophole*. The block letters painted in black and shadowed in red on the white stern of the large fishing boat registered just as she was about to walk toward the next slip. With a frown she glanced again at the name on the scrap of paper. A fishing boat? The last time she had seen Cade Santerre he had been the wealthy business-executive owner of a customized yacht.

"Hello, Jamie."

The dark husky tone brought Jamie's head up with a snap. She was suddenly very grateful she was wearing her sunglasses. At least they provided some semblance of concealment. For a long moment she simply stared at Cade as he leaned on the stern railing with the easy graceful nonchalance she recalled so vividly.

"Hello, Cade," she finally said slowly. He was wearing jeans that were faded from several washings, a cocoa colored short-sleeved shirt and a pair of rather worn-looking deck shoes that had been white once. The heavy leather belt that clasped his waist appeared to have been around even longer than the shoes. Cade had always dressed casually in Santa Barbara but the clothes he had worn there had been several times more expensive than the ones he had on now.

The harshly etched lines of his face and the tawny gold hunting eyes hadn't changed, Jamie thought. Nor had the sensation of quiet, controlled strength that emanated from Cade. He was watching her with an indefinable expression, an expression that made Jamie unexpectedly nervous. It was as if she had just walked into a trap he had set.

"It took you long enough to get here," Cade said gently. "Come aboard. I've got a couple of extra cans of beer." Suddenly his brows came together as though he had just recalled a stray fact. "Or are you supposed to have any alcohol? It seemed to me I remember reading something—"

"A beer," Jamie interrupted firmly, determined to take control of the situation right from the start, "sounds great." She decided to ignore the implication that somehow he had been expecting her, and his even odder reference to alcohol. She went aboard the *Loophole* with the knowledge that she must stay in charge.

"Have a seat, Jamie. I'll get the beer." Cade motioned her to a deck chair and disappeared for a moment into the forward cabin. When he returned he was holding two frosty, opened cans. Silently he handed one to her and then lifted his own in a too casual salute as he sank down into the seat across from her. His eyes never left her face.

Realizing that Cade wasn't going to say anything more to break the ice, Jamie drew a breath and asked the first obvious question that came to mind. "What happened to *Dreamer* II?"

"She wasn't mine. Belonged to a friend." Cade sipped his beer and waited.

Jamie nodded. "I always had a feeling she wasn't quite real." It was the truth. Nothing about the two months with Cade this past summer seemed real anymore.

"*Dreamer* II was real enough. She just doesn't happen to belong to me," Cade said roughly, as though he sensed Jamie's thoughts. "I needed her to make the right impression on Fitzgerald."

"I see." Jamie's mouth tightened as she lifted the can of beer to her lips. "I imagine that *Loophole* is a much more suitable name for a boat that belongs to you. A realistic, practical man would always have an escape route available, wouldn't he? You're hardly a dreamer, are you, Cade?"

Cade frowned. "Dreams aren't very useful things for a man. He needs clearer, more defined goals if he's going to get what he wants."

"You may be right," Jamie agreed thoughtfully. "The same theory would apply to women, too. You do have a talent for logic and decisive action, don't you, Cade? You were always so good at manipulating people and situations."

He didn't respond to the faint taunting in her voice. Instead, his own question was oddly quiet. "Have you been doing a little logical thinking yourself, Jamie? Is that why you're here?"

Jamie leaned back in her deck chair, wondering where to begin. "I'm not here because of any rational decision on my part. As a matter of fact, I voted not to come at all. Miss Isabel outvoted me. I'm here to carry out my employer's wishes." The lie came relatively easily to her lips. It should; she'd practiced it often during the drive down from Big Sur.

Cade's gaze pinned her abruptly. He appeared genuinely startled. "Miss Isabel sent you?"

"You seem disconcerted, Cade. Why did you think I'd tracked you down? Because I couldn't bear to live without you any longer?"

Sudden understanding seemed to flare in Cade's gleaming eyes. "Perhaps Miss Isabel knows what's best for you in this situation. She probably thought you'd be too proud to come looking for me unless she prodded you into it."

"She knows very well I didn't approve of this business of recontacting you." Irritably, aware that her present state of tension was making it difficult to think clearly, Jamie downed some more of the cold beer and got to her feet. She walked toward the bow of the boat, absently noting the neatly arranged array of gear. Assorted nets, fishing knives and tackle were all carefully stowed. She glanced into the front cabin.

"Jamie," Cade said, having risen silently to follow her. "Don't be afraid of me." He reached out to touch her hair. "I won't let you down."

Jamie stepped out from under his touch, conscious of the shock of awareness that had gone through her. She had to stay in control, she reminded herself yet again. Idly she pretended to examine some coils of rope that were lying neatly on the deck. "Quite a change from *Dreamer II*, isn't it? Do you really own this boat, Cade?"

"I own her," he replied softly. "I make my living with her. The *Loophole* is a charter boat. I take people deep-sea fishing."

Jamie shook her head in mild wonder. "I would never have guessed this past summer that you made a living as a charter-boat captain. You certainly had me fooled. I believed, along with everyone else, that you were a successful, wealthy executive. Amazing. Absolutely amazing."

Cade stepped closer, his expression suddenly dark and intense in the bright sunlight. "Are you shocked, Jamie? I told myself this summer that when you found out what I really did for a living, it wouldn't matter to you."

"It doesn't," she assured him, swinging around to confront him fully. She managed a lightly defiant smile. "Makes no difference to me at all as long as you're still for hire."

Long lashes briefly concealed the tawny gold eyes, but not before Jamie was certain she had seen a flash of grim astonishment in his gaze.

"For hire?" Cade asked carefully. "What does that mean?"

"It's very simple," Jamie said coolly, sitting back down and picking up her can of beer. "Miss Isabel has instructed me to hire you."

Cade looked momentarily blank. "Hire me to do what? Fulfill my responsibilities to you? She can't possibly believe she'd have to pay me to do that!"

It was Jamie's turn to look blank. "What responsibilities? You don't owe me anything, Cade. We both know that. We shared a brief affair this past summer and now it's over. I'm here to talk business."

He gave her a wary glance as he resumed his own seat. "Maybe you'd better start at the beginning. Where is Miss Isabel, by the way?"

"We took your suggestion. I put her on a three-month cruise. She left two weeks ago."

Cade nodded. "It will be good for her. How did she take the news about her brother's suicide?"

Jamie had the distinct impression he was asking out of genuine concern, but she discounted the notion. Cade wasn't the type to become overly concerned about his victims.

"About the way you'd expect. She was shattered at first."

Cade shook his head. "I suppose that's not surprising. She adored him. I doubt that she would ever have believed him guilty of the tax-shelter fraud. You should have let me tell her about the suicide, Jamie. I know it must have been hard on you."

"It was," she said simply. "But I think it was easier coming from me than from the man who had pulled the rug out from under her beloved brother."

Cade's expression didn't change. He continued to look at her levelly. "You can forget the little barbs and taunts, honey. I don't feel guilty for what I did and nothing you say is going to make me feel responsible for Fitzgerald's death."

"You just did what you had to do, hmm?" Jamie allowed nothing but cool sarcasm to show in her tone. She refused to let him see the fragility of her self-control. "Nothing like genuine machismo to fall back on when the ethical side of things gets complicated."

"I think," Cade observed far too politely, "that we are straying from the subject. Let's go back to Miss Isabel's request to hire me."

"Ah, yes. Miss Isabel. I think you did your best work on her, Cade. She has great faith in you, in spite of everything. Or perhaps because of everything."

"Do you want to clarify that?" Cade asked patiently.

Jamie looked at him narrowly. "Miss Isabel, to put it succinctly, does not believe her brother committed suicide. She wants you to find out what happened to him. She seems to feel that because you investigated him so thoroughly in the first place, you probably have more of an idea of how to find him than anyone else possibly could. I have to agree with her, Cade. You're a thorough man. You probably know just about everything there is to know about Hadley Fitzgerald's way of operating."

"His way of operating?" Cade repeated. "That sounds as though you may believe he was a little less than innocent."

Jamie stirred uneasily, inwardly annoyed at her slip of the tongue. "The authorities seem to have found a great deal of evidence against him," she admitted austerely.

"He was guilty as hell."

Anger flared in Jamie. "I'm not here to discuss his guilt or innocence. I'm here to ask you if you'd like another investigative job. A simple 'yes' or 'no' will do."

Cade gave her an unexpectedly affectionate smile. "Are you quite certain that's why you're here, Jamie?"

"Of course I'm certain!"

"Are you sure it's the only reason?" he prodded softly.

"What other reason could there possibly be?" she challenged.

"You don't have to fake it, honey. Not with me." He put out a hand and captured one of hers. "We got very close this past summer, you and I. I know a lot about you."

"Such as?"

His mouth curved in gentle amusement and he moved the pad of his thumb across the fragile veins of her wrist. "Such as the fact that you don't lie well."

"Unlike you?" she couldn't resist saying recklessly.

His fingers closed around her wrist. "I know you've got your pride, Jamie, but I think you've had your pound of flesh. There's no need to go on hurling accusations."

Her mouth firmed as she met his eyes unwaveringly. "You're right. I'm not here to sling more accusations at you. It would be a pointless exercise, wouldn't it?"

"I told you I know you very well, Jamie Garland. And I knew you'd be showing up sooner or later."

"Your arrogance is rather charming in a way," she told him. "Somewhat outrageous and somewhat amusing, I suppose." Jamie pulled her hand free from his grasp and was surprised when he allowed her to escape. "But I don't have time to play games with you. I'm here to offer you a job. Take it or leave it."

Cade drummed his fingers absently on the arm of his chair while he studied her intently. "I thought Miss Isabel was out of the country."

"She is. She'd like you to work on finding her brother while she's gone. If you turn up anything, I can reach her by contacting her cruise ship. I have complete instructions on how to do so."

"You're serious, aren't you?"

"Miss Isabel's serious," Jamie corrected calmly. "I, personally, advised against hiring you for the job." White lies, Jamie assured herself, merely white lies. After all, in the end Miss Isabel had agreed to the idea.

"You're claiming you're just here to carry out her orders?"

"Since she was gracious enough not to fire me after that debacle six weeks ago, I figure carrying out her orders is the least I can do," Jamie snapped.

Cade scowled. "You're still viewing what happened between us as a disaster?"

"I'm trying to learn how to be realistic, just like you."

Cade's expression softened. "Such sweet bravado. Charming. A little outrageous and rather amusing, I suppose," he added with a small grin as he threw her own words back at her. "But totally unnecessary. You're here and that's all that counts. If you want to pretend it's because you're offering me a job, go ahead. I don't mind."

"I am not pretending! That's exactly why I am here. Now do you want the work or not?" Jamie glanced around meaningfully. "Perhaps your charter work doesn't leave you any time to accept this sort of assignment right now?"

"Don't sound so hopeful," he said dryly. "I can make the time. The part about finding out what happened to Fitzgerald is for real? Miss Isabel really wants me to look into it?"

"Yes."

"It does make a convenient excuse," Cade said, nodding thoughtfully.

"It's not an excuse," Jamie exploded tightly.

"Whatever you say, honey."

"Damn it, Cade, if you're not going to take the job seriously, then forget it."

"After Miss Isabel's gone to all this trouble to provide you with a way of approaching me that doesn't hurt your pride? I wouldn't dream of it. I accept the offer of employment." Cade took a long swallow of beer and grinned at Jamie's infuriated expression. "Did she happen to say how much she's paying?"

"I'm empowered to negotiate your fee. Miss Isabel assumed it would be quite high," Jamie said stiffly.

"Miss Isabel is a very astute woman."

"Well?" Jamie demanded, as calmly as she could. "How much?"

"For finding out whether or not Fitzgerald might still be alive? I'll have to think about it. I'll let you know over dinner tonight."

Jamie brushed aside the reference to dinner. "Why do you have to think about your fee? Don't you have an established amount? How much did you get paid for your work this summer?"

"You don't seem to understand exactly what it is I do for a living," he retorted smoothly. "I'm not a private investigator. I'm a charter-boat captain. There's a difference."

"But someone hired you to go after Hadley Fitzgerald in the first place," Jamie pointed out. "I remember you said something about your relatives having invested in one of his, uh, programs." She had almost tripped over the word 'scheme'. Something in her did not want to grant this man the satisfaction of knowing that she suspected he had been right about Hadley. She had already surrendered too much to Cade Santerre.

"My sister and her husband didn't hire me to do the job. They simply asked for some advice. They were desperate. I started looking into the situation and decided I might be able to put a stop to Fitzgerald's activities. Then I got in touch with the authorities, who already had a lot of questions and suspicions. We put together an operation designed to find Fitzgerald's real set of accounts, not the one available for public inspection at the L.A. office."

"And you found them at his home in Santa Barbara. With my help," Jamie tacked on disgustedly.

"I would have found them with or without your help. Jamie, we've been through this. You're a fool if you're feeling guilty. You have absolutely no reason to feel that way. Fitzgerald deserved to be exposed and you know it. You're too genuine and honest yourself to condone criminal behavior. Would you actually want to let someone like Fitzgerald continue operating just because you worked for his sister, who happened to be a nice old lady?"

"Now you're the one straying from the main subject," she retorted haughtily. "About your fee—"

"I've told you, I'll decide and let you know over dinner," Cade said with an air of finality. "Where are you staying?"

Jamie frowned. "At a little motel in town." She gave him the name.

"I know it. I'll pick you up around six."

"I don't think dinner is necessary!"

"Come on, Jamie," he coaxed with unexpected gentleness. "What about just for old times' sake?"

"When I think of the 'old times' we spent together, I have a tendency to lose my appetite."

"I'll pick you up at six," Cade repeated with a new touch of cold steel in his voice.

Jamie took one look at the chill in the tawny gold eyes and knew she couldn't win; not if she wanted to carry out Miss Isabel's wishes. Putting down her can of beer with unnecessary force, she acquiesced with a short nod and made her way off the *Loophole* without a backward glance.

Cade watched her leave, disconcerted by the abrupt departure. Whatever her real reasons for seeking him out, there was no doubt that her pride was still at full sail. She was just tense, he told himself. Maybe a little scared. She was clinging to Miss Isabel's plan to hire him as though it were the real reason she was here. But under the surface, Cade was sure he had seen the warm, vulnerable woman who had fallen so sweetly into his hands this summer. The Jamie Garland he had seduced so carefully and had come to know so intimately was still there under that protective veneer. She was just a bit frightened at the moment.

Tonight, after some good wine and reassuring conversation he would bring her back to the *Loophole* and recover what had been his this past summer. The difficult part was over. Jamie had come looking for him. He had told himself firmly that it was crucial she take the first major step. But now she'd done it and he could take over. The thought of seducing Jamie again awakened a throbbing heat in his veins that he'd had to keep bottled up for six long weeks.

Cade went to work, sharpening a knife he frequently used for filleting his clients' catch, unaware of his own smile of satisfaction. He looked forward to undoing the last of Jamie's fears this evening. It was good to be able to take action again. The waiting had been almost in-

tolerable. A man could become a nervous wreck waiting for a woman to come to her senses.

SEVERAL HOURS LATER, seated across from him at dinner, Jamie was intensely aware of Cade's smile. In fact,
she decided wryly, the anticipation and satisfaction in
Cade was evident in far more than the cool, pleased curve
of his mouth. The two blatantly masculine emotions
pervaded his fascinating eyes and lent a husky quality to
his dark voice. And they reminded her far too much of
the past summer.

"Excellent fish," she remarked, valiantly attempting
to keep the conversation on an impersonal level. The
comment was valid. Her broiled swordfish had been
cooked to perfection. The Caesar salad and crusty sour-
dough bread that accompanied it made a perfect combination. But she would have said the same words even
if the food had been lousy. She was experiencing a real
need for casual, remote dinner-table conversation.

She had made every effort to maintain a detached,
impersonal image this evening. The dress she had chosen was a sophisticated red wrap affair belted with a
wide, black leather sash. The ensemble had seemed suitable for a business dinner. Her hair was in its usual casual twist, but that was largely because she couldn't think
of anything else to do with it. She had deliberately not
put on one of the dinner dresses she'd worn in Santa
Barbara.

"The place is noted for its seafood," Cade told her easily. "But I chose it because it reminds me a little of that
restaurant we used to go to so often in Santa Barbara.
Remember? The one that looked out over the marina?"

"Vaguely," she replied unencouragingly. Actually she
recalled every evening there with unsettling clarity. Cade
had behaved then as he was behaving tonight; solici-

tous, rather possessive, deeply, intently aware of her. It was that attitude of total awareness that had seduced her so conveniently once before, she reminded herself. She must be wary of it now. "It seems to me you wore that jacket a time or two in Santa Barbara. I take it you didn't have to return it when you returned the yacht?"

Cade registered the faintly derisive words with a slightly raised brow and then shrugged beneath the fabric of the expensively tailored linen jacket. "I have a few clothes left over from the days when I did other things for a living besides run a charter service."

"What did you do for a living before getting into charter work?" Jamie asked. "Something that made your relatives think you could get them out of the trouble they'd gotten into by investing in Hadley's programs?"

"Something like that," he verified dryly. "I was an accountant."

"An accountant!" For some reason that startled her.

"Had my own firm in Los Angeles. If there's one thing a good accountant knows how to do, it's to dig for information relating to money."

"How big was this firm?"

"Big enough. Does it matter now? I sold out to some of my employees a couple of years ago and I don't have any intention of going back into that line of work."

Aware of the strength of the willpower that seemed to underlie the decision, Jamie grew curious. Curiosity was a dangerous element to introduce into the casual, remote pose she was attempting to maintain, but she couldn't seem to control it. "You acted the role of successful executive very well this summer. I take it, it's because you once were one?"

"Would it make any difference to you tonight if I still were the man I posed as this summer?" he asked. He was watching her intently.

"I don't know," she said honestly. "At least it would be one less thing you'd lied about."

His expression hardened briefly and then turned cool and analytical. "You're really determined to push me tonight, aren't you? Be careful, honey. I'm willing to tolerate a certain amount of feminine vengeance from you, but there are limits."

"What will you do if I make one too many nasty cracks? Quit working for Miss Isabel? That's not a very effective threat, Cade. I advised her not to hire you in the first place. And if it's true that your background is in accounting, not investigative work, then perhaps she really should try someone else. I think she was under the impression that you were a professional criminal investigator."

"Believe me, if Fitzgerald is alive, I'll have a better chance of finding him than a regular private eye would. A man like Hadley has a distinctive way of operating. The technique he uses to handle money, locate potential clients and set up scams is as unique to him as a fingerprint is to a burglar. If he's out there, I can find him sooner or later. He won't be able to resist getting right back to work. But frankly, I doubt he's still around. No one has turned up any evidence to contradict the impression that he took his boat out to sea and decided not to come back."

"Miss Isabel is convinced he's still alive," Jamie said with a sigh.

"Miss Isabel is trying to avoid having to face reality."

"You're real big on that, aren't you?" Jamie snapped. "Did you face reality when you decided to quit managing your own accounting firm and become a charter-boat captain? That sounds like a rather ridiculously romantic move to me. Come on, admit it. You had some wildly romantic view of making your living from the sea instead of a sterile office, right?"

Cade smiled faintly. "No. I sold my firm because I woke up one morning and realized that I didn't like being responsible for fifty employees and a lot of tense clients. Building up the business had been exciting. Running it was not. I needed a whole new career, and I knew that if I stayed with the firm I would eventually grow bored and burn out. So I made a logical decision to start over in an entirely unrelated line of work."

Jamie looked at him in faint astonishment. He really believed what he was saying. Perhaps he had made such a dramatic decision based purely on a logical assessment of his own needs, but deep down she wondered. A man who made love the way Cade had that night on the yacht must have a streak of passion and romance in him somewhere. Or was she only telling herself that because deep down she couldn't bring herself to believe he was completely devoid of that kind of emotion? She was more the fool for romanticizing him! There could easily have been another reason why he'd changed careers so drastically. Maybe the accounting business had failed. Perhaps he'd run it into the ground. But even as she speculated on that possibility, Jamie knew it wasn't very likely. Whatever Cade Santerre did, he would do well. The odds were strongly against him having a real romantic streak in his soul. On the other hand, the only thing you could call her scheme to contact Cade again was romantic, unless you wanted to label it stupid.

"We haven't yet discussed your fee," Jamie said firmly, determined to bring the conversation back in line. "Have you settled on a figure?"

"We can discuss it later," he replied carelessly. "Right now we're talking about personal job histories and I've got a few questions about yours."

"You do?"

"Hmm." Cade buttered a chunk of bread. "Are you going to stay with Miss Isabel indefinitely?"

"She pays me well and I like her very much. It's a good job so, yes, I suppose I will stay as long as she's willing to have me work for her. Besides, where else is someone who graduated with a degree in history going to find such a well-paying position that offers so much travel and variety? I get to make my home base at her beautiful house in the mountains of Big Sur up in northern California. I get to travel with her frequently when she takes vacations as she did this summer when she went to stay with Hadley. And she treats me almost as if I were her daughter. I did hear that the CIA occasionally hires liberal-arts types and it does offer travel, but other than that outfit, I don't think there's too much out there for people with my background," Jamie said lightly.

"I doubt that. I saw the variety of duties you handled for Miss Isabel this summer. There were a lot of skills involved and I'm sure you could easily market those skills elsewhere. You did just about everything for her," Cade recalled slowly. "You took care of her business affairs, her taxes, her clients, her entertaining."

"Miss Isabel likes to devote herself entirely to creating new works of art. She doesn't care to be bothered with the business side of life. She depends on me completely in those areas."

"And you, in turn, are suitably faithful, loyal and obedient, is that it?"

"It's a living," Jamie shot back coolly.

"I wasn't mocking you, Jamie," Cade said softly. "In fact, I admire your loyalty to Miss Isabel. But there comes a time in everyone's life when you have to think about going in new directions, making changes. You shouldn't feel completely tied to Miss Isabel. Working for her is, after all, only a job."

Confused at the way the conversation was going, Jamie stared at Cade. "What are you getting at?"

He hesitated, sorting out his words and then said, "It's just that this past summer and now tonight, when you describe your job I have the impression that maybe you're a little too devoted to dear Miss Isabel."

Cold resentment caused Jamie's eyes to narrow behind the lenses of her glasses. "There was a time when I seriously considered walking away from dear Miss Isabel and running off with a man who wanted to sail into the sunset. Fortunately reality intruded."

"And instead you went running right back to the security of working for Miss Isabel."

"There is nothing wrong with working for her! Or are you going to accuse her of being somehow involved with her brother's schemes?" Jamie demanded furiously. "If she is, then so am I, because I handle all of Miss Isabel's business affairs!"

Cade cut through the emotional outburst. "Calm down, Jamie. I never meant to imply any such thing. I was only pointing out that you're not obliged to stay with Miss Isabel forever simply because you feel guilty for what happened six weeks ago. You should feel free to move on when, uh, circumstances dictate a change in your life." He seemed to stumble over the last few words as if he weren't certain how to express himself.

"Circumstances have not yet dictated a change. As it turns out, I'm damn grateful for the job. It might have been a little hard to get another after that scandal six weeks ago!"

"Don't let your feelings of loyalty toward Miss Isabel govern all your actions," Cade went on harshly. "There are more important kinds of loyalty you should be concerned about other than the kind you feel toward Miss Isabel."

"Such as?" she challenged rashly.

"Such as the loyalty you owe to your lover," Cade declared bluntly. "The loyalty you owe to me. You've had six weeks to think about it, Jamie. But you're here now and that means that on some level, at least, you've realized that this is where you belong. I like Miss Isabel, and if you want the truth, I suspect she invented this little job of finding out what happened to her brother largely to give you an excuse to come down here and find me. But I'm willing to go through with it and see if I can verify the suicide if it will make her rest easier about her brother's fate. Afterward, though, I'm not going to continue to share you with her. She needs someone virtually living with her and you won't be able to do that because you'll be living with me."

3

"YOU'RE SERIOUS, aren't you?" The last forkful of tender swordfish halted halfway to Jamie's mouth as she stared at her escort in stunned amazement. "You're really serious. I can't believe it."

"Can't believe what? That I want you? I never made any secret of that. I told you six weeks ago that our relationship had nothing to do with getting Fitzgerald."

"Just an unfortunate coincidence, I suppose? I had no idea I appeared so incredibly naive. Look, Cade, I think this has gone far enough. Obviously Miss Isabel's plan to hire you is not going to work out. I think you'd better take me back to the motel." Jamie realized she had crumpled the napkin in her lap into a sorry state. With great care she made an attempt to smooth it out and refold it. It was difficult to keep her fingers from trembling. She was getting cold feet, she realized with a sense of anxiety. The knowledge angered her. Determinedly she gathered her willpower.

"Jamie, just relax, will you?" Cade invited in a low, reassuring murmur. "I'm not going to rush you. I know you need a little more time. But you've taken the first step. Trust me to handle the rest. I gave you plenty of time this summer, didn't I? All the time you needed."

All the time she'd needed to fall in love, Jamie thought bleakly. And when he'd sensed she was in the palm of his hand, he had shown her the full extent of her own passion for him. Oh, yes, he'd given her time. And enough rope to hang herself.

"I told Miss Isabel this was going to be a disaster. Will you please take me back to the motel, Cade?" It took a tremendous effort but Jamie was proud of herself for the control she exerted. Deliberately she placed her napkin on the table beside her plate, signaling her readiness to depart. She had to make it appear that she didn't care one way or the other if he accepted the job. She had to be cool and detached. It was the only manner in which she could stay in charge. It was crucially important to stay in control. Any other direction would only lead to disaster.

"Back down, Jamie. No one's going to push you. I don't want you getting upset. You know it's not good for you." Cade threw her a half annoyed, half concerned glare as the waiter hurried toward them.

The odd comment about not getting upset raised a few questions in Jamie's mind, but she brushed them aside as Cade asked for the bill. Her main goal at the moment was to conclude this evening, which, she had known from the outset, was going to be difficult.

In silence the dinner check was settled, and in silence Jamie allowed herself to be escorted out into the parking lot where Cade's black Mazda sports car waited. Jamie wondered what had happened to the expensive Mercedes-Benz he had driven this summer. Perhaps it had been returned to its rightful owner along with the yacht. It was difficult to know what had been real and what had been fiction about Cade Santerre during those two months in Santa Barbara. It was safest for her to assume that nothing had been as it seemed. Jamie had been telling herself that, morning, noon and night for the past six weeks. She didn't dare stop the litany now.

Jamie took refuge in the night-darkened interior of the car but she was fiercely aware of Cade's aggressive, controlled presence beside her. Whatever else had been accomplished this evening, at least she had managed to erase some of the pleased satisfaction from his smile. Unfortunately she wasn't sure she liked whatever it was that had replaced it. The silence as he drove began to wear on her nerves. She had a hunch he knew that and was deliberately letting the condition continue. One of the lessons she had learned this past summer was that Cade had an instinctive ability to manipulate people. When she could stand the subtle pressure no longer she struggled for a neutral topic.

"About Miss Isabel's job . . ."

"I've said I'll look into the situation for her," Cade reminded her stonily.

Jamie slid him a speculative glance, but other than the implacable set of his features in the darkness she could detect little. Then she decided to risk saying what must be said. "If you do decide to take her offer of employment, it must be with the understanding that I don't come with the deal."

Silence descended again as Cade failed to respond to the warning. Jamie could think of nothing else to say until she finally realized they were pulling into the parking lot of the marina. Belatedly she became alert to her surroundings.

"This isn't the motel, Cade."

"Since you don't seem to be abstaining from alcohol, I thought I'd invite you in for a nightcap," he replied too easily as he switched off the ignition. "Remember how pleasant it was to go back to the boat after dinner in Santa Barbara and have a glass of brandy?"

Jamie remembered very well. Fleeting images of nights spent under the influence of warm brandies, sea-scented air and Cade's gradually deepening embraces would stay with her the rest of her life. A brief wave of panic washed over Jamie before she regained control of herself. She knew what he was doing. He was trying to invoke the magic that they had shared those two months in Santa Barbara.

"It won't work, Cade, but I guess there's no harm in letting you see that for yourself." With a blitheness she didn't quite feel, Jamie stepped out of the car as Cade opened the door.

"We'll see, honey." He smiled down at her and then linked his fingers with hers as he started toward the marina gate. "Just relax and let things flow naturally. Everything's going to be all right."

For the first time genuine humor lightened Jamie's mood. "For a confirmed realist, you're doing an absolutely amazing job of deluding yourself, Cade Santerre."

"Am I?" But he didn't seem worried. The anticipation and satisfaction were again very evident in him. The small setback he had experienced during dinner no longer seemed to be troubling Cade.

"Yes, but perhaps after you've had a dose of reality we can settle down and do business together."

He grinned at her and tightened his grip on her hand. "You're not the one to teach me about reality, sweetheart. You're much too soft and gentle and trusting."

"I don't trust you!"

"A temporary state of affairs." He paused beside the *Loophole* and gallantly assisted her on board, his smile still faint and teasing. "After you. It's not exactly *Dreamer II* but it's home."

She looked at him in surprise. "You live on board?"

"Yes. Very convenient."

"Well, considering it's a fishing boat, I'm surprised the, uh, odor of fish isn't stronger."

"You know me, Jamie. I keep things clean and neat."

"Yes, you always were a thorough sort of man."

He led her down the steps of the forward cabin and waved her to a seat on the bunk. Then he opened a cupboard and brought out a bottle of brandy.

"I see your tastes are still expensive in some respects," Jamie noted dryly as she caught a glimpse of the label.

"I don't compromise on the important things." He handed her a snifter and toasted her lightly. "To Miss Isabel." Then he set down the glass and casually removed his coat and loosened his tie.

It was all very unthreatening on the surface. Just a man relaxing after a dinner out. But somehow the atmosphere in the small cabin began to vibrate with subtle masculine sensuality.

Jamie blinked and lifted her glass. "I can drink to that. I don't believe in compromising, either."

She glanced around the tidy, cramped quarters of the cabin. There was one bunk, a small galley and a great deal of cleverly designed cupboard space. Fine for a few days at sea, she decided, but hard to imagine living in on a permanent basis. She wondered what the exact state of Cade's income was. Somehow the idea of him not really being wealthy didn't reassure her as it should have. She ought to be feeling less intimidated by a man who was closer to her own income bracket. The brandy warmed her and she leaned back against the bulkhead just as Cade sat down beside her.

"Where are you staying while Miss Isabel is on her cruise?"

"At her house near Big Sur."

"I'm surprised she didn't want you to accompany her on the cruise."

Jamie shrugged. "She said the cruise was supposed to be therapy, not a genuine vacation. She didn't want to take me along and end up depressing me for three months. Besides, there's a lot to do at home."

Cade frowned. "Home? You're talking about her place in Big Sur?"

Jamie swirled the brandy at the bottom of her glass. "It's become my home during the two years that I've been working for her. I'll leave the phone number with you so that you'll be able to contact me if you learn anything about Hadley's fate."

Cade sipped his brandy and looked at her over the rim of the glass. "It will be easier if I work out of Miss Isabel's house."

Jamie's head came up in surprise. "But you have a business to run here."

"I have a friend who can take the boat out when there's a scheduled trip," he returned carelessly.

"Cade," she began firmly, "I don't see any need for you to move into Miss Isabel's home." That was the last thing she could allow, she decided in a brief flare of panic. She had to keep a careful distance between herself and Cade until she'd discovered whether or not there was any real hope of picking up the pieces of her love.

"I could do the job from here but it makes more sense to work there. I assume Miss Isabel will have all kinds of odd information about her brother available. Photos of him on vacation, for instance. He might have retreated to one of those spots again if he actually faked his suicide. A man like Fitzgerald would choose a familiar place in which to hide out because he doesn't like dealing with new environments. That was one of the characteristics that made it easy to track his activities. He tended to stay in a limited geographical area and operate in a certain, recognizable manner. A man doesn't generally change his fundamental way of doing things any more than he has to in order to survive. Especially a man of Fitzgerald's age and temperament."

"You seem to understand him very well," Jamie breathed, a little frightened by the cool, undoubtedly accurate assessment. Whatever else had changed about Cade, he was still a very logical, calculating man.

"I'm usually fairly good at analyzing the motives and actions of others," he said with unconscious arrogance.

"And at manipulating them?"

"One talent usually leads to the other." He set down his brandy glass and reached for the one in her hand. Gently he removed it and put it down beside his own. "Don't be afraid of my limited skills, honey. They're all I have to use against your magic."

Her senses shivered in warning, but Jamie didn't protest as Cade drew her slowly toward him. This moment had to be faced and conquered, she told herself bravely. She had known that from the instant she had decided to take the chance of contacting Cade. There was no way beyond proving to the man she had loved that he could no longer control her as easily as he had this summer. It wasn't just Cade who needed to realize that, Jamie thought bleakly. She needed to be certain of it, too. She would be living in a state of constant tension until she had faced the sensual questions and dealt with them.

"There's no magic, Cade," she whispered as he slid his hands gently around her throat and tilted her face upward. It was a soft, husky protest, uttered with desperate conviction because she could feel the tendrils of the sorcery she feared.

"There is always going to be magic between us." He brought his mouth down on hers, brushing her lips lightly, persuasively.

Jamie could feel the leashed control he was exerting and momentarily wondered at it. It seemed to her that he was having to use a great deal of strength to keep from overwhelming her defenses with sheer masculine aggression. The very fact that he was making the effort intrigued her. Did he want her so very much?

"Jamie, Jamie, I've missed you so. It's been hell waiting for you." Cade's thumbs moved in slow, luxurious circles just below her ears. The small caress was infinitely erotic. "Did you know what you were doing to me by making me wait so long?" He spoke the words against her mouth. "Do you know how many times I've lain awake remembering that last night we had together?"

"No, Cade," Jamie managed, as despairingly she recognized that on one level, at least, he was right. The physical magic they generated between them was still strong. "I don't know the answer to any of your questions." *That's why I'm here,* she added silently; *to discover the truth about you and me.*

"The answers don't matter now that you're here. I've wanted you so badly, sweetheart," he groaned, leaning backward and drawing her down on top of his chest.

Just for a moment, Jamie promised herself. She would allow her senses to be engulfed once more for only a moment. She barely felt it when he slipped the glasses off her nose. The strong hands, so excitingly familiar to her from six long weeks of unwelcome dreams, began to move on her body. Jamie knew she shuddered beneath the touch and was aware that Cade knew it also. A distant voice of warning reminded her that he was a man who would use such information. He had a talent for manipulation.

"Don't be afraid of me, Jamie. I only want to make love to you once again. I need you, honey. God, how I need you. Don't you remember how good it was that night?"

The passionate seductive words flowed over her, dark and coaxing. Jamie closed her eyes, knowing she had to put a stop to this soon or she was lost. She needed time, carefully structured and controlled time before she took this chance again.

Cade's blunt fingers traced the line of her throat to her shoulder and then followed the V-shaped collar of the red wrap dress down to the lowest point. The dress had seemed demure enough when Jamie had put it on this evening, but the feel of Cade's touch as he explored just under the edge of the fabric was electric. It was as if she were wearing only a nightgown meant to be discarded.

No man had ever had the effect on her that Cade did, and she knew that he probably realized it. The longing to touch him more intimately took control for a moment and Jamie's trembling fingers toyed with the buttons of his white shirt.

"Go ahead, sweetheart," he urged thickly.

She found herself obeying. A little awkwardly she undid the buttons, telling herself at each step along the way that she had to stop soon.

"Cade," she whispered achingly as her copper-colored nails laced through the curling hair on his chest. "Oh, Cade..."

"I think you've missed me a little, too," he murmured in satisfaction. Deliberately he let his palm slide across the fullness of her breast. Beneath the fabric of the dress he felt the added protection of the bra she had worn. It was a very well designed, very prim little bra made of rather sturdy, plain material. It was not a romantic scrap of lace and satin of the sort she had worn during the two months in Santa Barbara. "You didn't need all this armor just to go out to dinner with me, honey." He chuckled affectionately. "Did you think I was going to assault you?"

Something clicked in Jamie's head. "No, Cade. That's not your way, is it? You don't assault. You infiltrate and manipulate. You're a very devious man. I must be sure to remember that." She lifted her head to look down at him. Without the aid of her glasses his features weren't as clear as they might have been, but she had no trouble distinguishing the flare of displeasure that appeared in the tawny eyes.

"Jamie, hush. You don't know what you're saying."

"Oh, yes, I do, Cade. I know exactly what I'm saying. And I know what I'm doing." Taking a deep breath and a firm grip on her wayward emotions, Jamie pushed herself free of the treacherous embrace. She didn't know where she got the strength to summon up the cool little smile, but it came from somewhere. She reached casually across Cade to pluck her glasses off the shelf where he had put them. Then she glanced meaningfully at her watch. "My goodness, how did it get so late? Time I was going. Thanks for dinner and the brandy, Cade. Miss Isabel will be pleased to know you're going to accept her job offer. I'll send her a message when I get back to Big Sur."

"Now wait just a minute, Jamie. Where the hell do you think you're going?" He sat up quickly as she slipped off the bunk.

"Back to the motel, of course. Where else?" She glanced at him over her shoulder, gray-green eyes reflecting only mild surprise that he should have to ask the question. "Don't worry about driving me. I can walk from here. It's only a few blocks."

"You'll walk back to that motel over my dead body."

"Don't tempt me."

"Jamie, come back here. You don't want to spend the night alone in that motel and you know it. Why the devil are you being so obstinate? You're the one who came looking for me!" Shirt still unbuttoned and hanging loose, Cade got to his feet, confronting her in the narrow confines of the cabin.

Well aware of the domineering, intimidating threat of him, Jamie called on her inner nerve and stood her ground. His cool, questioning smile never wavered. "You seem to be under some trite romantic misconception about why I came looking for you. Amusing, isn't it? This past summer, I was the one who tended to romanticize events. Now the shoe appears to be on the other foot. Be careful, Cade. It gets tricky trying to view the world through a pink haze. Everything gets distorted. A word to the wise."

Cade glowered at her, clearly torn between anger and uncertainty. The conflict mirrored in his eyes only lasted for a few seconds, but that it should have been evident for even that length of time startled Jamie. Perhaps he wasn't as sure of her as he'd like her to believe.

"All right, lady. You want your revenge. I guess I can't deny you that much. Just don't push it too far, okay?" He took her arm and propelled her forcefully out on deck. "It's been a long six weeks, honey."

"Cade, I think you're leaving imprints in my arm," she pointed out tartly as he hustled her along the walk between the tethered boats. She didn't know whether to be relieved or alarmed at his change of mood.

"I'd like to be leaving a few imprints elsewhere on your anatomy. I would never have guessed this summer that you could be such a stubborn little creature."

"Maybe you didn't get to know me quite as well as you thought you did," she risked boldly as he stuffed her unceremoniously but not ungently into the passenger seat of the Mazda.

For a split second the tawny gold eyes gleamed in the glow of the parking-lot lights. During that brief moment of fierce tension Jamie forced herself to remember that Cade Santerre was a dangerous man.

"I know you very well, Jamie Garland. Don't you ever forget it."

Several pithy responses to that statement went through Jamie's head as they sped back toward the motel, but none of them seemed likely to give her the last word so she kept her mouth shut. A flash of common sense warned her that she was lucky to be ending the evening this coolly and decisively as it was. There was no point in tempting fate.

In the motel parking lot Jamie jumped out of the Mazda before Cade had even switched off the ignition.

"An evening with you is always interesting, Cade. Thanks for dinner. If you decide to go ahead with Miss Isabel's little project, even though I'm not part of the fee, you can reach me at this number." She delved into her huge bag and handed him one of Miss Isabel's cards with the address and phone number of the house in Big Sur on it.

Cade was out of the car, reaching to take her arm before she could escape into the motel lobby. He took the card and shoved it into his pocket without looking at it. "We'll talk about the details of this in the morning. I'll pick you up for breakfast."

Wisely Jamie didn't argue. "What time?" she asked demurely.

"Is seven too early?" He was making an obvious attempt at recovering some semblance of politeness.

"No. Seven will be fine."

"Jamie, there's no need to run from me tonight," he said quietly as they came to the lobby door.

"I would prefer to keep our relationship on a businesslike footing, Cade. You shouldn't have any trouble with that. After all, you managed to court me for two months this past summer without once forgetting your real business in Santa Barbara. I have every confidence that you can keep your mind on your work."

He shook his head in wry disbelief. "You're determined to make both of us suffer before you admit the truth, aren't you?"

"What truth?"

His powerful hands moved soothingly on her upper arms as he faced her in the shadowy light. "That you're here because you need me."

"I've admitted Miss Isabel needs you, or thinks she does."

"*You* need me, Jamie. I know it must have been difficult for you to come back to me, honey. But it was inevitable. One way or another we were bound to be together again. I knew if I just gave you some time you would realize that what we shared this summer wasn't a casual affair."

"It seemed quite casual to me," she remarked with forced brightness. It was infuriating to know that he'd been right in many ways. When he'd made no effort to contact her during the past six weeks, Jamie had known she couldn't stay away from him.

His temper flared briefly. "If it had been really casual, I would have taken you to bed the first night I took you out to dinner! It would have been easy enough to do. You were ready to fall into my hands from the moment we met. Maybe that was where I made my mistake. If I hadn't been so concerned with doing things properly, I wouldn't be standing here tonight having this ridiculous argument in front of a motel."

"Sleeping with me for two solid months and then letting me find out you'd been using me to trap Hadley wouldn't have endeared you to me any more than did sleeping with me for one night and letting me find out the truth. What I can't figure out is why you still think you can have your cake and eat it, too. If you need Miss Isabel's job, then do the work. You'll be paid. But don't think you can pull the same stunt you did this summer. A check for services rendered is all you'll be receiving. For the last time, Cade, I am not part of the deal."

Whirling, Jamie slipped through the sliding glass doors and into the motel lobby. She was gone in an instant, disappearing up the staircase to her room on the second floor.

The night clerk watched her go and then glanced curiously at Cade standing outside in the darkness. For an instant the clerk's eyes met Cade's in an ancient male expression of commiseration and then he shrugged and went back to the magazine he'd been reading. Cade could almost read the other man's mind. *Win a few, lose a few.*

Except that he hadn't lost yet, Cade told himself forcefully as he stalked back to the Mazda. And after waiting this long, he sure as hell didn't intend to lose at all. Things had gotten a little rocky at times this evening, and the night hadn't concluded quite the way he'd planned, but progress had been made. She was here and she had accepted a dinner invitation. Afterward she had almost let herself be persuaded back into his bed. He'd come so close to having it all again. It had been a near thing. If he'd just kept his mouth shut at the appropriate moment, she wouldn't have taken fright. Next time he would be more cautious. He'd botched things this evening somehow and the knowledge annoyed him. What was the matter with him, anyway, he demanded in silent self-chastisement. Where was his normal finesse?

Cade slammed the key into the Mazda and yanked the car into gear. Next time matters would end properly. And after that it would be clear sailing. Because once Jamie had surrendered again, there would be no going back. He was done with waiting.

"Dance while you can, lady," he muttered as he sent the Mazda hurtling forward into the darkness. "Time is running out for you. The ball ends at midnight, in case you've forgotten." He might not be Prince Charming, Cade acknowledged grimly, but he was the one the lady would find waiting when she finally accepted her fate.

IT WAS LATE in the afternoon the following day when Jamie decided she'd better stop for groceries before driving the last fifty miles into the dramatic Big Sur country of northern California. The lonely highway ahead hugged the side of the mountains as the Santa Lucia Range swept down to meet the surging Pacific Ocean. It was a spectacularly scenic trip, but the region was very unpopulated. The few stores she would encounter during the last portion of her drive existed primarily to serve campers, and most would be closed by the time she reached them.

The fog was already gathering out at sea, Jamie noticed as she pulled into the parking lot of a small convenience store. She wanted to be home before it cloaked the land. The narrow highway that she would be following for the next several miles was precarious in places. Not a road to be driven in fog.

It had been a long, tiring trip. Jamie stifled a small groan as she climbed a little stiffly out of Miss Isabel's tomato-red Audi. She had left the motel at six-thirty that morning, praying earnestly that Cade would not decide to pick her up early for breakfast. But there had been no sign of him as she'd checked out and tossed her suitcase into the car. She turned left as she'd pulled out of the motel parking lot, deliberately avoiding the route out of town that would have taken her past the marina. The last thing she had wanted was to meet Cade coming the other way.

It had been quite easy to get up early, pack and leave well ahead of the seven o'clock deadline. After all, she hadn't been able to sleep well, anyway. She was half annoyed and half proud of the way she had handled the situation into which she'd so unwisely catapulted herself. Jamie winced as images of moths and flames came to mind.

The decision to tentatively, *cautiously* confront Cade again had been a reckless one, and Jamie knew it, but she had been unable to keep herself from doing it. Talking Miss Isabel into hiring him to search for her brother had been a way of providing protective cover for herself, but she wasn't sure it would work. The man she loved was shrewd and dangerous, and she hadn't been completely certain of her camouflage. But this time around, she'd vowed, she would be the one in control. She would not play the role of ripe peach again.

His utter confidence in his ability to rekindle the fires of their relationship was probably the only factor that had saved her from making a complete fool of herself last night, Jamie decided as she walked into the little store that adjoined a gas station. Never let it be said that pride couldn't give a woman fortitude. Who did he think he was to take the attitude that all he'd had to do was wait for her to come to him? The fact that he had been partially right was galling. She pushed the knowledge aside.

Brows drawn together in a severe little frown, Jamie selected some low-fat milk, cereal and a few vegetables. The small assortment of items, together with the supply of canned and frozen goods at the house, would tide her over for a few days. She could always drive into Carmel in a day or two if she ran out of anything. It was fun to spend time in the self-consciously quaint little town by the sea.

As she deliberated between whole-wheat bread and rye, she found herself once again asking the question that had been plaguing her since the previous evening. When all was said and done, why should Cade show such a strong intention to renew the relationship? She had, after all, dismissed him very haughtily from her life.

She understood her own actions. She knew what had driven her to seek him out. She was obviously a woman who loved unwisely but completely. Jamie was not, however, certain about what motivated Cade.

He had only been using her during those two months this past summer. There had been no words of undying love from him that night on *Dreamer II*. Nothing to indicate he had suddenly fallen head over heels in love with her. He hadn't claimed he couldn't live without her. In fact, he hadn't claimed as much last night, she thought ruefully as she decided on the whole-wheat bread. Cade had misled her, even used her in some ways, but to give the devil his due, he hadn't lied to her about something as important as his own feelings for her. He had wanted her this past summer and apparently he still wanted her, but he hadn't claimed to love her.

She ought to be grateful for finding some element of honesty in him, Jamie decided wrathfully as she carried the small basket over to the checkout counter. After all, a woman liked to know that the man to whom she had given her heart had a couple of good points in his character!

At least she had made a strong start at reclaiming her pride, if not her heart, last night.

"Will that be all?" the high-school boy behind the counter asked disinterestedly as he began totaling up the contents of Jamie's basket. It was obvious the youth was not viewing his after-school job as a stepping stone toward a career in the retail business. He appeared quite bored.

"That's it for the groceries. I'll need some gas, though."

"It's self-service. Help yourself. You pay my dad next door."

Automatically Jamie glanced out the window at the stand of gas pumps that adjoined the convenience store. A nondescript dark Buick stood waiting for its owner to finish paying for fuel. As soon as the Buick was driven off, she could pull the Audi into position. Jamie hated pumping her own gas. On the other hand, she hated paying the extra few cents per gallon that it cost to refuel at a full service station. Ah, well, she'd be home soon, and she could tolerate the smell of gasoline on her hands until then, she supposed.

She was about to refocus her attention on her groceries, when something about the silver head of the man who had just finished paying for his gas caught her attention. His back was toward her as he climbed into the Buick, but there was a familiarity about him that caused her to try to get a good look at his face. There was no chance. The man slammed the door of the Buick and set the car in motion, without once glancing sideways or back over his shoulder.

Jamie stood staring out at the car as it pulled onto Highway 1 and headed north. The man had been in his late fifties, she estimated, with a well-styled wealth of aristocratically gray hair.

"Eight ninety-five, ma'am," the clerk said in a prompting tone.

"What?" Confused by the incredible thought that had struck her as she watched the man in the Buick, Jamie belatedly pulled her attention back to the business of paying for her groceries. "Sorry, I was thinking about something else." Quickly she dug out a ten and waited for change.

Silver hair. Somewhere in his fifties. A certain, familiar dignity in his bearing. If only she'd gotten a better look.

Jamie shook her head impatiently as she hurried out to the waiting Audi. She was letting her imagination, or perhaps Miss Isabel's imagination, run away with her. It wasn't possible that she'd really seen Hadley Fitzgerald. She had simply seen someone who reminded her of him.

As much as she hated to give Cade Santerre credit, she had to admit that he was undoubtedly right in arguing that Fitzgerald had died at sea. The authorities who had investigated the incident had agreed. Jamie decided that she had spent too much time listening to Miss Isabel trying to pretend her brother was still alive. The poor woman had simply not wanted to accept the truth. And because she was so fond of her employer, Jamie had found herself occasionally beginning to doubt the facts. Well, it was only fair enough, she supposed. After all, it was Miss Isabel's belief that her brother was still alive that had given Jamie the excuse she needed to seek out Cade.

"WHAT THE HELL do you mean, she checked out half an hour ago?" Cade roared at the startled desk clerk. "She was supposed to be ready for breakfast at seven o'clock!"

"I'm sorry, Mr. Santerre," the middle-aged woman said for the tenth time. She was clearly affronted. "She said nothing about having an appointment with you. She simply paid her bill and left. Said she had a long drive ahead of her."

Cade leaned forward, both large hands spread flat on the desk. "That means she's headed for Big Sur."

The woman backed up a step, uncertain of the temperament of this man who was practically accusing her of aiding and abetting Jamie Garland's escape. "Possibly, Mr. Santerre. Yes, quite possibly she's headed home. A, uh, logical destination, I imagine."

"That house in Big Sur isn't her *home*," Cade growled dangerously. "It's her office. Her place of employment. She doesn't have a real home of her own."

"Oh."

"She thinks it's charming and adventurous and rather romantic to work for an eccentric artist and live in a picturesque place like Big Sur."

"Well, it does sound kind of interesting," the woman said placatingly, clearly having no idea at all about the subject at hand. "I mean, isn't it close to Carmel? Such a lovely little town, Carmel."

Cade showed his teeth in a smile that would have done justice to a wolf. "It is not charming or adventurous or romantic to me. As far as I am concerned, it is not even interesting. Her job has become a damned nuisance, in fact! It would have made things a lot simpler if Miss Isabel had fired her six weeks ago."

"Miss Isabel?" the clerk inquired warily.

"If Miss Isabel had fired her, Jamie wouldn't be suffering from a case of excessive, misplaced loyalty. Nor would Jamie have had someone to shelter her for the past six weeks. She wouldn't have had any place to run this morning. She would have been forced to accept the fact that she needs me and that deep down she wants me."

"I see." The clerk nodded very cautiously.

With an abrupt restless movement Cade straightened and turned toward the door. "Why am I standing here yelling at you?"

"I was wondering the same thing myself."

Cade didn't hear the muttered answer to his rhetorical question. He was already halfway out to the parking lot. The little idiot had flown the coop. More evidence than ever that she must be pregnant. He'd always heard pregnant women tended to be high-strung and occasionally irrational. It seemed to him that he remembered his brother-in-law complaining, albeit good-naturedly, about Meg's moods when their first child was due last year.

Then again, it wasn't strictly accurate to call Jamie the idiot. He was the fool for letting her get away last night. He should have taken a firmer stand with her, overwhelmed her sensually, shown her that he could crush any defense she had raised against him.

But he hadn't thought it necessary to push her that hard. He'd been under the impression that the battle had been won already. After all, she'd come looking for him, hadn't she? That trumped-up excuse about checking into Fitzgerald's death was clearly just that: an excuse.

Cade wrenched open the Mazda door and slid inside. It was perfectly possible that Miss Isabel did, indeed, want some confirmation of her brother's death, but she was an intelligent woman. She had been aware of the rapidly intensifying relationship growing between her personal assistant and Cade Santerre during the summer. She was not above playing matchmaker.

It was obvious now to Cade why Miss Isabel had resorted to creating this "job." The woman had probably been as startled as Cade had been by Jamie's streak of feminine pride. Jamie had always seemed so sweet-tempered, so gentle and understanding. Spirited but amenable. Good-natured. Cade had been certain that after the shock of discovering his true business in Santa Barbara, she would forgive and understand.

Apparently, finding out that she was pregnant had stirred up a surprisingly primitive streak of vengefulness. She seemed very much inclined to make him run in circles for a while before she surrendered again, Cade decided in gathering irritation. She wanted revenge.

But she couldn't play games for long. Being pregnant put her on a strict timetable.

Even so, Cade knew, he was no longer willing to wait out her moods. He'd already cooled his heels for six weeks and that was long enough. She'd taken the first step, and he had no intention of letting her retreat.

Cade drove back to the marina to pack his bag and make a few phone calls. It was a long drive up to Big Sur.

4

JAMIE TURNED THE KEY in the door of Miss Isabel's home with a vast sense of relief. The fog had been thickening rapidly along the coastal highway, and she was lucky to have finished the trip without having to deal with the worst of it. It was creeping inland swiftly and would soon blanket the cheerfully bizarre structure Jamie and Miss Isabel termed "home."

Jamie remembered liking the house on sight when she had arrived for her interview two years ago. It seemed exactly the sort of place in which a brilliant, eccentric artist ought to live. Clinging precariously to the edge of the heavily wooded mountain, it had a distant view of the crashing Pacific, seen through a primeval forest. Miss Isabel had proudly explained that the house had been designed and constructed by members of a local commune that had flourished briefly during the late sixties and early seventies. The earnest young men and women who had been experimenting with an alternative lifestyle on the edge of the Pacific had long since left the mountains to become stockbrokers and lawyers. But while they had lived their dream in Big Sur, they had applied their creativity to house design. The results were original, to say the least.

Fashioned of timber and glass, the structure consisted of a variety of oddly shaped rooms, none of them conventionally square or rectangular. Some were domed, some faceted, some pie-shaped and some simply strange. All of them had fantastic views and all of them were filled with the overflow of Miss Isabel's labor. When working, the older woman was driven by a tremendous energy that resulted in an incredible quantity of art.

"Why don't you sell some of these, Miss Isabel?" Jamie had asked after she had been working for her new employer for a month. "You've got a fortune in your own work hanging on the walls."

Miss Isabel had grimaced and then proceeded to explain the facts of an artist's life. "If I put too much out on the market, it would bring the prices down on all my work. Simple economics, my dear. The law of supply and demand. Too much product and the demand goes down. When the demand goes down, the prices drop. Keep the supply limited and people fight to get an Isabel Fitzgerald work. And the prices stay high."

"But in the meantime you're stuck with lots of extra paintings and ceramics because you can't stop working, can you?" Jamie had nodded perceptively. She was quickly coming to realize that her employer was not quite as scatterbrained and eccentric as she appeared on the surface. Isabel Fitzgerald was a very smart woman. Smart enough to maintain a healthy balance between business and art.

"Unfortunately, when the mood is on me, all I can do is go into the studio and work," Isabel had said with a sigh. "So the stuff piles up. That's one of the reasons I bought this place. It's big enough to hold it all."

Jamie's own room was filled with a selection that Miss Isabel had allowed her to choose from the vast array of art hanging on walls or sitting on tables throughout the house. As she walked into the unabashedly exotic art deco bedroom, Jamie felt her customary sense of pleasure. The room was octagonally shaped, with every other facet of the eight-sided wall sheathed in painted mirrors. The designs on the glass were flowing ornamental trees that had come straight from the depths of Miss Isabel's imagination during a period when she had become fascinated with glass painting. A flamboyantly graceful and rather erotic ceramic figure of a nude female stood on the round black lacquer table beside the bed. A huge beautiful cloisonné jar stood on an end table near the pillowed window seat. The carpet was a thick plush patterned in swirls of ivory, and the bed was covered in burgundy.

It had been home to Jamie for two years, and as she unpacked she told herself she was infinitely grateful to be back. The thought of risking another evening in Cade Santerre's vicinity was enough to send a nervous chill down her spine. She had gotten lucky last night, but that kind of luck didn't last. From the first time she had met him Jamie had been aware of a sense of inevitability about her relationship with Cade. A part of her had known from the start that sooner or later she was fated to wind up in his arms. Fate had accomplished its goal this past summer. She would be a fool to give it another opportunity without first asserting herself as his equal, not some easily manipulated little fluff-headed female.

She needed to let Cade know she was not the brainless creature who had dropped into his palm like a ripe peach. This time around she would set the terms of the relationship, or there would be no relationship.

But the sense of relief at temporarily having escaped was tempered with a strange, wistful sadness that hovered at the edges of her awareness as she finished unpacking and went into the kitchen to find something to eat. In spite of the end result, Cade had brought something unique into her life. She had undoubtedly fallen heedlessly in love with the wrong man, and there was no doubt at all that she had taken a great risk by contacting him again. The idea had seemed much more workable when she'd been occupied with Miss Isabel's problems, but now Miss Isabel was several thousand miles away. The house seemed empty and the idea no longer seemed so workable.

Puttering around the sleek black-and-white tiled kitchen, Jamie fixed herself a salad and opened a bottle of an interesting Sauvignon Blanc. She deserved the glass of wine, she decided as she dug out a corkscrew. She wondered how Cade had reacted this morning when he'd learned she had left town. She hoped the kindly-looking desk clerk hadn't had to bear the brunt of Santerre's displeasure.

The cork was half out of the bottle when she heard the car in the driveway. Jamie hesitated for a moment in surprise. Unbidden, a faint trickle of uneasiness pervaded her bloodstream. This was ridiculous, she thought. Probably a result of that fleeting glimpse of a man who had vaguely reminded her of Hadley Fitzgerald. Determinedly she finished removing the cork, set it down on the counter and went toward the front door. If there was a nondescript Buick parked in the drive, she was going to be very nervous indeed, she decided ruefully.

It was a black Mazda that was occupying the space beside the Audi. Tendrils of fog ebbed and swirled around it as the driver cut the lights and opened the door. It was no nondescript Buick, but there was no doubt about whose car it was.

"This," Jamie gritted through her teeth, "is what comes of getting involved with a thorough, tenacious sort of male." She flung open the door and stood on the threshold, jeaned legs spread apart, her hands on her hips. Seething, she glowered at the solid, lean figure coming toward her through the damp fog and shadows. "What the devil do you think you're doing following me like this, Cade?"

"There's nothing like a sweet-tongued, loving woman waiting at the end of a long trip," he observed laconically as he strode forward with a leather flight bag slung over his shoulder. "Good evening, Jamie. Have a nice drive? You forgot something this morning."

"Like what?" she challenged.

"Like breakfast. We were supposed to have it together, remember?"

"It must have slipped my mind."

"So I'll take dinner instead." He came to a halt directly in front of her and bent his head to drop a short, hard kiss on her startled mouth. Then, without waiting for a response, he pushed past her into the curving living room. "What a crazy place. Looks just like something you'd choose in which to live. I'll bet you think it's delightfully artsy and wonderfully eccentric."

"It is."

"The hell it is. Looks like a bunch of hippies designed it back in the sixties."

"Nobody asked your opinion!"

He stood for a moment examining the room, which was designed in a half circle. The curving portion was comprised of floor-to-ceiling windows and during the daytime provided a dramatic view of mountain and sea. It had been furnished in wicker and bamboo to create a romantically tropical look. Several of Miss Isabel's collages provided eye-stopping counterpoints to the charming serenity of the room.

Cade shook his head in mild disgust and dropped the leather flight bag on the sisal matting that covered the floor. He swung around to face his unwilling hostess. "I suppose you have a good explanation for sneaking off this morning?"

Jamie used the excuse of shutting the door to avoid the brooding examination of those tawny eyes. He wasn't supposed to be here, she thought on a note of hysteria. He was supposed to stay down south while she manipulated the contact between them. Everything was going wrong. "A perfectly good explanation. I felt like leaving, so I did."

"Nervous after last night?"

"You can stop looking so damn smug. No, I was not nervous after last night. I simply decided we had nothing more to say to each other until you have a progress report for Miss Isabel." Jamie stalked past him into the kitchen and headed for the counter where she had left the wine. "Don't tell me you've got news already!" Yanking a glass from the cupboard, she splashed wine into it and turned to face him. She peered wrathfully at him through the lenses of her glasses. "But, then, you always were a fast worker."

"Not fast enough, apparently. Give me a glass of that stuff. I need it. That's a hell of a drive on a night like this."

"Good thing you've had some recent practice," she shot back. "It will help you when you get back in the car in a few minutes and start toward Carmel. I do think Carmel is your best bet. You'll stand a much better chance of finding a motel there than you will if you go back toward San Simeon."

He came forward and poured his own glass of wine when Jamie made no effort to oblige. "Nice try, honey, but you know it's not going to work. I'm staying here tonight. Nobody but a complete idiot would attempt to drive that road in this fog."

"Since you just drove it, what does that make you?"

His mouth twisted in self-mockery as he raised his glass. "A very annoyed, very irritated idiot. Wise young women do not try to provoke such creatures. What's for dinner? I'm starving."

"Do you really think you can just land on my door-step and announce you're staying the night?" Jamie demanded, outraged.

"It's not your doorstep," he pointed out far too politely. "It's Miss Isabel's. And I am currently working for Miss Isabel. That gives me a few privileges."

"According to whom?"

"Me. Jamie, for your own sake, I'm warning you not to give me any more trouble today. I've about had it. I was not in a good mood this morning when I discovered you'd taken to your heels. That state of mind has not improved in the past several hundred miles of driving. I'm tired and I'm hungry and I badly need this drink. If you display half the intelligence I credited you with this summer, you will close your mouth and fix me some dinner. What's that you're eating?"

"Salad," she grumbled, aware that the advice she was receiving was probably sound. Cade was definitely in a temperamental mood at the moment, and instinct warned her to tread warily. Damn it, she wanted him to be the one who had to tread carefully. She wanted to be the one to stipulate the terms of this arrangement.

"Is that all you've got?"

"There's some canned soup and the makings for some sandwiches," she grudgingly acknowledged.

"Fix us both some. You should be eating more than a salad."

Blankly, Jamie looked at him. "Why?"

He frowned. "Because you need to eat properly at a time like this."

"What are you? A nutritionist? I'll admit I'm under some stress at the moment, but I don't think a salad will hurt me."

"We can discuss proper diet over a proper meal. Which room is mine? I'll put my bag in it."

"Now wait a minute, Cade."

"Shall I find one for myself?"

Knowing she was fighting a losing battle, Jamie surrendered with bad grace. "There are only two bedrooms made up, mine and Miss Isabel's. I suppose you'd better take mine. I'll move into Miss Isabel's room." Setting the wineglass down on the tile counter with an angry snap, Jamie whirled to lead the way.

Behind her Cade paced along the curving hallways, staring at the wealth of artwork.

"Good Lord, I had no idea Miss Isabel was so prolific."

"She holds a lot of her work off the market," Jamie muttered.

"Of course. The last thing she'd want to do is flood the galleries. It would ruin her image, not to mention her income."

At the door of her bedroom Jamie turned her head to glance at him in mild astonishment. "That's exactly what she told me. Law of supply and demand. How did you know?"

"I used to be an accountant, remember?"

"Oh, yes, I remember. An *investigative* accountant." She nodded derisively as she walked into the bedroom. "I'll collect a few of my things and take them into Miss Isabel's room. Honestly, Cade, I don't know why you had to show up like this. There was absolutely no point in trailing after me."

"No?" He examined his surroundings. "Are you sure you weren't expecting me, Jamie? I have a hunch I'm playing right into your hands." He tossed the bag down onto the bed before meeting Jamie's shocked eyes. His own gaze mocked her with both indulgence and irritation. "Come on, honey. We both know you're trying to salvage a little of your pride. After all, you had to swallow a big chunk of it to come looking for me in the first place. I'm trying to be generous, but it's beginning to wear on my temper. Does it give you a certain amount of satisfaction to know I came chasing after you on such short notice?"

"Not particularly!" Jamie exploded.

"That's too bad, because you're probably not going to get a whole lot more in the way of revenge. I don't like games. Time is running out for you, honey."

"Believe me, I have no intention of playing games with you!" Infuriated, Jamie wrenched open a few drawers and removed a supply of underwear, and a nightgown as well. Without another word she stomped out of the room and went across the hall into Miss Isabel's oddly angled bedroom.

The first thing that greeted her as she flipped on the light was the portrait of Hadley that Miss Isabel had finished shortly before she had consented to leave on the cruise.

"Oh, Hadley," Jamie muttered to herself, "a great deal of this is your fault. If it hadn't been for you, I wouldn't be in this mess."

Miss Isabel had worked in her usual frenzy to finish the picture of her brother. The painting was a modernistic combination of collage and heavily daubed acrylics that resulted in a full-length, haunting portrait of Hadley Fitzgerald. The work of art had gone directly into Miss Isabel's bedroom the moment it had been completed, and Jamie had privately decided that it had been her employer's way of coming to terms with her brother's fate. Jamie hadn't had a good look at it at the time it was finished and hadn't wanted to press Miss Isabel on the subject.

Now she saw that while Hadley's features were quite clear and finely drawn, the rest of the canvas contained some bizarre elements. A dollar bill had been lacquered in among the brilliant daubs of acrylic paint, along with a portion of a letter to one of Hadley's clients. All over the canvas there were bits and pieces of objects that Jamie guessed represented Hadley's life and business. Even a broken pencil had been attached in one corner, together with a sheet from an account book. Jamie studied the portrait for a moment and then turned away. She had more important matters to handle. There would be time enough later to scrutinize Miss Isabel's most recent creation.

"Miss Isabel is a fan of minimalism?"

Jamie glared at Cade, who had walked across the hall to stand in the doorway. He ran a quick eye over the spare, clean lines of the white-on-white room.

"I guess you could say that." She threw her underwear into an empty drawer in the white lacquer and stainless steel dresser.

"Your room, on the other hand, is a romantic, exotic hideaway, for you, isn't it?" Cade smiled for the first time since he had arrived. "But you can't hide in it any longer, sweetheart."

"Cade . . ." she began with a sudden ache in her voice. "What did you think you could accomplish by following me like this?"

"Let's go eat," he said easily. "I really am starving."

THREE HOURS LATER Jamie climbed into the white-covered bed, which had been placed right in the middle of the strangely angled room. She lay staring at the ceiling and wondered whether she was seriously misleading herself by thinking that she had maintained control of the potentially volcanic situation this evening.

She had not been in control of anything this past summer, and it was probably folly to tell herself that things were different this time around. Yet it seemed to her that although he was being unbelievably persistent all of a sudden, Cade was also exhibiting a streak of caution. He had chewed her out for leaving without notice this morning, but he implied he understood her actions. He had settled down on a sofa with his feet propped up on an old sea chest and eaten his meal beside her in relative good humor. Jamie had been suspicious.

"There really is no way you can stay, Cade. You'll have to leave in the morning," she had said quite firmly at several points during the evening.

"Miss Isabel is my employer, not you. And she's not around to evict me, is she?" Cade had answered with a smile.

"What is it you want from me?" Jamie had demanded, beginning to feel desperate.

"You know the answer to that." His smile deepened with alarming persuasion. "I've missed you during the past six weeks, honey."

"If you had really wanted me in the first place, you wouldn't have used me to get Hadley this summer. And if you had really missed me, you wouldn't have spent the past six weeks lounging around on that boat of yours," she'd eventually shot back rashly. "You would have spent the time trying to apologize and explain your actions!"

He'd appeared momentarily taken aback. Then he'd given her a long, considering look. "I thought it would be better if you took the first step."

"Another of your theories on how to manipulate and control people? Cade, I didn't come crawling back to you. In case you haven't noticed, I contacted you for strictly business reasons."

"Honey, I never wanted you to come crawling back. I just wanted you to realize that what we had together was good. Too good to throw away because of anger and pride."

"Well, I sought you out on business. Nothing else is involved. I want that to be quite clear, Cade."

He'd only smiled again with that oddly indulgent curve of his mouth that contained so much quiet sureness and satisfaction. Jamie had finally excused herself and stalked off to bed. There was no dealing with the man that night. He was in the house and she was stuck with him until she could figure out a way to get rid of him.

But if he thought she'd looked him up because she wanted to throw herself back into his arms, he was out of his arrogant male head, she vowed as she lay in the darkness of Miss Isabel's room. Apparently he hadn't paid any attention to the lesson she'd tried to teach him last night when she'd coolly ended the sensual scene on the boat's bunk and gone back to the motel.

Except she hadn't been that cool about it at all, she admitted with a small sigh. A primitive restlessness had kept her awake for a good portion of the night following her dramatic little scene. There was no denying that a strong, deeply feminine part of her would have rejoiced in another act of love. She had never stopped wanting Cade, even though there were times when she thought she hated him. Fortunately, Jamie told herself firmly, she was in control of that portion of her psyche these days. The new relationship with Cade would be governed by her brains, not her emotions. The latter had ruled her long enough this summer. With that assurance, she eventually slipped into sleep.

She didn't know what it was that awakened her a long time later: perhaps the sound of rain on the windows; perhaps just the fact that she was sleeping in someone else's bed instead of her own.

Whatever it was, it brought her to drowsy wakefulness. She stirred and rolled over onto her side. And quite suddenly her heart began to pound.

The portrait of Hadley Fitzgerald had come alive.

Jamie's breath caught in her throat. *I don't have my glasses on,* she thought in panic. *That's all it is. I just can't see properly. It's an optical illusion.*

Hadley's silvered head moved slightly. The whole portrait seemed to shift, and for an instant Jamie could have sworn there were two images of Hadley Fitzgerald.

More frightened than she could ever remember being in her life, Jamie nevertheless fought for self-control. It must be her eyes. She needed her glasses. Squeezing her lashes shut for several seconds, Jamie frantically willed the effects of the double vision to disappear. Then, still keeping her eyes closed, she reached out to grope for the glasses she had left on the cylindrical night table.

A new wave of heart-stopping panic washed over her as her fingers brushed across the surface of the table and failed to make contact with the chic designer frames. Her lashes flew open as her pulse raced into high gear. *Where are my glasses?*

Dreading what her improperly focused eyes would see, Jamie jerked her gaze back to the portrait that stood in the shadows. Only one gray-haired image seemed to be staring at her from the darkness now, thank heaven. But she couldn't be sure. She couldn't be sure of anything at the moment. The urge to scream was almost overpowering. Jamie wasn't sure how she controlled it.

Getting out of the room seemed of paramount importance suddenly. Glasses or no glasses, she had to get away from the nightmare her sleepy brain had conjured.

Shoving aside the covers with an act of will that seemed tremendous, in fact, almost more than she could manage, Jamie struggled out of bed. Her bare feet found the white carpet and then she was running toward the closed door of the bedroom. Reaching it, she pulled it open and darted out into the hall without glancing back over her shoulder. The door closed rather loudly behind her.

Ridiculous to let the nightmare affect her this way. As soon as she was safe in the hall, Jamie began lecturing herself. Absolutely ridiculous. She stood there in the expensive, unabashedly sexy French nightgown she had bought last summer when she had begun to realize she was in love and told herself she was acting like an idiot.

She was still standing there, willing her pulse to calm down, when the door across the hall opened and Cade materialized. For some reason her uncorrected vision had no trouble with the details of his image.

He stood there wearing only a pair of briefs, his dark hair slightly tousled from the pillow, sleek shoulders looming powerfully in the shadows. He should have looked dangerous, but instead the sight of him offered great comfort.

"At least," she noted quite carefully, "there aren't two of you."

"Just as well. I wouldn't be willing to share you. Come on in, Jamie. I've been waiting for you."

The dark, persuasive words soothed and beckoned, promising warmth and passion in place of irrational fear. As if in a trance, Jamie took a step toward Cade. "I had a bad dream," she whispered.

"Did you? Come here, honey, and I'll help you forget all about it."

Jamie drew a long, steadying breath. She was awake. She knew what she was doing. "Silly of me to overreact. Haven't done that since I was a kid."

Cade's teeth gleamed for a moment in the darkness, and she heard the trace of masculine amusement in his voice. "You don't need any excuses to come to me, sweetheart." He held out his strong square hand. "But if it makes it easier for you, by all means use them."

She trembled, but not with fear. Slowly she put out her own hand and let his fingers swallow hers. Instantly she was caught and held. Cade drew her closer. "It's not an excuse, Cade. I really did have a nightmare." His nearness was extraordinarily comforting, she realized.

"You won't have any nightmares in my bed," he promised huskily as he tugged her gently forward. "I'll make certain all your dreams are very pleasant."

The elegant French nightgown whispered encouragingly around her ankles as Jamie allowed herself to be drawn into the shadows of the bedroom. She felt as though she were drifting, floating, gliding. Like a beautiful sailing yacht upon a warm tropical sea. Her senses were spinning.

"You'll assume too much...." she managed awkwardly, trying to put her uncertainties into words. "You'll think everything is settled; that you have it all back under control."

"Does it matter?" he whispered, closing the bedroom door behind her.

"Probably," she said softly. "It will be harder than ever to convince you that I'm not the same ripe plum I was this past summer."

"When I have you nestled in the palm of my hand again, you could probably convince me of just about anything," he said whimsically.

"You don't understand, Cade," she began earnestly.

He cut off the hint of urgency in her tone by sealing her mouth with his own. With a tremulous sigh, Jamie accepted the inevitable. Just as she had known this summer that the affair with Cade would end in bed, she knew tonight that there was no point trying to resist the pull he had on her senses. Cade was instantly aware of the surrender.

"Jamie, Jamie, you won't regret it. Here in my arms is where you were meant to be. We both know it." The words were murmured achingly against her lips as Cade's blunt fingers found the delicate fastenings of the French nightgown.

"It will be different this time, Cade," she tried to warn. Her senses were already responding to the magic in his touch as he slipped the gown off her shoulders.

"Better. It will be better this time."

"You don't understand . . ."

"Hush, sweetheart. I understand everything. You don't have to explain a thing," he soothed. "And you don't have to worry about a thing, either. I'll take care of you. You can trust me. Just the way you trusted me this summer. I'll make everything all right again. I promise."

The gown slid to her feet, and Cade groaned as he let his palms glide from Jamie's shoulders to the budding peaks of her breasts.

"Oh, Cade," she whispered as desire unfurled within her.

"How could you ever pretend to yourself that there wasn't real magic between us?" he asked thickly.

"I don't know," she admitted simply and lifted her arms to wrap them around his neck.

"Jamie!"

She was locked against him, her breasts crushed tantalizingly against the hardness of his chest. Cade's hand flattened along her back, sliding down to the full curve of her hips. There his fingers sank erotically into the soft resilient flesh. Cade's body reacted fiercely, and Jamie took deep, feminine pleasure in the knowledge. He was right. There was magic between them. Why should she deny it or herself? This time, she vowed, she would stay in control.

"I've been going crazy for the past six weeks!" With an abrupt, decisive movement, Cade lifted her high into his arms and carried her across the room to the bed. "This time you're not going to run out on me. I'd lose my mind if you did."

Jamie felt herself lowered to the sheets, and then she lifted her lashes to watch as Cade stepped impatiently out of his briefs. She didn't need glasses to read the signs of surging male hunger in him, and her own body responded to it. He sat down beside her on the edge of the bed and spread his fingers across her stomach. He seemed both possessive and at the same time entranced. Jamie shivered.

Cade reached out with his other hand, caught hers and brought her fingers to his thigh. Jamie needed no further encouragement. She stroked upward, delighting in the ripple of sensation that coursed through him at her touch. His skin was excitingly textured with dark, crisp hair. She could feel the long, smooth swell of muscle in his upper leg. When she dared to cup him intimately in the palm of her hand, he groaned heavily and stretched out beside her. His mouth found hers while he slowly grazed her nipple with the pad of his thumb. The sensual strength in his body was a driving force in the room.

"I've spent too many nights remembering how you react when I touch you," Cade gritted, and then his probing tongue was invading the territory behind her lips, reestablishing his right to complete intimacy.

Jamie moaned softly and her leg shifted, twining itself around his. Cade's hand slid down her breast, finding the already taut nipples and pausing to hold the fullness of her. Then his hand continued downward, following the path that led toward the dampening heat at the apex of her thighs. When his strong, sensitive fingers suddenly flicked across the exquisitely vulnerable focus of her erotic feelings, Jamie cried out and set her teeth lightly against his shoulder.

"Little vixen. Go ahead and use your teeth on me. You'll only succeed in setting me even more on fire." He nipped passionately at the curve of her throat, returning the sexy caress in full measure.

"Cade, I'm going out of my head. I thought I'd forgotten how it was between us."

"I won't let you forget again," he vowed. His fingers stroked deeply, intimately, until her whole body was lifting and arching in response. "That's it, sweetheart. I want to see you go up in flames. I've missed your heat so much."

Jamie's breath came more quickly, and her aroused body moved with unconscious invitation as she twisted in sensual torment. With growing abandon she pulled Cade's mouth back down to her own, her fingers locking in the thickness of his hair.

"Tell me how much you want me, honey," he ordered softly as his body strained against hers.

"Come to me Cade. I want you. More than I realized. More than I could possibly admit."

A part of her mind knew that if he had asked for words of love she would have been compelled to give them to him along with the words of need. But Cade didn't ask for them and the dangerous words remained unsaid.

"In the future you're going to learn just how easy it is to tell me you want me. By morning you will have had a lot of practice." Cade shifted, covering her body heavily with his own. "Wrap yourself around me, sweetheart. Give yourself to me."

He moved between her legs aggressively, making a place for himself between her soft, warm thighs, and then he paused as if savoring the moment. Jamie looked up at him through her passion-heavy lashes and saw the flaring gold in his eyes. Anticipation, satisfaction and desire were reflected in Cade's tawny gaze.

He was reclaiming what he felt he owned, Jamie realized suddenly. Before she could deny that claim by word or action, he was moving to stake it. She gasped as she felt the hardened power of his manhood thrust heavily into her softness.

"Cade!"

His mouth took hers again, swallowing her small cry. Jamie felt the surging rhythm he imposed on her and gave herself up to it. She loved him, and in this moment of ultimate intimacy she could not pretend otherwise. Jamie was unaware of the tiny marks she made in Cade's bronzed back as her passion took control. She only knew there was nothing else in the world to compare with having Cade Santerre make love to her. She gloried in his desire, his undisguised need of her, and she took infinite pleasure in her own flaring passion.

Heedlessly, recklessly, totally, she surrendered to the demands he was making on her. At the same time she generated her own demands, and he answered them hungrily, making it clear he wanted to please. For a timeless interval they drank thirstily of each other, engaged in a sensual battle that brought the shared excitement to higher and higher levels.

Then the spiraling, tightening sensation deep in Jamie's body spun abruptly out of control, dragging her into the vortex of a throbbing, tumultuous storm. It was the same storm she had encountered that night on the yacht six weeks ago, and it brought the same sob of wonder to her lips. She sensed the man above her lose his fierce control.

With a muffled shout of satisfaction, Cade followed her into the heart of the whirling winds of passion. For an endless time they had the universe to themselves. And afterward Jamie refused to open her eyes. She nestled into the welcoming heat of Cade's arms and went to sleep. When all was said and done, this was the way it was supposed to be.

Awareness returned a long time later, when a shaft of light from the bathroom angled across the bed. Stirring sleepily, Jamie turned over and belatedly realized she was in her own bed. Memories of the night filtered back with disconcerting suddenness.

There had been the strange nightmare and then there had been Cade. Jamie shook her head, trying to clear the remnants of sleep from it. The bed was empty beside her.

"Cade?"

"In here," he called from the bathroom. "Just wanted a glass of water. I'll be right back."

She heard the door of the mirrored cabinet open, and then there was silence from the other room. Jamie blinked in the darkness and snuggled back down into the pillows. But now she was wide awake, her mind alive with the problem she had created for herself tonight.

She had just allowed herself to be drawn back into the arms of a man who had once callously used her; a man whose arrogance knew few bounds; a man she had promised herself she would not allow back into her life unless she was in full control of him. She had meant to keep sex out of the picture until she was convinced she could handle it.

It would be simpler to pretend to be asleep when he emerged from the bathroom. Jamie had a feeling it would be difficult enough to deal with Cade Santerre in the morning, let alone the middle of the night. When you weren't sure how to handle a volatile situation it was best to put it off for a while. Determinedly she kept her eyes closed.

But she wasn't going to have the opportunity of postponing the inevitable confrontation.

"What the hell is this?"

Cade's gritted question was laced with fury. A small object landed on the quilt a few inches from Jamie's wide-open eyes. At the same moment the overhead light blazed as Cade hit the switch.

Startled, Jamie levered herself up on one elbow. Her unfocused eyes went from Cade's thunderous features to the object he had tossed down on the bed. She couldn't see well enough without her glasses to read the printing on the box, but she knew by its general size and shape what it was.

"My birth control pills," she answered with a calm she was far from feeling.

"I can see that. How long have you been taking them?"

"Cade, what's the matter with you? Why are you so enraged?" She stared at him in confusion, trying to understand what was happening. This was the last reaction she had expected. Possessiveness, arrogance, satisfaction—any of a variety of masculine emotions would have seemed within the realm of probability from what she knew of Cade Santerre. But not this fury over a bottle of pills.

"How long have you been taking them?" he repeated savagely.

"I took them this summer," she said simply. No need to mention that she had gone off them last month on the assumption she wouldn't be needing them again for a long while.

"You were taking them this summer? You were on them when I made love to you that last night on the yacht?"

Jamie licked her lips, aware of the shimmering tension in him, but unable to comprehend the reason behind it. "Yes."

"That's impossible!"

"Why?" she asked blankly.

"Because you're supposed to be pregnant!" he roared.

5

"PREGNANT!" Jamie could only stare at him, stunned. "You thought I was pregnant?"

"It was the most logical explanation," Cade bit out roughly. He stalked across the room and flung himself into a chair. Totally unconcerned with his own nakedness he sprawled there, watching Jamie through brooding, narrowed eyes. "The timing was right."

"Timing?" she asked helplessly. Cade's state of undress might not bother him but her own similar condition was beginning to make her feel quite vulnerable. Jamie held the sheet to her breasts while she leaned over the edge of the bed and scrabbled around on the floor for the expensive French nightie.

"Six weeks," he explained impatiently. "It took you six weeks to come looking for me. That's about the length of time it would take you to suspect you might be pregnant."

"You're an authority on that sort of thing?"

"I had high-school biology just like everyone else!"

"I think you went to a more progressive high school than I did," she tried flippantly.

"This is not a joke, damn it!"

Jamie's hand closed around the gossamer material of the gown and she sat up quickly, tugging it over her head. "I don't understand, Cade. I told you I came to find you because Miss Isabel wanted you to verify her brother's suicide. Where did you get the idea I was pregnant?"

"I've just told you where I got the idea! Because of the amount of time that had elapsed," he nearly shouted. "And because I knew I had uncovered a streak of dumb, stubborn female pride in you. I figured that because of it, you would resist coming back to me as long as you could. When you showed up in six weeks, I decided it must be because you'd discovered you were pregnant. Otherwise, I'd decided, you'd probably wait two or three months. Long enough for your pride to have a chance to die down and for you to realize . . . Oh, forget it."

Slowly light began to dawn in Jamie's confused brain. She saw the beginnings of a way to salvage control and pride. She crouched on the bed, staring at him. "I see. You thought you had me all figured out, didn't you? Analyzed, pigeonholed and under control. Cade, the Great Manipulator. I don't know what makes you think you're such a good judge of other people's motives and actions! Whatever gave you the idea you understood me so well you could predict my behavior down to the minute?"

"I spent two months getting to know you, damn it! Two whole months," he repeated bluntly. "At the end of which I had you in the palm of my hand. I know I did. Don't you dare deny it."

A wave of impotent anger washed over Jamie. He spoke the truth and they both knew it. She would have done anything for him at the end of those two months. Desperately she struggled for a loophole. "If you knew me so well, why didn't you guess I was taking birth-control pills?"

"The subject never arose," he muttered.

"So you just assumed I'd plunge into a passionate little interlude with you without bothering to protect myself? Cade, I'm twenty-nine years old and I'm not exactly stupid, despite some recent evidence to the contrary. I knew within a few days of meeting you that the odds were good I'd wind up in bed with you. I went to a doctor and got a prescription."

"Why didn't you say anything about it?" he demanded.

"It's not exactly the sort of thing one casually mentions over the dinner table. Not to a man who hasn't yet asked you to go to bed with him," Jamie said between clenched teeth. She concentrated on the cloissoné jar beside him, unwilling to meet his eyes. "Actually, you never did ask. You just sort of assumed I'd follow where you led." *Right into bed*, she added silently.

"I get it. It didn't strike you as terribly romantic, right?" he mocked, concentrating on her first complaint and ignoring the second. "'I had a wonderful evening, Cade. By the way, I'm taking the pill, just in case you're interested in hopping into bed'"

"You see what I mean?" Jamie responded austerely. "It has a tacky sound to it. Getting accidentally pregnant is even tackier, however. Tacky is not romantic." She'd had two months to anticipate that one night with Cade. Two months of knowing where the relationship with him would lead. Two months of knowing she was falling in love and realizing where that love was bound to lead.

Cade swore softly. "I can't believe I didn't realize you'd been busy behind the scenes making plans and taking precautions."

"That's because you seem to have formed the impression that I'm some kind of naive, romantic, emptyheaded little bit of fluff. I'm a woman, Cade. I can think for myself. And I can take care of myself." Proudly she swung her gaze back to meet his, but without her glasses the effect was somewhat diminished. All she could really detect in his face was the brooding storm that seemed to be simmering there.

"So you're not pregnant?" he pressed once more.

She shook her head, wondering at the strange combination of frustration and dashed hope in his voice. This was not quite what a woman expected when she assured a man she wasn't pregnant. Men were reputed to be exceedingly relieved in such circumstances. "I should think you'd be grateful."

He ignored that. "You really came looking for me just to offer me this crazy job of Miss Isabel's?" He sounded dazed now.

"That's the only reason," Jamie emphasized.

"Then why did you come traipsing across the hall tonight?" he demanded. "Straight into my arms and my bed?"

Feeling braver and more sure of herself by the second as she witnessed the corresponding uncertainty in Cade, Jamie seized the opportunity. "I had a bad dream. I decided to get a glass of milk or something from the kitchen. Almost as soon as I stepped out of my bedroom, you appeared."

"And you figured, what the hell, why not jump into bed with me again since I'm conveniently located, obviously willing and you're on the pill?"

Jamie sucked in her breath and stuck to her newly developing image. There seemed to be a measure of safety in it. "Any objections?" Uneasily her fingers curled around the small box lying beside her. Belatedly she began to wonder how long the effects of the contraceptive lasted after a woman stopped taking pills. Especially when she'd only been on them a short time. Mentally she counted the days since she had gone off the medication. It had definitely been almost a month now.

"I can hardly object, can I? I got what I wanted."

"Did you?" Jamie edged her feet out from under the covers and sat up on the side of the bed. "Will you be leaving in the morning, then?"

His eyes narrowed dangerously. "I'll think about it."

"You do that!" Now she was getting angry.

"Jamie, don't push me."

She flicked him a curious glance. "You're really furious, aren't you?"

"Why should I be furious?"

"Come on, Cade. You look like you'd enjoy chewing on nails." Jamie's sense of insight deepened. "There is no logical reason why you should be angry except for one thing."

"What's that?" he challenged coolly.

"You may have gotten what you wanted but you didn't get it for the reasons you assumed you were getting it."

"You're not making any sense," he told her repressively.

Jamie nodded her head once in growing comprehension. "It's throwing you, isn't it?"

"What's throwing me?"

"The knowledge that I didn't come looking for you because I was pregnant, or because I couldn't bring myself to give up our relationship. I came looking for you for purely business reasons, and you don't like that one little bit. It means you missed something this summer when you were busy analyzing, assessing and seducing me. You failed to properly pigeonhole me and therefore you failed to predict my actions properly. That makes you nervous because you pride yourself on being able to manipulate and control people. You can't manipulate and control someone whose motives you can't fully analyze, can you, Cade? You got me back into bed but you're not quite sure why I'm there, and that makes you fretful, doesn't it? Well, you don't have to worry the problem to death. I'll be glad to explain."

"I can't wait."

"It's simple enough," she declared loftily. "Physical attraction. You don't have to look any further than that for a logical explanation. I'm not pregnant and I didn't find myself unable to live without you. I do, however, find you still physically attractive. As long as you're living in such convenient proximity as you are tonight, I suppose it's not unreasonable to expect me to traipse across the hall now and again." In that moment it seemed a near-brilliant excuse for her actions this evening. Why hadn't she thought of it before? Physical attraction. No need to admit to love.

She didn't need glasses to see the dark red color that stained his face. A little late, Jamie's new perception warned her that she might have gone too far with that last taunting remark. But she had been unable to hold her tongue. She'd found a way to recoup some of her crumbling emotional defenses and she'd grabbed it with both hands, making it sound as though she saw nothing wrong in treating Cade Santerre as a casual and occasional lover.

"You're saying that's all this was tonight? A mildly entertaining one-night stand?" he asked dangerously.

"Why should it mean any more to me than it did to you?" She shrugged. "That's all our affair was for you this summer, wasn't it? A convenient one-night stand?"

Cade came out of the chair and was across the room in three long strides. He reached her before she could get to her feet. Seizing her by the shoulders, he hauled her up to stand in front of him. "I spent two full months working toward that one night. I planned that night right down to the fifty dollar bottle of cognac I had on hand in the galley for an after-dinner drink. I had to slip the maître d' at the restaurant ten bucks just to get the seat you liked by the window. I had to order those yellow roses I gave you before dinner a week ahead of time at the florist's. You were like melted butter in my hands this summer. It was no casual roll in the hay for you and you know it."

Jamie held on to her pride and her temper. A strange, driving force was motivating her now. She had no trouble putting a name to it. Revenge. Jamie was learning that when a woman found herself cornered it was possible to want a little revenge even though she was passionately in love.

"I had no idea you spent so much money in one evening! Trust an accountant to have it all tabulated right down to the penny."

His fingers flexed on her shoulders. "At the time I thought it was worth every penny."

"Summer was a long time ago," she said.

"Six weeks isn't very long."

"Believe it or not, six weeks is quite long enough to get over a man who used me the way you did. Actually six hours took care of most of the problem. By the end of six days I was totally cured. I came looking for you yesterday for one reason and one reason only. Miss Isabel assigned me the job."

"And you always do what Miss Isabel tells you to do?" he growled.

"As long as I work for her, yes." Jamie tried to sound cool about it. "In this case, it wasn't all that traumatic having to carry out her instructions. In spite of what you seemed to have assumed, I suffered no lingering effects from that night on the yacht, either emotional or physical."

"But when you saw me again you did manage to recall that the sex was pretty good, is that it?"

"That's it," she agreed blandly.

"And tonight you just decided to let yourself enjoy it again? No strings attached this time?"

"Why not?"

"I don't believe you." Cade's words were laced with steel and ice.

"You can, of course, believe anything you wish. I know how pleasant self-deception can be. I certainly had enough experience with it this summer. I'll give you some advice, however. It's risky to paint things in a falsely romantic light. Very naive, Cade. Leads to all sorts of rude awakenings. You taught me that. If I were you, I'd pay attention to your own excellent lessons on the subject."

"I'm not the one who's prone to view the world through romantic lenses, damn it!"

"I don't have that problem any longer myself," she assured him easily.

"You expect me to believe that in six weeks you've transformed yourself into a cool, tough little lady who can handle a casual affair on her own terms?"

"Safer than letting you handle that kind of affair on your terms, isn't it? Safer for me, that is. If you decide you don't mind the fact that you're no longer in control of my emotions and able to manipulate me at will, then stick around, Cade. Who knows? This time we might manage a rational, even-handed affair that won't leave either one of us feeling the fool when it's over. If that sort of straightforward, honest arrangement doesn't appeal to you, then you'd better leave."

His mouth hardened. "Because if I stay you'll run the show?"

"I won't play the role of melted butter again," she vowed. "You'll never hold me in the palm of your hand a second time, Cade Santerre. I'm not quite as naive and empty-headed as you seemed to have assumed."

Without waiting for his response, Jamie swung around on one heel and walked out of the bedroom. Her head tilted proudly, her pulse racing with adrenaline, her stomach twisting with tension, she headed straight back across the hall, opened the door to Miss Isabel's room and shut it decisively behind her.

Then she collapsed into a trembling heap on the bed. It had been a grand exit but it had taken nearly everything she'd had to pull it off successfully.

Pride, revenge and the need to assert some control over the man who had once hurt her so badly had kept her going during the confrontation. But alone in the bedroom it was difficult to keep the fires of pride and revenge burning at their hottest. Sitting forlornly on the edge of the bed, Jamie was aware of a chill that seemed to seep all the way into her bones.

Cade had assumed she was pregnant. He thought that, knowing she was going to have his baby, she had lowered her defenses far enough to dream up an excuse to get in touch with him again. And if that hadn't worked, he would just as confidently have expected her to show up in a few more weeks, simply because she couldn't bear to end the affair.

He must think she was truly a mindless little twit at the mercy of her feminine emotions, Jamie told herself violently.

If he could see her now, he'd know he wasn't far off in that assessment. She was shivering with reaction and cold. What would he do now, she wondered unhappily. She'd as good as told him that if he stayed it would be on her terms, and that her terms involved treating their relationship as a very casual sexual affair. Nothing more.

Cade wouldn't like that. It wasn't that he had any qualms about treating her callously or casually, she reminded herself. But he'd savagely resent being treated that way himself. He was far too accustomed to being the one working the strings.

At every point this past summer he had set the pace, manipulating her emotions with consummate ease until she was practically begging for him on every level. Melted butter. Jamie winced, recalling how wrapped up in him she had been. She would have done anything for him. She had fallen in love with the man. Never in her life had she been so much involved with another human being. Never had she wanted to give herself so completely. At the time it had seemed totally rational.

With a sigh Jamie reached out to switch on the bedside light. She'd better find her glasses before she accidentally stepped on them. Frowning, she peered down at the white carpet beside the bed. She must have brushed them off the night table at some point.

Unable to spot the chic frames, she got down on her hands and knees and began to grope around under the bed. Her fingers closed over the glasses just as the bedroom door opened behind her.

"Jamie?" Cade's inquiry was gruff. There was a pause as he looked around the room for her. Then he spotted her. "What are you doing?"

"Looking for my glasses. I couldn't find them earlier this evening when I had that nightmare." She pushed the frames onto her nose and got to her feet, aware of the see-through quality of the nightgown. Trying to appear unselfconscious, she walked quickly across the room to yank a robe out of Miss Isabel's closet. Hastily she donned the garment. Cade, she was relieved to see, had pulled on a pair of jeans.

"I came to talk to you about that nightmare you said you had," Cade began a little too casually.

Jamie's head snapped up as she finished tying the sash of the robe. The bland expression on his face didn't fool her for a moment. "Still looking for angles? I didn't make up that bit about having had a bad dream and I definitely did not use it as an excuse to throw myself into your arms, if that's what you're thinking."

"I just wanted to ask you about it," he said, but she could tell she'd effectively cut off his latest tactic. He'd obviously been about to convince himself that she'd run instinctively into his arms when she'd been afraid. No telling what he might do with such an assumption. That was Cade to the core. Always looking for a motive so that he could manipulate.

"Forget the nightmare. I've got an interesting question to ask you," Jamie said before he could pursue his own line of logic. "What on earth would you have done if I'd shown up pregnant at the marina?" She hadn't actually meant to ask that question. Jamie wasn't certain she wanted to hear the answer. She'd probably get some assurance that he would gladly have footed the bill for an abortion.

He gave her a long, steady look. "Married you."

"Married me!" Thoroughly astounded at the answer, Jamie found herself staring openmouthedly at him.

"What else?" he growled. Then he moved, stepping past her toward the French door that opened onto the terrace. "It's freezing in here. For pete's sake. Why is the door open? Are you trying to make yourself sick?"

Still struggling to assimilate what he had just said, Jamie turned to watch him. Belatedly she realized that one of the glass-paned doors was indeed standing ajar. That fact finally registered just as Cade slammed and locked the door. Jamie swallowed, her mouth abruptly quite dry.

"Cade, I didn't open that door."

He glanced at her over his shoulder, frowning. "What do you mean, you didn't open it?"

"Just what I said." Weakly Jamie sank down into a white, curving chair. "About that nightmare, Cade. Maybe . . . maybe we should talk about it."

"It has something to do with the door being open?" he demanded, moving back across the oddly shaped room to drop into the chair opposite hers.

Jamie chewed reflectively on her lower lip and glanced uneasily up at the portrait that occupied the wall between the two white chairs. "I know this sounds crazy but when I woke up . . ." She broke off and tried again, because obviously she couldn't have been fully awake when she'd seen the portrait come alive. "I mean, just before I really woke up the thing that made me nervous was the funny sensation that Hadley's picture here sort of, well, moved."

"Moved?" Cade watched her warily. "What do you mean, moved? The whole picture shifted position?"

Jamie shook her head. "Not quite," she said, feeling embarrassed, which only angered her further. She was very conscious of needing to maintain a cool reserved image in front of Cade. Anything less and he would pounce. This sort of thing could become very stressful, she realized. "It was more an impression that the man in the portrait moved. For a while after I first woke up, I thought there might be two portraits. That was probably the effects of double vision, though," she explained hastily. "Sometimes that happens when I'm not wearing my glasses. I have to concentrate to focus properly, especially in darkness. It was just one of those things, Cade. A bad dream. To be honest, it bothered me enough that I wanted to get out of the room for a few minutes."

"Which is how you wound up standing in the hall outside my door at two in the morning, wearing something that looks like it came from Fredericks of Hollywood?"

"This gown was designed in Paris!" Incensed, Jamie momentarily forgot the nightmare of Hadley's portrait. "Paris, *France*, you heathen! And it cost a fortune! I did not get it out of some Fredericks of Hollywood catalog. I spent days shopping for it at the most exclusive boutiques in Santa Barbara!"

"Santa Barbara? You bought it this past summer?" The tawny eyes were suddenly quite brilliantly gold.

"At about the same time I got the prescription for those damn pills," Jamie confirmed bitterly. Then she realized it would also have been around the same time he had been buying a fifty-dollar bottle of cognac and ordering perfect yellow roses. Talk about irony. They'd each privately spent small fortunes preparing for that evening.

"You're saying you bought the nightgown to wear for me?" Cade asked gently.

"I got my money's worth out of the pills but I didn't out of the nightgown," she informed him in what she hoped was a suitably sarcastic tone of voice. "You may recall we went directly back to the *Dreamer II* after we left the restaurant. I couldn't figure out a way to pack the gown without seeming a tad obvious. I've been wearing it a lot lately so I wouldn't feel that I wasted the two hundred ninety-seven dollars and ninety-eight cents."

Cade looked dumbfounded. "Two hundred and ninety-seven dollars? For a nightie?"

"And ninety-eight cents. Say no more, Cade. I fully agree with what you're thinking. An utter waste of money. I tried to take it back the day after you left town, but the shop wouldn't refund my money," she explained flippantly. That was an outright fabrication. She'd had her hands full, dealing with her hurt and anger as well as trying to comfort Miss Isabel and fight off reporters. She had forgotten all about the nightgown until she'd discovered it in her suitcase when she'd unpacked here at the house.

"Two hundred and ninety-seven dollars for a night-ie," Cade repeated, still sounding dazed. "To wear for me."

"As you have noted more than once, I was a romantic little idiot this summer. Could we please get back to the subject at hand? It's nearly five o'clock in the morning."

Slowly but obediently Cade nodded. "The door."

"Yes. The door. I didn't open it, Cade." She was very sure of that. The knowledge sent a chill down her spine.

"Any chance it had been left open earlier? After all, you just got back to the house yourself a few hours ahead of me. Had you been in this room before you moved in for the night?"

"No, I hadn't wandered in here," Jamie admitted, dark brows making an intent line above the rims of her glasses. "I suppose it's possible Annie opened it and forgot to lock it the last time she was here."

"Annie?"

"Annie is the woman who comes in to clean once a week."

"She probably wouldn't remember one way or the other," Cade muttered.

"No. She might have left it open. But I didn't notice it earlier when I was getting ready for bed," Jamie said, trying to think. "Of course, if it was only unlatched, not actually standing open, I might not have been aware of it. A gust of wind could have blown it ajar later."

"About the same time you thought you were seeing Hadley's portrait move?" Cade asked quietly.

She gave him a quick, hopeful look. "You think the wind might have made the portrait shift, too?"

Cade idly reached out to push experimentally against the heavy frame of the big painting. It didn't budge.

"No," he stated categorically. "I don't think a small gust of wind would have made this sucker move."

"I didn't think so." Jamie's mouth curved wryly. "Miss Isabel and I had a heck of a time getting it hung in the first place. Weighs a ton."

"When did Miss Isabel do it?" Cade examined the strange conglomeration of objects embedded in the acrylic paint. "The date on that letter is fairly recent."

"She did it when we got back from Santa Barbara. Worked night and day, poor thing. I think she was trying to deal with her grief. It was after she finished it that she started talking about the possibility of Hadley still being alive. He was the only family she had, and I guess she couldn't bring herself to believe he'd gone. I could tell she needed to have it confirmed so that she would be able to accept the facts and get on with her own life." Jamie stopped talking, aware that she was perilously close to saying too much on that score. The last thing she wanted to surface just now was the exact manner in which the idea of hiring Cade Santerre had been put into Miss Isabel's brain.

"So when she came up with the bright idea of having me investigate, you let her talk you into it," Cade concluded in a flat tone of voice.

"Uh, yes. Something like that." Determinedly Jamie pressed on to the next subject that had occurred to her. "There's one other thing, Cade. I didn't think too much of it at the time, but now I'm not so sure."

He gave her a patiently inquiring glance. "Go on."

"Well, yesterday when I stopped for groceries outside of San Simeon, I caught a fleeting glimpse of someone at the gas pump who reminded me a little of Hadley."

Cade jumped on that, the hard planes of his face tightening abruptly. "He only reminded you a little of Fitzgerald?"

"I just got a small glimpse and I only saw the back of his head. But his hair was the same color and the general build of the man was similar. There was something about the way he carried himself that actually put me in mind of Hadley." When Cade said nothing, merely continued to watch her, Jamie shook her head in self-denial. "No, it couldn't have been him. It was just my imagination. Besides, even if he were alive, why would he show up around here?"

"Looking for his sister."

"But he knows I'd be with her. If he wanted to keep everyone thinking the suicide was for real, he wouldn't dare let me see him."

"He undoubtedly knows of your beyond-the-call-of-duty sense of loyalty to Miss Isabel," Cade observed dryly. "He might figure he could count on that if you should become aware of him."

"That really bothers you, doesn't it?" Jamie muttered.

"Your sense of loyalty to your employer? I've told you I think it's a little extreme. Not to mention misplaced. But it fits in with your general view of life, I suppose. You'd have done well in the age of chivalry and honor when unquestioning loyalty was a virtue."

"Perhaps," she shot back caustically. "But I'm finally learning to adjust to my own era. You've already taught me not to believe in knights in shining armor, for example."

Cade closed his eyes for a prolonged instant, and Jamie honestly couldn't tell if he was concealing genuine pain or blazing fury. When he lifted his lashes, the tawny gaze was unreadable, but the force with which his powerful hands gripped the arms of the chair was evident in the paleness around the knuckles.

"Are you going to slash me with that sharp little tongue of yours every chance you get?" he asked with almost detached interest.

"Possibly," Jamie retorted. "No, *probably*. It's the new me."

"A harsh mistress," he murmured.

Jamie lifted her head angrily. "I'm not your mistress."

He shrugged. "Lover?"

"At the moment," she snapped, "I am the woman who is supervising your work for my employer. I suggest you start performing in an investigative capacity or head south to your boat."

He got to his feet with a lithe movement, his features set in cold, austere lines. "Yes, ma'am. Since it's almost dawn, I think I'll take a shower and get dressed. I will go to work as soon as a few offices in Los Angeles are open. I'll try to do a reasonably satisfactory job for you, Jamie."

He was at the door of her bedroom before Jamie could find the last words. "Just do as good a job proving Hadley's dead as you did ruining him in the first place, and I'll be satisfied."

Cade, who had fully intended to shut the door behind him quite coolly, wound up slamming it instead. Furiously he stormed across the hall and then slammed the door of the room he had been using. Shocked at the lack of control, he came to a halt in the middle of Jamie's bedroom and stared down at his hands. His fingers were almost trembling with the force of his anger and frustration.

"Settle down and think, Santerre," he chided himself. "Losing your self-control isn't going to do any good. Damn it to hell. What a mess."

He stripped off his jeans and headed for the shower. First things first. He needed to calm down and start dealing rationally with the situation, or else he would be farther up the creek without a paddle than he already was.

He found the burgundy-and-white tiled bathroom pleasantly littered with Jamie's personal choices in soap, shampoo, hair rinse and body lotions. They were all exotically scented and flamboyantly packaged by shrewd manufacturers who knew how to appeal to the romantic element in a woman's nature. The names on the bottles conjured up mysterious locales, seductive sensations and heady fragrances. Cade was momentarily fascinated with the assortment. He was seeing a private side of Jamie that he'd never before had a chance to investigate. Although, he thought in satisfaction, if anyone had invited him to describe her bathroom sight unseen, he would have come fairly close to the reality. He'd have guessed it would look something like this.

He sniffed a soap that was carved in the shape of a rose. Sure enough, it smelled like a rose. He dropped it back in the seashell dish and picked up Jamie's hair rinse. It reminded him of peaches. Methodically he went through the array of lotions and potions, opening jars and inhaling the scents. The woman must have spent a month's salary on this stuff, Cade decided. That thought reminded him of the concoction of lace and satin she had worn to bed.

Two hundred and ninety-seven dollars for a nightie! And she'd bought it this past summer to wear for him. Too bad he hadn't given her a chance to pick it up and bring it with her the night he'd taken her back to the yacht and made love to her!

Cade set down the last of the bottles, opting to use the lemon-scented soap on the grounds that it would be the least objectionable scent on a man.

She must have purchased that nightie while under the influence of a particularly reckless state of romantic anticipation, Cade thought as he soaped himself. He wrinkled his nose in mild disgust as the lemon scent permeated the shower.

It would be like Jamie to do that sort of thing. If she had made up her mind to cast herself wholeheartedly into the fires of a passionate affair, she would exert every effort to make everything perfect.

Cade paused, staring unseeingly at the line of burgundy tile in front of him. Water cascaded down his chest as he considered his last thought. That explained the birth-control pills, of course. After all, she'd seen that night on board the yacht coming for two months. He'd made no secret of his desire. It had been only a matter of time, and they'd both known it. Jamie, being a woman, would have had to consider possible consequences. She probably hadn't wanted to spoil the romantic illusion by discussing such a mundane matter with him. Hadn't she admitted a few minutes ago that she'd found it a difficult topic to bring up in casual conversation when the man involved hadn't yet issued the invitation to bed? The problem was that he simply hadn't viewed the situation from this perspective. That explained why he'd been laboring under a false assumption.

Absently Cade began to shave himself, going by instinct as his mind worked on the problem. A woman's whole nature didn't alter in the course of six weeks, he assured himself. Jamie's gentle, romantic nature was too fundamental to change in that short a time. Just look at all this junk in her bathroom.

And remember the way she had unfolded like a flower in his arms last night. A passionflower. Once back in his bed, she had been the same Jamie he had been seeing in his dreams for six long weeks. During the night she had held him with hot desire and shimmering need. She had given herself to him completely, just as she had that night on the yacht. His body started to react just at the memory. With a grimace he turned off the hot-water tap and let the shower go cold. After a couple of moments of the drastic treatment Cade reached out to turn off the water and shook the spray out of his hair. He groped for a towel and came up with a fluffy burgundy one that had a rose embroidered on it. Briskly he went to work with it, trying to marshal his thoughts.

All right, he decided grimly, so he'd underestimated the full extent of her anger. He should have realized that her passion for revenge and her fear of getting hurt again would be strong. After all, she was a woman in every sense of the word. Passionate, intelligent, proud and not a little reckless in some ways. None of that contradicted his assessment of her basic nature. He just hadn't made proper allowance for the full strength of that nature.

Cade slung the towel over the rack and glanced in the mirror to make certain the shaving job had been accurate. Satisfied, he walked back out into the bedroom and began to dress.

The only real miscalculation he'd made so far was in assuming she was pregnant, he told himself as he tugged on a dark-hued pullover. Stupid of him, really. What were the odds that a woman would get pregnant after spending one night with a man, even if she hadn't been using a contraceptive? Probably exceedingly slim. He glowered at himself in the mirror. Dumb assumption. Dumb high-school biology class. The teacher probably had just been trying to terrorize the students when she'd warned them all those years ago about how easy it was for a woman to get pregnant.

Cade sighed, wondering briefly how he'd managed to convince himself so completely that he'd gotten Jamie pregnant. He wasn't usually naive, nor did he normally jump to conclusions without evidence. He promptly dismissed that useless line of inquiry.

It led, however, to another issue. His glowering expression intensified as he zipped up his jeans and fastened the snap. Jamie had seemed quite startled at the notion of him offering marriage in the event she was pregnant.

That bothered him, Cade realized. What the hell did she think he would do? Toss her out into the cold? If he hadn't wanted her to get pregnant, he would have taken preventive measures himself. She should have understood that. She should have trusted him to take care of her. She must not have much faith in his willingness to carry out his responsibilities.

Somehow that last realization irritated him more than anything else. Damn it, she ought to have known that he would have taken care of her.

Perhaps not, he thought savagely. She hadn't believed that he'd never intended for her to get caught in the crunch when the authorities moved in on Hadley. Given that, it made sense that she might not believe he would really have offered marriage if he'd gotten her pregnant. The little idiot.

Swearing in exasperation, Cade swung around to head out of the room in search of breakfast. Okay, so he'd made a false assumption and a tactical miscalculation or two. That didn't change the basic situation.

He'd spent two months this past summer seducing Jamie Garland. He was a patient man. He'd do it all over again, if necessary. But this time around he wouldn't deny himself the warmth of her bed for long. A man had his limits.

6

JAMIE REALIZED WITH DISGUST that she was having to devote an unnatural amount of concentration to the simple routine of getting breakfast ready. She found herself intently gnawing on her lower lip while watching the toast browning under the oven broiler and tried to shake off the sensation that things were on the verge of getting out of control. She was only fixing breakfast, for heaven's sake, not working on a solution to the problem of the national debt.

But everything seemed to be requiring undue caution this morning. It was as if she dare not relax or something would blow up in her face. Maybe this was what people meant when they said they felt as though they were walking on eggs. Even the simple act of showering and pulling on a pair of jeans and an oversize blue work shirt had taken more than the necessary amount of attention. Her hair still wasn't right. After several attempts in front of the mirror Jamie had abandoned her efforts, and now the dark auburn mass was clamped in an exceedingly casual twist. Tendrils were already coming loose.

It was all Cade's fault. He had been a disturbing influence in her life since the moment she had met him. Matters were not improving with time. They would disintegrate entirely if he ever discovered that it had been her idea, not Miss Isabel's, to contact him with the offer of a job.

Jamie yanked the rack partway out from under the broiler, flipped the toast and shoved it back. She wondered if Cade liked peanut-butter toast for breakfast.

On the other hand, she asked herself resolutely, who cared what he liked for breakfast? He could take it or leave it. That was supposed to be part of the new arrangement. Casual. Sophisticated. Independent. The second time around with Cade was going to be on her terms. She might not be able to resist playing with fire but she would darn well run the risks in her own way, not his. Last time he had played the tune and she had danced to his measure. This time the process was going to be reversed.

Jamie pushed her glasses more firmly onto her nose as she straightened away from the oven, and then she went to the refrigerator to find the carton of freshly ground peanut butter. The whole problem, she realized forlornly, was that it was almost impossible to be casual, sophisticated and completely independent around Cade. Take now, for instance. A part of her did care about fixing him a breakfast he would enjoy.

It made no sense at all. The man deserved absolutely no consideration from her. But telling herself that indisputable truth did not absolve her of the uneasy feeling that she had been unfair to him early this morning. That crack about telling him to do as good a job of proving Hadley Fitzgerald dead as he had done ruining the man in first place had been rather harsh. When all was said and done, it wasn't exactly Cade's fault that Hadley had apparently been a very shady businessman.

If only Hadley had not been Miss Isabel's brother and if only Miss Isabel wasn't both her close friend and her employer, Jamie thought wistfully. And if only Cade hadn't spent two months seducing her while he was investigating Hadley. Life could be full of "if onlys."

"Something's burning."

Startled, Jamie jerked around as Cade spoke from the doorway. Simultaneously her nose caught the whiff of overdone bread. "Oh, Lord, the toast!" She darted over to the oven and pulled the rack out. The toast had been caught in time. Barely. It was definitely very dark but still edible.

"You should use a toaster. Then you wouldn't have to watch it so closely. You also wouldn't waste excess electricity by heating up the whole oven just to brown toast." Cade sauntered over to the counter and took one of the stools. He reached for the pot of coffee Jamie had just finished making.

"As usual, your advice is extremely well-timed, well thought out and highly intelligent," Jamie muttered. "However, I didn't ask for it."

He sipped coffee and watched her over the rim of the cup. "Are you ever going to ask for anything from me, Jamie?"

"Not if I can help it. Do you like peanut-butter toast?" She began slathering peanut butter on a slice of darkly browned bread.

"For breakfast?"

"This isn't dinner I'm working on here."

He winced. "I love peanut-butter toast for breakfast."

"Then this is your lucky day."

"Jamie, honey, are you going to spend the whole day snapping at me?" Cade asked plaintively.

She looked up, glowering at him from behind her glasses. "I don't know. I suppose it will depend on how you behave yourself. Keep in mind that you're here to do a job, and perhaps we can make it through the day without slitting each other's throats."

"You're really determined to make sure I know who's boss this time around, aren't you?" he asked wonderingly.

"It seems the best way to prevent any unpleasant surprises such as I had to endure six weeks ago." Briskly she finished spreading peanut butter.

"Are you ever going to believe that I never meant things to end the way they did six weeks ago?"

"Oh, I believe that your pal Gallagher and his men apparently moved a little earlier than you had planned. I even believe it's possible you thought you'd have me out of the way the day the roof fell in on Hadley. But that doesn't change the fact that you used me. It also doesn't change the fact that you never told me the truth about why you were spending so much time with the Fitzgeralds. Our relationship lacked an essential element, Cade. It's called mutual trust."

"I did not use you. And as for telling you the truth about why I was hanging around Fitzgerald, I couldn't risk it. You would have felt it your duty to warn Isabel that her brother was in danger. I couldn't take a chance on your divided loyalties. The whole mess didn't concern you, anyway," Cade said bluntly.

"Didn't concern me! How can you say that? I was practically a member of the household," Jamie flared. "I was the one who had to fend off the reporters after you left. I was the one who had to help Miss Isabel cope with the fact that her brother had probably committed suicide. I was the one who had to deal with Mr. Gallagher and his men while they went through Hadley's private belongings. I was the one who had to close up the house in Santa Barbara. Shall I continue with the list of all the ways in which I was not involved in that mess?"

"I think we had better go back to discussing peanut butter on toast," Cade said with a sigh. "And then we can go on to discussing the job at hand."

Jamie flinched from the grimness in his voice. She wished she hadn't brought up the past, but unless she kept that firmly in mind she was in danger of forgetting it the way she had last night when he'd taken her in his arms. Last night should be a lesson to her. She had forgotten everything but the wonder of being in his arms again. Things were happening too fast this time around. Determinedly she faced him, the plate of peanut-butter toast in her hand.

"Cade, we need to make certain we understand each other. If you're going to finish this job for Miss Isabel . . ."

"I am."

"And if you're going to stay here while you do it . . ."

"I am."

"Then you must understand that the only way I can allow that is . . ."

"On your terms," he finished succinctly. He gave her a brooding, level glance. "I understand. I know you need to work it out."

She frowned. "Work what out?"

"The revenge. You have to have a chance to reassert yourself. I left you feeling used and vulnerable six weeks ago. God knows I didn't mean for you to feel that way, Jamie. I meant to keep you safe, clear of what was coming down. It didn't work out that way, and now you're wary and angry. I didn't think your resentment would go so deep or last this long. I guess I misjudged the situation between us, took too much for granted. I thought you would figure out for yourself that I really hadn't used you. I was wrong."

"You sound as though you're busy analyzing and assessing again," she grumbled, slicing toast. It made her uneasy to hear him admit that he might have been wrong. But it made her even more uneasy to hear him going through a logical reassessment of what it was he had done wrong.

"Analyzing and assessing situations is something I usually do fairly well," Cade reminded her gently. "Apparently I blew it this time."

"A slight miscalculation. The same kind of mistake you made assuming I must be coming back to you because I was pregnant." She tossed the plate of toast onto the counter and stood on the opposite side, nibbling at her own breakfast.

Cade examined the peanut-butter toast. "As you said, a slight miscalculation. It doesn't change things, honey. The only thing it affects is timing."

"Timing?"

He looked up. "I need to give you time to work out your feelings. I'm willing to do that."

She shook her head wryly. "Even when you're *trying* to be humble, you can't quite manage it, can you?"

"Give me a chance, Jamie." There was a genuine plea in his quiet words. "That's all I'm asking. You're usually so willing to give everyone else in the world, including a crook like Fitzgerald, the benefit of a doubt. Why can't you extend the courtesy to me?"

Jamie hesitated. Across the counter their eyes met. She felt as though she were hovering on the edge of a precipice. The important thing to remember was, she decided, that she didn't have to choose between hurling herself over the edge or retreating completely. She could find another, safer way down the mountain. As long as she kept control of the situation and her own emotions, she would be able to make her own way off the edge. She had known from the beginning that approaching Cade Santerre a second time had to be done with great caution.

"We have to do it my way, Cade. And I'm making no guarantees."

Something cold and relentless flashed for an instant in the tawny gaze and then it was gone. "We'll do it your way, Jamie."

She munched toast for a moment before finding a way to break the unnatural silence that followed his comment. She wanted to ask for clarification, wanted to demand that he repeat what he'd just promised, but she was a little afraid to push it. "I suppose we should get down to business."

"I told you I'd call some people in L.A. after eight o'clock."

"That Gallagher person?" she hazarded.

"Yeah, Gallagher. He can update me. Maybe he's learned something useful in the past six weeks. After I left Santa Barbara I washed my hands of the whole mess. I also should make a start on whatever information I can dig up around here. I've been thinking about that business of your door being ajar."

"So have I," Jamie admitted, "and the more I think about it, the more certain I am that Annie must have unlocked it and forgotten to relock it before she left. It wouldn't be the first time she's made a simple mistake like that."

"What about your nightmare?"

"I've had lots of instances of double vision before, when I wasn't wearing my glasses," she said, shrugging. "I told you, I have trouble focusing properly without them." In the light of day it was easy to face that kind of logic.

"Well, maybe . . ."

"You said you wanted personal information on Hadley," Jamie went on, grateful for the change of topic.

"Does Miss Isabel keep photo albums or letters? Did she ever let her brother handle any of her own investments?"

"Sometimes," Jamie said slowly, answering the last question first.

"As the person who managed Miss Isabel's business affairs, were you ever approached by Hadley?"

"Everything Hadley recommended for his sister in the investment line was conservative and rock solid. She never suffered any significant losses because of his advice, and at various times she made a great deal of money. I never had enough spare cash to take any risks. My money's all in the bank. Hadley certainly never tried to take advantage of me. He used to say I was wise to bank my savings until I had enough to play with," Jamie defended stoutly.

Cade backed off, clearly reluctant to push her on that score. He was obviously going to resist the temptation to comment on her naïveté regarding Hadley. His hesitation to do so gave her courage. It was obvious she wasn't the only one trying to walk on eggs this morning. A part of her wondered at Cade's attempt at diplomacy. He was trying, Jamie realized with a start. He was making an effort to mend his side of the fence. The thought sent a rush of hope and longing through her that she couldn't banish completely, not even with a litany of repeated warnings.

"Okay, presumably he was fond of his sister and would not have involved her in any of his schemes. In his own right, Hadley was quite shrewd. There's no reason he wouldn't have given Miss Isabel sound advice. What I'm interested in are the records of the various transactions he might have recommended. I'd like to see which brokerage houses he told her to use, for example. What contacts he had. I'd like a look at the files of any of the real estate or investment deals he fixed up for her. I want the names of the people he used to conclude the arrangements. Were those records your responsibility?"

"Yes." Jamie concentrated on pouring herself a cup of coffee. "I can get those for you. Anything else?"

Cade considered his words. "Jamie, I'm not sure how to ask this without making you bristle . . ."

"Try." She discovered she liked it when he was being careful around her.

"Well, was there anything that Miss Isabel brought home from the house in Santa Barbara besides the baggage she arrived with at the beginning of the summer? Anything that might have belonged to Hadley?"

Jamie regarded him silently for a long moment. "Not exactly," she finally said.

Cade closed his eyes in what was obviously a silent plea for patience. "Not exactly. Care to expand on that a bit further?"

Jamie tapped one fingernail on the counter while she considered her answer. "I'm not sure how much I should tell you, Cade. It's very personal information."

"You might keep in mind that this time around I'm working for Miss Isabel," he said evenly.

"I know, but I'm not sure that having the wolf on our side changes the basic fact that he's still a predator. You must see that I'm walking a very fine line here. I'm responsible for supervising you. I realize I have to give you enough room to work. But I also have to be certain I don't do anything Miss Isabel wouldn't want done. I don't want to accidentally give you information that she might want kept confidential."

"If you want me to do a decent job, you can't tie my hands."

"That is, of course, a lovely rationale for turning you loose, but I don't think I'll buy it completely," she responded coolly. "I will try to answer your question, however. I don't want you claiming that I made it impossible for you to work at all. Miss Isabel wouldn't appreciate that."

"And you're determined to please Miss Isabel."

"She's my employer." Jamie shrugged with a nonchalance she didn't feel.

"For a while this summer you used to worry about pleasing me," Cade said quite deliberately.

"For a while this summer I lost my head," she retorted. "Working for Miss Isabel may not be quite as exciting as getting myself seduced by a professional business spy, but it has its compensations."

She knew a split second too late that she'd gone too far. Cade's hand moved so quickly that she couldn't have backed away in time to escape even if she had been warned. He reached across the counter, powerful fingers closing around her wrist, capturing her. His eyes blazed with temper.

"I am not a professional spy, damn it. I had my reasons for what I did this summer. I've explained them and I refuse to apologize for them. If you have any sense, Jamie Garland, you will learn to exercise a bit of caution. I'm aware that you're feeling vengeful, but there are limits, lady. Keep it in mind."

"Is this what you meant about doing things my way?" she dared, aware of the strength in his hand. He wasn't hurting her, but she knew she could never have broken the grip.

Abruptly he released her and picked up his coffee. Jamie could read the seething annoyance in him, but he was firmly tethered on the self-imposed leash. When he spoke again it was with extreme politeness. "I believe you were about to explain what you meant when you said Miss Isabel had 'not exactly' taken anything with her when she left Santa Barbara?"

Jamie blinked owlishly behind the lenses of her glasses, peering at him dubiously. Had he really backed down or was he tricking her? This was ridiculous. She had to have more faith in herself. She lounged against the counter, sipping coffee with great casualness. Damned if she would allow him to see how nervous he made her.

"There was a letter and a package," she began quietly.

"That she took with her?"

"No. Waiting for us here when we got home."

"Mailed or privately delivered?" Cade demanded.

"Mailed. It was waiting in the box when we got here." Jamie hesitated. "It was addressed to Miss Isabel. She opened it and told me it had been sent by Hadley. Mailed before he disappeared."

Cade was fully alert. "What was in the package?"

Jamie took another sip of coffee before admitting, "I don't know. Miss Isabel never told me. She said it was personal."

"I thought she shared just about everything with you."

"Normally she does, but you have to understand, Cade, she was very upset about her brother's death. Very depressed. She wasn't acting normally."

He thought about that. "So what happened to the contents of the package?"

"She took whatever it was and put it in my safe-deposit box at the bank in Carmel."

"Your safe-deposit box?" He looked astonished.

"I got it free when I opened the account at the bank," Jamie explained impatiently. "But since I never had anything all that valuable to put into it, I let Miss Isabel use it. We're both authorized to get into it. She never got around to getting one of her own. She doesn't like to be bothered with petty details. That's why she hired me in the first place, remember?"

Cade swore softly. "Whatever is in that package must have been important."

"I think it was something *personal*," Jamie stressed. "Something he wanted her to have. Don't you see? He must have known things were about to collapse. Perhaps he was already contemplating suicide at that point. In any event, he couldn't talk to his sister about it. He probably wrote something extremely personal by way of a farewell note to her and mailed it shortly before taking the boat out for the last time."

"Unless we can find out what's in that safe-deposit box, we'll never know for sure." Cade drummed his fingers lightly on the tiled counter.

"Don't look at me like that Cade. Miss Isabel *trusts* me with her personal affairs. I have earned that trust. I won't betray it." Jamie stood tensely on the other side of the counter, preparing herself to remain firm against what she knew was coming next.

"I'm not about to suggest that you betray her," Cade said quietly. "As I keep reminding you, I'm looking after Miss Isabel's interests these days. There might be information in that safe-deposit box that I could use to figure out for certain what happened to Fitzgerald. And it is your safe-deposit box, you said, not hers . . ."

Jamie shook her head stubbornly. "If there had been anything useful along those lines, Miss Isabel would have told me about it. I don't think she learned anything at all for certain about his fate from the contents of that package. If she had, she wouldn't have told me to go ahead and hire you, would she?"

"We won't know that until we see what's in the box," Cade shot back smoothly.

Jamie thought about the way Miss Isabel had handled the contents of the package from her brother. Never before had the older woman been so quiet and secretive. Whatever was in the envelope had obviously been of a deeply personal nature. It was equally obvious that it hadn't shed any light on Hadley's disappearance. If it had, Jamie felt certain Miss Isabel would have said something, or maybe she would have vetoed the idea of hiring Cade. No, at this point it was clear to Jamie where her duty lay. Miss Isabel did not want the contents of that package made public.

"I won't let you into the safe-deposit box, Cade."

"You don't trust me, do you? Not even an inch. What's the matter now? Do you think I'm still looking for more evidence to pin on Fitzgerald?"

"I have an obligation to look after Miss Isabel's interests. Whatever was in that package was obviously of a private nature."

"Most stuff that gets put into safe-deposit boxes is of a private nature," Cade growled. "That's precisely the reason I want to see whatever it was that Hadley sent to his sister. Jamie, I—"

"No, Cade."

For a moment a silent battle of wills raged over the breakfast counter, and then Cade moved his head in disgust. "You and your sense of loyalty. You're carrying it to extremes, Jamie."

"I don't see it that way."

"I wonder what the hell you'll do if you ever have to make a choice."

Her mouth tightened. "What kind of choice?"

"Never mind. Can I have another slice of that peanut-butter toast? It sticks so nicely to the roof of my mouth."

But she knew what he meant. He was wondering what she would do if she ever again had to choose between him and her sense of duty to Miss Isabel. Let him worry about her decision. It would keep him on his toes, Jamie decided. Besides, she couldn't have answered the question, anyway. She didn't know the answer. And she shied inwardly from examining the dangerous possibilities inherent in the problem.

Breakfast was finished in silence, somewhat sullen on Jamie's part, thoughtful on Cade's. When it was over, Jamie stiffly volunteered to show him her office. With a polite nod he stood aside, waiting for her to lead the way.

"I keep all of Miss Isabel's records in here," Jamie said as she flung open the door of the round room that served as her office. "Her tax information is in that file cabinet over there. I don't do the actual tax forms for her. I send them to her accountant. Records of the sales of her paintings are here in this drawer. The details on her various investments are all over there under the tax data." She swung around challengingly. "Anything else you want to know?"

Cade scanned the windowed room, examining the old-fashioned rolltop desk, the file cabinets and the array of plants that stood near the window. He shook his head. "This will make an interesting place to start. I don't suppose you have any journal or ledger? Some sort of index to everything that's in that file cabinet? A written record of her business transactions?"

She tilted her head, a trace of mockery in her small smile. "You mean you don't feel like going through every item in each drawer? I thought you were a thorough sort of investigator."

"I am," he said blandly, "but I also believe in doing things efficiently."

"How could I forget? I know all about your efficiency, don't I?" She turned away and opened one of the desk drawers. Withdrawing two notebooks, she set them on the desk. A pang of embarrassed uncertainty assailed her. "I guess you could call those a journal and a ledger."

"What do you mean, you 'guess'?" Idly he walked over to the desk and flipped open the cover of the top book. It revealed a page filled out in Jamie's slightly irregular handwriting.

Jamie's sense of embarrassment grew. She could feel the red flush staining her cheeks. "Well, you have to remember that when I first came to work for Miss Isabel I didn't have any formal training in this sort of thing. I, uh, majored in history in college, if you'll recall," she added with a humbleness that appalled her. Why on earth should she be apologizing to him for her unprofessional record-keeping systems?

"Even if you hadn't told me the knowledge wouldn't surprise me. I wouldn't have assumed you were the type to get a really practical education," he mused as he flipped through a few more pages of the notebook. "The journal is kept by the month?"

"I didn't know how else to start tracking things. Everything was in such a mess when I arrived two years ago. I talked to Miss Isabel's accountant, and he told me the kind of information he would need to keep her taxes straight. From there on I was on my own. I sort of made it up as I went along."

"You made up the details of her tax records?" Cade murmured interestedly.

Jamie's flush deepened. "Of course not. I meant I invented the record-keeping system. I didn't know anything about double-entry bookkeeping or account books or journals or ledgers. So I had to fake it. There's so much to keep track of," she went on, feeling pressed and growing slightly agitated under the pressure. Jamie waved a hand around the room. "Honestly, Cade, it's a big job. There are dealings with galleries, all this artwork that has to be kept inventoried, her personal finances. We're thinking of getting her incorporated, which will mean even more work. It goes on and on!"

"Another romantic, dreamy-eyed history major overwhelmed by reality." Cade grinned.

Jamie ignored that and stalked to the door. "Call me if you have any questions."

"Just one more thing."

"Yes?" She paused, glaring back at him over her shoulder.

"There's a desk in Miss Isabel's bedroom," Cade began slowly. "What does she keep in there?"

"Not much," Jamie said honestly. "Some personal correspondence, photographs, a few trinkets. Just odds and ends. She turned all the important financial stuff over to me when I arrived."

Cade nodded. "Okay. I'll have a look through it after I've gone over this stuff." He sat down at the rolltop desk and pulled the handwritten journal toward himself. It was apparent that he was immediately and completely absorbed in the task at hand.

Jamie hesitated and then decided that there was no way he could possibly get through the contents of her office before lunch. She would worry later about how much of Miss Isabel's personal correspondence to turn over to him. She walked out into the hall and stood there for a moment, fretting over what Cade would think about her unprofessional bookkeeping system.

It was ridiculous to be nervous or embarrassed. After all, she had done the best she could. Still, she had just left her poor, handwritten, unsophisticated records with a man whose business had once involved analyzing and tearing apart highly complex accounting systems. He was bound to find her unskilled attempts at record keeping rather laughable.

Well, there was nothing she could do about it now, Jamie told herself philosophically and went into the kitchen to get another cup of coffee. Then, feeling restless, she wandered out into the living room and picked up a volume she had been reading on the history of how the British had lost their American colonies.

But the foibles and follies and occasional acts of idealism that had characterized the eighteenth century failed to hold her attention this morning. She had her own foibles, follies and idealism with which to contend. Jamie realized she also had a lot of memories.

She found herself gazing out the window through the trees into the distance where the Pacific Ocean stretched forever. It was the same ocean that had extended into forever off the coast of Santa Barbara. This summer her dreams had extended into forever, too. Time had taken on curious properties during the two months she had known Cade Santerre. It had seemed to stop in some ways and in others it had appeared to be rushing past far too quickly. In its wake time had left images that were indelibly etched in her memory.

A few of those images returned to haunt her now just as they had haunted her steadily for the past six weeks. Sometimes it was the little things that seemed so vivid. She recalled the clasp of Cade's hand around her own as she had walked on the beach with him. His fingers contained such strength, and yet he had always touched her with a gentleness that had never failed to amaze her. The combination of power and tenderness in Cade had been deeply compelling. It was one of the reasons she had not been able to push him out of her mind during the past six weeks; one of the reasons she would never be able to forget him. Last night he had held her in his arms with that same enthralling combination of strength and gentleness. Jamie knew she was dangerously close to the brink of forever.

During the next few hours she tried very hard to read the book in her lap, but the words on the page wouldn't stay together in coherent sentences. Too many stray thoughts and memories intruded. She thought of Cade working in her study and wondered about his past. How could such a coolheaded, pragmatic man ever have walked away from a lucrative career in accounting in favor of the far more unpredictable life of a charter-boat captain?

Then her mind skipped along to scenes from Santa Barbara. Scenes that always involved Cade. Pâté and French bread shared on a secluded stretch of beach, an afternoon spent wandering through the beautiful Spanish mission together, a morning drive along the coast. And always there were memories of the evenings spent talking over wine and good food. They had talked about so many things, Jamie realized: the history that she loved, the sailing that Cade enjoyed, art, politics, their own personal philosophies. Jamie's mouth twisted wryly. Everything under the California sun except the truth had been discussed during those two months in Santa Barbara. Cade had had priorities that had precluded discussing that topic.

Priorities. Loyalties. Commitments.

The words tumbled around in her mind. She wasn't the only one who was capable of feeling the pull of such demands. For the first time Jamie allowed herself to openly recognize that Cade, too, might have been struggling with loyalties and commitments this summer. She thought about Cade's sister. Faced with a similar situation, Jamie acknowledged, she might have tried to walk the same line Cade had walked for two months in Santa Barbara.

Then she remembered his comment at breakfast and shivered. She hoped she would never have to choose between her own loyalties.

Cade emerged a few minutes before noon, stretching hugely as he walked into the living room to find Jamie. She glanced up anxiously from the book she had been trying to read.

"How did it go?" she asked cautiously.

"It was *interesting*." He nodded. "Yes, I think that's the word. Interesting. You have a novel approach to the task of bookkeeping, Jamie."

"Never mind the cracks about my bookkeeping. Did you find anything useful?"

"Possibly." Cade sank down on the wicker lounge across from her, shoving his jeaned legs out in front of him. He laced his fingers behind his head and regarded her as if she were a specimen under a microscope. "Possibly not. Hard to know at this point. There are the names of some companies Fitzgerald dealt with that should be checked out. They might provide some leads." He paused. "Did I ever tell you just how much you can learn about a person by studying the way they keep track of financial matters?"

"You were not in that office to study me," she gritted.

"I know, but I couldn't help but pick up a few items of interest along the way. Actually I was quite impressed with your creativity at times. A case of '79 Bordeaux is a business expense?"

"Miss Isabel needs it for occasional artistic inspiration and I need it to get through the job of doing the monthly entries in that dumb journal."

"Four hundred dollars a month for petty cash?"

"I discovered it was easier to create a petty-cash fund rather than note down every itty-bitty little purchase in the journal," Jamie explained austerely. "Much more efficient."

"Fifty percent of the utilities written off as a business expense?"

"You can't expect Miss Isabel to paint in the dark!"

"A thousand-dollar television set put down as office furniture?"

"Miss Isabel is a great fan of soap operas," Jamie defended. "They give her a lot of creative ideas. Look, Cade, I didn't send you into that office to nitpick every little detail of my present record-keeping system. You were supposed to be looking for ways to track down Hadley!"

"It was a fascinating experience. I can't even begin to imagine the inventiveness a full-scale IRS audit might reveal. You have a really imaginative approach to bookkeeping, Jamie. A definite flair and style all your own. I told you record-keeping techniques are almost as unique to individuals as fingerprints." Tawny eyes gleamed with amusement.

"Did you learn anything about Hadley while you were snooping through my books?" Jamie asked in chilled tones.

"I learned that he kept his sister's investments conservative, as you said. I called Gallagher on your office phone, by the way."

"Did he have any news?"

"No. Just that there's been nothing yet to contradict the suicide theory. I asked him to check a couple of names on the board of directors of one of the real estate partnerships in which Fitzgerald had his sister invest. Thought I recognized at least one of them as a man who was distantly involved with Fitzgerald on a land-fraud scheme five years ago. It probably won't lead us anywhere useful." Again Cade stretched luxuriously. "What's for lunch?"

Jamie considered the matter along with her own tentative desire to understand this man better than she had this summer. "How about driving into Carmel? I know a couple of nice places there. Besides, I need some groceries. I only picked up a few things yesterday."

"Suits me." Cade got to his feet and reached for her hand. "Come along, my creative little accountant. We might as well eat, drink and be merry as long as we can, for tomorrow they may slap you in jail"

"Jail!" Horrified, Jamie dug in her heels and stared up at him.

"I'm only teasing you," Cade said, chuckling.

"Are you sure? Cade, I wasn't deliberately doing anything dishonest. I was only trying to interpret things to Miss Isabel's advantage. Everyone says you have to use every available loophole or else you wind up paying a lot of excess taxes."

"Stop worrying," he growled, propelling her out through the front door and into the waiting Mazda. "If worse comes to worst, I'll bake you a cake with a file in it."

"Cade!"

He slid in beside her, turned the key in the ignition and slanted her a strangely compelling glance. "Better be nice to me, honey. You may need my professional skills one of these days. I'm real good at finding loopholes."

"How much would you charge for keeping me out of trouble with the IRS?" Jamie grumbled as she fastened her seat belt.

"You'd be indebted to me for the rest of your life."

THE OUTING TO CARMEL proved to be unexpectedly pleasant for Jamie. Cade seemed to be in a lighthearted, easygoing mood. He chatted casually with her over lunch in a tiny European-style café, offered to spend some time browsing through the myriad little boutiques that lined Carmel's quaint streets and generally made himself agreeable. Jamie wasn't quite sure how to interpret the good-naturedness, but she found herself taking advantage of it.

She took him into one of the local galleries where Miss Isabel had some work on display, and later they shared a cup of espresso. When it was finally time to leave the wealthy picturesque village of the sea, Jamie realized she had forgotten for a while just why she and Cade were again spending time together. The lovely afternoon was all too reminiscent of the many such days they had spent in Santa Barbara.

It was only as Cade guided the Mazda back along the narrow, curving highway hugging the cliff above the sea that Jamie questioned Cade's motives. She wouldn't put it past him to deliberately re-create a day that brought back warm memories of the time spent in Santa Barbara. She must be constantly on the alert, she told herself firmly. And then she realized that she had willingly participated in the fantasy that afternoon. She, too, wanted to re-create the feelings they had shared this summer. That way lay danger. The safest way to maintain the uneasy status quo was to keep everything on a business basis. For a while this afternoon she had neglected to do that. The reward for allowing her guard to slip had been a wonderful day spent with Cade.

"I've thought about letting you at Miss Isabel's private desk," she began as Cade pulled into the drive in front of the house.

"Have you?" He didn't seem unduly concerned.

"I think it would be all right. I don't know if there's anything useful to be found there, but I don't believe she'd mind if you had a look."

"I'll do it in the morning."

She slanted him a quick glance. "Not this evening?"

"Morning will be soon enough."

"Oh."

"Now about this evening," he went on imperturbably as he climbed out of the car.

"What about it?"

"I was going to suggest we examine the details of one of those business expenses of yours."

Jamie eyed him uneasily as she followed him to the door.

"Which expense?"

"The '79 Bordeaux."

"You don't think it's a legitimate deduction?"

"I suspect I'll have to sample a bottle or two in order to determine that."

"Ah, I see," Jamie said sweetly. "I'll bring one up from the cellar. You can open the smoked oysters."

"Yes, ma'am."

CADE'S GOOD MOOD lasted through the dinner of tortellini, salad and crusty bread. It took two bottles of the '79 Bordeaux to determine its legitimacy as a business expense, but in the end Cade agreed with Jamie that it did, indeed, inspire creativity.

It wasn't until the dishes had been washed that Jamie began to wonder how she would handle the rest of the evening. There had been no pressure from Cade, but it would soon be time to go to bed and she had to be prepared to deal with the inevitable confrontation.

She would be polite but firm, she told herself.

She would assert her control over the situation by making certain he knew he would sleep alone.

She would maintain the friendly atmosphere without allowing it to become intimate.

Jamie was adding to the list, fine-tuning her proposed responses in preparation for the moment Cade would make his move, when she happened to step into her office. She was on her way down the hall to the bathroom at the time and simply decided to have a look inside.

It was curiosity as much as anything else that made her want to see how the place looked after Cade had been through it with a fine-tooth comb.

She discovered that it appeared almost distractingly neat. The excessively pristine condition of all the papers and records on the shelves made her wander over to the desk and glance inside a drawer. Jamie couldn't help wondering how far Cade's inclination to tidy things up had gone.

The first thing she noticed was that the envelope of keys that she kept in the top desk drawer had been opened. She always kept it sealed.

For a long moment she simply stood there, contemplating the full meaning of the small change in her office environment. She didn't have to dump the packet of keys onto the desk top to confirm what she already had begun to suspect.

The safe-deposit-box key was missing. Jamie chilled.

Hardly surprising, she thought sadly. After all, she had been fool enough to leave Cade alone in her office all morning. He'd had ample opportunity to examine the keys in the envelope. Safe-deposit-box keys were distinctive things. Easy to identify and remove from a pile. Cade wouldn't have had any trouble selecting it and pocketing it.

7

Perhaps Cade hadn't taken the key. Perhaps she had misplaced it. After all, it had been ages since she'd needed it. The last time she had actually seen the safe-deposit-box key was the day she had taken some of Miss Isabel's insurance policies down to the bank for her. That had been months ago. Isabel had used the extra key Jamie had once given her when she'd put Hadley's package in the vault.

Besides, Jamie thought desperately as she lay wide awake in Miss Isabel's bed, what good was the key without an authorized signature to go with it? You had to sign to get into the vault at the bank. Or did a smart investigative accountant with government contacts know how to get around that barrier? If Cade showed up at the bank with the proper key and some sort of government clearance he might be able to get into the box. Jamie just didn't know.

Whether or not he could pull off that trick didn't bother her nearly as much as the possibility of his having taken the key in the first place. As she lay staring at the dancing shadows on the ceiling, Jamie realized the real problem.

She didn't want to believe he was capable of that kind of deceit.

What an idiot she was. Jamie reminded herself grimly that she'd had proof enough of his unscrupulous tactics this summer. If Cade Santerre wanted something, he didn't let anything stand in his way.

But she had spent the past six weeks making excuses for him, telling herself that he'd had his reasons for what he'd done. She'd even begun to believe the evidence against Hadley, although she had been careful not to voice such traitorous thoughts to Miss Isabel. Jamie didn't even want to think about the nights she had lain awake dreaming various and sundry ways of confronting Cade again. The notion of using him to verify Hadley's death had seemed a stroke of genius at the time. The perfect way for Jamie to give Cade another chance without dragging her own pride through the mud a second time.

"He knows more about Hadley than anyone else except yourself, Miss Isabel," Jamie had reasoned when she presented the idea to her employer. "What's more, he's got all sorts of contacts with various authorities. If anyone could find out for certain what happened to your brother, it would be Cade."

"But he must hate poor Hadley!" Miss Isabel had protested.

"Not necessarily. Someone hired Cade to do a job and he did it. I think it's as simple as that. We could hire him ourselves and if he accepts, I think he'll do what we want him to do. I believe he's something of a, uh, professional in his own way."

"Do you really think he could tell us anything more about my brother?"

Jamie regarded her employer with compassion. "I think he might be able to set your mind at ease by verifying the facts."

"If I knew for certain he was dead, I could cope with the knowledge," Miss Isabel had admitted softly. "It's just that I have the oddest sensation that he is alive. I won't be able to rest until I can be sure."

"I understand."

"I always liked Mr. Santerre. He seemed like such a nice man. Even at the end he seemed to be worried about you and me. Perhaps he was just doing a job and sincerely regretted having to hurt us in the process. Do you think Mr. Santerre would accept an offer of employment from us?" There was a flicker of hope in Miss Isabel's eyes. "After everything that happened this summer?"

"I'm not sure. But I think it's possible."

Jamie hadn't known why she thought it was possible. It was just that, like her employer, she had a restless feeling of her own. It had nothing to do with Hadley Fitzgerald, but she couldn't rest until she'd satisfied herself that Cade's motives this summer hadn't been as deceitful as she'd believed. His final words as he'd left the Fitzgerald home in Santa Barbara still rang in her ears. He was waiting for her. All she had to do was to go and find him.

Now, as she faced the prospect of his having stolen the safe-deposit-box key, Jamie realized just how much hope she had been living with for the past six weeks. He must have taken it, she told herself for the fiftieth time.

But it was just barely possible she herself had lost it. There was even the off chance that Miss Isabel had taken Jamie's key instead of her own the day she had driven into Carmel with that package from Hadley.

The other possibilities didn't change the fact that the most likely one was that Cade had simply come across the key this morning while going through Jamie's desk and helped himself. He certainly had been in a good mood for the rest of the day, she thought resentfully. She didn't want to believe it was because he'd gotten what he'd wanted. This afternoon had been a romantic fantasy, a re-creation of the magic that had existed this summer. It would be unbearable if the hours of happiness had existed simply because Cade had gotten hold of the damn safe-deposit-box key.

If only she knew for certain what was going through his mind! Jamie turned onto her side, eyes wide open in the darkness. She was behaving like some sort of silly moth around a flame again; wary, but drawn toward the fire in spite of all the logical reasons why she should flee. She felt torn by the separate but powerful forces operating on her. Love and the dangerously reckless emotional commitment she felt toward Cade were at war with logic and evidence.

Desperately she tried to decide what motives Cade might have for taking the key. He could be looking for further information on Hadley, with the intention of turning it over to the authorities. He might simply be governed by his own determined curiosity and his decision to do the job for which he'd been hired. There was a relentless streak in him that Jamie knew well. And he didn't appreciate anyone standing in his path the way she had today when she'd refused him access to the box.

It was conceivable he had taken the key because he felt that whatever was in the safe-deposit box would help him complete his task. The task for which Jamie herself had hired him. There were definite risks in hiring predators. They tended to do things in their own way.

She was dwelling on that bit of wisdom when the door to the bedroom opened. There was no light from the hall to illuminate Cade but his presence in the room was unmistakable. Jamie felt it in all her senses. She lay very still in the darkness and wondered what to do next.

"Jamie?" Cade came toward the bed, moving silently across the carpet.

Jamie sensed his approach and a very primitive part of her urged her to run. Another part of her whispered that there were answers to all her questions and that the only thing that counted tonight was the chance to spend another night in Cade's arms.

"You . . . you shouldn't be here, Cade." She didn't like the tremor in her voice, but she couldn't seem to control it.

"Where else would I be?" he asked gently, dropping to one knee beside the bed and reaching out to touch the side of her face. In the shadows his tawny eyes seemed deep and beguilingly dark. "Why did you disappear tonight? Hasn't the day been good? Just like the days we used to spend in Santa Barbara. Why did you leave so abruptly? I've been sitting alone by myself wondering what I did wrong. Please, Jamie, tell me. Whatever it is, I'm sorry. I would sell my soul not to ruin things between us tonight."

Jamie swallowed, wanting to turn her lips into the palm of his hand as he stroked her. "It was late. We were up very early this morning, and I was tired."

"I'm tired, too," he murmured, his strong, blunt fingers trailing down the line of her throat. "I came to ask if I could sleep in your arms."

"Oh, Cade," she whispered starkly, "don't do this to me."

"Don't do what? Tell you that I want you? That I need you? That I've spent the past six weeks dreaming about holding you again? Jamie, I felt that I'd finally emerged from a cave last night. It's as though I've spent those six weeks in darkness. I'm so hungry for you, sweetheart. I don't want to push you. I swear I won't. Just let me crawl into bed beside you and hold you for a while."

The words were honey and fire, pouring over Jamie until she trembled. This was the man she had fallen in love with this summer and here he was, pleading for her tonight. Surely her instincts could not have been totally wrong about him. He was right: the day had been similar to one of those magic days of their summer. And she longed to recapture that magic completely.

"I wish I knew you better, Cade. I wish I knew how you think," she said wistfully. *Then, perhaps, I could learn to trust you completely again,* she added silently.

"All I can think about at the moment is you."

"And what were you thinking of earlier today?"

"You. In one way or another, you've been on my mind since the moment we met. Last night you let me make love to you. Jamie, I'll give you anything you ask if you'll let me make love to you again tonight."

She caught her breath. "The truth, Cade? Will you give me the truth?"

The hardening of his features was barely visible in the darkness, but Jamie sensed it. "What truth do you want, honey? The truth about the way I feel? That's easy enough to give you. I'm on fire for you. I want nothing more than to take that two hundred-and-ninety-seven-dollar nightgown off you and dump it on the floor."

"I thought you only wanted to crawl into bed and hold me."

"I'll take whatever you choose to give. No more, no less. I won't push you into giving me more than you can, Jamie."

"You sound very humble tonight, Cade. I don't think I've ever heard you sound quite that way before," she murmured wonderingly.

"When a man is on his knees begging a woman for anything she cares to give, he's bound to sound a little humble. Jamie, please. Trust me, sweetheart." His hand moved to her shoulder, and the heat of it sank through the fabric of the expensive French nightgown, warming Jamie.

All of her own inner warnings grew mute. Jamie realized on some distant level that she was being captivated by this new side of Cade's personality. He wasn't demanding anything from her; rather he was pleading. It gave her a sense of safety, a sense of being in command of the potentially dangerous situation.

"Cade, are you really here only because of me?"

"Don't you know the answer to that yet?" He leaned close and brushed his mouth against hers. "Please, Jamie. I want you so . . ."

The soft caress unraveled the last barriers. She wanted this man; more than that she still loved him. Jamie had learned the hard way that becoming involved with him was risky, but tonight there was something new to be considered. Cade was no longer the seducer. Tonight he was begging to be seduced.

Jamie looked up at him through her lashes and silently held out her arms.

"Jamie, honey . . . !"

He came down beside her in a fierce but carefully restrained rush. She realized he was still wearing his jeans, but that was all. When he gathered her into his arms she kissed the bare skin of his smoothly muscled chest, delighting in the hard, sure feel of him. Cade's husky groan of response sent a shiver of pleasure through Jamie.

"I've got to get out of these damn jeans," Cade muttered, his hand going to his zipper.

"I'll get you out of them." Jamie rose to her knees. "Just lie still, Cade. I'll undress you." Her own gentle aggression was a new source of excitement to her. She felt wonderfully wanton and free and uninhibited. She also felt strangely secure.

That sense of security increased as Cade meekly allowed her to tug the denims down his lean hips. His hands moved through the auburn tumble of her hair as she worked at the task of undressing him. And when she leaned forward to drop a warm, damp kiss on his thigh, the fingers in her hair went tense with masculine excitement.

"Jamie, you must know by now that you have the power to drive me crazy. Oh, God, honey, I'm burning up. I don't know how I lasted six weeks without you!"

His arousal fascinated Jamie and sent an answering response flickering through her veins. Her obvious power over him was a heady thing, leading her faster and faster down the paths of desire. When Cade's hands dropped from her hair to the flimsy fastenings of her nightgown, she barely noticed.

Her own hands moved with delicate tantalizing rhythms, gliding along Cade's hard thighs, holding him intimately until he groaned aloud. When she caught his flat male nipple between her teeth, he ground out her name in tones of aching need. With growing excitement Jamie continued to torment and tease. Glorying in the level of passion she was invoking, she gave herself up to playing the role of seductress. Finally Cade's hoarse pleas and her own desire overcame her fascination with the enthralling new game she had been playing.

"Please, Jamie. I can't take much more. Come and take me, honey. *Take me!*"

It came as a distant surprise to Jamie to discover that she was no longer wearing her nightgown. She couldn't remember taking it off. Not that it mattered. All she wanted now was to complete the lovemaking. She wanted to bring Cade to shuddering fulfillment and know that she was the cause of that fulfillment.

She flowed over his strength, fitting her soft, womanly body to his with a slow impact that made both of them suck air into their lungs. Her nails bit deeply into his shoulders as she sat boldly astride him, absorbing his power into herself. Cade's palms lifted to cup the soft weight of her breasts, and his eyes gleamed with hunger.

"You're a witch," he breathed as he felt the tight warmth of her body surrounding him. "A sweet, fiery, passionate little witch who doesn't yet know her own power. But you will after tonight, won't you, sweetheart? You'll be sure of both of us by morning."

He was right, she decided exultantly as she began to move against him. Always before he had been the one in control of the lovemaking. Cade was the one who had teased and seduced her this summer. He was the one who had taken the lead last night, sweeping her up and carrying her to bed. But tonight everything was reversed, and Jamie was suddenly and vividly aware of her own power over this man. For the first time she felt truly confident of it.

The knowledge drove her up a spiral of excitement that thrilled her. Cade was swept along with her. His hands were on Jamie's hips, holding her tautly as she guided them both to the heights. Again and again he lifted himself in obedient, eager response to her feminine demands, until with a startled cry Jamie felt herself tighten in unbearable pleasure. Then she was shivering violently, collapsing against his chest even as he called her name and shuddered deeply.

"Jamie, Jamie, my sweet Jamie . . ." The big hands moved on her body in slow, soothing motions as Cade cradled the soft, limp weight of the woman who lay along his length.

She was so full of fire and passion when she let herself go, he thought wonderingly. He would never get his fill of her. He had been needing her so, and it was infinitely reassuring to know that she needed him. It was also very satisfying to see the feminine pride and sureness come to the surface tonight. It had been touch and go there for a while this evening. He had been certain that she was relaxing around him earlier today, and dinner had been reminiscent of the evenings out they had spent in Santa Barbara. A good sign. Everything had seemed to be on track until an hour ago when her mood had suddenly altered, and she had disappeared into the bedroom.

Cade had been dismayed and annoyed. He had been so sure he was recovering all the ground he had lost: sure that when it was time to go to bed tonight she would follow him without any qualms.

But again he had miscalculated. It was astonishing to Cade that he did that so damn frequently with Jamie. He seldom made such mistakes with other people.

So once more he had been forced to take a new tack. As he had lounged broodingly in the living room, realizing that Jamie had gone to bed without him, he had finally decided to try the humble approach. Maybe if she were more confident of her power over him, she would not be so wary. It had been worth a try.

The experiment had some unexpected side effects, Cade thought in wry amusement as he toyed with a strand of Jamie's hair. He had gotten a surprising degree of satisfaction out of the sensual game. Accustomed to being the aggressor, he hadn't realized how much pleasure there was in having a woman take the lead. Maybe he'd try it again sometime. But meanwhile, he decided in unmitigated relief, his tactics appeared to have achieved a large measure of success. Aware of a pleasantly lethargic feeling of sensual satisfaction, he noted that the success was on several levels. Being around Jamie had that effect on him. He always seemed to be aware of her on more than one level at a time.

He felt Jamie stir in his arms, and he smiled down into her heavy-lidded eyes. She was cute without her glasses, he thought. The gray-green eyes were always so intent, so very serious as she tried to focus clearly.

Jamie saw the satisfied amusement in the curve of his mouth, and she hoped she hadn't played the fool once more. He had responded to her, she reminded herself. She had led and he had followed willingly, making no secret of his need. She had been in control. She must remain in control now. She must get some answers, or she would go out of her mind.

"There's something I have to know, Cade."

"Ask," he ordered easily, bending down to nuzzle the hollow of her throat.

Jamie touched his hair. He felt heavy and deeply relaxed as he lay against her. His bare feet were tangled intimately with her own. Jamie realized she was afraid to ask her question. But she had to know the truth. Closing her eyes, she forced out the words.

"Did you take the safe-deposit-box key in my desk out of its envelope this morning?" she managed in a rush.

Instantly the languid male relaxation in him vanished. Cade stiffened, lifting his head again to meet her eyes. "What did you say?"

She licked her lips nervously and opened her eyes. But Jamie refused to retreat. "You heard me. The safe-deposit-box key that was in my desk is missing. I know you wanted to get your hands on it. So I'm asking if you took it."

He looked dumbfounded at first and then, with menacing swiftness, glittering anger lit his eyes. "You're saying I stole that damn key?"

"I'm asking," she emphasized desperately, beginning to wish she'd chosen a more opportune time. Then again, how did a woman find an opportune time to ask a man if he'd stolen from her?

"You're accusing me of theft?" Cade sat up abruptly. "I don't believe it! After making love to me like that?

How the hell can you turn around and accuse me of stealing from you?"

"I'm not accusing you!" she gasped, inching toward the side of the bed. "I went into my office this evening and found the key was missing. You spent the whole morning in that office going through everything. And you had been angry because I refused to open the safe-deposit box for you."

"So you assumed that because the key is now missing, I took it!" Cade surged to his feet beside the bed and stood glowering down at her. The rage in him was plain.

"I'm just asking for the truth," Jamie countered, torn between wariness and a rising sense of anger. "Is that too much? I won't have you playing games with me, Cade. You played one too many this summer. You're working for me now, and if you won't be honest with me I'll fire you!"

"I'm working for Miss Isabel!" he shot back tightly.

"I'm in charge!"

"The hell you are! I will tell you one thing, however. I did not steal the damn key. Show me where it was supposed to be in your desk."

"Believe me, it's gone," she muttered.

"Show me!"

"All right, I will!" Furiously she slid from the bed, grabbing for her glasses and then her nightgown, which she slid quickly over her head. Then, the soft fabric floating behind her, she led the way down the hall to her desk. A few minutes later she yanked open the drawer and displayed the torn packet of keys. "See? It's gone."

"What does the key look like?" Cade dumped out the remaining keys and flipped through them quickly.

"Like a safe-deposit-box key!"

"You're sure it's not one of these?"

"Yes, I'm sure. Miss Isabel has one just like it. I can show you what it looks like, but I don't see why—"

"Let's have a look," he interrupted bluntly.

"But Cade . . . !"

"I said, let's have a look," he bit out savagely.

Jamie spun around and again led the way back down the curving hall. Throwing on the light switch in Miss Isabel's room, she went over to the delicate-looking desk and wrenched open a drawer. Quickly she rummaged around until she found the velvet-lined tray in which Miss Isabel kept important keys. Triumphantly Jamie flung open the lid. Then her eyes widened in shock.

"Oh, no," she breathed.

Cade peered into the tray. "So? Which one is the safe-deposit-box key?"

"It's gone," Jamie said weakly. Startled and dismayed, she glanced up to find Cade watching her through narrowed eyes.

"Are you accusing me of taking this one, too?" he asked dangerously.

"No . . . I, that is, you couldn't have known about this one. And you haven't had a chance to go through Miss Isabel's desk yet. Cade, I . . . I don't understand . . ."

"You have got a problem, haven't you? Both keys are missing, and you can't link me to the second theft, which means you have to ask some serious questions about the first. Careful, Jamie. You're going to get all tangled up in your own idiotic logic." He turned on his heel, scooped up his jeans from the floor and started out the door.

"Wait!" she called anxiously. "Where are you going?"

"Back to my own room," he said without bothering to glance over his shoulder. "I'll leave you alone to work on your little puzzle. Let me know if you come to any brilliant conclusions."

His scathing words echoed in Jamie's ears as she sank down onto one of the curved chairs beneath the painting of Hadley Fitzgerald. He was furious, she realized. And apparently with good reason. She sighed and looked down at the velvet tray she still clutched in one hand. All things considered, she was inclined to believe his protestations of innocence.

All things considered, of course, probably meant that she was a woman in love and would seize any excuse that exonerated her lover. But in this instance there did appear to be some fairly hard evidence in his favor. Thank God.

Mouth twisting wryly, Jamie tossed the small tray onto an end table and sat huddled in the chair, staring at nothing. She hadn't accused him of taking the key, she tried to reassure herself. She had only asked for the truth. She had grounds for questioning his actions. It wasn't as though he had never done anything to make her wonder about his scruples.

No, that wasn't completely fair. She might not have approved of his actions this summer, but she was forced to respect his reasons. Everyone had his or her own loyalties. Jamie's had been firmly with Miss Isabel and therefore, to a certain extent, with Miss Isabel's brother. Cade's loyalties, understandably enough, had been with his sister and brother-in-law. Jamie had been unlucky enough to get in the middle. And when all was said and done, Cade had tried to get her clear before the authorities moved in on Hadley. She didn't doubt his intentions. On the other hand, she didn't like being manipulated, either. Cade was a master at that sort of thing.

But she loved him. That was the bitter irony that lay at the bottom of this whole mess. She loved him and she wanted him to love her.

Could a man who was accustomed to always being in control, whose instincts about people were so good that he could analyze and assess and manipulate them with consummate ease, ever really be able to love, Jamie wondered. The next question was whether or not she could ever completely trust such a man. Even when he claimed to be acting in her best interests, he tended to do things his own way, without bothering to consult her. He certainly hadn't bothered to explain the real reason he wanted her to take an unplanned vacation with him this summer. Probably because he had known she would have felt obliged to warn Miss Isabel about what was going to happen, Jamie acknowledged.

Loyalties. She and Cade had been caught in a set of conflicting loyalties. Perhaps in his mind he'd had no choice but to handle her the way he had; not if he wanted to offer her some protection from the impending disaster. A part of her did not doubt that had been his intention.

None of that changed the facts. She had perfectly adequate reasons to be cautious around him. And she had not actually accused him of stealing the safe-deposit-box key, Jamie told herself once again. She had merely asked for the truth. He had been enraged at her lack of trust.

It was all very confusing, Jamie decided wearily, and it didn't answer the immediate questions. What had happened to the safe-deposit-box keys if Cade hadn't confiscated them? It didn't make any sense that Miss Isabel would have taken them with her on the cruise. She could have no possible use for them. Besides, she probably would have mentioned the fact to Jamie if she had decided to take them. The missing keys made that last letter from Hadley Fitzgerald more mysterious than ever.

"Hadley, what were you up to there at the last?" Jamie asked aloud, glancing at the painting. Hadley's aristocratic, gentlemanly features stared back at her. He looked every inch the successful, ethical businessman of the old school. The kind of man who took grave care of his sister's financial investments. And then promptly turned around and fleeced others without a moment's hesitation.

Jamie continued to stare at the man in the painting, remembering her nightmare in which there had seemed to be two Hadleys. The thick globs of paint and assorted artifacts that surrounded the central figure caught her attention. Miss Isabel had achieved a very interesting effect by including bits and pieces of Hadley's life in the final painting.

Jamie found herself staring even more intently at the picture, examining it in far greater detail than she'd bothered to do before. The bits and pieces that Miss Isabel had mired in the paint included a wide variety of ordinary objects.

Jamie took a deep breath and stared harder. Ordinary objects, all of them. Papers, pencils, part of a watch. There was even a small bit of metal poking out of one glob of acrylic, a bit of metal that resembled the tip of a key.

Across the hall in his own room, Cade paced the floor, scowling. She still didn't trust him. He couldn't believe it. The knowledge alternately enraged him and frightened him. Cade could understand the first emotion. The last perplexed him. He couldn't recall ever being this fundamentally nervous. He'd certainly known certain kinds of fear. There had been moments at sea that had a way of impressing upon a man that life was an extremely precarious thing, for example.

But this fear was of a different kind. It stemmed from a panicky feeling that Jamie might be slipping away from him. He had been so sure of Jamie at every step along the way, and at the last minute she always succeeded in surprising him. Why he couldn't calculate and control her actions the way he normally did other people's, Cade couldn't understand. It left him extremely worried. More than that, it left him strangely insecure. It also left him mad.

She had a lot of nerve accusing him of stealing that key. Who did she think she was to level a charge of outright dishonesty against him? And after he'd taken such care to give her a dose of feminine self-confidence this evening, too! He'd been trying so hard all day to reassure her and remind her of how good it had been between them in the summer. He'd been intent on rebuilding the relationship, and he'd thought he was making great progress until a few minutes ago.

The realization that her distrust of him went very deep was shattering. Cade sat down on the foot of the bed and locked his hands together in a fist as he thought about the subject. It was Miss Isabel's fault, he decided grimly. Somehow the older woman had established a bond of loyalty that kept getting in the way of Cade's efforts to establish his own bonds. Sweet, charming, brilliantly creative Miss Isabel. A woman who had obviously played the role of confidante, friend and mentor to Jamie for the past two years. Tough competition.

He had time, Cade reminded himself. He mustn't get panicked at this stage. Things weren't going as smoothly as he'd hoped, but he had time. Perhaps he had pushed too quickly tonight. Maybe the smart thing to do now was simply to keep at the job for which he'd been hired. *Take things one step at a time, Santerre.*

The problem, of course, was that he really had very little interest in working on the task of proving Fitzgerald dead. For one thing, he was reasonably convinced that the man had, indeed, committed suicide. A number of other men before him had done so when faced with ruin and scandal. Trying to prove otherwise seemed a pointless waste of time. Gallagher had assured him that the authorities were sure of their facts. But the job served to keep him near Jamie while he tried to unravel the twisted threads of her distrust and wariness.

There were one or two small matters he'd like to settle, just out of curiosity. He'd give a great deal to know what had been in that last package from Hadley, and he'd be very interested to discover exactly what had happened to the missing safe-deposit-box keys.

The keys. Cade focused on that element of the problem with abrupt attention. Yes, the questions surrounding them needed answers because they were so closely related to the questions concerning Fitzgerald's last letter.

The trouble was, Cade knew, he didn't stand much chance of getting his answers until he'd won Jamie's confidence again. He swore savagely. In that moment he could have strangled Hadley Fitzgerald and said some extremely unkind things to Isabel. Both of them seemed to be standing in the path that led to Jamie.

Cade got to his feet with sudden decision. First things first, he reminded himself. He had a job to do. In three long strides he reached the door and pulled it open. Then he padded softly across the hall to the room Jamie was using. Determinedly he flung open the door.

"Jamie, I know you're feeling hostile, resentful and generally uncooperative," he began roughly, "but that doesn't change the fact that I'm supposed to be working on a problem for Miss Isabel. We're going to have to cooperate with each other. And that means we're going to have to sit down and discuss a few matters."

She swung around as he entered the room, a small frown indicating the intensity with which she had been studying the portrait of Hadley Fitzgerald.

"I shouldn't have asked if you'd taken the key from my desk," she said in an odd little voice.

Cade eyed her narrowly. "That's nice to hear," he retorted sarcastically. "Mind telling me what gave you that bit of insight?"

She shook her head slowly. "You couldn't have taken that nor the one in Miss Isabel's desk, either."

"What makes you so sure?"

"I've found them."

That startled him. "Where?"

She glanced back at the picture on the wall. "Miss Isabel painted them into the portrait of Hadley. Why do you suppose she'd do that, Cade?"

Cade stared at the portrait as his analytical mind finally went to work. *About time you started thinking, Santerre,* he told himself in disgust.

"I don't think," he stated succinctly, "that there are any good reasons why she would do that. Only unpleasant ones."

8

"I WAS AFRAID you were going to say something along those lines." Jamie walked over to the closet to find a robe. The action was out of a need to give herself time to think as much as a desire to shield herself from Cade's hard, brilliant gaze. She had the awful sensation that everything was closing in on her, seeking to trap her and force her into confronting her loyalties. Soon she would be forced to make a decision that would take her perilously close to the borders of her duty to Miss Isabel. A sudden premonition assailed her that she might actually have to cross the border of loyalty entirely. She pushed the feeling aside.

"Jamie, you must realize now that we've got to find out what's in that safe-deposit box." Cade stood unyieldingly in the center of the room. It didn't take any unusual degree of perception to realize he'd made up his mind.

Jamie refused to meet his eyes as she tied the sash of the robe and walked slowly back to face the painting. "I don't understand, Cade. She finished that portrait the day before she left on the cruise. She didn't say anything about the keys or why she would make them a part of the picture. Why did she do it?"

"The answer is obvious," Cade said flatly. "She wanted to hide the keys."

"Because she didn't want anyone going into that box at the bank while she was gone," Jamie concluded bleakly. "She didn't trust me to protect her interests."

Cade moved, taking a step forward. His powerful hands settled on Jamie's shoulders. "Probably because whatever is in that letter from Hadley is very explosive or very incriminating. Jamie, this puts a whole new light on a couple of things."

"Such as?" she challenged, not liking the direction in which she saw herself heading. Unfortunately she didn't see any alternative.

"Such as your thinking you might have seen Fitzgerald at that gas station." Cade's voice hardened. "It makes me wonder just how your terrace door got opened last night. It also makes me wonder if perhaps you weren't having a bad dream or a case of double vision when you thought you saw the portrait move."

Jamie flinched. "You don't believe Hadley was in this room prowling around, do you?"

"I don't know what to believe at this point."

"Oh, my God." The thought staggered her.

"I'm not saying he was in here, but we can't take any more chances, honey. You must see that. We've got to find out what it is that Miss Isabel took such care to hide. Until we know what's in that last letter from Fitzgerald, we're working blind. That could be very dangerous."

"Dangerous! Why should it be dangerous? Hadley was never involved in anything violent. He was a businessman. Even if he was mixed up in some shady deals they were *business* deals, not . . . not armed robbery or murder, for heaven's sake!"

Cade's mouth curved sardonically. "What you don't seem to understand, my naive, loyal little personal assistant, is that when the money is as big as it was in most of Fitzgerald's deals, you can't make any assumptions about how far someone would go to protect himself. People have been known to commit murder for a good deal less than even the smallest of one of Hadley Fitzgerald's transactions."

"You're saying Hadley is a murderer?" Jamie yelped.

"Jamie, I'm not saying anything for certain at this point except that we have to find out what we're dealing with before we get caught in something dangerous. Already there's a possibility that someone might have entered your room."

"We don't know that for certain. It could have been a dream," Jamie protested.

"I want a look at the contents of that package."

"That's all you've wanted since I mentioned it. A real single-track mind. I always said you were a thorough man," she muttered, pulling free of his grasp.

Cade watched her in cold silence for a moment before saying quietly, "If you won't let me have a look at whatever it was Miss Isabel stashed in that safe-deposit box, then I'm going to have to take you away from here."

Her head came around abruptly, eyes widening in shock. "Take me away! What on earth are you talking about? This is my home!"

"This is not your home, damn it. This is your place of employment and I have reason to believe that the working conditions may no longer be safe!"

"I'm not going to let you bully me into opening that safe-deposit box for you. The only thing you want is a look at that letter so you can satisfy your own curiosity!"

"Jamie, that's not true. You once admitted I've got good instincts when it comes to figuring out other people's motives and actions. Well, those instincts are in full sail right now and they're all telling me this whole scene is very big trouble. You never knew the side of Hadley Fitzgerald I uncovered. He was an unscrupulous man who didn't care one bit whom he hurt as long as the take was big. If he hasn't actually been involved in violence up to this point, it's probably only because violence hasn't been necessary. It doesn't mean he's not capable of it."

"You're talking as if he might still be alive."

"The possibility exists. Gallagher found nothing but an empty boat, remember. People have faked suicides before."

Jamie felt the pressure increasing. The trap was closing on her. Desperately she fought to keep her options open, struggling to avoid being pushed against the wall and forced to make a choice. Hands laced tightly in her lap, she sat down at the foot of the bed and tried to think.

"Miss Isabel believes so strongly that her brother is still alive," Jamie murmured aloud. "She just couldn't accept the evidence of his death."

"Perhaps her instincts were valid," Cade offered softly. "Jamie, she hired me to find out the truth. Whatever is in that safe-deposit box might give us the truth. I have to see that package."

"If it leads you to the conclusion that Hadley is still alive, you'll go straight back to your friend Gallagher with the information, won't you?" Jamie charged.

Cade hesitated before saying cautiously, "It's the logical thing to do."

"I knew it! That would hardly be what Miss Isabel would want and you're supposed to be working on her behalf."

"Look at it this way," Cade said, trying to reason with her. "If he is still alive, presumably he has the sense to stay out of the country. He's safe as long as he does that. If I can prove he's alive and figure out where he's living, Miss Isabel can contact him."

"But what if he's not safely out of the country?" Jamie said wildly. "What if he's here? What if it was him I saw the other day?"

"And what if it was him in your room last night? Then the situation is dangerous." Cade spoke coldly and deliberately. "You must see that, Jamie. I'll have to act. If I can't settle the issue by getting into that safe-deposit box, then I'll have to take you away from here in order to be sure of your safety."

"You don't have a right to make such arbitrary decisions where I'm concerned, Cade Santerre."

"I'm your lover," he stated uncompromisingly. "I have the right to protect you."

"Even if I don't want that protection?" she mocked angrily.

"Even if you're letting your sense of duty blind you to the danger in which you're involved. Yes."

"I still don't think there's any danger," she retorted. His overpowering certainty that he had the right to dictate her actions angered her. It also made her extremely nervous. She wasn't quite sure she could fight and win if it came to all-out war with Cade.

"That's because you don't want to acknowledge the possibility. Just as you're afraid to acknowledge that I'm your lover," Cade said almost gently. "Honey, you have a real knack for ignoring the obvious when it conflicts with the way you think the world should be. But I'm not going to let you go on ignoring the obvious much longer. There are too many risks involved."

"You can't force me to leave here," she flared.

"Are you going to stand there and tell me that you'd have no qualms at all now about staying in this house alone? That you wouldn't lie awake nights wondering why Miss Isabel hid your key as well as her own in that portrait? That every time you found a door or a window open you wouldn't wonder if someone had been prowling through the house? Come on, Jamie. You're inclined to be naive, but you're not exactly stupid. Furthermore, one of your talents is a very active imagination. Do you really want me to leave you alone? Maybe I should do exactly that. Why the hell am I banging my head against a brick wall? There are easier ways to get a headache."

She stared at him and realized that it had not occurred to her that Cade would leave her alone here. Somehow she had assumed he would remain in the vicinity now that questions had been raised. She had been subconsciously counting on his presence ever since she had seen the tips of the keys buried in the portrait. Some elemental instinct had told her that he wouldn't leave her alone with the mystery. Miss Isabel's house suddenly seemed isolated and huge. It no longer seemed like a home. Homes were places that held no unanswered questions: places where a person felt comfortable and sure of herself. As long as the keys remained mired in the portrait, Jamie knew she would be neither comfortable nor sure of herself in Miss Isabel's house.

"Oh, Jamie," Cade groaned, striding forward to pull her fiercely into his arms. "Don't look so shocked. You know damn well I wouldn't leave you alone in this house. I was only saying that to make you realize this situation requires some answers. And the only way we're going to get them is by taking a look at whatever is in that last letter from Fitzgerald."

The wave of unadulterated relief that washed over Jamie irritated her. She countered it by saying gruffly into his bare chest. "You're perfectly free to leave whenever you wish."

"Do you honestly think I'd leave without taking you with me? Tell me the truth, Jamie." He stroked her slender back and she quivered a little under the touch of his strong hand.

"No," she admitted on a sigh. "You're a very stubborn, determined, thorough man. You don't walk away from problems unless you've got another plan for solving them."

"You're right," he growled into her hair. "I see you did learn something about me, after all, during those two months in Santa Barbara. Something real."

"Yes. I learned something." It was the truth.

For a long moment they stood in silence. Jamie closed her eyes, her head on Cade's shoulder and tried to analyze her alternatives. They seemed very limited. The trap was almost closed. "Oh, Cade, I don't know what to do. I feel I should protect Miss Isabel's privacy—"

"There's one aspect of this situation you haven't considered," he interrupted quietly.

"What's that?"

"The risks involved might affect Miss Isabel."

Jamie lifted her head in surprise. "Miss Isabel! How could they affect her?"

Cade buried his hands in her tousled hair. "If someone was in this room last night looking for the letter or the safe-deposit-box key, that person didn't have to be Hadley Fitzgerald."

Shock went through Jamie as she absorbed the ramifications of his words. It was frightening enough to think of Hadley prowling around; the notion of a complete stranger in the house was terrifying. "I never thought of that."

"There are a lot of possibilities you haven't considered. Probably because your mind doesn't work along devious paths," he pointed out dryly.

"The way yours does, you mean?"

He winced. "The way mine does when the occasion requires," he temporized. "One problem we have to face is the possibility that someone else might be involved here. Someone very dangerous."

"But Hadley always worked alone!"

"The thing about big business is that it's never done in a vacuum. Someone else is always involved. It could be someone he fleeced. It could be a partner we don't know about. It could be anyone."

"We don't even know if there is someone prowling around," Jamie said desperately.

"Jamie, we know that whatever is in that package from Hadley, it was serious enough that Miss Isabel felt obliged to conceal it in a place of safekeeping. She didn't even confide in you and from what I've seen, that alone is cause for speculation."

"Yes," Jamie agreed wearily. "I didn't think she and I had any secrets from each other."

"She might have thought she was protecting you in some way by not letting you know what was in the package. But by concealing it, she might have been putting herself in danger."

"Perhaps. I don't know, Cade. I just don't know."

"Think about it, honey. In the morning we've got to act." Cade continued to run his fingers through her hair, his touch soothing and reassuring. "One way or another, we've got to do something."

He was right. Jamie knew he was right, but she didn't want to admit it. "In the morning," she repeated, buying herself a few more hours of time. "In the morning I'll decide what I'm going to do."

She felt him tighten and then relax as he accepted her words. "Then that leaves us with the rest of the night," he finally whispered. "I think we both could use some sleep."

Jamie realized she was being led back toward the bed. Belatedly she understood his intention. "Oh, no, Cade Santerre. You're not going to seduce me into doing what you want in the morning," she announced bluntly.

"You want to stay alone in this room tonight?" He smiled beguilingly down at her as he stopped beside the bed and began undoing the sash of her robe.

"Not particularly, but I also don't want you using any undue influence on me, either," she said tartly. "Cade, I mean it. I've got to have time to think. I want to consider my options." She put her hands over his, stopping him from unfastening the robe. Earnestly she looked up at him, willing him to understand.

"I know, sweetheart," he said seriously. "I know. I won't touch you. But I don't want to leave you alone, either."

"Where will you sleep?" she asked cautiously, glancing around the room.

"It's a big bed. I'll stay on my side. At least admit that you'll feel more comfortable with me in the room."

"What about you? Will you feel more comfortable staying here?" she countered wryly.

"It will be a very long night. But I've spent a lot of long nights during the past six weeks. I can handle another. Get into bed, honey. I'll check the locks and get the lights." He gave her a gentle push toward the bed and started across the room toward the door.

"Cade?"

He didn't look up from where he was examining the door lock. "What is it, honey?"

"Did you really spend a lot of long nights during the past six weeks?" She didn't know what made her ask and as soon as the words were out of her mouth she wished she hadn't spoken. The question shed far too much light on how she had spent her own nights during the past month and a half. Her pride protested violently.

"Lady, I spent more hours pacing the *Loophole*'s deck than I want to count." He shoved home the door's bolt with totally unnecessary force. Then he flipped the light switch.

Nestled in the shadows on her side of the bed, Jamie wondered if she was being naive and foolishly romantic to believe him.

CADE WAITED for Jamie's decision the next morning with the patience of a hunter. He knew he'd used the one lure Jamie would not be able to ignore. He had deliberately implied that the secret in the safe-deposit box might be a threat to Miss Isabel. The chance that her employer could be in potential jeopardy should give Jamie the final rationale she needed to unlock the bank box.

The thing was, he admitted to himself as he silently sipped coffee and munched peanut-butter toast, the lure wasn't exactly a fake. There was valid reason to suspect that the contents of Fitzgerald's letter were dangerous, both to Miss Isabel and to Jamie. Miss Isabel would not have taken such pains to hide the keys otherwise. He knew people and he knew motives. He'd had two months in the Fitzgerald household this summer, and he'd learned a lot about Miss Isabel. In spite of her flamboyantly artistic temperament, the older woman would not have hidden the keys in the painting unless she was very nervous about the contents of the safe-deposit box.

Cade was trying to manipulate Jamie again, and he knew it. But there was no other option this time. He had to protect her and that meant finding out the answer to the puzzle the keys represented. Damn it, none of the manipulation would be necessary if she would just trust him! Couldn't she see that he was only trying to take care of her?

Out of the corner of his eye Cade watched Jamie munch her own toast, her expression troubled and deeply thoughtful. Soon, he decided. She would let him know her decision very soon. She was on the brink. The minutes ticked past on the kitchen clock.

"All right," she finally said calmly, setting down her slice of toast. "If we can get the keys out of the painting, I'll take a look inside the safe-deposit box."

"Thank you, Jamie. It's for the best." Cade drew a deep breath, trying to conceal his sense of relief. "You're doing this for Miss Isabel's sake as well as your own, you know."

"I have a feeling I'm doing this because you pushed me into it," she tossed back bluntly.

Cade looked at her. "I'm not forcing you to open the box."

"You dragged Miss Isabel's name into this so that I'd be able to tell myself I was still looking after her interests, didn't you?" She eyed him with speculation.

Briefly startled by her perception, Cade shook his head ruefully. "Maybe. But the reasoning holds. She could be in danger. She wouldn't have hidden those keys if she hadn't been worried about something, Jamie."

"I know."

"Jamie, I'm doing this for your own good."

She shot him a disgusted glance. "Don't you know that's just about the worst reason in the whole world to do something for anybody?"

Cade sighed. "Is it? I'm not used to deliberately doing things that are for someone else's good. Maybe I haven't handled it well."

Jamie grinned unexpectedly. "But you mean well, don't you, Cade? That's the only reason I'm doing this, you know. I've decided that although you are shrewd, manipulative and downright overbearing on occasion, I think you really do mean well this time."

"Your gratitude and praise are going to my head," he grumbled, reaching for his coffee.

"Well, don't let yourself feel too terribly giddy because I've got news for you. We're going to do this my way." Jamie took a certain satisfaction in the manner in which he received that bit of information.

"You want to run that by me again?" he asked coolly, watching her intently.

"Sure," she responded with a carelessness she was far from feeling. "We will not carry out this little project together. I will go into the safe-deposit box and I will take a look at the letter from Hadley. I will then tell you what I think you should know."

There was a rather menacing silence before Cade repeated far too softly, "You will tell me what you think I should know?"

She nodded once with just a hint of defiance. "I have been authorized to handle Miss Isabel's private affairs and make decisions regarding them. Furthermore, that safe-deposit box belongs to me, even though I never use it. Anyway you slice it, this is my job, Cade. Not yours. I did a lot of thinking about it last night and my decision is made. We do it my way or not at all."

Cade drew a deep breath before saying carefully, "Jamie, I think we had better discuss this."

She smiled brilliantly, feeling on top of the situation once more. "There is nothing to discuss."

"What would it take to make you trust me completely again?" he demanded with a harshness generated by frustration. "The way you trusted me this past summer? Just tell me, Jamie! Do I have to get down on my hands and knees and beg? Walk on coals? Sell my soul? Tell me what it will take, damn it!"

Jamie's brilliant smile faded. "We'd better get started. It's a long drive into Carmel and we still have to decide how to get the keys out of the painting."

Cade swore softly. "With a knife."

"I hate having to harm a piece of Miss Isabel's work," Jamie said worriedly.

"I'll take the responsibility."

"It won't bother you at all, will it? Getting answers is all that concerns you."

He threw her a savage glance as he got to his feet. Then he strode around the kitchen counter and yanked open a cutlery drawer. Selecting one of Miss Isabel's finest knives, he headed for the bedroom without a word.

Belatedly Jamie scrambled off her stool and followed. She was involved in this, and regardless of what Cade said about taking responsibility, there was no way she could abdicate her own role in that respect. She arrived in the bedroom doorway in time to see Cade insert the knife into the painting as if he were filleting a fish. Jamie winced at the cool act of destruction. It was all over very quickly: neat and clean, if somehow shocking. Hadley Fitzgerald continued to gaze seriously out into the room, oblivious to the secrets that had just been exposed.

Silently Cade held up a small paint-encrusted plastic sandwich bag. The two keys were inside. Then he headed down the hall, pausing impatiently while Jamie collected her oversize shoulder bag. As he walked through the kitchen, Cade casually tossed the knife onto the counter.

He remained silent until he had Jamie ensconced in the Mazda and they were headed down the winding road toward Carmel. When he did speak his voice was cool and detached, almost clinical. A change had come over him since he'd freed the keys from the painting. He was very definitely all business.

"Since you won't let me look over your shoulder while you're going through the contents of that safe-deposit box, I want your promise to describe whatever it is as completely as possible. I need data, Jamie, if I'm ever going to figure this out. I must have a complete report on what you find. Do you understand?"

Uneasily Jamie nodded, realizing that he was right. "I understand."

"It would be a great relief to know that for a fact," he muttered.

Jamie said nothing in response, moodily watching the clouds that were gathering out at sea. There would be rain this afternoon, she thought distractedly.

In Carmel Cade parked the Mazda between a Mercedes and a Ferrari near the bank and escorted Jamie inside. At the gate to the safe-deposit vault he watched as she dutifully signed in and held out her key to the attendant. The bank clerk smiled and nodded and led her inside the steel-lined room. Nervously Jamie glanced back at Cade.

"Just be sure you look at every detail," he advised grimly.

Jamie nodded and quickly turned away. Inside the vault the clerk handed her the box and directed her to a private little cubicle.

"Ring the bell when you're finished. I'll put the box away for you," the woman said cheerfully and closed the door.

Alone at last, Jamie thought ruefully and flipped open the lid of the box. She sat down at the single chair that had been provided and pulled out the letter from Hadley Fitzgerald. As she did so she disturbed a couple of small flat containers that were nestled deep inside the steel box. Curiously she reached out and picked one up, recognizing it by its shape. "Cade," she whispered to herself, "your famous instincts may be right. We may, indeed, have trouble."

For a long time Jamie sat staring at the small packages of recording tapes, wondering what Hadley had concealed on them. She read the letter to Miss Isabel a half-dozen times, and then she made up her mind. The trap she had sensed closing in around her seemed to shut just a little tighter. Instinct told her that soon there would be no room at all in which to maneuver. She would have to make a choice. Perhaps, she thought uneasily, she had made that choice when she had decided to contact Cade again. With a sigh Jamie removed the tapes and the letter, closed the box and rang for the attendant.

Cade waited with barely concealed impatience outside the little gate. When she came through he swung around quickly, his eyes going instantly to the letter and the tapes in her hand.

"Tapes?" he asked roughly.

Jamie nodded, not offering them to him. She dropped the packages of tapes into her oversize leather shoulder bag. "The letter doesn't say what's on them, only that Miss Isabel is to hide them."

"What's the date on the letter?" Cade demanded as he guided her out of the bank.

Jamie could feel the tension in him. The predator was very close to the prey, requiring enormous restraint for Cade not to simply pounce. She had seen the glittering anticipation in his eyes when she'd emerged from the cubicle with the contents of the safe-deposit box in her hand. No doubt he'd been very much afraid she would put them back in the vault.

"It's dated the twenty-first."

"The day before Hadley took the boat and disappeared," Cade muttered thoughtfully as he seated her in the Mazda. He closed the door and walked around the hood of the car to get in on the driver's side.

"The day you first made love to me," Jamie whispered to herself.

She watched him move lithely around the car and slide into the driver's seat. Apparently the personal significance of the date did not affect Cade one way or the other. He was busy sinking his teeth into the problem.

"So the letter by itself doesn't prove whether or not Fitzgerald's still alive." He expertly slid the Mazda out of the parking slot.

"No."

"We'll have to get a tape player so we can listen to what's on those tapes," he mused as he carefully negotiated the narrow Carmel street. It was Friday, and the weekend visitors were already arriving in droves to inundate the small village. Cars and pedestrians crowded the little streets. Behind the Mazda a plain dark Buick with heavily tinted windows struggled through the same throng.

"Miss Isabel has a machine," Jamie offered slowly. She fingered the strap of her bag as it lay in her lap, not at all certain about what to do next. "Though I'm not sure we have any right to listen to them, Cade."

"Jamie, the tapes are no different than the letter in that sense. Just another form of communication. We'll have to listen to them if we're going to figure out this mess."

"I suppose I could play them and then tell you if there's anything useful on them," she said slowly.

Cade's fingers tightened so severely on the wheel that his knuckles went white. But his voice was low and calm. "Yes," he agreed. "We can do it that way. It's a waste of time but we can do it. Given your lack of trust in me, I suppose it's the only alternative."

Jamie stared out the window, wondering if it was really pain she thought she heard in his words. She must make him understand that while her own trust in him was growing she was still torn by her sense of loyalty to her employer. Cade was beginning to demand that she make choices: choices that were dangerous and emotionally wrenching. "It's not a question of trust. Not exactly," she defended herself. "It's a matter of obligation to Miss Isabel. Can't you understand that, Cade?"

"It's a matter of trust," he countered bleakly. "Don't try to label it anything else."

The bitterness in his words lashed at her. *Oh, Cade,* Jamie thought, *you've got just about all I have to give. Do you need my complete and total loyalty, too?*

The clouds had grown heavy by the time Cade and Jamie reached the highway. Rain started before they had gone more than a couple of miles along the coastal road. The precipitation was driven by a sharp wind and drastically reduced visibility. Cade prudently slowed the Mazda and paid attention to his driving. He turned on the lights at about the same time the driver in the car behind turned on his. Cade glanced irritably into the rearview mirror.

"That's all I need in weather like this. A tailgater."

Automatically Jamie glanced back. The dark car was following rather close. "Probably scared to death on this road in this rain. Maybe he's using your taillights to navigate."

"Not a cheerful thought," Cade gritted.

Jamie slanted her companion an expressive glance. "You're in a lousy mood today, you know that?"

"I'm aware of it." Cade hit a fairly straight stretch of road and accelerated. The dark car picked up speed, too.

On the right the cliffs fell away to a wind-whipped surf. Jamie caught glimpses of the water foaming on the rocks as the rain swirled around the car. It was a spectacular sight, primeval and raw. Up ahead the short stretch of straight two-lane highway disappeared abruptly around a hairpin curve. Cade reluctantly began to ease off the accelerator.

"Son of a—" The rough, clipped oath was bitten off savagely as Cade glanced once again into the rearview mirror. "The fool's going to try to pass!"

Startled at the act of folly, Jamie swung her head around in time to see the dark car maneuver out into the opposite lane and pick up speed with alarming suddenness. "You know, Cade, there's something familiar... Oh, my God!" Her breath caught as she realized what was about to happen.

"Cade, he's going to hit us!"

The warning came almost simultaneously with the impact. The dark car brushed the Mazda's side heavily and then seemed to bounce away. Cade was already reacting. He fought the dangerous curve and the protesting Mazda with a fierce grip on the wheel and ruthless footwork on the brakes and the accelerator.

The heavy dark car sideswiped the Mazda again, nearly sending it into the guardrail. Tires screeched and rubber burned as the battle for control of the little sports car was played out. The hairpin curve seemed to jackknife in front of Jamie's eyes, and for a timeless instant she was certain the next stop would be the bottom of the cliff. There was the violent sound of metal on metal as the Mazda scraped the rail.

Dimly aware that the dark car had surged ahead and was already out of sight around the sharp corner, Jamie dug her nails into the leather of her purse and wished she could squeeze shut her eyes. For some reason the small physical act seemed impossible. She was fated to watch the approaching doom through wide open eyes.

The world seemed to spin around her as Cade hauled the Mazda back from the brink and forced it into a twisting turn. A few seconds later the car came to a halt with nerve-shattering abruptness. Jamie finally managed to blink. She found herself staring at the face of the mountain instead of the sea. The Mazda seemed to be tilted at a precarious angle, but at least it wasn't hanging over a sheer drop. Cade had swung it into the opposite lane and brought it to a stop against the rocky cliff. Jamie started to speak, swallowed and tried again.

"I have the oddest feeling this isn't going to do anything to improve your mood," she managed in an unnaturally thin voice.

"Full marks for your intuition," Cade growled. He flexed his hands on the steering wheel and looked at Jamie. His eyes moved quickly over her. "Are you all right?"

She nodded, wishing her pulse would slow. "Thanks to your driving. By any reasonable assessment of the situation we should be at the bottom of the cliff right now, trying to swim! My God, Cade, what on earth was that other driver thinking of?"

"An interesting question." Cade unlatched the door and pushed it open. "If I ever get my hands on him, I'll get an answer."

Jamie heard the ruthless fury in his cold words and shivered. "Where are you going, Cade?"

"We'll never get the car out of this ditch by ourselves. We'll have to walk. We're only a couple of miles from Miss Isabel's house. Get your jacket on, Jamie. The sooner we get started, the sooner we'll get there."

"I wish I'd brought an umbrella," Jamie groaned, trying to open her own door. It was impossible. The angle at which the car had come to rest prevented the door from opening more than a couple of inches.

"You'll have to get out on my side." Cade's hair was already soaked as he bent down to take her huge purse so that she could scramble out over the driver's seat.

Jamie handed the encumbering purse to him before she quite realized what she was doing. It was only as she saw his strong fingers close around the bag containing the tapes that it occurred to her it might be very difficult to regain possession.

"Uh, Cade . . . ?"

"Hurry up, Jamie. I'm wet and I'm mad, and as you have already noted, I am not in the best of moods. This isn't a good time to bring up the subject of trust, loyalty and obligation. You'll get your damn purse back as soon as you get out of the car. You think I want to hike two miles carrying this forty-pound sucker?"

"Probably not," she agreed as she found her footing in the mud. "I . . . I wasn't accusing you of trying to take it," she began uncertainly.

"Jamie, right now, the less said, the better. For both of us."

It was a long, wet and thoroughly miserable walk. The rain made Jamie's glasses more of a hindrance than a help. She removed them and stuck them into her purse. There were several points along the way when Jamie wished devoutly that it was Cade and not herself carting the heavy shoulder bag, but she could hardly ask for help after that little scene at the car. By the time they reached the driveway of Miss Isabel's house, she felt as though the purse really did weigh forty pounds.

"I've been hallucinating about a hot shower and a warm brandy for the past half hour," Jamie said as she slogged toward the front door, head down against the driving rain.

"You're going to have to go on dreaming a while longer," Cade declared softly as he came to an unexpected halt. His hands closed over Jamie's shoulder, bringing her to a stop.

Annoyed, Jamie squinted up at him through the pouring rain. "What on earth are you talking about?"

"We've got company."

Jamie turned her head, able to perceive that there were lights on inside the house. She knew she had turned them off before leaving earlier in the day. "Good heavens! Who in the world could be inside? Burglars?"

"I'm not sure, but I have a hunch it's not your ordinary, run-of-the-mill burglar. Not today and not with the way my luck has been running lately."

"You and your instincts," Jamie muttered, trying to peer through the rain-dark afternoon. She reached inside her purse for her glasses and succeeded in shoving them onto her nose just as the front door opened. The sight of the familiar silver-haired figure standing on the threshold sent a jolt of alarm along Jamie's senses.

"Miss Isabel!" she gasped.

9

"JAMIE, WAIT!" Cade caught hold of her shoulder just as Jamie lifted her arm to wave to Miss Isabel. "Listen to me before you dash over there."

The harsh urgency in his words stopped Jamie in her tracks. Through rain-streaked lenses she stared at him, waiting impatiently for whatever it was he felt obliged to say. Miss Isabel stood several yards away, sheltered in the doorway.

"What is it now, Cade? Can't it wait until we're in the house? I'm soaked to the skin, and I can't wait to ask Miss Isabel what happened to bring her home early from the cruise. Maybe she discovered something important about Hadley. Or maybe she got ill."

He held her full attention with the cold hard gold in his eyes. Cade's face was set in steel, and the strong hand on her shoulder conveyed the overwhelming volume of his will. "Jamie, I'm going to ask something of you. Something crucial. It's for your sake as well as mine, although I don't expect you'll believe me."

"Cade, I'm not in the mood for heavy drama. What are you trying to say?"

"I want you to promise me you won't tell Miss Isabel you've got those tapes in your purse. Let me handle that part of the story."

"But, Cade, that's ridiculous! Why shouldn't I tell her? They belong to her. After all, they're from her brother."

"I'm not going to steal them from her, I'm just trying to buy some time!"

"Time for what?" Jamie flared, moving uneasily under the hard pressure of his hand. She sensed the determination in him, and knew he was deadly serious.

"Time to figure out what in hell is going on," he snapped. "Jamie, that car that sideswiped us back there on the highway . . ."

"What about it?" she asked, frowning.

"I think the timing of that accident was rather coincidental. It didn't take place until after we had those tapes in our possession."

"Cade, that's absurd." But her eyes narrowed as she took in the full implications of his words. She remembered thinking just before the accident that there had been something familiar about the plain dark Buick. Was it the car she had seen at the gas station, she wondered. The one that had been driven by the man who resembled Hadley Fitzgerald?

"I also think that whatever is on those tapes is dangerous. If it weren't, Fitzgerald wouldn't have asked Miss Isabel to hide them. Jamie, I haven't got time to convince you logically of what I'm saying. All I can tell you is that every instinct I've got is screaming. I'm going to have to ask you to trust me. I know that's demanding a lot under the circumstances—"

"Yes, it is, Cade," she interrupted coolly.

His mouth tightened. "Damn it, woman, I love you and I think that once you're through punishing both of us for what happened this summer, you'll realize you love me. That relationship gives me the right to make a few demands, especially when your life may be at stake!"

Jamie's mouth fell open. She closed it immediately when she tasted rain. Behind the lenses of her glasses her eyes widened in astonishment. "You love me?" she squeaked. Her brain ignored the rest of his statement, focusing entirely on the first few words. She couldn't believe he'd said them. "You love me," she whispered wonderingly.

He looked down at her rain-drenched face. "Why in hell do you think I agreed to get involved with Miss Isabel's screwy hunt for her brother? Why would I be putting up with your temperamental moods and your notions of revenge if I didn't love you? For God's sake, Jamie, this isn't the time to discuss that subject in detail, either. You're going to have to trust me."

Vividly aware of Miss Isabel waiting in the doorway, Jamie knew she couldn't stand around in the rain asking for explanations and protestations of love. There would be time for that later. Cade was right. At the moment she had to make a decision. She gripped the leather bag more fiercely as she tried to search his rain-streaked face for the truth.

"I'll . . . I'll agree to follow your lead until I decide for certain what's going on," she temporized.

Cade wanted to shake her. Couldn't she see the danger they were in? There was no time to go over all the details for her benefit. No time to add up the various and sundry little things that went together to form an alarming pattern. He was going on instinct and a view of the world that was far more cynical than Jamie's. After his investigations this summer he knew for a fact just how deeply involved in criminal activity Hadley Fitzgerald had been. Whatever was on those tapes had to be incriminating and therefore dangerous.

Jamie, however, functioned under an entirely different view of the universe, one that inclined toward the benefit of the doubt until proven otherwise. As far as she was concerned, Cade had given up his right to that benefit of a doubt by his actions this summer. Miss Isabel, on the other hand, had two full years of friendship going for her. She had done nothing to crush Jamie's belief in her integrity the way Cade knew he had.

Cade felt a devastating wave of helplessness. It was too late to try to reason with Jamie. He could only hope that her underlying feelings for him would surface in this moment of crisis. On top of that hope, he was counting on love being a stronger bond than the loyalty she felt toward Miss Isabel.

Cade was all too well aware that he was pinning a great deal on a very insubstantial and unproven foundation. He had, after all, no proof that Jamie loved him. On top of that he had ample proof that she distrusted him. The fact that her life might depend on the outcome of her decision only served to infuriate him because it reinforced his sense of helplessness.

"Jamie, please trust me," he heard himself say, but he didn't know if she heard him. She was already turning away and starting toward the house. Unable to do anything else, Cade followed.

"Miss Isabel! What on earth are you doing here? Why aren't you in Samoa? What happened?" Jamie's questions bubbled over as she hurried to get under the shelter of the eaves. "Watch out," she added quickly as Miss Isabel started to hug her, "I'm soaking wet!"

"So I see. And Cade is also. Whatever made you two decide to take a walk in this weather?" Miss Isabel stepped back into the hall and held the door.

"It's a long story," Cade began calmly as he bent down to remove his mud-splattered shoes. "And before we start explanations, I think Jamie and I had better have a shower and get into some warm clothes."

"Yes, of course," Miss Isabel agreed instantly. "Run along, both of you, and I'll fix some hot tea."

"But, Miss Isabel, what happened?" Jamie asked as Cade took her arm and started her down the hall to the bedrooms.

Miss Isabel smiled, her eyes animated. "Mine is a long story, too, dear. Suffice it to say that I've found Hadley. Or perhaps I should say he found me."

"Hadley!" Jamie gasped. "He's alive?"

"I told you I had a feeling he was," Miss Isabel said. "Now hurry up with that shower. I'll see you in the kitchen."

Jamie lifted a perplexed face to Cade as he strode down the hall with her in tow. "Cade, she says he's alive!"

"I heard."

"What in the world is going on?" Jamie wondered aloud, feeling dazed by the turn of events.

"Let me have the tapes, Jamie," Cade ordered softly as he pushed open the door to the bedroom he had been using.

"Why? What are you going to do with them?"

"Nothing brilliantly clever, unfortunately. I just thought I'd try to make them a little more inaccessible than they are at the moment." His eyes never leaving hers, Cade shut the bedroom door and reached for the leather bag.

For a wary moment Jamie hesitated. Then slowly, reluctantly she released the purse. Without a word Cade unzipped it, removed the packages of tapes and dumped them into the big cloisonné jar.

"What good will that do?" Jamie asked bewilderedly.

"You never know. Sometimes it pays to have something with which to bargain," Cade said cryptically. He gave her a level glance. "Of course, bargaining doesn't do much good if one party insists on giving away the objects with which one is negotiating. You might keep that in mind later, Jamie."

"I don't understand what you're talking about," she protested.

"You will soon enough," he said, sighing. "Get into the shower, Jamie."

"My clothes . . ."

"I'll dig some out and leave them in the dressing room."

"What about you? You need a shower, too," she pointed out gently.

"I'll skip the shower and use a towel." His mouth crooked wryly. "What's the matter? Afraid I was going to insist on sharing? You don't have to worry about that today. I've got other things on my mind." He peeled off his wet shirt.

Jamie eyed him for a moment, and then the light dawned. "You're going to stand guard out here, aren't you?"

"Let's just say I don't think this is a good time for both of us to be playing water games."

"Cade, you can't possibly believe Miss Isabel is plotting to . . . to harm us!"

"Jamie, I don't know what to believe," Cade said wearily. "I only know we've got to take a few precautions until we get this mess sorted out. Now go take your shower."

She turned to obey and then paused once more to ask tremulously, "Cade, did you mean what you said out there? Do you really love me?"

"I love you, Jamie."

Jamie's heart sang with hope. "Oh, Cade, when did you first realize it? This past summer or during those six weeks we were apart?" An instant later she knew her eagerness was a mistake.

"For crying out loud, Jamie, we've got a serious situation on our hands in case you haven't noticed," Cade snapped. "This is hardly the time for that sort of discussion!"

Jamie bit her lip. "You don't sound like a man in love."

"Go take your shower." Cade turned away and began to unzip the wet jeans he was wearing. His tension was plain in the taut lines of his bare shoulders.

Jamie stepped into the bathroom and closed the door behind her, wondering at her curious sense of hovering again on the edge of a precipice. It was the unknowns that plagued her, she thought as she stepped under the hot shower. For a few moments she had truly believed Cade loved her. Now she was not so sure. He was very intent on gaining her cooperation at the moment. He was a very perceptive man in some respects and he might have realized that the surest way of gaining her allegiance was to claim he loved her. If he had come to realize that she loved him, he would know what a powerful tool he held. *Please*, she thought desperately, *please Cade, don't use my love to try and control me. I can handle anything else, but not that.*

Out in the other room Cade finished drying himself, pulled on fresh clothes and paced the floor, questioning his approach to the problem he faced. He had been a fool to let those six weeks go by without contacting Jamie. He realized that now. At the time it had seemed the best way to handle her. But those six weeks had apparently given her plenty of opportunity to question him and his motives, rather than to make her long for him.

Bad timing and bad planning. Cade was disgusted with himself. But everything had been like that around Jamie. Nothing seemed to go right. Now he was trapped, forced to rely on her very weak trust in him.

While Miss Isabel seemed to enjoy unlimited loyalty from Jamie.

He whirled too abruptly when Jamie emerged from the bathroom, dressed in the jeans and red knit top he had selected for her. Instantly he realized that his quick movement came across as somehow menacing. Cade swore silently and forced himself to exert the full measure of his self-control.

"Ready? Remember, I'm not saying that Miss Isabel is a criminal . . ."

"I should hope not!"

"All I'm asking," Cade continued doggedly, "is that you let me take the lead. Let me be the one to give her information. Just back me up, okay?"

Jamie nodded unwillingly, wishing desperately that she could read his mind. Then she started toward the door.

Miss Isabel was waiting in the kitchen, busying herself with the teakettle. She looked up as Jamie and Cade walked into the warm, cozy room. "Ah, there you are. You look much better now. Not like a couple of drowned rats. Here, have some tea." She poured into the two cups she had set out. The atmosphere in the room was charming and gracious. Jamie began to relax. Cade's sense of urgency had really begun to affect her, she realized.

"Tell us what happened, Miss Isabel," Jamie said, sliding onto a stool beside Cade. The knife Cade had used earlier to pry the keys out of the painting was still lying on the counter where he had tossed it. Jamie swallowed a guilty feeling as she saw the flecks of paint on the blade. She wondered if Miss Isabel had noticed the damaged painting in the bedroom. Apparently not, or probably she would have already said something about it. "How did Hadley find you?"

"He was waiting in Tahiti. Met me at the ship when we docked. I was never so astounded in my entire life!"

"How did he know where to find you?"

"Oh, that was simple enough. He contacted his lawyer a week ago and found out from him that I had left on the cruise a week earlier. It wasn't hard to get the ship's itinerary." Miss Isabel poured herself a cup of tea.

"Where is he now?" Cade asked calmly.

"Still out of the country. He doesn't dare come back until he can prove his innocence." Miss Isabel turned bright, excited eyes on Jamie. "Remember that package that was waiting for me when we got back from Santa Barbara?"

Jamie swallowed as more guilt assailed her. "Yes," she managed in a reasonably steady voice. Beside her she felt Cade's increasing tension.

"Well, that package contains the proof of Hadley's innocence," Miss Isabel declared triumphantly. She went on in a rush. "We have to get it out of the bank vault and play the tapes for that Mr. Gallagher person. Hadley says everything will be all right once Gallagher understands who was really behind the land-fraud deals. Hadley was just a pawn. He didn't realize what was going on behind the scenes, you see. He had simply agreed to broker the deals. Naturally he assumed things were legitimate. But the people who had set it all up let him take the blame when things went wrong. Hadley was forced to run."

"I see," Jamie said slowly, trying to think. Now was the time. She had to tell Miss Isabel she already had the tapes. Jamie realized the only thing that was preventing her from blurting out the full truth was Cade's silent command. She could feel him willing her not to say the words, and for the life of her, Jamie found herself keeping her mouth shut.

"Miss Isabel," Cade began quietly, "I think you should know that Jamie and I have already been to the bank."

Miss Isabel looked startled. "But the keys . . ."

"We found the keys in the painting. I convinced Jamie that it was necessary to see what was in the package from your brother."

Miss Isabel turned apologetic eyes on Jamie. "Forgive me for hiding your keys, my dear. At the time I thought it was for the best. I had no idea what was in that package, you see, and I wanted to protect you."

Jamie exhaled on a sigh of relief and gratitude. Cade had decided not to lie to Miss Isabel. She started to smile reassuringly at her employer, but the expression faded as Cade went on coolly.

"We picked up the tapes, but as yet we haven't played them."

"Where are they?" Miss Isabel demanded, some of her gracious manner fading as she turned to gaze intently at Cade.

"In a safe place," Cade told her neutrally.

"I don't understand." The older woman's brow furrowed.

"I hid them," Cade said simply. "You see there was an accident on the way back from the bank this afternoon."

"An accident!" Miss Isabel looked thunderstruck. "Is that why you two were walking? Something happened to your car?"

"We were sideswiped by another car," Jamie put in quickly. "Almost sent us off the road into the ocean. Fortunately Cade managed to hold things together. We ended up in a ditch instead of the sea."

"Good heavens!"

"It was a little grim for a few minutes," Cade said dryly. "And afterward I was left wondering if the incident hadn't been deliberate. As Jamie can tell you, I tend to take a rather cynical view of life."

"But who would do such a thing deliberately?" Miss Isabel asked.

"Someone who wanted the tapes." Cade let the words hang in the air for a moment before adding smoothly, "Perhaps the people your brother claims framed him."

Jamie's head came around, her eyes as startled as Miss Isabel's. "Cade, do you really think . . . ?"

"I don't know what to think at this point," Cade said patiently, his eyes on Miss Isabel. "I'm trying to put all the pieces of the puzzle together but I'm still missing a few answers."

Some of the animation left Miss Isabel's face. "Where did you hide the tapes?"

"I stuffed them into a plastic sack and left them under a rock about halfway between here and the spot where the Mazda got shoved off the road," Cade said quite casually. "If that accident had been deliberate, the wrong people might have been waiting for us here, you see. I didn't want to take any chances." He didn't even glance at Jamie, who went very still as she listened to the outright lie.

"Oh, my God," Miss Isabel whispered, looking stricken. "We've got to get them!"

"They'll be safe," Cade soothed. "The plastic bag will protect them from the moisture."

"No, you don't understand," Miss Isabel said agitatedly.

Jamie couldn't abide her employer's obvious distress. "Miss Isabel, stop worrying. The tapes are safe, believe me. You said your brother wants them played for Gallagher and his team. Well, we'll do exactly that. We'll get them and take them down to L.A. and play them for Gallagher. Won't we, Cade?" she added deliberately.

Cade shrugged easily. "Sounds like a logical plan to me."

Miss Isabel shook her head quickly. "Hadley wants me to get them and take them to him. He wants to be the one to go to Gallagher. Don't you see? That way there won't be any question of his innocence. He can interpret them properly to the authorities. If someone else is after those tapes we've got to move quickly. It would be terrible if the others discovered them first!"

"No one will find them, Miss Isabel," Cade told her.

She studied his calm, controlled face for a long moment and then appeared to reach a decision. She turned to Jamie.

"Jamie, dear, I'm afraid I must insist that you fetch the tapes," Miss Isabel ordered very softly. "We can go and get them together."

"No," Cade interrupted quietly. "Jamie's not going to get the tapes for you."

Jamie tensed, sensing that the trap in which she had found herself was finally about to close completely. She knew she was going to be forced to choose between her duty to Miss Isabel and her trust in Cade.

"Miss Isabel, Cade thinks it would be dangerous for you to have the tapes. If someone is out to get them then whoever has them is in jeopardy," Jamie argued desperately, seeking a way to resolve the dilemma without being forced to hurt Miss Isabel.

"You must trust me to know what's best, Jamie," Miss Isabel told her gently. "I'm the one who's seen Hadley. I know how he wants this matter handled. Now go get your rain coat, dear. We must hurry."

Jamie turned appealing eyes on Cade, but there was no help from that quarter. "Everyone around here seems to be acting in my best interests," she observed dryly.

"Don't move, Jamie. The tapes are safe enough for the moment, and I don't want you near them."

Miss Isabel frowned. "Jamie, I really must insist. You are, after all, my employee, and I'm afraid that if necessary I'll have to make this request an order. Please don't forget that the tapes are rightfully mine."

"I know, Miss Isabel, but if they're dangerous—"

"They're dangerous," Cade interrupted coldly. "Believe me. If you turn them over to Miss Isabel, all of us will be in danger."

"Cade!"

"What are you talking about, Cade?" Miss Isabel demanded.

"Just that right now the location of the tapes is the only bargaining point Jamie and I've got. I intend to hang on to it for both our sakes. I'm not going to let her risk her neck by turning them over to you."

"Risk my neck!" Jamie exclaimed. "What *are* you talking about, Cade? You said it was Miss Isabel you were trying to protect."

"I'm trying to protect all of us, but I'm not getting a hell of a lot of cooperation." Cade reached out and caught hold of her chin, forcing her to face him. Tawny eyes burned down into her anxious gaze. "I mean it, Jamie. If you care about what happens to yourself, to me or even to Miss Isabel, you will do as I say."

She had to make a choice. In that moment Jamie hated both Miss Isabel and Cade for forcing her into the painful decision. She had seen this moment bearing down on her for a long while, and now that it was here she was strangely furious. She had striven to avoid having to take this risk, but she should have known that there was no way around it. For a timeless moment she studied Cade's implacable gaze, and then she turned wearily to her employer. The reason she had always feared finding herself up against the wall was because deep down she had known what her choice would be. The trap had closed. She loved Cade, and now she had to trust him. Completely. She was being forced to make a final statement about her loyalties and her priorities. Faced with no other alternative, Jamie made the only choice she could. She had to back her lover.

"I'm sorry, Miss Isabel, but I think Cade is right. The tapes are dangerous, and we'd better let him handle them. He'll know what to do with them." Beside her she felt Cade inhale deeply, as though he had just finished a long race. She was vaguely astounded that he had been so tense about her decision.

"This is ridiculous!" Miss Isabel bit out. "Jamie, you can't do this. You work for me! We're friends. You have to do as I say."

"You're quite right," declared a cultivated male voice from behind Jamie. "This is ridiculous. I told you your way wasn't going to work, Isabel. I know Cade Santerre too well. I think it's time we put a stop to this silly game. Foolish of me to let you try your approach first, Isabel. It's obvious that Mr. Santerre has already been put on alert. And once Mr. Santerre has the scent, he never lets up until he's bagged his quarry. Isn't that correct, Cade?"

"I do my best to finish things, Fitzgerald," Cade said calmly. Of all the people in the room, he seemed the least surprised to see Hadley.

Jamie swung around on the stool, staring at Hadley Fitzgerald. The polished, cultured appearance of Miss Isabel's charming brother was rather marred by the gun he held in one hand. He was gripping the weapon very tightly, as if he were not at ease with it. She watched him, frozen in astonishment, and wondered inanely why she had never noticed the lack of warmth in Hadley's eyes. Good manners could certainly cover a multitude of secrets, she realized, feeling dazed.

"I thought you were waiting somewhere outside the country for the tapes." Jamie felt stupid and shaken. She decided then and there that Cade's concerns had been valid, to say the least.

"And instead he was waiting in the pantry. He couldn't risk turning this little job over to his sister, could you, Fitzgerald?" Cade swiveled slowly on the stool so that he was facing Hadley and the gun. His eyes went briefly to the overly fierce grip Fitzgerald was applying to the weapon. With an absent movement Cade rested his arm on the counter, his hand near the kitchen knife. "Too much is riding on getting back those tapes. What exactly is on them, anyway? Details of how you worked other scams? Blackmail information? Conversations with people who didn't know they were being recorded and who would probably react violently if they found out?"

"Proof of his innocence is on those tapes!" Miss Isabel cried.

Hadley nodded pleasantly. "Exactly. So I'm afraid I really must ask you to fetch them, Jamie. I find I don't want to spend the rest of my life living outside the country. So inconvenient. So few places like Santa Barbara. Once I play those tapes for Gallagher and explain the entire situation, I'll be free to return."

Cade said nothing, his derisive disbelief clear in his seemingly relaxed pose.

Jamie licked her lower lip. "Are you really going to play the tapes for Gallagher?"

"Just as soon as I get my hands on them," Hadley Fitzgerald declared vehemently. "Isabel told me she had put them in your safe-deposit box, and that either you or she had access. I slipped back into the country a couple of days ago. Isabel flew in late yesterday. After all, it wouldn't have done me any good just to get my hands on the keys. I needed Isabel to open the safe-deposit box. When she told me Santerre was probably starting to search for me, I knew there would be trouble. And I was right, wasn't I, Santerre? You'll do anything to see me in jail. You're never going to accept the fact that your sister and her husband got into financial trouble out of sheer stupidity, not because I victimized them. You were out for revenge this summer, not justice. So you came looking for me. You managed to plant enough false evidence around my home to convince Gallagher that I was guilty of fraud."

Jamie moved restlessly and glanced at Miss Isabel. The older woman looked distraught.

"If only I'd known, Jamie," she said sadly. "I would never have allowed you to talk me into hiring Cade to find Hadley."

"It was Jamie's idea to hire me?" Cade sounded only mildly interested, but Jamie sensed his acute attention.

"Yes. She said you were a very thorough man, and that by the end of the summer you probably knew more about Hadley's way of doing things than anyone else on earth, even me. And I suppose she was right." Miss Isabel sighed. "She and I both made the mistake of thinking you were only doing a job when you went after poor Hadley the first time. Now I know you were out for revenge because you thought he had defrauded your sister. You must have been very angry when my brother slipped through your fingers. When Jamie showed up offering you the task of finding out whether or not he was still alive, you couldn't resist having another go at him, could you?"

"Your brother did defraud my sister and a lot of others, as well," Cade said flatly. "If he weren't guilty as hell why would he be holding a gun on me now?"

"Because I know there's no other way to get those tapes back from you," Hadley put in. "Jamie, my dear, you've been used. Santerre has used you from the first."

"Yes, Jamie," Miss Isabel said quickly. "It's the truth. You must realize that by now. The fact that he won't turn the tapes over to their rightful owner is proof enough. Surely this time around you can see him for what he is."

Jamie didn't look at Cade as she answered the other woman. "Yes, Miss Isabel, I can see him for what he is. He's the man I love. And that doesn't leave me much choice. I have to trust him."

"Jamie, no!" Isabel pleaded.

"Not a smart move, Jamie." But Hadley didn't appear surprised by her words. He seemed to have expected something like that.

"Perhaps not," Cade agreed sardonically, his eyes on Jamie. "But for better or worse she's made her decision. And that leaves you with a problem, Fitzgerald."

"The same problem I've had all along. I need those tapes."

"I know. So why don't we get down to business?"

Not understanding, Jamie snapped her head around to stare at Cade. "What business?"

Cade wasn't looking at her now. His whole attention was on Hadley. "The business of trading those tapes for our lives."

Jamie's breath seemed to falter, and Miss Isabel bit back a small scream as she glanced at her brother and then at Cade.

"Your lives!" Isabel managed in tones of shock. "No, no, you don't understand . . ."

"I'm very much afraid he does, Isabel." Hadley smiled genially. "We appear to have arrived at the bargaining point."

"You're going to kill us?" Jamie could feel the fear crawling unpleasantly through her stomach. She hoped she wouldn't be sick all over the kitchen floor. "For those tapes?"

"No, no, my dear," Hadley corrected her. "I'm only going to kill you if your lover doesn't turn the tapes over to me. But I'm sure Mr. Santerre will be reasonable about this, won't you, Cade?"

Cade inclined his head politely. "Very reasonable."

"Where are the tapes?"

"In a safe place."

"Please, Cade," Miss Isabel interjected, wringing her hands, "tell him where they are."

"If I do that, Isabel, Jamie and I won't leave here alive. We need to work out the terms of the trade, don't we Hadley? You need the tapes, and Jamie and I want to live. Just out of curiosity, what will you do once you have your hands on those recordings?"

"Leave the country again. I plan to invest in some land-development projects down in the Caribbean. I'll keep myself amused there for a few years until everyone here in the States has forgotten about me. People always forget about this sort of thing in time."

"But if you plan to stay out of the country, why did you risk coming back for the tapes?" Jamie asked.

"I'm afraid one of Mr. Santerre's guesses a few minutes ago was accurate. There are conversations on those tapes. Conversations with people who would be most incensed if they knew they had been recorded. If those tapes were ever played for Gallagher or someone like him, they would lead to all sorts of interesting investigations. And they would probably get me killed. The people whose voices are on those tapes would likely go to jail, and they wouldn't care for that. They have the power and the, shall we say, inclination to punish people responsible for causing them that sort of inconvenience. Regardless of where I was living, they'd find me. They were, I'm afraid, less than respectable business associates of mine who occasionally backed some of my projects."

"Why did you record them?" Jamie struggled to put it all together.

"At the time it probably seemed like an insurance policy, didn't it, Fitzgerald?" Cade supplied the answer easily. "You thought that if your business partners ever turned threatening or nasty, you'd have the tapes. You could have used them as blackmail or to trade with someone like Gallagher for protective custody."

Hadley nodded easily. "As you say, at the time it seemed like a good idea. But I started getting nervous about you in Santa Barbara, Santerre. So I thought I'd take a few protective measures and drop the tapes in the mail to Isabel along with instructions to hide them until I could collect them. I didn't want them in the house. Unfortunately, I didn't know just how dangerous the situation was. The day after I mailed them I realized everything was going to collapse much sooner than I had expected. I got a warning from a business acquaintance who had received word that Mr. Gallagher knew Mr. Santerre. More of a coincidence than I cared to contemplate. I decided to leave everything and run. I thought the fake suicide was a nice touch. I hired a certain person whom I had occasionally used for other purposes to take the boat out to sea and abandon it."

"While you left the country under another name?" Cade concluded.

"Exactly. You're very astute, Santerre. A most perceptive man."

"I try," Cade said dryly. "Sometimes I'm a little slow on the uptake, but I try."

"You should have tried a little harder. Now you're in a rather awkward situation, aren't you?"

"I know where the tapes are, and I'm willing to deal," Cade reminded him.

"How do you propose we go about this little trade?"

"You and I will go together to get the tapes. Jamie leaves here in the meantime and heads for a motel where she will wait until I contact her."

Jamie panicked. "No, I won't leave you behind with him!"

"You will do as I say, Jamie," Cade told her icily.

"On the contrary," Fitzgerald said. "You will both do as I say. And I'm not sure your plan provides me with adequate protection, Santerre. Jamie could go to the cops instead of a motel."

"She won't. Not if she knows my life would be forfeit." Cade sounded absolutely certain of that.

Miss Isabel interrupted in painful tones. "Please, Hadley. Is all this necessary?"

"I'm afraid so, Isabel."

Isabel turned unhappy eyes on Jamie. "Jamie, dear, I'm so sorry it had to be like this. Please believe me, I never meant you any harm. It's just that when Hadley explained to me what serious jeopardy he was in because of what was on those tapes, I knew I didn't have any choice but to get them back for him. Surely you can understand?"

Jamie looked at her and then said slowly, "I understand, Miss Isabel. We all have our own priorities when it comes to giving our loyalty and trust to another human being, don't we?" She thought she saw tears in Miss Isabel's eyes, and she wanted to put her arms around the older woman and offer comfort. But that was impossible. Isabel stood on the other side of the invisible line of loyalty that had been drawn down the middle of the kitchen. Everyone in the room had made his or her own choice, and now there was no going back.

Hadley Fitzgerald eyed Jamie with a shrewd gaze and came to a decision. "All right, Santerre, I'm inclined to believe your analysis of the situation is correct. You always seemed to have a knack for knowing what motivates people, and I think you're right about Jamie. She's in love with you, and she won't do anything to put you in greater danger than you already are. I'll go along with your plan with one modification."

"What's that?"

"My sister accompanies Jamie to the motel just to make certain there are no last minute complications."

Cade thought about that. "All right," he agreed. "When do we leave?"

"Immediately. I don't wish to stay in the country any longer than absolutely necessary. Run along and get your things, Jamie. Isabel, go with her."

Wordlessly Jamie looked at Cade, willing him to change his mind. She felt panicked: no longer trusting either Hadley or Miss Isabel, and very much afraid that there was far more risk involved for Cade than he seemed to acknowledge. The last thing she wanted to do was leave Cade alone with Hadley and the gun.

"Do as he says," Cade said gently. "Run along and get your purse and keys. Then take Isabel's Audi and drive to San Francisco."

"How will you contact me later?" she asked desperately.

"Phone the marina and leave a return phone number. I'll call there and get the message. Then I'll call you."

"Cade, I don't think this is a good idea," she said urgently.

"Get going, Jamie," he commanded softly. "Just get the hell out of here, will you?"

Jamie knew he meant it. Swallowing the rest of her protests, she spun around and started down the hall to her bedroom. After an anxious glance at her brother, Miss Isabel quickly followed.

Something wasn't right about the trade that had been arranged, Jamie thought distractedly as she opened the door to the bedroom. Hadley had agreed to it too readily, for one thing.

"I'm so sorry, Jamie. You can't imagine how upset I am about all this," Isabel said unhappily as she watched Jamie cross the room to pick up the oversize purse. "But there really is no choice. I must help protect Hadley. He's my brother."

"I understand, Miss Isabel."

"And he's explained to me just how vengeful and relentless Cade can be. Hadley says he's like a lion on the hunt. He's clever and ruthless. He'll do anything to bring down his prey."

"Hadley may be right," Jamie began wryly and then realized what she was saying. Hadley *was* right! And Fitzgerald was shrewd enough to know what to expect from his enemy if he turned him loose. No place on earth would be safe for Hadley Fitzgerald after this confrontation. Cade would track him down and make him pay for having put Jamie in such danger. It was probably Hadley who had tried to force the Mazda off the road this afternoon, Jamie realized. Then he'd threatened her with a gun.

Cade would be cold-bloodedly furious. He would also be relentless about bringing Hadley to justice. Failing that, he would deal out his own justice.

Jamie knew it and so did Hadley Fitzgerald, she was certain. Fitzgerald could simply not afford to let Cade live. If she meekly left the house with Miss Isabel, she would be leaving Cade alone with a man who fully intended to kill him. She would be abandoning the man she loved to his executioner.

10

"MISS ISABEL, I can't leave here with you." Jamie turned at the window, the heavy shoulder bag in her hand. She looked straight into the older woman's eyes. "Hadley will kill Cade."

Miss Isabel stared back, her face crumpling. When she spoke there was a new, almost hysterical harshness in her voice. "I'm afraid you have no choice, Jamie." She reached into her pocket and withdrew a tiny but lethal looking handgun. Her fingers trembled, and she held the weapon as though she hated it, but she pointed it straight at Jamie. "And I don't have any choice, either. I must help Hadley. You and I will leave here while Cade shows Hadley where the tapes are. You must, Jamie. It's the only way. I must help Hadley! He's my brother."

"Miss Isabel!" Dumbfounded by the appearance of the gun in Isabel's talented fingers, Jamie could barely speak.

"I'm sorry, Jamie. Please believe me. I'm very, very sorry."

"So am I." Jamie's next action was not premeditated. She only knew that she had to do something. Miss Isabel held a gun, and that gun would provide the edge Jamie needed to help Cade. In that moment nothing seemed as important as taking the weapon from Miss Isabel.

She flung out her hand, sending the heavy purse straight into the huge cloisonné jar that held the tapes. The elegant vase toppled and crashed to the floor. The carpet was not sufficient padding to protect it. The jar broke into a hundred pieces with a shattering sound, and the tapes tumbled free.

Miss Isabel shrieked, whether at the destruction of the beautiful object she had created or at the sight of the tapes, Jamie never knew. As Isabel whirled to stare in shock at the shattered vase, Jamie leaped forward.

There was an enraged scream of pain from the kitchen just as Jamie grabbed Isabel's arm. It sent a jolt of terror through Jamie until she realized it was Hadley's and not Cade's voice she had heard. Frantically she grabbed at the gun in her employer's hand.

It was a simple matter to wrench the small weapon from Miss Isabel's fingers. The older woman didn't even seem to notice. She was mesmerized by the sight of the destroyed vase.

Holding the gun uncertainly—she had never held one before in her life—Jamie took a last look at Isabel and decided there was no danger from that quarter. Desperately she spun around and flung open the door.

"Jamie!" Cade's voice came from the kitchen, fierce and demanding.

"I'm okay, Cade! What's going on?"

"It's all right, Jamie," he shouted from the kitchen. "Get in here where I can see you. I don't trust Isabel."

Jamie ran down the hall, halting abruptly in the kitchen doorway to stare at Hadley's sprawled form. He was lying on the floor, clutching his arm in obvious agony. The kitchen knife that had been sitting on the counter was sticking out of his shoulder. Dazedly Jamie lifted her eyes to Cade, who was going down on one knee beside his victim. He looked up, giving her a quick assessing glance.

"Where the hell did you get the gun?" Cade asked roughly.

"It's Miss Isabel's . . ." Jamie broke off and started the explanation again. "I mean, Miss Isabel pulled it on me, and I knocked over the jar."

"That was the crashing sound? The cloisonné jar going over?" Cade examined Hadley's wound while the other man glared at him in helpless pain and fury.

"I threw my purse at it."

Cade's mouth crooked laconically. "I knew that forty-pound bag must be good for something. When he heard the crash and Isabel's scream, Fitzgerald lost his concentration for a moment, didn't you, Hadley? Luckily that knife I used this morning was still on the counter. I'm usually neater than that. But I guess I was feeling distracted this morning. Lie still, Fitzgerald. I'm going to take it out. Jamie, have you got a first-aid kit?"

"In the bathroom. I'll get it." Transfixed by the blood on Hadley's sleeve, Jamie backed up a couple of steps and then turned to hurry down the hall to the bathroom. When she returned to the kitchen a few minutes later, she found Cade applying pressure to staunch the bleeding.

"You're sure you're all right?" he demanded anxiously.

"I'm fine," Jamie told him again and hesitated before asking, "Where did you learn to handle a knife like that?"

"I've cleaned a lot of fish," he told her dryly. "Where did you learn to disarm people who hold guns on you?"

"I probably watched too much television in my youth."

"The hell you did. Are you sure you're all right?"

"I'm fine," she said. Jamie wondered if that was technically correct. She seemed to have developed a trembling in her fingers. Shock, she assured herself. "You're okay?"

Cade's expression was wry. "Other than being thoroughly disgusted with myself for getting you into this situation, I'm fine."

"But it wasn't your fault!" she protested, surprised.

"That's highly debatable. If I'd taken a firmer hand, listened to my hunches . . . Never mind. How's Miss Isabel?"

"Sitting on the bed, crying," Jamie said quietly. "If you don't need me here, I'll go to her."

"Jamie, remember where she stands in all this. At the moment she can't be your friend. She's got other priorities."

"I know, Cade. I'll be careful."

Hadley interrupted then, appealing to Cade. "Santerre, I didn't lose everything when you brought Gallagher down on me." He broke off, wincing in pain. "I've got a nice cushion stashed away in an island bank. You can have half if you'll help me get back out of the country. It's a fair-size amount. Say a hundred thousand?"

"Forget it, Fitzgerald."

"Come on, Santerre. This business you're in doesn't pay as well as I'm willing to pay. What can Gallagher give you? Five or ten grand at the most for each job."

"I've got news for you, Fitzgerald," Cade said sighing. "I haven't made a cent on you. But I have received a very valuable payoff. It's been worth the trouble." He looked at Jamie as he said the last words, and the tawny eyes were dark with meaning.

Jamie smiled back tremulously. "I've just got one question, Hadley," she said to the man on the floor. "Was it you in my room the other night?"

Hadley glowered at her. "Isabel said she'd hidden the keys in the painting. I've been watching the house. I thought her room would be empty so I went in to see if

I could find them. I didn't realize you'd be sleeping in there."

"And it was you who tried to force us off the road this afternoon," Cade added, finishing his bandaging work.

"I followed you into Carmel," Hadley groaned. "When I saw you go into the bank, I knew there could be only one reason. You'd found out about the tapes. One way or another I had to stop you and get rid of the recordings. I thought if you and the tapes all went into the sea I would be saved a great deal of effort. When that didn't work, I picked up Isabel at the motel down the road and told her we had to do whatever it took to get hold of the tapes. Then we came back here and waited for you and Jamie to arrive. Isabel wanted to try coaxing Jamie into cooperating." Hadley shot Jamie a disgusted glance. "Jamie was always so cooperative."

"Jamie and I are together now," Cade informed the older man. "That means our first loyalty is to each other."

Jamie thought about his words as she walked back down the hall to tend to Miss Isabel. *Our first loyalty is to each other.* There was no doubt in her mind about her own feelings. She had known since the affair in Santa Barbara that she was in love with Cade Santerre. She would drive herself crazy wondering if he'd declared his feelings merely to secure her cooperation. Whatever he'd done, it had been to protect her. Regardless of whether or not he really was in love, she didn't have to doubt his commitment. She sensed the strength of it and took comfort from the knowledge. It was a strong foundation on which to build, she assured herself.

It was hours before Jamie and Cade were free of the demands of the authorities who came to collect Hadley. Miss Isabel had remained behind in the big house, although she had been questioned closely. Jamie had simply refused to mention the way her former employer had held a gun on her, and Cade had allowed her silence on the subject to stand.

"She's suffered enough," Jamie said as Cade bundled her into the Mazda, which had been pulled out of the ditch and declared operational.

"I agree." He turned the key in the ignition. "In any event, Hadley was the dangerous one. I'm willing to let Gallagher handle it from here on in, and as far as I know, he only wants Fitzgerald. Got everything?"

"Yes." She looked back at the forlorn figure of Miss Isabel standing in the doorway. "Except a job and a good friend."

IT WAS NEARLY eight o'clock that evening before Cade finally pulled into the parking lot of a motel that promised a lounge and a restaurant. Jamie had the feeling he'd wanted to put as many miles as possible between them and Miss Isabel's house. She had the oddest feeling he disliked the place intensely. She didn't complain. She had no desire to stay in the vicinity, either.

"God, I could use a drink." Cade climbed out of the Mazda and stretched like a big cat. The words were almost the first he had spoken during the long drive. "What a day. Let's get the suitcases into the room, honey, and then head for the bar. We both deserve something after what we've been through."

Jamie agreed wholeheartedly. She felt utterly drained. She was tired, and she was also feeling strangely wary. The physical exhaustion was certainly understandable. The wariness had an explanation, too, but she was reluctant to face it. The truth was that during the long hours of driving, Cade had said nothing concerning his feelings for her or his plans for the future. He seemed totally preoccupied.

Well, you haven't been exactly chatty on the subject, either, she reminded herself as they found a private booth in the motel lounge. A rather bored pianist played cocktail music on the other side of the room for the small crowd.

Jamie sipped at her glass of wine and wondered why it had been easier to declare her love while facing a gun than it was now when she was alone with Cade.

Cade took two or three grateful swallows of his Scotch, his expression severe and thoughtful. When it became apparent he was not going to break the long silence, Jamie spoke.

"I won't hold you to it, you know," she murmured.

As if she'd interrupted his chain of thought, Cade frowned in mild surprise. "Hold me to what?"

"Your declaration of love this afternoon. I know you were desperate to maintain control of a very dangerous situation, and telling me you loved me was one way of doing that." She focused on the piano player across the room. She was unprepared for Cade's swift movement. He reached across the table, caught her chin and turned her to face him.

"You may not hold me to my claim of love, lady, but you can damn well bet I'm holding you to yours!"

"Cade!"

"What makes you think I didn't mean everything I said about loving you?" he demanded. "You think I go around telling women I love them just to make them cooperative? I thought you'd finally decided you could trust me."

"Yes, but . . ."

"So trust me!"

Jamie stared at him, unable to repress the hope that had never been very far from the surface. She had lived on that hope since this summer. "I do trust you, Cade.

It's not that, it's just that I didn't want you to feel, well, obligated."

"I feel obligated," he growled. "I feel committed, obligated, and very, very determined. I've felt that way since I first met you. And since Miss Isabel slipped this afternoon and admitted it was your idea to contact me again, I've been assuming that nothing has changed for you since that time in Santa Barbara."

"Then why have you been so quiet for the past few hours?" she asked cautiously.

"I've been thinking."

"About what, for heaven's sake!"

"About what a fool I was for letting you get involved in that mess, if you want to know the truth! I've been calling myself every name in the book," he exploded softly. "Adding up all my mistakes."

"But, Cade . . . !"

"But nothing. I should never have played that waiting game after Santa Barbara. That was my biggest mistake. I should have refused to let you accompany Miss Isabel back to Big Sur. If I'd taken you with me when I left Santa Barbara, none of this would have happened. You would have been safe. I seem to always miscalculate around you, Jamie," he finished on a groan.

"That's probably what gave me hope for our relationship," she confided gently.

"You do want me, don't you, Jamie? I've been bouncing back and forth between heaven and hell, thinking one moment that I knew you still cared and the next that you didn't trust me. Don't put me back on that seesaw. I'll go out of my mind."

He closed his eyes in silent supplication. When he opened them again, Jamie could see the golden heat burning in the tawny gaze. "The only thing I've been absolutely certain of is how much I want you, how much I love you."

"Did you know you loved me when you walked out the door in Santa Barbara?"

"No," he admitted, his eyes never wavering in intensity. "I only knew I had to have you. I was convinced you wouldn't be able to ignore what we'd found together. I think I realized that what I was feeling was love when I found those birth-control pills in your bathroom."

Jamie blinked. "The pills?"

"That's right. When I realized just how much I'd been counting on the fact that you were pregnant, I had to really analyze my feelings. The last thing I'd ever wanted to do was get a woman with whom I was having an affair pregnant! I'd been so busy calculating, analyzing and assessing your feelings that I'd forgotten to look closely at my own. When I did, I saw the obvious truth. I love you, Jamie. I wanted you to trust me completely. It enraged me to think that you couldn't give me your complete trust. I want to make a home with you, a real home. Don't worry, I won't make you live on a fishing boat. We'll buy a nice place near the water, close enough to San Diego so that you can find another job if you like. Whatever you want. I'll do your taxes for you . . ."

"Joint return?" she asked softly.

He grinned briefly, a slash of sheer masculine amusement. "Most definitely a joint return. In case you haven't noticed, I'm proposing to you, Jamie Garland. All that's required from you is your acceptance."

"I will certainly give your proposal my closest consideration . . ."

"Jamie, don't tease me," he pleaded, the grin fading instantly. "I can't stand any more uncertainty where you're concerned."

"Having given it due consideration," she went on as if he hadn't interrupted, "I've decided to accept."

"Thank God. Jamie, you really do love me, don't you?"

"Oh, yes, Cade. I really do love you."

"I've miscalculated so frequently with you that I need the reassurance," he explained.

"Want some advice?"

"What's that?"

"Give up trying to calculate, analyze and manage me. Save your skills to use on others. Just love me, Cade. That's all that's necessary to keep me close."

"You may have a good idea there. Something seems to go awry with my skills when it comes to dealing with you, anyway." Cade reached for his wallet and tossed some bills down on the table. He got to his feet.

"Where are we going?"

"I said something happens to my business skills when I'm dealing with you," he murmured as he led her from the bar, "but my more basic instincts seem to be functioning. Come with me, my love, and let me show you just how sound my instincts are."

She went with him unprotestingly as he led her out of the lounge and up the stairs to the room. Cade's hand was warm and compelling on hers, the intensity of his grip signaling the intensity of his emotions. She sensed the fine trembling in his strong fingers as he opened the door and led her inside. Then he turned to her without bothering to switch on the light.

"Jamie, I love you so," he whispered huskily. "Please believe me."

"I do, Cade. And I trust you. I always will." Even as she said the simple words, Jamie was aware of the truth behind them. There would be no more doubts about this man. His first loyalty would always be to her, just as hers was to him. She put her arms around his neck as he began to undress her there in the darkness.

Slowly, with infinite care and tenderness, he slipped off her clothing and then his own. When they were both naked, Cade bent to lift Jamie into his arms and carry her to the bed.

Moonlight seeped through a crack in the curtains, dancing across Jamie's breasts as Cade came down beside her. He followed the path of the pale light with his fingertips, finding the tautening buds of her nipples as his mouth closed over hers.

Jamie twisted luxuriously, turning to him with gentle invitation. Her hands stroked the sleek curves of his shoulders and the bold planes of his thighs.

"Cade," she whispered throatily as he trailed his palm down her hip to the inside of her leg. "I love you so very much."

"Just go on reassuring me for the rest of my life, sweetheart. I need you. I'll always need you."

Together in the shadowy depths of the bed they explored the physical side of their love, glorying in the knowledge that there was nothing to hide, no longer any need for wariness. Jamie gave herself up to the increasingly exciting caresses. Cade's hands moved on her with unconcealed joy, parting her legs to tantalize the soft silk of her inner thighs and then moving upward to tease the sensitive flower of her passion.

"You respond so beautifully," he breathed raggedly. "You make me want to devour you." He bent his head to take a small nip at the skin of her shoulder. The wickedly exciting caress thrilled her senses. The flower he probed suddenly grew hot and moist.

His own response to her was aggressively evident. Cade's body had hardened instantly to Jamie's touch. She sensed his throbbing desire and knew he was only waiting until her own need matched his. When she moaned and instinctively closed her legs around his hand, pleading for more, he levered himself over her.

"Open for me, sweetheart. Take me inside. I need your warmth."

Willingly she put her arms around him, and then she wrapped her legs around him. Cade came down to her with an exclamation of male need, thrusting deeply into the waiting feminine heat.

"Jamie . . . *Jamie!*"

He held her fiercely, sharing the passionate journey totally. Jamie lost herself in Cade's embrace, knowing that he was equally lost in her arms. They clung together, abandoning themselves to the ancient rhythm, until the tightening sensation within them burst into a thrilling, convulsive release. And then they rode the descending path as one, united physically and emotionally.

Afterward Jamie lay enmeshed in the soft intimacy. She was vaguely aware of Cade's leg thrown across her thighs and of his quiet breath fanning her ear as he lay beside her. She knew he was awake and that he was lazily studying her face in the shadows. With a faint smile she turned to him.

"What are you thinking?" she whispered, stroking his arm with her fingertips.

"I was wondering why I made so many mistakes during this crazy courtship," he answered wryly.

She grinned. "Ah, that's because deep down there's a very strong romantic streak in you."

He glowered at her with mock ferocity. "Nonsense. I've been a rational, pragmatic man all my life. You're the romantic, not me."

"Rational, pragmatic businessmen do not throw away successful careers in order to go live on a boat," Jamie pointed out calmly.

"I've explained that," he began on a note of protest.

"Oh, you've worked up some reasons, but nothing can disguise the basically romantic impulse. You fell victim to the call of the sea and the lure of adventure. You want another example? How about the way you took two whole months to get me into bed this summer?"

"What about it?" he asked suspiciously.

"Wonderfully romantic," she breathed in fond memory.

"I just wanted everything to be right, that's all."

"It was. It was perfect. Only a true romantic would devote that much attention to the details of a seduction," Jamie teased.

"Afterward you thought I'd just been spinning a web."

"Well, you were in a way. A romantic web. And then there was the way you assumed after only one night with me that I was probably pregnant. Only a true romantic would so completely convince himself of that without proof. You actually wanted me to be pregnant. Very endearing. And then there was the way you chased after me when I left your marina the other morning. Fantastically romantic. Then, of course, you topped it all off by saving my neck."

"I think you may be interpreting events in the light of your own distinctly rosy view of life," Cade complained good-naturedly.

"Not at all. Cade, you've done an excellent job of hiding your basic romantic impulses beneath a veneer of hard-headed pragmatism, but underneath you're a lot like me. It's only natural that when you ran into another romantic you'd have trouble predicting and manipulating her actions."

"I fail to follow the logic of that."

"Romance and love have no logic," she informed him wisely.

"You've got an answer for everything, don't you?" he asked admiringly.

She laughed softly. "I'm working on it."

"There's one small detail you're forgetting."

"What's that?"

"I was right about one thing: you did come looking for me after that scene in Santa Barbara. Miss Isabel said it was all your idea, remember?"

"Are you going to hold that over my head for the rest of my life?" she complained.

"Probably. But I won't tease you about it right now. I've got better things to do."

"Such as?" she challenged throatily, her fingers stroking languidly down his chest.

"I'm going to put a few of my romantic impulses into practice." Cade lowered his head and kissed the hollow of her throat.

Jamie felt the renewed tautness in his body, sensed the rising hunger in him. "This is romance?"

"The hell with romance. This is love."

She didn't doubt him. Cade Santerre might not recognize the genuine streak of romance in his soul, but he knew all about the important things in life.

PENNY JORDAN

Sins and infidelities...
Dreams and obsessions...
Shattering secrets
unfold in...

THE HIDDEN YEARS

SAGE — stunning, sensual and vibrant, she spent a lifetime distancing herself from a past too painful to confront... the mother who seemed to hold her at bay, the father who resented her and the heartache of unfulfilled love. To the world, Sage was independent and invulnerable— but it was a mask she cultivated to hide a desperation she herself couldn't quite understand... until an unforeseen turn of events drew her into the discovery of the hidden years, finally allowing Sage to open her heart to a passion denied for so long.

The Hidden Years—a compelling novel of truth and passion that will unlock the heart and soul of every woman.

AVAILABLE IN OCTOBER!
Watch for your opportunity to complete your Penny Jordan set.
POWER PLAY and SILVER will also be available in October.

HIDDEN-RR

HARLEQUIN

Romance®

**This September, travel to England
with Harlequin Romance
FIRST CLASS title #3149,
ROSES HAVE THORNS
by Betty Neels**

It was Radolf Nauta's fault that Sarah lost her job at the hospital and was forced to look elsewhere for a living. So she wasn't particulary pleased to meet him again in a totally different environment. Not that he seemed disposed to be gracious to her: arrogant, opinionated and entirely too sure of himself, Radolf was just the sort of man Sarah disliked most. And yet, the more she saw of him, the more she found herself wondering what he really thought about her—which was stupid, because he was the last man on earth she could ever love....